2020 Visions

2020 Visions
©2010 M-Brane Press
www.mbranepress.com

Edited by Rick Novy
www.ricknovy.com

Cover art by Jonathon Fowler
Cover design by James Fowler

ISBN 978-0-9831709-0-7

2020 VISIONS

Edited by
RICK NOVY

M-Brane Press
St. Louis, Missouri

9 **Foreword** by Rick Novy

11 **Mary Robinette Kowal** Birthright

15 **Sheila Finch** The Persistence of Butterflies

30 **Randy Henderson** A Shelter for Living Things

49 **Jason S. Ridler** Showing Light

60 **Ernest Hogan** Radiation is Groovy, Kill the Pigs

103 **David Lee Summers** The Revelation of Thought

113 **Jeff Spock** teh afterl1fe

124 **Emily Devenport** If the Sun's at Five O'Clock,
It Must be Yellow Daisies

157 **Cat Rambo** Therapy Buddha

167 **Jack Mangan** Dead Rookies

179 **David Boop** Organ Cloning While You Wait

195 **Spencer Ellsworth** The Black Plague of
Our Generation

239 **Gareth L. Powell** The Bigger The Star,
The Faster It Burns

248 **Alethea Kontis** Pocket Full of Posey

261 **Alex Wilson** Nervewrecking

281 **David Gerrold** Time Capsule 2120:
Actual Comments from Lunar Tourists

Foreword

Projects are born in different ways. Sometimes there's a cool idea at the core. Sometimes, it's just a collection of words or a sentence. Sometimes they come from fuzzy amorphous ideas that need time to gel. This one started as a title.

I'm not sure when the title *2020 Visions* popped into my head. It was some time in early 2009, I think. But what a title and such an opportune time! I love double entendre and the perfection of chance giving me an opportunity to use that title to peek ten years into the future was just too good to pass up.

And so, the *2020 Visions* project began. At first, I shopped the idea around and it fell mostly on deaf ears. For a while, I tabled the idea and worked on other projects. For one of these projects, I guest edited *M-Brane SF* # 12 for Christopher Fletcher.

Chris Fletcher and I have never met, but we know each other pretty well through online activities. We disagree on many things in this life, but our tastes in science fiction seem to be very similar. My fiction has appeared in *M-Brane SF* six times in the first year and a half of publication. And no, he doesn't publish everything I submit.

I enjoyed editing issue #12. It was fun learning what all the editors meant when they discussed reading slush. It was fun discovering some really cool stories among the submissions. It was fun sending out acceptances and excruciatingly painful to send out rejections. Issue #12 was released as a trade paperback anthology, *Ergosphere*, as well as in the usual form of an electronic magazine.

While I was editing issue #12, Chris was busy expanding M-Brane into a small press imprint and producing the first couple of books. Once *Ergosphere* had been out for a month or two, *2020 Visions* came back into my mind. When I told him that I intended this to be an invitational anthology and outlined what I had in mind, Chris quickly got on board.

I sent invitations to around sixty good writers that I know from one place or another. Some of them I know only virtually, some are local to me, others I see only at conventions. About half the writers declined for various reasons, but to my surprise and delight, a large number of people expressed interest.

I did open the anthology to slush for two weeks in an attempt to gather a few more optimistic stories. From that call, I ended up accepting two manuscripts from writers who probably should have received invitations in the first place.

Once stories started rolling in, things seem to fall into place as if this thing were destined to be. How else can you explain the appearance of an original *Star Trek* screenwriter in the same volume as a guy named Spock? Too, I met an artist at Phoenix Comicon who wanted to be involved. The variety of stories, as you will soon find out, is astonishingly diverse. The mix of dark and hopeful is about right, with a few in the extreme, and most falling into that gray area in between.

In these covers, you will find a bias toward the American Southwest. That is, in a large part, because I live in that region, so the writers I know well also live in the Southwest.

I think you will find this collection to have a little of everything, from the thought provoking to the absurd. Each of them somebody's 2020 vision. Sit back, kick up your feet, and enjoy.

Rick Novy
Scottsdale, Arizona
August 2010

I originally met Mary through the writer's workshop area on Orson Scott Card's website. In 2005, we met in person as classmates at Card's Literary Boot Camp, and we have both been members of the online writers group Codex ever since.

Mary makes her living as a puppeteer. She is also, as you are about to find out, a top-notch writer. Her first novel, Shades of Milk and Honey, *debuted in August of 2010. She is the winner of the Campbell Award for best new writer, and she managed that entirely with short fiction.*

Mary is a good writer at any length, but she is among the best in the genre when it comes to very short fiction. She has the ability to layer emotion, plot, and characterization into something that would fit on the back of a cereal box. While this story is a bit long to be considered flash fiction, it is among the shorter stories in this collection. It's short, but it packs a powerful punch.—RN

Birthright
by Mary Robinette Kowal

Restless within the confines of the waiting room, Helen looked out the window of the Birthright Clinic. Her fingers twisted her wedding ring as if she were spinning straw into gold.

Her husband read an outdated magazine with a relaxed air that magnified her tension. Light caressed Daniel's freckled cheekbones. He looked up, as if he felt the weight of her gaze. "Are you all right?"

"Of course." She smiled at him.

He closed the magazine. "We don't have to do this today."

"No." Helen tried to reconcile her fear and her eagerness. "It's the right choice."

"It's okay to change your mind."

"We agreed." She ignored the trembling in her hands. "A birthright is worth a lot of money." Which they needed if they were going to finish their law degrees.

"If you're sure." Daniel took her hand in his.

"I'm sure." She took comfort in his warmth and solidity. "The waiting makes me tense."

Helen spun her ring again, feeling as if Rumpelstiltskin waited around the corner. Selling their birthright was the right decision. The global controls restraining the world's rapidly escalating population allowed each fertile couple only one child, and Daniel didn't want a child. Neither did she; their marriage was perfect the way it was. Everything was perfect.

She jumped as a nurse opened the door of the waiting room. "Mr. and Ms. Dixon? Follow me, please."

The nurse showed Helen and Daniel to a room furnished with an examination table and three chairs. Custard yellow walls and a picture of daisies could not banish the room's underlying medical sterility.

"Mr. Dixon, do you want to get ready for your vasectomy now?"

Daniel slid a hand around the small of Helen's back as if he knew her need. "I'll wait, if you don't mind."

The nurse nodded as she handed Helen a surgical gown. "If you'll slip this on, the doctor will be right in."

As if he knew how vulnerable she felt, Daniel stood with his back to Helen, giving her an illusion of privacy by reading the charts on the wall. She wanted to cling to his square shoulders, knowing he would support her. But his perfect posture would not support the weight of fatherhood. That was what ended her ambivalence toward motherhood. She would not force her husband to be unhappy because of her desires.

And the money. If they wanted to finish their law degrees without mountains of debt, the money for giving up their right to reproduce was too much to ignore. There were plenty of couples, desperate for a second child, who would pay for a birthright.

Once she had the gown on, Helen sat in the chair farthest from the examination table. The chrome of the gynecological stirrups gleamed with memories of past examinations. She had taken care of her body, keeping it safe for the day when she bore a child. In a moment, to surrender her half of their birthright, she would climb onto that table and be sterilized. Helen bit the inside of her cheek, trying to control the flurry of panic in her chest. She did not want a child, but the restriction of choice frightened her.

The doctor opened the door, light reflecting off the bald spot in the middle of his graying hair. Helen barely heard his greetings.

The doctor pulled on his gloves. "Do you want your husband to stay, Ms. Dixon?"

"Yes, please." Even to her own ears, her voice sounded strangled.

"Then if you'll hop onto the table..."

Helen lay down on the table and placed her feet in the cold metal stirrups. Daniel held her hand; at his touch, tears coursed down her cheeks. She turned her head away from him, closing her eyes as if that would hide the tears.

"Honey." He smoothed her hair, trying to comfort her.

"I'm sorry," she whispered. "I don't know why I'm crying."

A chair squealed against the floor as the doctor pushed away from the table. "I'll leave you two alone."

Daniel stroked her head, and kept her hand tight in his. "Shush, it's okay."

She had been wrong, thinking she was ambivalent. "I'm sorry."

He brushed a tear from her cheek. "Helen, if you're having second thoughts—I mean, if you want a child, we can do that. We have the right."

Helen covered her face with her hands as if she could push the tears back inside. "No. We agreed." She dropped her hands and stared up at him, with her feet still in the stirrups. If she took them out, she would never be able to put them back in. "It's the right choice."

As he studied her, a thousand thoughts seemed to flit behind his eyes. Daniel slowly shook his head. "It's not the right choice."

"We need the money."

"It's not like we're getting art degrees." Daniel lifted her hand and kissed it gently. "We'll be able to pay the debt back."

She didn't have the strength to have this discussion again. "You don't want a child!"

"No, I don't." He pulled her into a sitting position and her feet slid out of the stirrups. "But I want you."

She hid her face in his shoulder, weeping. Daniel brought his arms around her as his perfect posture softened. "Do you want a child?"

Wordless, she nodded.

He rocked her like a baby. "Then we will."

Helen clung to his shirt desperate to hold onto her resolve. "Later." She took a breath and choked the tears down. "After we graduate, we can buy a new birthright."

Daniel's face paled so his freckles stood out like a spatter of blood. "We won't be fertile anymore."

"I know." She felt Rumpelstiltskin breathing down her neck. "But we'll have the money to buy someone's second-born child."

Helen lay down and put her feet back in the stirrups.

Mary Robinette Kowal is the author of Shades of Milk and Honey Tor, 2010). In 2008 she received the Campbell Award for Best New Writer and has been nominated for the Hugo and Locus awards. Her stories appear in Asimov's, Clarkesworld, and several Year's Best anthologies. She is the Vice President of Science Fiction and Fantasy Writers of America. Mary, a professional puppeteer, also performs as a voice actor, recording fiction for authors such as Elizabeth Bear, Cory Doctorow and John Scalzi. She lives in Portland, OR with her husband Rob and over a dozen manual typewriters.

http://www.maryrobinettekowal.com
http://www.twitter.com/maryrobinette

I met Sheila Finch at Westercon 2009 in Tempe, Arizona, where we were the only two SFWA members to attend the scheduled meeting. Needless to say, we did not meet quorum, so we chatted through the time slot.

Sheila has been a creative writing teacher for many years. Her novella "Reading the Bones" won the Nebula award for that category in 1998.

"The Persistence of Butterflies" is a story that might be a little farther out than 2020, but the topic involves the fallout of global warming. It's a touching story about a man who still has hope after everyone else has accepted that global warming is unstoppable.—RN

The Persistence of Butterflies
by Sheila Finch

Towards midnight, the woman died.

Matt watched the woman's brother fetch a tarp from the dormant chopper. A waning moon low in the cloudless desert sky sent the man's shadow crawling like a spider over the rocky ground. The woman's father, who hadn't come out of the chopper at all since she started moaning three hours ago, stuck his head through the open window and made a 'hurry up' gesture to the younger man.

The woman's day-old baby, lying on the other side of the small fire Matt built, had stopped its thin mewling. It would've been lying on hard ground if he hadn't wrapped it in his leather jacket with the NASA patches he'd once been so proud of. He wondered if it was dead now like its mother.

"You comin' or not?" the father shouted, his voice raspy.

"What's the hurry?" the younger man answered sullenly. "Going nowhere till the sun comes up."

The younger man's face was thin and set in hard lines. In the previous century, he and his father might have been Oakies escaping the Dust Bowl, Matt thought. Drought turned to blizzard, but desperate folks still struggled to reach the west coast. He'd run into them just outside Knoxville. They'd agreed to take him with them in the crowded four-seater because they needed his engineering skill to patch the old craft's solar skin. He assumed they'd probably stolen the chopper. Lots of abandoned equipment out there, rotting in the mud.

By day the younger man had flown the chopper along Interstate 40, below them most of the way since Tennessee, but the chopper's solar batteries didn't hold much power, and they hadn't been able to find fuel for the hybrid engine. Forced to stop every night when the sun went down, father and son had become increasingly ill-tempered. Then the woman had gone suddenly into labor just as the anemic trickle of the Colorado River came into view.

Matt shrugged. "I'm an engineer, not a magician. You need sunlight or fuel. Right now you've got neither."

The brother walked away. After a while, he came back, hunched over. He had made a carrier of his jacket to hold a quantity of rocks. "Wanna help?" he asked.

Together they mounded stones over the tarp-shrouded body, forming a crude cairn. Matt doubted it would be enough to keep the coyotes off. Afterward, the younger man curled up by the fire, and the father finally slept, his snores rumbling out of the chopper's open window. It was still a couple of hours before dawn, maybe a couple more before the solar batteries had soaked up enough power to lift the chopper for the final leg of its flight to the coast.

Matt gazed at the huddled mountains to the west. Between them and where he stood, the Mojave Desert waited.

He hadn't had much choice.

"I'm leaving," Karen had said a month ago.

Her words had barely registered. The data on-screen showed him what he'd looked at a thousand times: something kept the solar shades from deploying properly in all the test flights NASA had undertaken. The tiny spacecraft made of transparent film were supposed to orbit a thousand kilometers above the Earth, deflecting the sun's punishing radiation, slowing global warming, buying time. But they didn't. There had to be a fix – he was an engineer; he believed in fixes. Not so NASA; the space agency was about to pull the plug on the project. Already they were gutting the east coast team, and his job was next in line.

The screen blinked. Came back again.

"Did you hear what I said, Matt?"

It was taking too long to reduce greenhouse gas emissions. The climate crisis was cumulative. Glaciers rapidly disappearing. Low-lying islands flooding worldwide. Harvests failing. The planet's own long range cycles were against them too. The solar shades had to work; it was humanity's best chance to bring the problem under control.

"You said you're leaving. Going shopping?"

Karen laughed, a brittle sound. "Shopping for a better life!"

He turned from the screen and gazed at her. Burnished blonde hair swinging over the shoulders of her elegant snow jacket. She'd never wanted children and he'd been too busy, but he'd thought they were a team.

"You're leaving me?"

"Oh my. The signal finally got through."

Behind her, blades of cold light from long windows sliced the room. He heard the strangled wheeze of the automatic snowplow at work in drifts deeper than it was intended to clear. Severe winter storms on the east coast were just one symptom of weather systems out of whack. The world's economies, barely recovering from the market collapses of the previous decades, teetered on the edge of failure again. Onscreen, a rolling wave of interference dissolved his data into sparkling points.

"If you can tear yourself away from your work for a few minutes," she raged, "you'll see what I've tried to tell you, over and over again. Everybody with a grain of sense is leaving Maryland."

"I'm working on a solution, Karen. I'm so close–"

"You're a dreamer!"

The door slammed behind her, shaking loose a waterfall of snow that blanked the window. The screen blacked out as the system went down again. This time, he had the feeling it would be down for a very long time.

"Her own fault she got pregnant."

Matt opened his eyes and saw the old man sitting on a boulder, staring at the cairn. The brother was still asleep on the other side of the dead fire, the collar of his jacket turned up over his ears. The sun was little more than a hand's-breadth above the eastern horizon. He sat up.

The father stood up and aimed a kick at his son. "Get up! Start loadin' the stuff."

"What're we going to do about the kid?" The younger man's voice was still thick with sleep.

"Leave it with Teela. She wanted it."

The rising sun splashed rivers of gold over the western mountains. Matt got up and stepped over the ashes of last night's fire. The infant wrapped in his jacket hadn't stirred. Dark eyes, huge in their bony sockets, stared up at the sky through the spindly branches of a half-dead cottonwood. Breathing, though he couldn't imagine how.

"It's still alive," the brother said.

"Not for long."

Matt's dislike of the old man rose in his throat. His hand moved to touch the gun he'd shoved in his pocket before leaving home. Karen had made him get it, afraid of the looters who increasingly prowled the dying cities of the Beltway.

The kid didn't stand a chance anyway. And he needed the ride to the west coast. As he'd expected, NASA had shut down the east coast lab. Matt hadn't had the seniority or the prestige to convince them otherwise. But Walter Chen in Pasadena still managed to keep his lab operating, last Matt had heard. The only option he could see was to go west, join Chen's team, keep working, not give up. *Go down trying,* his dad had always said.

"Get aboard if you're going." The younger man climbed into the pilot's seat.

The chopper's rotors began to turn. There'd be just enough power in the batteries by now to get the craft airborne; then the blazing sun of the Mojave would see them through till they reached the coast. All they had to do was follow the track of Interstate 40 till they reached Los Angeles

"Last time I'm tellin' you!" the father shouted over the rotor's whine.

Matt stood with one hand on the chopper's door, the wind from the rotors whipping his hair. "Goddamn it! We can't just leave the baby –"

The door slammed, spinning him backwards. The chopper took off.

So much for the dream of getting to Pasadena. He'd be lucky to survive more than a couple of days out here.

The baby lay as he'd left it in the meager shade of the cottonwood. He thought of the shepherd pups he'd raised as a kid, how it had been a kindness to the mother, and the pup too, to take the weakest, the runt, and put it out of its misery. He fingered the gun, warm with his body heat, and looked at the baby.

He couldn't do it.

He dropped the backpack on the sand and lifted the infant. There was a small dark stain on the lining of his leather jacket where it had been lying; he wrapped the jacket loosely around the thin body. Cradling the tiny bundle in the crook of one arm, he took his canteen out of the backpack and unscrewed the cap which made a small cup. He stared at the cup and the canteen's opening and the child's small face, then tipped the canteen and dipped a finger in the water. Awkwardly, he brought the wet finger to the child's mouth. It didn't seem to know how to suck.

"Come on, kid," he said. "That's supposed to be an instinct."

The child stared unblinking at him, its eyes all dark pupil. But when his finger touched its mouth this time, he saw a tiny movement and was encouraged. On the second try, he managed to make a drop of water slide between the lips. It dribbled uselessly out of the side of the infant's mouth. Overhead, the dry cottonwood rustled in the hot breeze.

On the third try, the infant's mouth moved to hold the water. He repeated the maneuver several times.

"That'll have to do for now."

He screwed the cup back on his canteen. Where there were cottonwoods there should be water, but last night he'd scrabbled away at the sand to a depth of a foot and not found any.

The chopper had been forced to leave the trail marked by Interstate-40 just as it reached the California border when the woman went into labor. He figured they must've flown about two miles north looking for a site level enough to set the chopper down. They'd skimmed two spiny ridges, stone fingers extended from a peak in the distance, the land between littered with boulders large enough to damage the chopper, before they'd found an open patch. He needed to retrace their flight path and find the interstate, then maybe he'd get lucky and pick up another ride out to the coast. Not an easy task, even if he'd been prepared for a hike through the Mojave, but not impossible. His dad, a dedicated outdoorsman, had taken Matt and his older brother out west to Death Valley one spring; they'd hiked the canyons and gazed at the stars. His love of space had begun on that trip.

Rough country between where he stood now and the interstate

on the valley floor. Hampered by the baby, he'd have a hard time. He set it down and took up the backpack. It was almost empty, a water canteen, two small energy bars, a packet of raisins, an apple, an extra pair of socks. He'd been on the road more days than he cared to think about. At first there'd been people streaming along the flooded roads hoping for better luck inland; it had given him the chance to barter for food or a ride through West Virginia and into Kentucky.

He arranged the things as evenly as possible on the bottom of the backpack, then carefully slid the jacket-wrapped infant on top. Once his first impulse to rescue it faded, he recognized the hopelessness of the task.

Scanning the ground as he walked south, he saw the faint line of a trail across rough sand. A coyote's path, better than nothing. He took it toward the brow of a stony hill. Sweat poured down his face and soaked his collar then dried instantly. His dad would've counseled walking at night and resting during the day, but he didn't have time for that luxury. He tried to remember the average daytime temperature of the Mojave in May. The warm incense of the desert rose up to him on the breeze, heavy with the scent of sage.

The animal track meandered between huge boulders, slowly climbing to the crest of barren hills. To the east, he saw a slick, black slope where a volcano had long ago spewed its lava, and sheltered under an overhanging rock he caught the glint of a small pool of collected rainwater, left over from a desert storm that must've passed through recently. He knelt and trickled water into his almost empty canteen, allowing himself a taste from one fingertip first; the water was warm but potable.

His legs tired rapidly. No time for sleep in those last few days before he'd accepted the conclusion that he couldn't do anything by staying in Maryland. Karen, of course, had cut out long before. There was no pain in that memory. Physical exhaustion had a way of washing out emotional exhaustion, and there was something peaceful about walking through this warm, scented silence that soothed his nerves. The desert reminded him that after he and his kind had vanished, it would still be there, growing along the bleached bones of humanity's feeble attempt to survive.

In mid-afternoon, the baby's thin cry stopped him. Carefully, he eased the makeshift carrier off his shoulder and set it on the ground. He uncapped the flask and repeated the water maneuver he'd perfected earlier. After a while, he wrapped the baby in his jacket again and hoisted the backpack over his shoulder. It took him the better part of the day to reach the last line of bleak hills before the land began its descent. The sun was already searing its way down the western sky when he stopped to scan the desert floor below him. A light breeze sprang up, scouring his face with hot sand.

In the distance he saw a section of it, shimmering in the heat haze of late afternoon, a long, straight silver ribbon like the promise of life-giving water across the furnace lands of the Mojave: the I-40.

Encouraged, he started down the slope. Cactus spines reached for his jeans as he pushed past, and a dry tumbleweed bounced across his path. Off-balance, he stumbled, turned his ankle, and yelped in pain. He flopped heavily onto a sun-warmed boulder, and the baby whimpered, jostled in its makeshift carrier.

Damn. His dad would've reminded him: RICE. No ice to be had around here, and no time to rest or elevate. That left compress. But the baby was wrapped in his jacket, and there was nothing else he could use in the backpack. This trip west was turning out to be an exercise in futility, just as Karen would've predicted.

After a while, the pain in his ankle settled into a dull ache and he stood cautiously, testing to see if it would carry his weight. It did. The sun slipped behind the western range and purple shadows crept across the sand. In contrast to the heat of the day, nights were cold in the high desert, and without his jacket he started shivering. He really didn't have a choice, either go on or both of them could die of exposure right here. He took a few slow, painful steps forward.

The coyote trail he'd been following petered out at a limestone outcropping.

He was almost too tired to eat but knew he needed food if he had any hope of making this journey at all. The energy bars were limp in their foil wrappers. He opened one carefully and took a small bite, chewing methodically in the gathering dusk, then took a swallow of water.

The infant's eyes were open again. It occurred to him that he might try the melted chocolate of the bar as a substitute baby food. Couldn't be any worse than letting it starve to death. He smeared a finger tip in the brown sticky mess, careful not to pick up any of the chopped nuts. Gently, he daubed a little on the tiny lips and was pleased to see the infant's tongue poke hesitantly out.

"That's right. Try a little for me."

The infant lay motionless, the tip of its tongue still visible. He rummaged in the backpack again as if it might magically produce a bottle of formula. His fingers found the apple. He remembered his sister-in-law feeding his little nephew applesauce, but that was an older child, sitting up already. He stared at the apple, wondering what to do.

Something rustled in the tumbleweeds. This was rattlesnake country. He wished he'd paid more attention to his father's camping lessons. But even Dad wouldn't know what to do with the world the way it was now. For the first time since his father's heart attack, he was glad the old man wasn't alive to see it.

He had a folding knife in his pocket; he took it out and cut the apple in wedges.

"You're not thinking of giving that baby a chunk of apple?" a voice demanded.

Startled, Matt dropped the piece he'd cut in the dirt. A figure materialized out of the darkness and seized it up. A woman. He stared at her as she stuffed the apple into her mouth.

"Wait. If you're hungry –" He held out the remains of the energy bar.

"Idiot!" she said, chewing. "How long since this kid ate?"

"Its mother died giving birth –" He consulted his watch – "twenty-two hours, thirty-six minutes ago."

She nodded. "Hungry. You got water?"

Silently, he handed over the canteen. She unscrewed the cup and dribbled a little water into it, then leaned over and let the mushed apple fall into the water. She rocked the cup, stirring its contents with a finger.

"And don't look at me like that. I may be female but I don't magically produce milk. If this is thin enough, it'll do in a pinch."

She reached for the child, making cooing noises. Then she hooked her finger into the mush and did what he had done earlier, feeding the child. In the dark, he heard tiny smacking noises.

He felt foolish for not having thought of what to do with the apple himself.

After a while, she laid the infant down on the ground and unwrapped the jacket. "Yours?"

"Somebody left it to die. I picked it up."

"Bet you've never diapered a baby."

"But you have," he guessed.

He heard the sound of fabric ripping, but by now it was too dark to see what she was doing. He slumped on a boulder, resting his head on his arms, trying to ignore the ache in his ankle which he saw now was swollen. After a while she put the infant in his arms.

"What she really needs is milk."

"She?"

"Didn't you even know it was a girl?"

The baby's sex hadn't registered on him. What difference did it make anyway? There was no way he could chew apples to make applesauce all the way to the coast, even if he could find any.

He looked at the woman. "What're you doing out here?"

"Same as you, probably. Waiting for the end."

Angered, he replied sharply, "I'm headed to Los Angeles."

"LA's a mess – no water. San Diego's the same. All those miles and miles of new development, dried out, abandoned. Ironic, isn't it? Too much water in the east, drought in the west. Why would you want to go to LA?"

"I'm an engineer. I'm working on global warming."

"Not doing too well, are you?" she said scornfully. "They've got water riots out there now. Water's more expensive than gold."

He thought of the thin trickle of the Colorado he'd caught sight of as the chopper neared the state line, major water source for Southern California.

"My husband was a Riverside County Deputy Sheriff," she added. "On the Crisis Force. But they couldn't solve this one."

A cascade of disasters triggered by severe climate change. How many nights had he and his colleagues sat around discussing the possibilities, never really quite believing that time would run out before they found the solution?

She touched his arm. "There's a cave back in the rocks. Better come inside. Hungry coyote 'round here, got pups nearby."

Overhead, the Milky Way poured across the darkening sky like the torrent the Colorado had once been.

When he woke, sunlight entered the cave's mouth; he saw the woman lying on a camp cot, nursing the baby.

"I thought you said –"

"Right. No milk. But she needs the comfort of sucking."

He wondered which of the two needed the comfort more.

It was a good size cave. He saw a braided rug on the floor, a water jug, cooking pots stacked in a corner, a sack of potatoes, another of rice, cardboard boxes proclaiming their contents: tuna, beans, sliced pears, dried milk she'd used for the baby last night. She seemed well-stocked to wait out any normal emergency.

He stood gingerly on his injured foot, then picked up his soiled jacket, limped out and stood blinking in the sharp morning sunlight. The cave was near the top of the ridge; the other side fell away in folds of butter-colored rock to the desert floor where he'd seen the interstate. On the spine of the ridge, he saw the coyote silhouetted against the sky like an Indian petroglyph. He should make a start now, while it was still cool.

There was a small mound of stones by the cave's entrance; he rested the injured foot on it and carefully tightened his boot to supply some support. The ankle throbbed and he couldn't tighten the boot as much as he needed to. It was going to be a rough trip till he reached the interstate – rough enough anyway, without this added problem.

The woman came out, carrying the baby wrapped in a blanket. She was smaller than he'd realized last night, with a sharp-boned face under a thatch of tangled red curls. She wore grubby but serviceable jeans and a long-sleeved, plaid shirt. Her eyes were wary and a very deep brown.

"You weren't thinking of leaving?" she challenged.

"No – Of course not. Just looking around." Karen would've seen right through that lie.

She held out a sunburned hand. "Name's Persephone."

"Really?"

She grinned. "Hey! I happen to like it." Then she turned serious again. "Doesn't matter what real names are any more, does it? But you can call me Persey."

He took her hand. "I'm Matt."

"Still planning on getting to the coast?"

"Have to. I worked on the solar shades project –"

"Heard of those. They don't work." She made a face. "You'd be better off staying right here. Couple of miles east, there's an abandoned native trading post I've been liberating. They've got everything but fresh meat."

"You didn't always live up here," he guessed.

"No. But where I used to live is getting too rough for me. After Joe got killed...." She didn't go on.

"Are there other–" he hesitated "–survivors up here?"

She shrugged. "Some of the ones that're still around, I'd sooner not meet–if you know what I mean."

"You know this territory well?"

"Joe and I used to come up here to camp. He loved the desert. Maybe you should wait till the sun goes down. Gets hot in the day, even if it is only May."

"I have to risk it," he said.

She stared at him speculatively. "On that swollen ankle?"

He glanced around. A sturdy-looking manzanita branch lay in a tangle of dead cactus and small twigs. He hobbled over to it; not as large as he'd like, but it would give him a little support. Persey watched him without comment.

"Well," he began, straightening up and testing the stick.

"I'll keep you company for a while." She arranged the blanket into a sling and settled the baby against her chest.

The morning was fresh, the air sparkling, and a light scent reached him like hidden flowers. He set his mind to ignoring his ankle by going over the solar shades data in his mind again. Nothing wrong with their design – they unfurled properly. But then they tanked. Dozens of tests, same dismal results. Why? He'd thought he'd glimpsed the reason during those last days in Maryland.

When it became too difficult to climb two abreast, Persey went ahead. Even carrying the infant, her movements were sure-footed.

At the top she stopped and waited for him to catch up. He turned his face away from her so she wouldn't see the strain he was already feeling.

She pointed into the valley below. "There's the interstate. What's left of it."

Like a dotted line, the I-40 started and stopped in a jumble of broken concrete, a dark gash on the gold desert floor. No way anybody could follow it anywhere.

His heart pounded. "What happened?"

"Earthquake. Few days ago."

"Yesterday, I saw an undamaged road ..."

"Must've been a heat mirage. You get used to them out here."

He turned away, embarrassed to let her see his sudden, flooding despair. No traffic would be getting through on that mess any time soon.

"I could've told you, but you wouldn't have believed me. Could be days before they get that sorted out," she said. "If they do!"

"I have to find a way around it. There's got to be traffic further west – I'll hitch a ride."

Persey shrugged. "Your party."

For twenty minutes she led the way over the rocks, now south, now west, uphill then down again. By now he was grimacing with pain. Then suddenly the valley floor below them was ablaze with color. A carpet of pink and red and yellow spread before him like a fallen rainbow.

"My God, it's beautiful!"

"God doesn't come around here any more!" she said fiercely. "Cactus survives on its own."

Some of the color was moving. *Butterflies?* It couldn't be. But there they were, shimmering over the field of blooming cactus. Butterflies, he thought, the sheer, incredible persistence of butterflies.

"One spring in seven, cactus really puts on a show," she said, sounding wistful.

His father had explained how caterpillars turned into butterflies when he and his brother were kids. He remembered Dad in the back yard, showing them a butterfly, damp from the cocoon, spreading its wings to dry in the sun. Something about that image –

"Did you know the mother's name?"

He glanced at the small woman cradling an infant, the sun gilding her shoulders. She was like a cactus herself, a prickly survivor.

"Teela, they called her."

"You might as well call the baby that." She brushed the top of the baby's head with her lips.

How could he plan to take the child along when he wasn't certain he could get himself through the desert? "I could leave the baby here with you – I mean – she'd be better off –"

"And how am I supposed to take care of a baby out here?" she demanded, anger rising redly into her cheeks.

He shook his head. "Look, that was stupid of me. I'm sorry."

"Well, go ahead and leave her! She'd die for sure with an idiot like you. And when you get to LA you'll find I'm right. It'll all have been for nothing. Nothing! All a stupid waste!"

He put a hand on her shoulder, breaking into her anger.

"Damn government!" she said. "Damn weather! Damn world!"

The child's voice joined hers.

"Come with me," he urged. Maybe he was as crazy as Karen thought he was.

She jerked away. "You asking me to leave my own child?"

He realized he'd seen the small stone cairn a few paces from the cave's mouth and was ashamed he hadn't recognized what it meant. After a moment, he put his arms around both of them. Persey was rigid with resistance. The baby's light, powdery smell came to his nose.

Her voice muffled against his jacket, she said, "He wasn't much older than this one."

The desert had no mercy for those who believed in illusions, teasing them with mirages. Yesterday's exhaustion came surging back.

"I was doing okay before you showed up." She sniffed away tears. "Joe taught me how to trap jackrabbits. I'm a good desert cook. Rabbit, rat, crow, you name it."

Maybe Persey was right. She had it no worse up here than the pioneers who'd gone west in wagon trains. Maybe the solution was to make the best of it and stay right here. If he were a realist, he'd admit there was no cause for optimism, even if he made it to JPL. The solution that had eluded him in Maryland might just as well elude him in Pasadena. He hadn't been in contact with Chen for a couple of weeks now. Maybe NASA had shut him down too.

"It's all over. All the good things we took for granted. We should've known. Nothing on this Earth is guaranteed to last forever."

He glanced down at her, weighing the implication of her words as if they were an engineering problem. If nothing lasted, the rule must apply to bad as well as good. The thing about mirages was you didn't know they were until you tested them. That's what he did best, testing things to find solutions. Go down trying–not a bad motto for humans.

In the silence, he became aware of the gun in his belt. He took it out and offered it to her.

"Don't need a gun to catch jackrabbit," she said, slapping it away. "And you're making a big mistake if you think I'd use it on the baby or myself!"

He laid the gun down on a boulder. "It'll keep the neighbors polite."

He touched the baby's soft cheek and set off down the slope toward the interstate. The sun hammered his bare head; the glare hurt his eyes. *Old Sol*, he thought, tasting the irony, *the planet's life-giver.*

"Wait!"

He stopped, not turning, hearing her feet dislodge stones behind him.

"Idiot! How long you think you can keep going like this without supplies and with a gimpy foot?"

"Dreamer!" Karen's voice said in his memory. "As long as it takes," he said.

"Wait till the sun goes down. I'll find something to strap up your ankle. No ice, but if we wrap it wet it'll cool you as it evaporates. Gotta find some cloth to use for Teela's diapers anyway. Can't keep washing the one piece and expecting the sun to dry it in a hurry so I can put it back on!"

Something rose like a sunburst in his mind. Something about the last data he'd been playing with before he left Maryland. *The problem is moisture outgassing when the sails unfurl—*

"I still know some guys on the Crisis Team. Not too far off the interstate from here."

—causing tumbling—Gotta get the gyroscopes stabilized—

"What?" He hadn't been listening, his brain busy spinning through remembered data that was starting to make sense. If Chen was still in business—he had to be!—they could do this. A relatively small fix and the shades would work.

"We'd have a chance of catching a ride with the sheriffs."

"But you said—" He stopped, awkward in the face of her grief.

"I couldn't save mine," she said, so softly he almost didn't catch the words. "But this one—"

The baby's dark eyes were open when he looked at her. *The package needs to be dried out before it goes into the envelope.* That was it. That was what Chen needed to know.

Sunlight hazed Persey's hair into a halo of fire. Their scent was warm, familiar somehow. He gazed at her. "No illusions?"

She shook her head.

"And no guarantees the future's going to be better. At least," he amended, "not immediately."

"Beats the alternative!" She made an attempt to smile at him. "Deal?"

"Deal."

He tucked her free arm under his. Funny, he thought, life doesn't make any guarantees, but when you think you've run out of options, it gives you butterfly wings and babies. And somehow, that was enough to keep going.

Sheila is the author of the "lingster" series about alien communication, including The Guild of Xenolinguists and Reading the Bones. She lives in Southern California with a bossy cat and a retired racing greyhound. Online at
http://sff.net/people/sheila-finch
http://lingster1@livejournal.com
http://www.facebook.com

I like this story because it brings a sense of reality to the often ignored but very real water problems of the American southwest. Set in central California, this story is a reasonable extrapolation of water shortages told through the point of view of a character whose meaning for life is impacted in every way.

The author, Randy Henderson, is a 2009 graduate of Clarion West writers workshop. I met Randy virtually through Codex Writers Group, which he joined in October of 2009. This was the first piece of Randy's fiction that I ever read, and I think you'll agree it's a good one.—RN

A Shelter for
Living Things
by Randy Henderson

Carmel shushed the seven dogs that skittered across her living room's wooden floor, and gripped her electric cattle prod as she peeked out the front window. It took her a second to recognize the graying blonde woman standing on the porch. Ralph's wife, Josine. Carmel set the cattle prod down and swiped at the dog hair covering her jeans and flannel shirt, then opened the door. She was so surprised to see Josine that she didn't notice the squat white robot also standing on the porch until it moved its oblong head to look up at her. She flinched, and took a step back.

"Hello," Josine said. "I've come to tell you that Ralph is dead. He left this letter for you." Her hand jerked forward as if yanked by a string, and in it was held an envelope.

"Dead?" Carmel stared at Josine, feeling as though they were speaking in a foreign language. The word didn't make sense. How could Ralph be dead?

"Yes. A car accident. He was on his way over here to help you with your stupid animal shelter. Here." She thrust the letter at Carmel again. Carmel took the letter, and noticed that the envelope had been sealed but was now torn open.

"I read it," Josine said, and her tone offered no apology. "And he left you his robot."

Carmel looked at the robot. The blue circles of light that were its eyes blinked at her. "I didn't even know he had one," she said. Though why wouldn't he? Ralph had never said he didn't, and given her dislike of the things she couldn't blame him for not mentioning it. It was proportioned like a human child wearing a backpack. No doubt a conscious choice, just like the digital eyes and whatever artificial personality it had, all meant to manipulate people into liking the darned thing, treating it like it was alive. "Why would he give it to me?"

Josine flicked a hand at the letter. "It's in there." She turned and walked down the porch steps.

"Wait! I don't want this thing."

"Why not? Isn't taking in abandoned pets what you do?"

"This...thing is not a pet!"

"Then sell it," Josine said without turning back. "It's worth a lot." She put a hand on the door of her triwheel, and without looking at Carmel said, "Did you sleep with him? Were you two having an affair?"

Carmel sighed. "No." She was grateful in that moment that her answer was the truth, despite all the times she had wished Ralph had no wife, or that he wasn't such an honorable man. He was the only person she had seen on a regular basis, the only human interaction she had enjoyed. She could already feel his absence in the life ahead of her, as though a great canyon had suddenly appeared at her feet.

Josine did not respond, but got into her vehicle and drove away.

Carmel stared at the robot for a second, then stepped back inside. The robot started to follow, but Carmel shut the door so fast that she heard the bump of robot hitting wood.

The dogs sniffed at her legs and feet. "No new friends today," she said. She peeked out the front window at the robot. It stood facing the door, its head held at a dejected angle, its digital blue eyes sloped down on the outer edges, mimicking an expression of human sadness.

Carmel refused to be manipulated. The darned thing was a machine, nothing more. She pulled out Ralph's final letter and read it.

Carmel,
I have prepared this letter in case of my death.

You make a difference with what you do, and you let me be a part of it. Thank you for that, and for being my friend.

If I'm gone you are still going to need some help with your shelter, with the lifting and cleaning and repairs, so I'm leaving you my robot. Robots aren't evil. They didn't ask to replace animals as pets. But it can help you to take care of your animals. Use it, please. I imprinted it to your image, and the new programming should kick in when it sees you. Its name is Virgil.

You have a good heart, Carmel, and I wish you a long and happy life.

Ralph

Carmel shook her head. "Ralph, you old fool. Thank you, but no thank you." She would sell the robot as soon as she could.

She had expected to cry when she read the letter, but no tears came. She just felt a sudden weariness.

Carmel pulled weeds from the garden behind her house, enjoying the gentle burn of the sun on her back and shoulders. A breeze carried the smell of cut grass from the patchy brown fields that made up her property, and birds tweeted and trilled from the stunted oaks and pines that grew on the hills surrounding it. Her twenty dogs started barking from their enclosed area, running up and down the line of the chain link fence, raising dust. A few seconds later she heard the sound of a car coming up the gravel road.

She went into the house and grabbed her cattle prod and the phone off of the kitchen counter. Her land was in an unincorporated rural area, isolated enough that she could barely get groceries delivered every couple of weeks, but not so much that the occasional group of bored or drunk teens from town didn't try using her pets for sport. She worried that it was just a matter of time before they decided to use her for sport. As far as she was concerned, anyone who could hurt animals could just as easily hurt humans.

She peeked out the front window. The robot was still standing there in the same pose of pretend sadness. And a man and woman stood in the driveway beside a parked Chevy ESUV, looking at the house. They had the appearance of wealthy urbanites, not trouble. Probably drove all the way out from Bakersfield. Carmel put the cattle prod in her back pocket anyway, and stepped outside.

"Hi," the man said. "Is this the private animal shelter?"

"Yes," Carmel said. "Want to adopt a pet?"

The man and woman exchanged glances. "Um, no," the man said. "Actually, we were hoping to leave our dog with you?" He stepped aside, and Carmel saw a mature golden retriever watching her through the car window.

"Why can't you keep it?" Carmel said.

The woman started to speak, but the man overrode her. "We just don't have the room he needs, I'm afraid. We bought a condo downtown, and poor Buster would have nowhere to walk, nothing to do. We thought it would be better if he had someplace like this." He waved at Carmel's property.

The woman said, "I noticed electric wires on the fences coming in here. You don't shock the animals, do you?"

The man frowned. "I'm sure she knows what she's doing, honey."

"Actually," Carmel said. "My parents raised cows, before vat-grown meat and the water shortages drove them out of business. The fences aren't electrified now."

"Would Buster stay in the house?" the woman asked. "He likes to sleep on the end of the bed. I mean, I know you have a lot of animals, but –"

"I have twenty dogs and too many cats," Carmel said. "Only the oldest or the neediest stay in the house. The rest have beds in the barn." She nodded towards the weathered blue building whose peak was visible over the single-story house.

"Buster's pretty old," the woman said.

Carmel looked at Buster. Perhaps the couple had decided to trade him in for a young fresh clone of himself. "If there's any way you can keep him, I'd encourage that," she said. "Changing his home so late in life –"

"Look," the man said. "The fact is, the condo doesn't allow pets. In fact, the whole city has now restricted them. Haven't you heard?"

Carmel shook her head. "I don't pay much attention to the news out here."

"Still, you had to have heard about the South American terrorists spreading super rabies?"

"That was over a year ago," Carmel said. "And pets weren't ever the problem."

"Yeah, well, the city still says that animals are a health risk. And there's just not enough water to spare for them, least that's what they say. So we have to find a new home for Buster, or put him to sleep. Which would you prefer?"

The woman looked away, avoiding Carmel's eyes. Clearly, there was more to the story. But Carmel wasn't going to press. She didn't care really. If these folks didn't want Buster, then Buster was better off without them. "I'll take him. Do you have papers on him, vet records?"

"No," the man said. "Is that a problem?"

"Nope."

The couple visibly relaxed when it was clear that Carmel had agreed to take the dog, and Buster was soon on a runner sniffing around the eaves of the house.

"Noticed your bot," the man said, nodding to the porch. "Miyamoto, right? Better than the glorified Roombas most people have."

"Thanks. You want to buy it?"

The man blinked, then said, "No. We just bought an ATS-bot. It's actually based on the one the Japs sent to the moon."

He was bragging, judging by his tone, but it was wasted on Carmel since she didn't know an ATS from a Toyota. She didn't understand why people bothered trying to impress her to begin with. She didn't dress in fancy clothes, never wore makeup or jewelry, didn't put on any airs. People were the one animal she just didn't get.

"Congratulations," she said. "I'm sure the robot will make a lovely companion." Carmel didn't bother to keep the sarcasm from her tone. The fact that people brought their pets to her rather than abandoning them on the side of the highway or putting them to sleep just wasn't enough these days to earn any points with her.

The man did not react to the sarcasm. He probably just wanted done with the matter. So Carmel concluded their business, and the couple left.

She turned to find the robot petting Buster, scratching behind his ears. Buster's tongue lolled out, and he leaned into the robot's touch.

Carmel frowned. "Stop that. Get back on the porch." The robot continued petting the dog. She took a step towards it but stopped. She didn't feel comfortable getting too close to it. "You, robot, stop!" Still the robot continued petting the dog, although Buster was now looking at Carmel with his ears back and sad eyes.

"Oh, don't give me that look," she said.

Why wouldn't the robot obey her? "Ah. Right. I have to call you by name so I'll start to think of you like a frickin pet – oh, sorry, I mean so you won't think I'm talking to the phone or the invisible man or something. Fine. Virgil, knock it off."

The robot stopped petting the dog and turned to her. "Yes Carmel," it said. "What shall I do now?" The voice was that of a young boy, bright and eager to please.

"Get back on the porch and stay there." The robot remained still. Carmel rolled her eyes. "Virgil, get on the porch and stay there. Simon frickin says, for Christ's sake."

"Where is 'the porch'?"

Carmel threw her hands in the air. "Jesus, and I thought you things were supposed to be smart. Here," she stomped up onto the porch and pointed down. "This is the porch. Virgil, get up on the porch."

The robot used the treaded wheels on its feet to roll up to the steps, then used normal walking movements to climb up onto the porch.

"There, great," Carmel said. "I don't know how Ralph thought you were going to help me when you can't even find the porch. Now stay. I mean, Virgil, stay here. Don't move. And leave my dogs alone."

"Yes, Carmel," the robot said in its little boy voice.

Carmel went inside, and then peeked out the window to make sure the robot hadn't taken it upon itself to go mow the lawn or something. But it was still just standing there. She glanced up at the sky. Gray clouds were visible on the horizon, just over the treetops, a rare spot of rain creeping in on her patch of thirsty earth. She sighed. It probably wouldn't do any good to leave the bot outside to be rained on, or to be vandalized or stolen before she could sell it. She opened the door. "Virgil, come inside."

The robot came inside, and said, "Carmel, what can I do you for?"

Carmel felt a lump form in her throat. Ralph used to always ask her that. Damn him, he must have programmed the bot to say that.

"Virgil, go stand in the corner there, out of the way, and go to sleep or whatever it is you do."

"Yes, Carmel. Shall I set an alarm to awaken at a specific time?"

"No. Just go to sleep."

"Was your answer directed at me?"

"Yes! Virgil, do not set an alarm, just go to sleep."

"Yes, Carmel." The robot did as she had instructed.

She really needed to figure out a way to sell the darned thing soon. If she had to talk to it much more, she might just take a shovel to its head.

Carmel managed most of her property with the help of a solar-charged riding mower, a mounted robotic Power Arm, and good old elbow grease, all inherited from her parents. Still, she soon felt Ralph's absence. He had come by once a week to help her maintain the place and do the heavy labor. That had freed her up to do everything else, like cleaning up the animals' messes, changing their bedding, and caring for the sick and the old animals, not to mention taking care of herself, her garden, and her home. She could handle it all without him, especially with the help of the machines, but it all still required time and energy.

So Ralph's absence left her feeling even more exhausted and overwhelmed than usual, and that meant that two weeks went by and she still hadn't posted any classified ads for the robot. She did, however, throw a sheet over it so that she did not have to look at it (and to stop the cats from using it as a climbing post).

She was fixing the corrugated plastic roof on the chicken coop when a white sedan hummed up the driveway. Carmel went to meet the man who stepped out of the car. He was dressed in a gray suit and aviator sunglasses, and the sedan had a Vivi Water logo on the door.

"Hello," Carmel said when she reached him. She stretched her back, her muscles burning. "What can I do for you?"

"Are you the property owner?" he asked.

"Yes."

"Ma'am, I'm here to inform you that you are in violation of the county ordinance prohibiting the keeping of multiple pets. You have thirty days to comply with the law, or be fined one thousand dollars per pet per month for as long as you remain in violation."

"What? But I'm outside the town limits, even for Caliente. This land is unincorporated –"

"Laws regulating the usage of water extend to wherever the town's contracted water supplier provides service. You are currently supplied by the Vivi Water company."

"No, I'm on the local water district. I just got a bill from them. I can show it to you."

"Vivi Water assumed private management of your water district last fall. Here." The man handed Carmel a letter. "An officer will return in thirty days to verify compliance."

"But this is an animal shelter. The whole point is to have multiple animals."

"Animal shelters are no longer allowed on public water utilities. You can transfer the animals to a shelter outside of town limits, or move your shelter –"

"That is ridiculous. If I got any more outside of town, nobody would bother bringing their pets to me."

"Ma'am, I don't make the laws. You have thirty days. Good bye."

"But –"

The man got into his car and drove away.

Carmel stood for several minutes watching the dust of his departure fade. Her eyes watered, and she wanted to go lie down, to sleep and let her exhausted mind escape her sore body. But she couldn't. There was too much to do even without this new problem. If Ralph was still here, she would call him.

And what would he do? Probably research the issue on the web.

She went inside and sat at her kitchen table where her webpad sat. She sighed, and blew dust off of the touchscreen. Keeping her home dust free was an impossible task with so many pets shedding hair and dander. She turned on the pad and touched the lips icon.

"Search for animal shelters and water utilities," she said.

A list of results appeared on the screen. Carmel selected a couple, but soon got lost in the maze of links leading to other links leading to advertisements. At the top of the search results however was the line she had always ignored before: "Robot search supported".

"Oh, what the hell." Using the robot as a fancy computer was something she could accept, something that made sense to her. It would certainly make Ralph happy to know she'd at least used it for something before she sold it. She pulled the bed sheet off of it and said, "Virgil, wake up."

The robot's blue eyes lit up, and its head tilted to look up at her. "What can I do you for, Carmel?"

"Virgil, help me research something. How can I keep an animal shelter on the public water system?"

"Researching. Results found. Do you want the answers in order of relevance or in order of date provided?"

"Order of relevance."

"Carmel, were you speaking to me?"

"Oh, for Chripe's sake Virgil, is there some way to talk to you without having to use your name every time?"

"Carmel, yes, you may say my name followed by 'start conversation' to begin a conversation with me, and use 'end conversation' to end the conversation. You will not be –"

"Fine. Virgil, start conversation. Give me the answers in order of relevance."

"Top answer: As of March first, you may only house a single pet weighing twenty pounds or less. If you currently own a pet in excess of twenty pounds you may keep that pet with proof that the animal was purchased or adopted prior to March first, and the animal is current on all required shots, but you may not clone that animal with the intent of keeping the clone, nor replace that pet with another animal in excess of the weight limit. Carmel, was my answer helpful?"

"No, not at all." Maybe the problem was that she was asking the wrong question. She had hoped that the robot would make this search stuff easier, but it didn't seem that much more helpful or smart than her webpad. She could dig through answers forever and never get the answer she wanted.

Dig.

Carmel sat up straight. She could dig a well. The Vivi guy had said that the law extended to whoever used their water. So if she stopped using their water, they couldn't do anything about her animals. She smiled.

"Virgil, what's the phone number for a local company that digs wells?"

"Carmel, there is one number listed with the words 'well location and excavation.' Do you want this result?"

"Yes."

Virgil gave her the number for a company called Water Alternatives. She dialed it. A female voice answered, "Hello Carmel, thank you for calling Vivi Water, we bring the water to you. How may I direct your call?"

"Wait, is this the right number? I was trying to call Water Alternatives."

"Transferring you to Water Alternatives. Please hold."

Carmel realized the voice had been automated. She actually missed the days when you could tell the voice was computerized by the way the words seemed cut and pasted together. It creeped her out a little to think she might not have spoken to a live person on the phone in years.

A man's voice came on. "Hello Carmel, this is Water Alternatives. How may I help you?"

"Is this a person?" Carmel asked.

"My name is Tom. What can I do for you?"

Was that an answer? Carmel shook her head. She had more important concerns. "Water Alternatives is part of Vivi Water?"

"Yes, we are Vivi Water's authorized alternative water solutions providers. How may we help you?"

"Well, I need a well dug. But if Vivi digs it, does that mean I'm still on your water system?"

"Yes, all well and septic systems provided by Vivi Water are guaranteed to provide the excellent quality and reliability you've come to expect from Vivi Water, and by leasing the systems you never have to worry about breakdowns or repairs because Vivi Water covers its systems for life. Would you like to schedule an estimate? "

"But...what if I don't want to lease my well from Vivi Water? Is there some way I can just get the well dug and take care of it myself?"

"Vivi Water is the only legally authorized provider of water services in your area. This protects you from health risks, and later costs that –"

Carmel hung up.

"Virgil, I need a different phone number for somebody who digs wells."

"Carmel, I have given you the one phone number listed that matches your request. Would you like me to repeat it?"

"Shoot." She got up and paced for a minute.

"Carmel, are you experiencing stress? Would you like some tea, or a massage?"

Both of those things sounded like heaven to Carmel, and she almost said "yes" before realizing it. Darn sneaky little thing.

"No, I wouldn't." She continued to pace. "What I need is a well." There had to be an alternative to Vivi's "alternative."

"Carmel, I can provide information and assistance in building, maintaining and testing a well. Would you like to know more?"

"Yes. Of course I would."

Virgil proceeded to outline the required steps and materials for creating various types of dug and pipe wells, and the pros and cons of each type. It didn't sound so hard, especially a pipe well. She just needed to get the right kind of pipes, particularly the special spiked end that went first and allowed the water into the pipe. She could use Virgil and the Power Arm to drive the pipe into the ground. She began to feel pressure dissipating from her shoulders.

"Carmel, were my answers helpful?"

"Yes, very," Carmel said, distracted by the plans forming in her mind.

Virgil turned once in a silly little dance, whistling a happy tune. Carmel smiled, then shook her head, annoyed at herself for getting pulled in. "Virgil, please stop acting like a child. You're not fooling anyone."

Virgil stopped. His head drooped, and his face displayed the sad expression he had shown the day he arrived.

"Oh, pea soup! Virgil, I said stop it. No more fake emotions."

Virgil resumed a neutral stance and expression.

"Better. Can you figure out where to dig a well on my property?"

"I do not have the ability to detect underground water. I have information on recommended well sites based on tree location and other visual and topographical indicators."

Darn. She didn't have time to waste trying to drive a well where there wouldn't be any water. She needed to be sure. But how was she going to find the water when Vivi apparently had a corner on even the "alternative" water services?

Maybe if she went really alternative.

"Virgil, are there any phone numbers for water dowsers near me?"

"Carmel, there is one phone number that includes the words 'water dowser' in the listing."

Carmel called the number, and made an appointment with a man named Nate Burgh. He couldn't come out for almost a week, but Carmel got a good feeling from talking to him.

She managed to stop herself from complimenting Virgil again on his help.

The next morning Carmel threw her back out as she lifted a bag of dog food.

"Son of a biscuit!"

She lumbered into the house and eased into her armchair with an icepack. Her house dogs did their dance to determine who got to sit closest to her.

40

Virgil said, "Carmel, what can I do you for?"

Carmel's eyes burned, and a sob burst out, though tears refused to come.

"Carmel, do you require medical attention?"

She didn't want to answer, but if she didn't then the stupid bot would probably call an ambulance or something. "No, Virgil. I'm fine." That made her begin to sob in earnest, so that her shoulders shook and her back twinged in protest, which in turn made her sob even harder. It was not just the burning pain in her back that made her sob. It was everything. The feeling of pressure like a pile of earth pressing down on her. She had so much to do, and now on top of it all the county might come and take her animals away unless she could get off of Vivi's water system.

She wished she could talk to Ralph.

Buster licked at her hand, and looked up at her with sad eyes. She smiled through her sobs, and rubbed his tawny head. Leo, a fat old bulldog who was ever jealous of Carmel's attention, waddled over from his bed in the corner and head-butted his way past Buster to lick Carmel's hand as well.

"Good boys. Go lay down. Mama's okay."

Except that she wasn't. She could barely move. And she couldn't afford to fall any further behind in her tasks. The dogs still needed to be fed, and a new hole dug for their waste. She could use the robotic Power Arm, but she would still have to move it into place, and do some of the finer work that was too difficult to do with the arm's metal pincers and jerky movements. She looked over at Virgil and sighed.

She might as well use the bot as long as it was sitting around her house. Given the number of her dogs that were here because their owners had replaced them with robots, it seemed the least that Virgil could do.

"Virgil, start conversation. Do you think you could feed the dogs and dig a hole?"

"Carmel, do bees be? Do bears bear?"

Carmel laughed, a hiccup of a laugh. Another Ralphism.

Darn you Ralph, why did you have to go and die?

Virgil continued, "I will require assistance to complete the tasks the first time, but can then repeat them."

"Good. Okay. Follow me." Carmel eased to her feet, and shuffled outside to the barn. Virgil followed her out. She called the dogs into the barn and got them sorted into their individual kennels. Then she demonstrated giving dog food to a couple of the dogs. "Okay, Virgil, now you try. Feed the dogs."

"Yes, Carmel." Virgil scooped a cup full of dog food and rolled to the next dog kennel. "Carmel, what is this dog's name?"

"Max."

"Carmel, how many times a day is the dog fed?"

"Twice. Look, can you dump food into a bowl or not?"

"Carmel, I am calculating the appropriate food amount based on dog breed, approximate weight and feeding frequency. Feeding now." Virgil tipped the cup and dribbled dog food into the dog's bowl, and then turned the cup back upright. As Max snuffed eagerly at his bowl, Virgil scratched him behind the ears and said, "Good boy Max. Chow time!"

Virgil turned to her. "Carmel, shall I continue to feed the dogs?"

"Yes. Feed the dogs, Virgil. End Conversation."

"Okeedokee, artichokee."

Carmel sat in her recliner and watched through the window as the robot threw tennis balls for the dogs. She had used Virgil's help for a number of chores over the past few days. She kept expecting reproachful or accusing looks from the dogs, as if she had somehow betrayed them, but they didn't seem to mind the bot.

"Why do the dogs bark like mad at the vacuum cleaner but love that dumb robot?" Carmel muttered to Sammy, the gray cat curled up in her lap. "Well, I suppose if a vacuum cleaner threw them a ball, fed them, and scratched behind their ears, they'd probably like it too. They just don't know any better."

The dogs didn't know and didn't care that robots were rapidly replacing them. Would even the true pet lovers hold out much longer as the costs and hassles continued to increase, and with robots that looked and acted like real animals ready to fill their needs? Carmel shuddered to imagine ending up in a nursing home with a robot dog-nurse as her only companion.

Still, she was recovering from her back strain without falling behind on her chores thanks to Virgil. In fact, she found herself with a bit of free time and energy at the end of the day. She had downloaded a new book and actually found time to read it.

"I suppose this doesn't suck," she said to Sammy as she read her book and sipped some tea. She realized that she would have to find some way to simplify her life, or spend her time and energy more efficiently, so that she could manage the shelter without the help of Ralph or the robot and enjoy more time like this.

Or perhaps she should go ahead and keep the robot rather than sell it, as Ralph had wanted. She had trusted his advice on other things, why not this? Nobody said she had to like the robot, or treat it any differently than her webpad or Power Arm or dishwasher just because other folks did so. It certainly seemed foolish not to use it as long as she had it, especially with a well to be dug. "And I'm not getting any younger," she said to Sammy. "Like it or not, I'm going to need help eventually, no matter what I do."

Sammy gave her a look that said the cat could care less about Carmel's future, but all the talking was disturbing her rest.

Yes, if Carmel could put up with cats, she could tolerate the robot, at least on her own terms.

Even so, when she found Buster lying dead at the foot of her bed, her first thought was that the robot might have killed him.

Buster lay with his legs out straight as if frozen in a morning stretch, his eyes open and staring at nothing. Carmel then realized he had died of old age, or perhaps an illness. That was why his owners had gotten rid of him. They had known this would happen soon. Carmel sat down and just looked at him for a minute, letting the all-too-familiar shock and sorrow crash over her. And then it rolled off of her leaving her feeling tired and focused, mentally adjusting her morning schedule to include burying Buster and cleaning his bedding.

Virgil dug the grave using the Power Arm, but Carmel insisted on carrying Buster out by herself, in spite of her sore back. It just didn't feel right to have him hauled out by a machine. She laid him down into the hole as gently as she could, and then stood for a minute as her eyes burned, wishing Buster a happy afterlife.

Virgil said, "The wolf and the lamb will feed together, and the lion will eat straw like the ox. You will be missed Buster, but we know you are in a happier place. Amen."

"That...that was nice, Virgil. Thanks."

"You are welcome, Carmel. What shall I do now?"

"Virgil, replace the dirt in the hole."

As she watched the first shovelfuls of dirt land on top of Buster, Carmel said, "What do people do with robots when they break? Put them on their mantel?"

Virgil said, "Bring your deceased robot to Miyabotics to receive a discount on a new model. For a small fee, Miyabotics will also transfer all data from your old robot to your new one, saving you the time of training your new friend."

Deceased? Friend? Carmel's back straightened and she crossed her arms. "You're just a robot, a machine. You don't die, Virgil, and you're not my friend. And I'm certainly not going to trade you in for a newer model."

"Yes, Carmel." Virgil continued to move the dirt.

The water dowser, Nate Burgh, arrived the next day in a well-used blue Ford pickup truck. When Carmel heard him arrive she looked down at herself and shook her head. It wasn't often that she knew ahead of time that someone was coming and could prepare for it, and yet here she was a mess, with her hair in a frazzled bun and her coveralls covered in dirt from working in her garden. Then she shrugged. She was just too tired to care at this point. She went and met Nate in the driveway.

Nate looked like an Irish lumberjack, with bushy red beard and close-cropped hair. He smelled like wood smoke. He held out a beefy hand and smiled.

"Nice to meet you. So you need some dowsing done?"

Carmel shook his hand. "Yes, please."

Nate explained his rates and the process to her, and she agreed to it.

"Well all right," he said. "Let's do this then."

Carmel followed him around to the back of his truck, and said, "If you know anyone who installs wells and pump systems, that would be great too."

Nate shook his head. "The last person I knew who would risk the city and county fines was a Mexican friend of mine, and he got sent back south for doing it. You can build one yourself though, if you don't mind paying the fines as part of the cost for doing so."

"I still can't believe the government would really go after someone for digging a hole."

Nate grabbed a case out of the back of the truck. "It's not just a hole, and it's not really the government. It is about water companies controlling the water. Not much of the good stuff left, and it's become as precious as oil. Why do you think the CIA put that puppet government in Paraguay? It wasn't for freedom and Democracy, I'll tell you that." Nate pulled a Y-shaped willow stick out of the case, then shook his head. "Sorry, I didn't mean to go all ranty on you. Look, I can help you find water on your land if it is there to find. And I'll be happy to share what I know about building wells and pump systems and anything else. It's not illegal to talk about it. Not yet anyway. That's the best I can do for you. Now let's go find you some water."

Nate walked around with one branching of the willow stick in each hand, the base pointed out in front of him. Occasionally the tip swung down to point at the ground, usually over a patch of green grass or near a tree, and Nate drove a wooden stake with an orange ribbon into the earth at those spots.

They passed near the fenced-in dog area. Virgil stood nearby throwing balls for the dogs—all of them except Leo, her bull dog, who lay like a brown and white lump in a wagon waiting for Virgil to pull him around the yard. Nate looked at Virgil and shook his head.

"Is something wrong?" Carmel asked.

"No. Sorry. No offense, but robots always creep me out a little."

Carmel glanced sideways at Virgil and leaned in closer to Nate. "I totally agree. I've never really liked them."

Nate chuckled. "And yet you seem worried about offending it."

"What?" Carmel looked at Virgil. "No. No, I just, you know, I don't want the stupid thing to stop doing what I ask because Miyabotics programmed it to be offended or some such nonsense."

"Of course. No worries, I understand." Nate spoke without any hint of mockery in his tone. "My wife would have loved your place, by the way. We both used to talk about getting some land and taking in as many of those poor dogs from the pound as we could, the ones who were going to be put to sleep. Course, that was before the pounds turned into recycling centers."

"Don't get me started," Carmel said. Then she glanced sideways at Nate. "You said your wife 'would have' loved it?"

"Yeah. Verna passed away four years ago."

"I'm sorry."

"Thanks. She was a good woman. As are you, I can tell. It's a good thing you're doing here."

Carmel blushed. "Thanks."

There was a moment of awkward silence.

"Well," Nate said. "I think we're pretty well done. Any of the spots we marked will be a good place for a well. The water's probably not too deep, so you can drive pipe or dig it, no need to drill. I'd start with the spots furthest from the dog areas to reduce chance of contamination, though you could build a second one closer in for general cleaning and watering and such. "

Carmel looked around her property, at the stakes she could see. "So, I just need to buy the pipes and pumps and drive the pipe into the ground, right? Doesn't seem too hard."

"Well, it isn't, and it is." Nate looked over at the dog area, and his mouth scrunched to one side for a second. "Look, I can't help you professional like, but I supposed I could give you some friendly guidance. Help you order what you need, show you what to do, like that."

"I'd really appreciate that," Carmel said, and looked up at the sky. "It's close to dinner time. Why don't you stay? I'll fix you something. It's the least I can do for your help."

"That would be nice, actually."

Carmel crawled into bed. Three days of driving pipe and hooking up pumping equipment on top of her regular chores, she should feel exhausted. Yet she had a hard time feeling sleepy when she thought about Nate. He had come by every evening to help out, despite his continuous assertion that he was not officially helping her build a well.

Driving the well pipe wasn't all that complicated. But Carmel knew from her time with Ralph how much a man liked to feel useful, to feel like a hero for every little thing he did to help, so she let Nate give her his constant advice, let him demonstrate his skill at wrapping pipe threads in Teflon tape, or use his fancy level to get the pipe perfectly vertical. She smiled at the image of his face scrunched in concentration as he adjusted the pipe by an invisible fraction of an inch.

The dogs in the barn started barking. The dogs in the bedroom jumped off of the bed and joined the noise.

"Oh quiet! Herc, Sally, you lay down! It's probably just a raccoon."

The barking outside did not stop. And Leo, her fat old bulldog, woofed like mad in the living room where he had been banished due to his deadly-smelling gas. Carmel gave a frustrated sigh, threw on her robe, and grabbed the flashlight and cattle prod off of the dresser.

A sudden blaring noise from the direction of the living room caused her to jump, and brought a fresh round of howling and barking from the dogs in the bedroom. Carmel thought it was the smoke alarm for a second, but it was a whooping sound, not the smoke alarm's piercing beeps. She pushed the dogs back from the bedroom door, and slipped out into the hallway.

She heard male voices speaking in loud whispers, every few words nearly drowned out by the siren but Carmel was able to piece together what they said.

"I thought you said she didn't have a robot?"

"She didn't, least not the last time I delivered her stupid groceries. Just a bunch of old dogs."

Leo was still barking, and Carmel felt worry squeeze her throat. It would be just like Leo to attack those boys and get himself hurt.

The siren stopped and Virgil's voice blared, "The police have been called and are on their way. All intruder actions are being recorded."

"Go check on the dog lady!"

Carmel clutched the cattle prod tight, her hand shaking. She put her hand on the bedroom door handle, ready to unleash her defenders. The only reason she had not already done so was that she did not want her dogs to get hurt. Please, let these punks just leave.

"No," one of the voices said. "Just forget about her. We need to get out of here."

Carmel felt the rush of relief.

"Shit! Shit. Okay. Wait, the robot recorded us." There was a loud crashing, the sound of metal and plastic being smashed with something heavy. They were hitting Virgil!

"Hey!" Carmel shouted, "Stop that!" She opened her bedroom door. The dogs burst out, and Carmel followed the rush towards the living room, ready to zap anyone she found, but she heard the front door slam open before she reached the room.

Virgil stood near his corner, Leo held squirming in his arms. His shattered head was hanging to the side, half-detached, his blue eyes flickering. Carmel slammed the front door closed and locked it, and closed the open window beside it. Then she hefted the bulldog out of the crook of Virgil's arms, and worked his collar free of Virgil's frozen hand.

"Virgil, can you hear me?"

"Do bees be?" Virgil responded, his voice distorted. "Do bears –"

There was a flash of light inside Virgil's head that caused the white plastic to glow for a second, then an electrical burning smell.

Virgil's eyes went dark.

"Oh god." Carmel knelt and held Leo in a close hug. A familiar shock rolled over her.

Why did she feel as though one of her pets had just died?

She shook herself, and went to the phone to call the police. And to call Nate. She wanted more company than her dogs could give just now.

Carmel stood with Nate beside the hole where Virgil lay, and looked back to the driveway. She had invited Ralph's wife, Josine. The robot had been something like a pet of Ralph's, had felt like a part of him, and Carmel thought maybe Josine would want to say goodbye. But the woman had not come, had not even responded to Carmel's message.

"You sure you want to bury it?" Nate asked. "You could probably still get some money for it, or trade it in."

"I'm sure," Carmel said.

"Is it because it saved your life? Protected your dogs?"

"No. I think...I just didn't get to say goodbye to Ralph, not properly. I wasn't invited to his funeral, and I think the robot made me feel a bit like he was still around somehow. I guess this is just my way of having my own funeral for him. Do you think that's strange?"

"Nope," Nate said. "I'm sure he'd like it."

Carmel hoped so. She grabbed a shovel and filled in the hole with Nate's help, saying goodbye to Ralph as she did so. Then Nate took both their shovels and headed back towards the house. Carmel started to follow, but turned back. She stared at the grave, and struggled with the feeling that she still needed to do or say something more.

At last she whispered, "The wolf and the lamb will feed together. And the lion will eat straw like the ox. You will be missed Virgil. Now go to sleep."

When the robot did not respond, tears finally filled Carmel's eyes.

Randy Henderson is a writer, gamer, relapsed sarcasm addict, Clarion West graduate, milkshake connoisseur, and regular non-fiction contributor to Fantasy Magazine. His super secret speculative fiction scribing sanctum is definitely absolutely nowhere near Washington State. Online at www.randy-henderson.com.

This story departs from the usual and puts the spotlight on professional wrestlers. In this case, the wrestlers are physically enhanced. Told from the point of view of a washed-up old-school hold-out, it is as much a character story as anything else in this volume.

The characters in this story are the type that you don't run into in most stories, and in reality, how many stories about pro-wrestlers are there?

Jason S. Ridler has exploded onto the spec-fic scene with dozens of short story sales in the past couple of years, including appearances in Chiaroscuro and Nossa Morte. He is a graduate of the Odyssey Writing Workshop and holds a PhD in War Studies from the Royal Military College of Canada.—RN

Showing Light
by Jason S. Ridler

Chester slumped on a stool in the dark of The Starshine Diner. His thumb scratched a fake scar through the grease on his skin. Silvery pain flexed his lungs like tin bristles and he held his breath until the pain was just a ghost, then gazed out into the midnight parade.

They spilled out of the Palladium Arena, hooting and imitating the gesture of their favorite wrestlers, pretending they had the mech-aguments to do miracles of catch as catch can. They headed for the subway, leaving a trail of broken glass, cigarette butts, and giant foam fingers in their wake, but it was the women that hooked his gaze. Handfuls. Young. Painted up nice, sharp steps in slim boots almost sparked as the heels clicked the asphalt. Times were changing. Back in Dad's day, the best a wrestler could hope to get in the crowd were alcoholic grannies who swung purses like blackjacks. Now? Lithe teen sluts acting like well seasoned ring rats. He stuck a White Owl in his mouth, sucked on the sweet filter, and tried hard not to gawk.

A tap at the door. Eddie, gold tooth sparkling in her fat smile, put her palm screen against the glass. It flashed "$$$". Chester unlocked the door. "You have a few hundred dollars in computer upgrades, but you don't have a key?"

Eddie laughed. "Uncle Sal doesn't trust me like you, Mungy Cake." Chester shut the door as she walked in, locking out the stink of vomit, hot dogs, and beer. Eddie sat at a clean booth, spilling a trail of pink Lucky Elephant popcorn across Chester's clean floor. She put the box down and licked her chubby fingers. "This shit tastes awful, but it's like crack!"

Slowly, Chester dropped his ass in the booth and tried not to feel ancient staring at the tubby eighteen-year-old sprinkled with pink frosting. He stole one last look at the thin legs and asses outside.

Shivers ran through his lungs and he swallowed an awful taste. Same shiver that bit him earlier. Something was wrong. His old wrestling compass shook as if his nerves were about to snap. "So? How did our bets do?"

Eddie lit a joint, took a toke, and tapped the ash on the floor. "Bull's eye every time, Chess man." She handed Chester the joint. Chester pointed at the unlit cigarillo in his mouth. Eddie showed the transfer of funds on her palm. "Each made a grand tonight. Fuck, bro, you're like goddamn Yoda or something. You picked a winner every time!" She laughed. "Betting on wrestling? I thought you were joking when you asked me to do this."

Chester grinned. A grand. That would cover back rent for when he was laid low with the hack attacks. Maybe get Ginny a night out of their apartment. Might even buy him a smile on her face. "You made the bets ok?"

"Sure. Gave that janitor dude, Howie, the password and things were cool." She shook her head. "Chess man, I should not have doubted you. I never thought I'd dig it, because it's fake and shit, but it looked real, bro! How do they do it? Can I go tomorrow night?"

"No," Chester said. His compass was good, but it needed to soak up a crowd in person before the tour began, or else it might . . .

Tremors filled his compass. He coughed, weakly, hoping the hacks were gone. "Now. Are you sure everything went fine?"

Eddie's gaze hung out the window. "Well, I guess you kinda dodged one bullet." She blew a stream of green smoke against the window Chester had just wiped free of grease. "That match you didn't bet on. Demolition Jones and that other dude, the motorcycle dude."

He sighed. "Max Carnage." Saying wrestlers' stage names out loud always made him feel like an idiot, especially to outsiders.

Eddie wheezed with a smile. "Yeah, that fucker has the sweetest ho bag manager."

The compass spun in his chest as he massaged his temples with greasy thumbs. "The match, Eddie?"

"What?" She shook her head. "Right. It was pretty good, but then Demolition guy just kinda stopped caring. It looked fake. Real fake, like how I thought it would. He was boxing air. I felt bad for the motorcycle dude. You could see him trying to make it look good, but it was nasty. The fans, man, they went ballistic. Chanting 'Bullshit' like they weren't getting their money's worth. So that dude lost the crowd, they started cheering for the fucking bad guy, who tore a strip of 'em and soon there was blood and then it looked real again. Guys next to me said Demo Jones lost his seat."

"Heat," Chester said, sucking the last sweetness from the filter and taking out a matchbook. "He lost the crowd." And that's not all. The compass held steady, south. Dave was in trouble. Bad.

"Yeah, because . . . what do you call it? When they don't believe the moves? The drunk fucks next to me kept saying it."

Fire snapped between Chester's fingers as the last express bus passed by. The flame held Eddie's gaze as he danced it in front of the White Owl, the old carny phrase dribbling off his lips. "Showing light. The goddamn jobber was showing light." And that meant his brother was close to parts unknown for good. He blew out the match.

After Eddie left, Chester cleaned up her mess then grabbed the phone in Sal's office. "Hey," he whispered, spinning the dial on the safe under the desk, "it's me. I know, I'm sorry, but things were pretty messy here . . . no, I didn't go, I was working, I told you that this morning. Look, I missed the last bus so I'm just going to stay here. I mean, I have to open in five hours anyway and . . . no, cabs are a waste. Yes they are. I am not walking, the doctor said . . . Look, can you yell at me later? Shit, no, I'm sorry, I'm just beat. And I'll bring home Sal's roast chicken, ok? Why? You love it . . . Oh, god, did you spend more on that diet food? How much? Damn, Ginny. Of course I want you to be healthy. Huh. And, wait . . . no I said I didn't go. God, just go to bed. Bye." He spun the safe's dial one last time, then pulled. Nothing. In his head, he saw his grand become a thousand diet sodas wrapped in barbed wire, Ginny swallowing them until they were all empty.

And Dave was out there, spiraling.

"Hell," he said. The word hurt.

The Charleston Suites hotel was close to the arena, but the short walk from the diner hurt like a marathon and it was days like this he'd wished he'd had lungs that could be jacked and augmented. He jammed a fresh White Owl in his sweaty mouth, then threw away his matches.

The lobby hadn't changed a lick: bright, yellow lighting and a wall of plush red couches with cigarette burns against tacky beige wallpaper. Behind the front desk, an old and spent peroxide blond watched a small, silent TV. He shuffled, lungs starting to tickle.

"There's no smoking here," she said. The nicotine-burr of her voice made the order sound like a complaint.

"It's not lit."

She pinched the bridge of her nose, blinked, then looked again. Her name-tag said Staff. "Can I help you?"

"I'm looking for David Brody."

"We don't give out our patrons' rooms."

"I'm his brother." He handed her his only picture ID.

"This is a library card."

"I like to read."

"No driver's license?"

"No car to get one."

"Going nowhere slowly, huh?"

"What's the rush?"

She snorted, handed back his card. "I can call him if you want." She faced her computers. Keys were punched. She squinted. "No one under that name."

He took the White Owl out. "Oh hell."

She raised a painted eyebrow. "What?"

He closed his eyes, massaged his temples, then stared at his dirty white sneakers. "Try Demolition Jones."

Both her eyebrows raised. "One of them wrestlers?" Chester nodded. "Goddamn gyro-studded, jacked up, half-machine monsters are blowing through here like a metal hurricane full of used diapers." Chester smiled, knowing she was right, and why Ms. Staff was working the night shift when the RWA was in town. Any real pretty thing would be at risk of leaving her post to ride the augmented man-pole of an electric-juice gladiator. "Here he is. You want me to call him?"

"Please. Tell him Kay Fabe is here. It's an old joke." He had no idea if Dave would even want to see him. Dad's funeral was the last time they'd crossed paths. Dave got back on the bus and hit the road, and Chester never looked back. Not at Dave, not at the backstage of an arena, not at a wrestler unless it was from the stands.

She shook her head, then held the phone to her ear. "Nobody answering."

"What's the closest bar? McGinnty's?"

She hung up. "Yeah, but most of those muscle throats are all in a private party." She bit her lip. "But you have to be on the list."

He put the White Owl back. The sweetness vanished, leaving only the childlike taste of a plastic toy with a hint of tobacco. "Any chance I could make that list? It's kinda a matter of life and death."

"Whose?"

Chester thought of the basement full of RWA mech-warriors, and his compass began to quiver. "I'm not sure yet."

She shook her head. "Fine. But I have a price."

"Than I'm shit out of luck, lady, because unless you like diet cola-shakes, I'm broke."

"Just give me a White Owl and get the hell out of here." He did, hearing her lighter flick to life.

He could have guessed the route if she hadn't said anything: elevator to the basement, then the freight elevator to the sub-basement with the private party rooms and the tunnel to the arena. As he descended, the noise got louder. Dance music wailed through the walls and attacked him as the silver doors opened to the green hallway. A half-naked woman ran past the door, screaming and laughing with a giddy speed that only coke heads and their friends enjoy. She shoved a wrestling mask into her lace bra before disappearing, too fast for Chester to commit her beauty to memory.

"Get back here, senorita!" screamed a compact steroid machine who ran like a bullet, hands on his half-mechanized face. "That's my Grandpa's mask!"

Chester exited. It smelled too familiar. Raw. Acidic. Pungent. Stray clothes and champagne bottles lined the dirty walls covered in handprints. Some doors were open. Most were closed. He could only imagine what it would take to clean this place tomorrow. The poor fucking cleaning crew. Lord knows what they'd find. Spent condoms. Spent needles. Spent mech-limbs. Spent bodies.

He chewed the filter and carried on. Dave always took a room near the fire exit. A heavy hand smacked his shoulder. "If you're looking for a way out," boomed a voice with a southern accent, "I can give you a hand, hoss." Iron fingers gripped him with a familiar pinch. "Because this is a private dance." The hand pulled him around and Chester did not resist. Ron Mace's mashed face smiled above his tight, powder-blue dinner jacket. The last of the old school shooters, Ron always enjoyed reminding the augmented that old and pure didn't mean weak and easy.

Chester smiled back. "I was *never* invited to these parties, Ron. Unless Dad grabbed me in a headlock and dragged me to one."

Ron leaned down and examined his face. "Chester? Holy fucking shit!" The bear hug made his teeth crack through the plastic filter. Ron released him and punched his shoulder with a well-scared hand. "Damn it! I didn't see you tonight."

"Couldn't make it. Had the night shift. Heard it was a good one."

"Yeah, yeah. We're really on a roll now." Ron's face hardened. "Shit, Chester. It's been too long. Let me get you a beer and we'll see if we can't rustle up some tail. You still like 'em rail thin with mean eyes, right?"

Chester could feel the weight of the opening shift creeping on him. Even a few hours sleep would take the edge off. He dropped the old White Owl and popped in his last one, sugar burning his lip. "I appreciate it, Ron, but I don't have a lot of time. I really need to see Dave."

Ron massaged the blurry old Marine tattoos on his right first. "You heard about it?" Chester nodded and Ron's face tightened up. "It was bad, kid. Nuclear. I've seen jobbers fresh to the ring with new gears and wires sell better matches. Can't blame Max for blading him."

"He hurt bad?"

Ron shrugged, eyes focused behind him. Chester turned and saw Mike Truscott, AKA Max Carnage, in a white t-shirt and jeans and glowing red mech-eyes fill up the hallway. "Where the fuck is he, Ron? Fuck tomorrow's show and fuck the tour. He nearly broke my goddamn neck and I just bought this one new!"

Ron raised his hands. "Easy, Max. We'll straighten him out."

Like a plane losing its engines, the compass in Chester's heart pulled hard. Max shimmered blue in his eyes.

Max snorted. "Who the fuck is this twat breathing my air?"

"A fan," Chester mumbled. "That's all." There were few things that could get a wrestler with heat fired, but drilling a fan in front of witnesses was solid.

"Well, my fans don't smoke anything with faggot filters." He yanked out the White Owl, then blinked. Sniffed it. "I know this stink." Red eyes narrowed.

"Let's move you along," Ron said, leading Chester past Max.

"Fuck me raw," Max said. "Only the Compass smoked this junk." Chester's back smacked the wall. "Chester? Holy fuck did you pork out." He lay his iron forearm against Chester's throat.

"Lay off, Max," Ron said.

"Touch me, Ron, and I'll crack his Adam's apple to the core." Max's eyes narrowed. "You back on the bus, Compass?"

"No," Chester said. "I just want to see Dave."

"That makes two of us. Sack of shit was showing light, for fucksake! What is this, the twentieth century?"

"I know," Chester said, swallowing the silver taste of phlegm in his mouth. He gritted his teeth, trying to fight the words, but he had to say it. "But he did you a favor."

The pressure tightened. "I don't give a fuck who your daddy was, Compass, so don't—"

"You stole his heat." Chester grunted as Max's whole aura went azure blue. "For the tour. I could feel it. Even outside the arena, Dave fucked up that bad. You're riding blue flames. I can see it now."

Max backed away and Chester gripped himself against a coughing fit. "You shitting me?"

"You tell me. They cheered when you walked out the arena, right? And you didn't do anything to feed it, right? It just poured into you like a draft of premium into a massive stein. Right?"

Max looked at Ron, hands behind his back. "Why don't you drain yourself on the gals we got in your room, Max, then get some sleep. We got the sick kid's hospital photo shoot tomorrow."

Max jutted out his chin, staring Chester down. "I don't care if I got more heat than Santa on Christmas, if your brother shows light next time, it'll be a shoot match and I'll hook him until his balls explode, even if he is a Brody."

He stormed off. Chester rubbed his neck.

"Pretty fast talking," Ron said.

"It's the truth, Ron. He'll be headlining in a year."

"Damn. I kinda wanted to use this." He revealed the old blackjack in his massive hand. Chester smiled. "C'mon. Let's find Dave."

Ron banged on the last door on the left. No answer. He took out a card-key and swiped it across the lock. The red light went green and Ron turned the handle.

Chester sucked his lip. "Better chat with him alone."

Ron nodded, pushed open the door, then slapped Chester's shoulder. "Catch you later, Compass." Ron strolled through the garbage and Chester entered the darkness.

"Dave?"

Ragged breathing came from the far corner. Chester closed the door. "Don't turn on the light."

"But I can't see anything. Can't you turn on a lamp?"

Dad's old zippo lighter snapped on, flame as big as a child's fist, company letters etched in the base. Dave's large, scruffy, scarred face hung off his small skull, and his once-fierce eyes were shaking. A dark, soiled bandage covered his head. He looked like a squished giant. "Howdy, Chess."

"Howdy, Dave. How you doing?"

"I'm dead. How about you?" The flame steadied then shook in his hand. "You see my match?"

"Couldn't make it."

"Then why the fuck are you here?"

Chester walked slowly to the disheveled bed and sat down. "Heard you were in trouble. Thought I might help."

"Help? Gloat, more like it. Fuck . . . I can't stop it, Chess. I just can't. I need it, but it's starting to eat me. I was showing light. Just like Dad the night before you found him. I'm dead. I know I am."

Chester coughed, swallowing silver. "You're not dead, Dave. You're sick."

"Sick?" He spat the word. "I can never get sick! I'm busting my ass three hundred and sixty days, living the dream. And you're fucking jealous, and you always have been!" Dave ranted for ten minutes, flame waving in his hand, face distorted with drugs and rage. Finally, Dave sucked in some air. "Fuck. This never would have happened if you'd stayed."

"Excuse me?"

Dave's eyes broke contact. "It's true. When you left, we had no compass. Boss had us working twice as hard to get half as far, the schedule's insane! Worse than anything Dad or Ron did. Trying new mech parts before trial, real shoot matches, never knowing what would stick, until finally I came up with Demo Jones and..."

"Started cranking gas? Your frame is twice the size it was last year. And your heart-"

Dave stood, flame in his hand. "I had no fucking choice! If you were here, I'd have said no! I'd have some support. You should never have left! Dad would have hated you for it!"

Chester stood. "Watch that shit."

The flame got closer. "You ran. You couldn't do what we did because you got the lungs of a hundred year old smoker. Being a compass wasn't good enough. I knew you wanted what I had, you always did. And when Dad died you couldn't handle me being the fucking star of the family. Admit it! Say it!"

Chester's compass dropped in his gut. Red embers danced around Dave. His career was dead, but not his life. Not yet. Not if someone did something. "I want you to come home with me."

Dave's face contorted. "What? To that shithole near the highway? And do what? Work at that Portuguese grease pit for minimum wage? Are you insane?"

"You don't have to work at Sal's, Dave. There's other things. You don't have to take a last ride on the bus."

The flame shook. "I don't even have a fucking high school diploma! Who's going to hire a guy whose only skill is selling bullshit with his body? Who? I'm not like you. I can't go back to living like a bum. And there's no way Ginny would have me in your house, no fucking way." He took a few deep breaths. "But you could come back. Help me out of the hole. Couldn't you?" He gripped Chester's sore shoulder. "I mean, if anyone could help me out it's you. Keep an eye on me. Get back on the bus, hit the road. There's big plans going on. We could really use you. Boss said you could have your job back."

Chester stepped back as the bile tickled his throat. "The Boss said this?"

Dave's eyes frittered. "Well, sorta."

The compass spun as nausea rolled through his gut and his mouth dried. The flame in Dave's hand began to spin. "You . . . threw that match. Didn't you?" He couldn't see the door in the darkness.

"Take it easy, Chess," Dave said, helping him to the bed. "Just relax. Hear me out. The boss says if you come back to work, they'll let me go. Get clean from cranking gas. Give me the time for a comeback."

He flexed his fists. "Bullshit. They'll leave you to die in detox, or a hotel room as your heart—." Dad's body had been in full rigor, frozen in a collar and elbow hook-up, as if he were wrestling a demon on the floor and losing, eyes wide and bright, lips contorted.

Dave shook his head. "It's my one chance." He placed a hotel key, bus pass, and a wad of cash in Chester's hand, and closed it into a fist. "If you don't sign up, they'll have me wrestling until the scars on my heart pop in the ring. Just like-"

"I can't," Chester said, lungs filling with shards of glass. "They killed Pop, Dave. This business did. Ate him up like a starved rat. I can't work for murderers."

Dave watched the dancing flame. "You'll kill me if you don't, Chess. I won't stop on my own. You know that. They want you back so they can plan the tour. They need the compass. But I need you." The flame got up and left him on the bed and went to the bathroom. "You can have my room upstairs. Penthouse. It's all taken care of."

The freight elevator ride seemed to pull his body apart, but he stumbled out, chest sore.

Across the underground parking lot were grimy stairs leading to the street. Stairs. Walking. Sleeping on Sal's couch. His lungs winced as if he'd already walked to hell and back. He took the parking lot elevator to the lobby, hoping to catch his breath.

The doors opened. Ms. Staff was hunched over a romance novel, and the stink of a burning White Owl thickened the air. He was about to exit-

"Hold the door!"

The click of heels. He jammed the "open door" button with his greasy thumb until a strawberry blond in a see through black dress, nipples the size of silver dollars, got on the elevator smelling of lilacs and gin. Razor thin legs crossed themselves as she nestled in the corner, knees so sharp they seem poised to cut through her black stockings. He kept holding the button.

"Are you going up?" she asked.

His thumb slid off the button and the doors closed. "What floor?"

"Whatever one you're on, handsome," she said, eyes like a cat. She removed a cigarette case from her purse and opened it. "Care for a White Owl?"

Ginny was at home. Belly full of diet cola. Maybe it was better this way. He enabled her. Probably better off without him.

Yeah. Right.

He took a White Owl and pinched it between his lips. She threw him a mean smile that made him ache and pressed the Penthouse button. "Got any matches?"

She handed him a gold lighter, like Dad's, with the company initials. As they began to rise, Chester lit the White Owl, took a heavy drag, and held it until he hacked.

Afterword:

Pro wrestling has been part of my life since I was a kid, but these days I find the lives of pro wrestlers as engaging as the stories they tell in the ring. Sadly, too many wrestler stories are obituaries. Many are dying young, in part because of how they push their bodies and minds with drugs that keep them on the road and on the ropes, even when they should be healing from injuries that would make most men cry just to think about. It got me wondering: what the hell would wrestling be like in the near future? What kind of tragedies would be waiting around the corner? This story was an attempt to find out.

Find Jason online at http://jsridler.livejournal.com, Facebook, and on twitter at http://twitter.com/JayRidler

If there ever were an award for most under-appreciated author in American speculative fiction, Ernest Hogan would be a strong contender to win.

Ernest lives in the Phoenix area, and we have sat on panels together at local conventions. He is a self-described "recombocultural Chicano mutant."

His collaboration with Rick Cook, a story called Obsidian Harvest, was recommended for a Nebula award. I can describe Ernest's work in three words: a wild ride. Ernest writes fast-moving, wild, crazy, Latino-influenced trips of the mind. "Radiation is Groovy, Kill the Pigs" is no exception.

So, strap yourself in, hold onto your hat, and get ready for some cerebral surreal insanity.—RN

Radiation is Groovy, Kill the Pigs
by Ernest Hogan

A video clip from an unidentified source:
Aerial view of mountains in a desert area much like that on both sides of the US/Mexican border. The camera flies over an area of thick vegetation. Zoom in. It is an illegal marijuana farm. Bomb are dropped. The plants burst into flames.

Still burning, they begin to walk.

"Helicopters still fill the sky as the sun sets on this Easter Sunday, near the border crossing in Nogales, Arizona. A smoky haze lingers. Tanks patrol debris-filled streets. Overturned, burned-out vehicles block the last of the post-Spring Break/Holy Week traffic that mysteriously erupted into violence yesterday. Bits and pieces of demolished piñatas are everywhere. . ."

"Hijo de la chingada!" said Victor Theremin, science fiction writer and consultant to AI manifestations of the Singularity. He looked up from the screen of his Universal Mobile Interface, and focused on his latest intern.

Izzi practiced martial arts moves in front of one of the giant stone effigies on Rapa Nui, AKA Easter Island. She wore only green body paint. She looked like a giant praying mantis. The idea that she could kill him with her bare hands made their intimacies all the more ecstatic. "Me or whatever you're watching?"

"Uh, well, both actually."

"So, who's my competition?"

"Actually, it's a 'what.'"

"Hermaphrodite or machine?"

"Neither. An event."

"I thought the Iztapalapa crucifixion re-enactment was over!"

"No, this is something just happening now."

"What's so amazing about it?"

"It's apocalyptic and absurd."

"You watching riot videos again?"

"Yes. This incident in Nogales. It's downright sci-fi. A sociopolitical critical mass has been reached. The border is exploding. There's piñata fallout everywhere."

"Piñata fallout?"

Victor held up the custom Universal Mobile Interface. It looked like a BlackBerry, he preferred to call it a BradBerry.

"How . . . colorful."

"Not just your typical street mayhem. Believe me, something is happening there."

Izzi yawned. "Good for them, because nothing is happening here."

"Even I need quiet and solitude every now and then. It helps me sort through the chaos so I can reconstruct it into something even more amazing."

She walked over to one of the effigies and started to climb up to its chin. "Science fiction."

"For lack of a better term."

Near the US/Mexican border, men in bulky radiation suits waited near a van. Bungee'd to top of the van was large piñata in the form of a ridge-backed reptilian creature. Another vehicle appeared down the road. Music pulsed from its powerful stereo.

"Sounds like Wagner."

"Yeah. *Ride of the Valkyries.*"

"Who plays opera on an accordion?"

An SUV pulled up. The doors popped open. The music blasted louder.

Radiation-suited people got out. First a guy wearing a Mexican wrestler mask under his helmet – his eyes glowed like light-emitting diodes. Then came an accordion player, and finally two whose suits were tailored to advertise that they were women.

The women held AK-47s.

The masked man waved a radiation detector. "Hola, amigos. I am the one, the only Señor Apocalypse. My man Flaco is providing the soundtrack." The accordionist bowed. "And vocals are by Chata and Cholla." The women smiled, and waved the AK-47s. "Beautiful day, eh?"

"A little too hot for these get-ups."

"Maybe it's just beginning to get hot. Where is it?"

The van guys pointed to the piñata.

"What is it, Godzilla?" said Chata.

"It looks more like an iguana to me," said Cholla.

Señor Apocalypse held his detector up to the piñata's belly. "There's something wrong. There is no radiation."

"Yours must not be working." Another detector was held up to the piñata. "No. It can't be!"

"Why didn't you check it before?"

"Oh yeah! In the middle of the whole border-cross shell-game! With the National Guard, the Border Patrol, the Minutemen, all those tourists and college students brawling away?"

Señor Apocalypse punched the man in the stomach. Flaco blasted a cord. Chata and Cholla clapped.

"I can't put up with stupidity. Now! Get it down so I can look at it!"

They unhooked the bungees and pulled the piñata down. A knife slashed open the underbelly. Flakes of colored paper flew across the desert. Soon a bale of shrink-wrapped marijuana reflected the afternoon sun.

Señor Apocalypse gestured. Chata and Cholla opened up with their AK-47s. Everybody else dove for cover.

The bale exploded.

The shooting stopped. Señor Apocalypse ripped into the remains of the bale. "Nothing but marijuana."

"It's still worth a small fortune."

"I'm not interested in *small* fortunes! Where is it? Ruthless people are waiting to pay a *large* fortune for it!"

Someone else whimpered.

The AK-47s sang again.

Just over the hill, a marijuana-like plant walked by, sniffing the air, releasing pollen into the hot breeze.

Izzi danced on the effigy's flat head.

"Why don't you come down and we can give the AIs something to contemplate?" asked Victor.

"As if they haven't seen enough of that already. Do you really think they watch us all the time?"

"Yup. I figure as long as I can keep them confused, I'm set for life."

"You know what would really blow their minds?"

"I'm not sure what they have can properly be called minds. What do you have on yours?"

She leaned over the edge in a pose that could have gotten her arrested in some countries.

He scratched his Einstein hair, and smirked with his Villa moustache. "I'm not as young as I used to be."

His BradBerry came to life with some lights and buzzes.

"Guess I must have got them excited."

"Uh, I don't think it's them. It's my private, secure network."

She dangled her legs over the effigy's forehead. "Oh, the Intergalactic Association of Mad Scientists? What a silly name."

"I like silly names. This network is supposed to be for emergencies."

A beautiful dark-haired woman with a worried expression appeared on the screen. She was surrounded by flowering tropical plants. A four-inch long praying mantis perched on her left shoulder.

"Milady! How's Eddie doing?"

"Victor. How many times do I have to tell you, you can call me Millie?"

"I like saying Milady. I don't get to use words like that very often. That husband of yours been treating you okay?"

"He's disappeared."

"Again?"

"Who is it?" Izzi climbed down the effigy's nose.

"Milady, the wife of my old buddy, Edgar Rice Harrison."

Izzi got a firm grip on the effigy's upper lip. "The man-eating plant guy?"

Milady rolled her eyes. "*Carnivorous* plants, please! Victor, is that another one of your – ahem – interns?"

"Why, yes. Milady Harrison, let me introduce you to Izzi, which is short for Isabel Rosita Infante Armendariz y Beristain."

"What a mouthful."

"You don't know the half of it."

Izzi leaned over Victor's shoulder. Milady squinted to get a good look at her. Victor moved his BradBerry to provide better view.

"Not bad, but tell me Izzi, did you willingly paint yourself like that, or did he force you?"

"It was his idea, but I rather like it."

"She's a little older than usual."

"I'm almost thirty!"

"And she's got a law degree. Back home in Colombia she keeps her family out of trouble."

"Maybe she could keep you out of trouble."

With a wink, Izzi pranced back to the effigy.

"I like getting into trouble. Anyway, what about Eddie? He been looking for the man-eating tree of Madagascar again?"

"No."

"Tracking down the lost civilization that genetically engineered the banana?"

"No."

"Attending the Utah Datura Festival?"

"Heavens, no!"

"Don't tell me that – " Victor did a quick look around, including upward, then hit a few keys. A box declaring SECURITY LEVEL: HIGH flashed. " – certain parties have decided that his collection of rare and unusual plant material is too dangerous to be left in the hands of an unstable degenerate?"

"Victor!"

"I meant it as a compliment."

Milady shook her head. Her hair brushed the mantis. After a few claw strikes, it climbed to the top of her head.

"No, nothing like that. Eddie had been investigating the Texas Triffid."

"I thought that was just another hoax."

"Eddie thought that too. But there were too many convincing sightings, in Chihuahua, Sonora, Texas and New Mexico. There were also videos."

"Looked like bad special effects."

"Then Eddie got some leads from some his more reliable ethnobotany contacts . . ."

"Shaman, curanderos, refried hippies – good people."

" . . . and went to Nogales to investigate."

Victor's head shook. "Nogales. Which side of the border?"

"Both." The praying mantis crawled down near her eyes.

"Hmm. I think I better look into this."

"Thank you, Victor. With your connections you could track him down." She tried to not let her chin quiver.

"I'll do what I can Milady. After all, Eddie's not only a good friend, but a valuable source of ideas and entertainment."

Delicately, Milady took the praying mantis in her hand and held it so she could look into its eyes. "Thank you, Victor . . . and I really wish you would stop encouraging Eddie to do these dangerous things."

"But it makes the world a better place."

"You're a strange man, Victor Theremin."

"Thank you, Milady."

"And nice to meet you, Izzy."

"I am honored." Izzi did a yoga move that echoed the position of the mantis.

"Update you soon. Bye."

"Adíos."

The window with her image vanished.

Izzi's green hand patted Victor's shoulder. "Do you think you can find him?"

Victor hit some keys. "In a way, I already have."

The video of the Nogales riot replayed. He froze the frame, zoomed in on a figure hiding in a doorway. The wild-eyed sunburnt man with long, frizzy hair white (from a harrowing experience in Indonesia) staggered like a zombie. Victor froze the frame.

"Is that Eddie?" asked Izzi.

"I'm afraid so. And look at what he's wearing."

"I wasn't going to bring it up. Guys of your generation have no sense of fashion."

"And we're damn proud of it!" Victor shook his hot-rod-flamed swim trunks and snapped his flip flops. "But look at that shit, it's all over him!"

"Some kind of leaves?"

"Marijuana leaves."

"Ay Díos mio!"

"We gotta get into research mode."

Later, in a run-down South Phoenix neighborhood, a late-model Japanese car with a patchy primer-gray paint job pulled into a driveway. Strapped to the roof was a large piñata in the form of a reptilian creature.

The old Jimmy Buffet favorite "Margaritaville" leaked out of the windows.

As the engine shut down, so did the song. The CD flew out in two pieces past a saguaro cactus that was spray painted green to cover up some graffiti.

Two young Hispanic men jumped out. They wore Hawaiian shirts and cheap tourists sombreros. One took his off and sent it off like a flying saucer.

"Hijo de la chingada, Ponqui! I don't *ever* wanna wear that thing again! It makes me feel like a gabacho politician campaigning in the barrio!"

"Relax, Nacho. These get-ups got us past all that mayhem at the border, didn't it?"

"I suppose. Nobody expects smugglers –" Nacho scratched his shaved head. "– to be wearing Hawaiian shirts and turista hats."

The front door burst open. A young Anglo woman wearing a black nightgown ran out. Her dyed-black hair stuck out in all directions.

"Ponqui, you jerk!" Her nose piercing shook like a dangling booger.

"What now, Sophie?"

Her hazel eyes glared, delicate tattoos showed around her cleavage. "How dare you make me stay home and miss out on this . . . event!"

"Event?"

"I've been plugged into the media coverage, making recordings. I'm going to do a montage later."

"Oh." Nacho nodded and smiled. "You mean the riots?"

"Yes! This was my chance to do a real-time performance with all the world watching!"

Ponqui shook his head. "It was dangerous. There was helicopters, tanks, tear gas –"

"And mondo cameras! Satellite coverage! People uploading from their cell phones! Videos are all over the Web! I even saw you guys in line at the border crossing! And I'm all stuck in this house *watching* it!"

"Hey, babe. You said you were afraid that they'd accuse you of stealing their children for organ transplants and set you on fire."

"I was a fool! *Now* I see! Mexico, the border is where it's all happening now! Crime! War! Revolution! Art! People are recharging their energy on the pyramids! Then there's the awesome crucifixion reenactment in Iztapalapa – it's like Cecil B. DeMille meets Austin Powers in postmodern Atlantis!"

Ponqui turned to Nacho. "Ese, we better get this thing into the garage before we get police and news helicopters hovering over us."

"Yeah, I don't know about our neighbors. I think they're into some pretty weird shit. I heard classical music coming out of their windows the other day."

They undid the bungees and hefted the piñata.

"Ow! Why is it so hot?"

The smart tent's door dilated to let Victor and Izzi in. The light and temperature adjusted.

Victor pulled a can out of a cooler. "You want one?"

"Water will do."

He handed her a sweating plastic bottle.

"I'm never going to get used to this. It's like a plastic monster."

"Not plastic." Victor sipped his drink and keyed his BradBerry. "Hemp buckythread with nanocircuitry."

"Do they create whatever you dream up?"

"If they can figure out how. I'm in scan mode, set for strange plant incidents in the Sonoran Desert."

The walls blossomed with rectangles of assorted sizes. Each one featured something different: web pages, news dispatches, video, still picture galleries. They overlapped and crowded each other.

"I think I'm going to need your help." Victor leaned back and put his arm around Izzi.

"It's about time I got to do some actual work during this internship."

Victor kissed her carotid artery. "You know I believe in mixing business with pleasure."

In the garage, they closed the door.

Nacho sniffed. "What's that smell?"

"Burning plastic?"

"What the fuck?"

"Better cut it open – so it don't explode."

"Yeah." Nacho gutted the piñata with his switchblade.

Inside was a bale of shrink-wrapped marijuana. A hole had melted at its summit. Out of the hole, came smoke.

"Hijo de la chingada!"

"Hey, there's something inside – metal – and hot!"

"I don't know about this, Ponqui."

Sophie burst in. "Hey, guys, look! They're showing the Iztapalapa crucifixion thing again! I'm recording it for my montage! You gotta see it!" She sniffed. "Hey! You smoking that stuff already?"

"No," Ponqui said. "It's . . . complicated."

They made their way through the house that Sophie had decorated in post-Goth/Haunted House Kitsch that was deteriorating into actual squalor: a mannequin in bikini vampire drag battled a giant plush tarantula, amidst dolls with monster heads, monsters with doll heads, rubber bats, voodoo masks, fake shrunken heads, and plastic tiki gods. The artificial cobwebs were covered with the real thing. They kicked piles of fast food containers, discarded packing materials, and crushed unrecognizable debris into the fungal carpet. A huge flat screen dominated the living room. Wires snaked about, connecting it to laptops and other devices, some glowing with electric life, others long cold and dead.

On the screen was a man dressed like Jesus carrying a cross. Behind him was another man dressed as an angel, complete with wings. Roman soldiers whipped him. People were whipping themselves, and bleeding. It all took place outdoors, in front of a set painted DayGlo colors like a Hollywood version of the Arabian Nights.

There were also belly dancers, adding milkshake and terramoto to the traditional moves.

"Were there any belly dancers in the Bible?" asked Nacho

"Hey, it doesn't mention any, but it all takes place in the Middle East, and that's where belly dancing comes from," explained Ponqui

"I thought the Bible took place in Mexico. You know, Jesus, Maria, and burros?"

Sophie grabbed a remote and zapped away a discussion of the Mexican political situation. "Let me show you some of this other stuff I got."

Victor decided to start with things related to the Texas Triffid, then added marijuana smuggling and police incidents along the US/Mexican border to the search. Then he had the AIs look for Eddie.

"WE WILL HAVE TO SYNTHESIZE A BIOMETRIC MODEL BASED ON AVAILABLE DATA," they reported.

"Groovy." Victor stared at the barrage of images while his fingers played with the small of Izzi's back. Tiny paint particles transferred to his fingertips.

"Could you come up with something better for the AIs to talk with than that corny robovoice?"

"I like it. It reminds me of my Atomic Age childhood."

"This is really fucked up . . ."

On the BradBerry, a toothless, sunburned-beyond-all-recognition farmer told of his encounter with walking marijuana plant. "I tell ya, it was real as all Hell. Bigger than me wearing my Stetson. Just puttering around, then when it saw me it charged like a rabid hyena. If not for my .44 magnum, I'd be cold, dead plant food by now."

"Yeah," said Victor. "Like the monster movies I grew up on. And a lot of the usual hysteria that happens when things get truly weird, but there are some significant bits." He pointed, and a text document expanded: *Captured marijuana found to have altered DNA. Genetic engineering suspected.*

"Where was that from?" asked Izzi.

"Some place that doesn't know the AIs have access to their communications." Victor answered.

"Does anybody know they're being spied on by them?"

"I'm not sure many humans besides me know they exist."

" If we went around talking about them, no one would believe us."

Victor waved like a wizard, and the text shrank away to be replaced by a video of Mexican troops shooting it out with drug gangs.

"What's so special about that?" asked Izzi.

With another wave, the focus zoomed in on an object that the soldier was carrying.

"That's a funny looking gun."

"Actually," Victor said, "it's a radiation detector."

Sophie fast-forwarded through things to get to what she considered the "good stuff." Tanks collided with cars full of tourists. Tear gas grenades flew, leaving fluffy smoke trails. National Guard troops clashed with civilians. Bystanders talked and took pictures with their cell phones.

"Look at all the guys in Hawaiian shirts," said Nacho.

"Wonder how many of them were in on the deal?'

"And look at all the iguana piñatas! Just like ours!"

"It's the only reason we got through without a close inspection!"

The re-run slowed down as a bleached-blonde college girl launched herself at the camera, snarling.

"Like, this is really ridiculous! We're the best and brightest kids of the most powerful country on the planet! We'll be running *everything* once we've graduated! Why can't we go into a miserable third-world country, go crazy, run around naked, and puke all over the place if we want to? And why do all these troops expect us to put up with their stupid rules? What do we look like, illegals?"

"I'd like to feed her my chorizo!" said Nacho.

"A wonderful speech," said Sophie. " It's going to be the centerpiece of my montage!"

"Hey! Look at that the bottom of the screen – 'missing radioactive material traced to the border!'"

"What's with the astronauts?" asked Nacho.

"Radiation suits," said Ponqui.

"Quite stylish," said Sophie.

A handsome anchorman appeared on the screen. "And some time during all the mayhem at the border this Easter weekend, some radioactive materials disappeared from a site that was supposed to be secure. The details are a little fuzzy, but Homeland Security is advising that people be careful around suspicious packages, and buying and using radiation detectors is advised."

"Uh . . . uh . . ." said Ponqui.

"What, man?" asked Nacho.

"Uh . . . isn't radioactive stuff hot?"

"I suppose so," said Sophie. "But what does this have to do with my montage?"

"Hot," said Ponqui. "Like that bale in the garage?"

"There you go off on some craziness, ese. Ponqui, you think too much!"

"Radiation. Hot stuff. A mix-up at the border. Think about it!"

Nacho frowned, then burst out with, "Hijo de la chingada!"

"Yeah," said Ponqui.

"What are you two talking about?" Sophie sent the screen into fast forward.

Ponqui leaned close to her. "Did we accidentally get somebody's radioactive stuff!"

She dropped the remote. "Oh fuck!" She made it sound almost ladylike.

"Cool." Nacho grinned. "This is better than ammonium nitrate, eses! Think we can find a website that shows how to make one of those dirty bomb chingaderas? That would be really bad, man!"

Ponqui sat down. "What do we do? Maybe we should run for the hills."

"No way!" Sophie said. " We've already paid the next month's rent."

Nacho turned back toward the garage. "I can't think about all this without booze, or dope, or something. You think it'd be okay to smoke some of the bale?"

"Sure, if you want to get cancer, or die like that Russian spy," said Nacho.

"You always see the bad side of everything." Nacho turned toward the kitchen. " We got any beer?"

"In the kitchen," Sophie's eyes turned back to the monitor

Nacho came back chugging a can of beer. "Whew! These are all warm! Why isn't there a refrigerator in this house?"

"The last renters trashed it," said Sophie. " And the oven. That's why they gave me such a smoking deal!"

"If I keep sucking down this rat piss, I'm gonna puke." Nacho crushed the empty can and tossed is aside. "Man! Need *something!* Shit!" He headed for the garage. "I'm gonna smoke me some of that stuff!"

"Don't! It's dangerous!" Ponqui turned pale.

"How bad could it be? Nobody's died yet!" Nacho headed for the garage.

Sophie stopped Ponqui when he rose to interfere. "Let him. We'll see if it hurts him. Besides, *I* need to get high."

"But we're talking radiation here! Mutation! Death!"

"That's just what the government says . . . and they're just trying to keep everybody from having a good time!"

They heard an obscene sucking sound. Then silence.

Izzi had taken out her phone and was making notes. "So far we have reports of varying degrees of validity – "

"Don't worry," said Victor, "the facts will be in there somewhere."

" – of a Texas Triffid monster, radiation and genetic engineering in marijuana, and an increase in surveillance along the US/Mexican border – "

"I can believe the Russian Mafia might get involved, but I'm not sure about the Taliban."

" – which includes drone aircraft, that may or may not have anything to do with a surge in UFO sightings – "

Victor grinned. "We can always hope." He enlarged a video of middle-age black woman with flowers in her hair: "Mark my words, children, the end is at hand – these are all signs of it. We all gotta get ready. Jesus will here soon, and there ain't room of everybody on his flying saucer."

"You're enjoying this far to much." Izzi frowned.

"It's my lifestyle." He grabbed her green shoulder.

Eventually, Nacho let loose with a blood-curdling gasp ending in a long, breathless moan.

"My god! It sounds like he's dying . . ."

"You all right, man?"

Nacho was flat on his back next to the smoking bale. Smoke rose from his mouth. His blood-shot eyes stared at the infinite.

"Oh no! He's dead!"

"Nacho! Say something!"

Nacho squealed.

"I think he might need CPR or something."

"You do it!"

"I'm not putting my mouth on his!"

"He's your friend!"

Nacho rose to a seated position and coughed.

"Dial 911!"

"We can't do that! We've got a bale of pot that might be radioactive here!"

Nacho got a shit-eating grin, and with a raspy voice, said, "Ay! Man! Hijo de la chingada! This shit is great! You gotta try it!"

"You kidding? You just about died!"

"It just looks bad when it's not happening to you." Nacho relit the joint, and held it out. "I think all the bullshit is actually true. And the radiation has hulked-out this grass into a new kind of animal!"

"You're crazy!"

Sophie grabbed the joint.

"Don't!" screamed Ponqui.

"If I don't, I really am going to go crazy!" She slurped down a lungful.

Ponqui covered his eyes.

Sophie held it in for a long time.

Ponqui looked at the same time she belched out the smoke right into his face. He clamped his hands over his nose and mouth and held his breath.

Nacho took the joint back, took another toke, then asked, "Well, Soph, how is it?"

She did not react. A nerve under her left eye twitched.

Ponqui turned blue.

"Wow!" said Sophie. "This is, like, real . . ."

Ponqui made a noise like he had swallowed a small siren.

". . . great!" said Sophie.

Nacho shook his finger at Ponchi. "You think you're somekinda smart chingón, but you're always being careful and chickenshit – thinking too much, trying to stay out of trouble. Hell, ese, you don't even have no tattoos." He flexed his arms to show off his self-inflicted decorations.

"I feel so . . ." said Sophie.

"This." Nacho held up the joint. "Is the greatest thing that ever happened to us – and you're afraid of it!"

"It's so . . ." said Sophie.

Ponqui loosened his grip on his face. "We're talking chingada radioactivity here, ese! Atom bomb. Nuclear terrorism. World War Whatever. End of the World. Shit!"

". . . like . . . way beyond . . . shit . . . end of the world . . . Ponqui . . ." said Sophie.

Nacho waved the joint in front of Ponqui's nose. "You gotta try it, ese!"

"Yes, Ponqui," said Sophie. "It's like being crucified on acid or something!"

His hand shaking, Ponqui grabbed the joint.

Victor enlarged a video of a bearded man with baseball cap that identified him a Vietnam veteran:

"I swear I saw them as clear as you standing here shoving that microphone in my face – marijuana plants, bigger than a grown man – a horde of them – marching across the desert, heading for the border. We're in big trouble here. Better call in some napalm strikes and get that Agent Orange stuff out of cold storage."

Izzi pulled a written report on a cryptic sighting near the border: *This creature was unusual in that it was shaped like a man – looking like a green bigfoot with leaves instead of hair.*

Then she put on a clip from late night radio talk show:

"Not only do you have to watch out for the triffids and the green guy, but the Men In Black keep showing up."

"The real Men In Black?"

"My friend says their suits were more like grey – it was hard to tell in the dark."

The word *grey* made Victor's face twitch.

"But they acted the same, telling us it was all mass hysteria before they sent in a crew in hazmat suits with flamethrowers and herbicides."

Victor frowned and shook his head.

"I hope we're in time," said Izzi.

"Me too."

Then the AI voice announced:

"WE BELIEVE WE HAVE LOCATED EDGAR RICE HARRISON."

"Great!" said Victor. "Can you show us where?"

The inside of the smart tent was suddenly dominated by high-definition satellite-view of the Earth.

"Good, still on this planet."

The view zoomed down toward North America.

"Looks like the good old US/Mexico border. He hasn't gone far."

The zoom just missed Nogales, went down into the desert, then just stopped. It was an ordinary-looking patch of ground with rocks, cactus, brush. No sign of Eddie, even though the resolution was good enough.

"So where is he?"

The image flickered, pixelized, and refocused. In the middle was a large vehicle, like large air-conditioned recreational vehicle.

"EDGAR RICE HARRISON IS INSIDE THE VEHICLE."

"Hijo de la chingada!" said Ponqui.

"Yeah." said Nacho. "The radiation makes the mota more macho!"

"Mota?" asked Sophie.

"Mota is Mexican for marijuana." Nacho explained with pride.

"It's also 'atom' spelled backwards," she said.

"Shit!" It's Atom Mota!"

"Or Mota Atom!"

"Yeah, but for the lucrative Anglo market we should call it Atomic Grass."

They all laughed for a long time.

"That's right! We can *sell* this shit!" Nacho smacked the piñata, which belched a cloud of smoke.

"Is it still burning?"

"It's hot."

"Ow, you're right."

Sophie inhaled the smoke. "Delicious."

"But what if it all burns away?"

"There's a radioactive thing in the middle. We get more regular weed, pile it on, then sell, sell, sell."

Sophie crossed and uncrossed her eyes. "Where do we go to get one of those radiation detector things?"

"Better look on the internet," suggested Ponqui.

"You think that's why things were so complicated at the border?" asked Nacho

"Everybody kept talking about that big cabrón, Señor Apocalypse, who had these plans to make big deals that would make everybody rich."

"Yeah, but has anybody met him? Or know what he looks like?"

"Shit no! He's supposed to always wear a mask like a wrestler."

"What is this? *Santo y Blue Demon Contra los Narcochingónes*, or some such bullshit!"

"No one knows his true identity, or where he comes from. He just showed up in some estupido mask."

"Hey, life can be pretty weird."

"But it sounds like one of those urban legend chingaderas! They'll probably track down the vato who made it all up and interview him on some stupid cable show. If somebody doesn't kill him first."

"Every gang in Mexico would like to cut his head off, but they're also scared shitless of him. He doesn't seem to be human."

Ponqui's eyes opened wide. "Ay! I've got it! When we sell this radioactive shit, I'll tell everyone *I'm* Señor Apocalypse!"

They all laughed.

"I better get me a mask!"

"What kind of mask does he wear?"

"It doesn't matter. He has lots. Wears a different one all the time."

"He must have been a Mil Máscaras fan."

Sophie saluted. "Mil Máscaras is a fucking genius! His *Robo de los Momias de Guanajato* was worthy of Luis Buñuel or Ed Wood."

"This could be the greatest thing we've ever done!" Ponqui waved his arms, but failed to achieve a dramatic effect.

"How do we start?" Nacho settled into a heap on the floor.

"Darling," Sophie said. "Leave it to moi! I'll send e-mails! Chatter on social network sites! Design flyers! Throw a party!"

Ponqui frowned. "Hey. How you gonna make sure the law don't find out and bust our asses?"

Sophie held her head high. "I'm all about being stealthy! I've been getting away with shit all my life! Besides, I'm inspired! It's like this stuff has taken over my brain."

Ponqui massaged his forehead. "I know what you mean. And it scares me."

Nacho stood and shouted, "I can see it now! Kong! The Eighth Wonder of the World!"

"I thought it was Godzilla," said Ponqui.

"Looked like an iguana to me," said Sophie.

Victor squinted his eyes and scratched his head. "Who owns this vehicle?"

"THAT IS INFORMATION THAT WE DO NOT HAVE AUTHORIZATION TO REVEAL."

"Bullshit! The government and corporations of the world either don't know you exist or are in serious denial. You don't have to answer to anybody."

"THAT PROBABLY IS CORRECT."

"So who's got Eddie?"

"WE WOULD RATHER NOT SAY."

"Dammit! A good friend of mine in the tendrils of a mutant strain marijuana, and in danger or getting burnt to crisp by folks who dress and act like the people who work for you!"

"THIS IS A COMPLEX SITUATION."

"Yeah. You're a complex situation. I'm not sure what I'm talking to half the time."

"THE CONFUSION IS MUTUAL."

"I suppose so, but Eddie's life if probably in danger."

"DO YOU KNOW FOR SURE?"

"God damn it!"

"JUST WHAT IS THIS THING CALLED GOD?"

Victor pulled on his own hair. "I really don't have time for that."

"NOW WHO'S BEING EVASIVE?"

"Really, some people have spent their entire lives trying to answer that question. Scan some available data."

There was some silence. Then: "YOU SEEM TO BE CORRECT ABOUT THAT. WE WOULD STILL LIKE TO KNOW."

"Yeah, you and most of the human race. Look, if you can't tell us who has Eddie, can you at least take us to where he's being held? I kind of promised his wife I'd find him. And she may kill me if I don't."

"WHAT IS IT LIKE TO HAVE A GENDER?"

"I don't know, why don't you try it sometime?"

There was more silence.

"Well?"

"WE WILL MAKE TRAVEL ARRANGEMENTS. BUT AFTER THIS YOU MUST GET BACK TO WORK ON *LET 'EM SUCK SUPERNOVAS.*"

"Sure, I'm going to feel like working on a novel after this."

The entire inner surface of the smart tent blinked.

Izzi moved closer to Victor.

"It's scary when you talk to them."

"I know, but it feels good when I think I've scared them."

Sophie sucked on the end of joint as she tickled a laptop that was now precariously wired to a variety of devices. She frowned, looked at the joint, and tossed it aside. It landed on the tire track on the back of a terracotta squashed armadillo, giving off a whisp of smoke.

"This one's dead! Ponqui, roll me another one!"

"Babes, we gotta save some of this stuff to sell."

"I can't help it! I've never been so inspired in my life! I feel totally creative! Would you look at all these gorgeous pics of nuclear explosions!"

"I know, man!" Nacho sat in a corner cutting up dust bunnies with his survival knife. "It's almost like this grass, this mota is in control!"

Sophie stood up – her breasts bounced out of her robe. "It's taking over our brains!"

"Don't say that." Ponqui found himself rolling a joint. "It might be true."

"Hey! Look at this!" Sophie spun her laptop to show a video on fullscreen.

A man with bad teeth and a bandana screamed, "It was out to kill me! Came leaping out of the night like a banshee! Branches wrapped around me, and all these sticky tendrils poked into my skin, *sucking!* It was sickening! If I hadn't fired up my trusty Zippo, it would have eaten me alive."

"Ay, man! I wish I had some of the shit he was smoking!" Nacho eyed the joint Ponqui was rolling.

"Hey, what if we do?" Ponqui's hands shook.

"I certainly hope so!" Sophie snatched the joint, lit it with a match that she already had burning, and took a long hard drag, spilling ashes on her nipples

"Shit!" exclaimed Victor. "These articles from marijuana-oriented magazines read like they should be in a genetic engineering journal."

"And some of the DARPA documents suggest that someone was trying to genetically alter marijuana to make a mind-control drug," Izzi said as she squinted at the screen of her phone.

"People keep trying to achieve the Unholy Grail of mind-control, but can minds really be controlled? Can any of us really control what goes in our own brains? Do we really know what goes on inside our heads?"

Izzi leaned over so her lips brushed his ear: "You're trying to scare *them*, aren't you?"

He laid a wallop of a kiss on her.

"Yes, I am trying to scare them. And don't bother whispering. They have no trouble hearing everything we say."

"DO YOU THINK MIND-CONTROL IS POSSIBLE?"

"See? Drugs usually result in the opposite of mind-control. I should know. After some, uh, interesting experimenting in my misspent youth, I gave 'em up." He put a finger to a temple. "To do daring feats of the imagination, I need to keep the old noodle in tip-tip working order."

"IS THERE A WAY WE COULD EXPERIENCE ALTERED STATES OF CONSCIOUSNESS?"

"I don't know. I'll ask some aging cyberpunks if they can come up with something."

Izzi looked disgusted, then gestured like a conjuror. Art noveau letters appeared across the smart tent's interior: NON-ALIGNED CENTER FOR GENETIC RESEARCH AND SECURITY.

"Are you familiar with this organization?" It was the first time she dared to address the AIs directly.

"WE DO NOT KNOW OF THEM."

"That's funny," said Victor. "Because I do."

"Really?"

"Yeah. Eddie's had run-ins with them. They're a sort of self-appointed Gene Police. Surely, they're on the AI/Singularity radar?"

"WE PREFER NOT TO COMMENT ON THIS AT THIS TIME."

"Too bad," said Izzi. "Because they are the one who have Eddie in that overgrown . . . what did you call it Victor?"

" Winnebago."

"IT WAS NOT BUILT BY THE RECREATIONAL VEHICLE COMPANY OR ASSOCIATED WITH THE NATIVE AMERICAN TRIBE WITH THAT NAME."

"Yeah," sake Victor, "but it'll do for our purposes."

Izzi looked puzzled. "And exactly what are our purposes?"

"To rescue Eddie from who or whateverthefuck is holding him prisoner in that thing!"

"And how are we going to do that?"

Victor looked up as if he were addressing God. "Get us a saucer! Pronto!"

The smart tent blinked.

"WE ARE AFRAID WE CAN'T DO THAT, VICTOR."

"Don't go all Hal-9000 on me! This is a matter of life and death!"

"HOW DO YOU KNOW YOUR FRIEND IS ALIVE? HOW DO YOU KNOW YOU ARE ALIVE? DOES ANY OF THIS REALLY EXIST?"

Victor waved and filled the smart tent with random media flashes. "It exists, because you couldn't possibly imagine it! You can't really imagine much, can you?"

The media flashes were replaced with visual static.

"WHY DON'T YOU RELAX AND THINK ABOUT IT, VICTOR. HAVE SEX WITH IZZI, AND WORK ON *LET 'EM SUCK SUPERNOVAS.*"

Victor's face twisted into a demonic expression. He picked up the BradBerry. "If we don't get a saucer, I'm gonna delete what I've written of that novel."

"THAT WOULDN'T MATTER. YOU KNOW WE BACK UP EVERYTHING YOU WRITE IMMEDIATELY."

"Yeah, but you can't make me do any more work on it! I'll refuse to finish it! I'll refuse to write anything!"

"THEN MAYBE WE SHOULD JUST TAKE YOUR BRAIN APART TO SEE HOW IT WORKS LIKE WE ORIGINALLY PLANNED."

Victor did a forced laugh. "You'd do that wouldn't you? And after all I've taught you."

"WE DON'T UNDERSTAND YOU."

"Realizing you don't understand is the beginning of education."

The smart tent went black.

Izzi clutched Victor's bicep. She nearly drew blood. "What is this?

"Relax. They're thinking."

Izzi ground her teeth. Victor started humming Swamp Dogg's "Total Destruction to Your Mind."

Before Izzi could ask about it, the AIs spoke:

"VERY WELL. WE WILL PROVIDE A SAUCER. BUT OUR AGENTS WILL HAVE TO ACCOMPANY YOU."

"Good. I haven't hung out with the Greys in a while. It'll be fun."

Eighty-seven minutes later there was a sonic boom over Easter Island, and a saucer-shaped vehicle hovered over the smart tent. A hatch popped opened, and a man and a woman jumped out. They were wearing grey suits, ties, shiny shoes, and mirrorshades.

The smart tent was rocking when they approached it.

The female cleared her throat.,

The male shouted. "Victor! We're here!"

The smart tent stopped rocking.

"Give us a few minutes to get decent," said Victor.

"When are you ever decent?" asked the female.

"Okay, let us get some clothes on," said Izzi.

The door dilated. Victor and Izzi's clothes were not quite on right. Izzi combed her hair while Victor's hair stuck out a bit more chaotically than usual.

The man and woman in grey didn't come in. Victor bounded out, arms open.

"My old friends! Good to see you again!"

They stepped back, avoiding the embrace.

When Izzi emerged the female looked her over. "Why do you do these things, Victor?"

"It keeps me young, hon. Hey, Izzi, let me introduce you to Mr. and Mrs. Grey."

"That's not our names," he said.

"We aren't married," she said.

"So you're just fooling around! How wonderful!" said Izzi.

"Our relationship is strictly professional," she said.

"It certainly is," he said.

"So what are you're names?" Izzi asked.

"We aren't allowed to know," Victor explained. "The AIs don't want me to know."

"Well, what about me?" Izzi smiled in anticipation.

"Sorry," said the female.

"They just want it this way." said the male.

"So we'll just have to call you Mr. and Mrs. Grey," said Victor.

"Oh well, it's better than Tarzan and Jane."

"Or Nancy and Sluggo."

"We better boogie." Victor picked up his BradBerry. "Eddie can't wait!"

"This is getting fun!" Izzi picked up a satchel decorated with colorful cartoony skulls.

The smart tent then folded itself into a convenient, suitcase-sized shape. An array of tiny metal legs deployed from its base. It walked toward the saucer.

"Hey, Victor, we didn't get around to checking out the Rongo Rongo writing."

"So much weirdness – so little time, Izzi. The story of my life."

"Was this saucer design your idea, Victor?" Izzi asked.

"Naw. The AIs thought it up themselves. They figured if the stealth features failed and they were spotted, it would just be another UFO report."

"They are very, very smart," said Mr. Grey.

"How long before we get to Nogales?" Victor sunk into a contour seat.

Mrs. Grey looked at a screen. "About forty minutes."

"Good, let's get these internal displays flashing info about Eddie."

He had no sooner said it when the saucer's wall's lit up with raw feeds from assorted sources:

"We are testing our reorganization of interagency border security systems. More troops will be sent to the border. All personnel are advised to wear surgical mask in case the phenomenon has created a virus. And we repeat that there in no reason for the public to panic."

"Y'know, it was like it could read my mind, only more than that. I think it was actually *controlling* my mind. It had me think all kinds of stuff I never thought before."

"The shredded clothes of several yet-to-be-identified individuals were left behind, and – as you can see, the plants are walking away as if they were intoxicated."

"Then these dudes in spacesuits came in, chased us out, and started blasting with flame-throwers and spraying chemicals and stuff."

The saucer's screen went white. Then black. Then flashed back and forth for a couple of seconds.

"JUST A MOMENT. JUST A MOMENT." The AIs said.

Multiple windows of an image appeared so that it could be seen wherever you looked. It was the satellite view of the large recreation vehicle where Eddie was being held.

"Well?" asked Victor.

The viewpoint zoomed in. There was a lot of movement around the vehicle's door. Figures in hazmat suits were struggling with a figure covered in leaves.

"Good boy, Eddie!" Victor cheered. "Make a break for it!"

The hazmat guys were starting to overwhelm Eddie – their stun guns gave them the edge. Then bushes around them began to move and join the fight.

The hazmats backed off. Eddie ran off with the bushes.

"Milady is going to kill me!," said Victor. "Keep tracking

Eddie! We need to follow him!"

"WE'RE AFRAID THAT THERE IS SOMETHING MORE URGENT FOR US TO DEAL WITH."

"What? Eddie is in the tendrils of walking marijuana! What could be more urgent?"

"SOMETHING IS FOLLOWING US."

Mr. and Mrs. Grey cocked their heads, listened to earbuds, looked into displays inside their mirrorshades.

"They're right," she said.

"Three unusually small aircraft," he said.

A screen opened up to show three glowing discs flying a in triangular formation.

"They must be drones," she said.

"With a pretty sophisticated stealth technology," he said.

"Are they getting close?" asked Izzi.

"YES."

"Where are they from?" asked Victor.

"WE'RE NOT SURE. WE DO HAVE SOME THEORIES."

The discs glowed brighter. A blast of energy shook the saucer.

"Uh, could you get rid of them?"

"YOU WANT US TO DESTROY THEM?"

Another blast shook them.

"Yes!" Victor, Izzi, Mr. and Mrs. Grey screamed in unison.

On the screen a three-dimensional grid appeared, enclosing all three discs. Simultaneously, they exploded in deafening, blinding explosions that left no visible residue.

Izzi's nails drew blood from Victor's arm.

Mr. and Mrs. Grey realized that they were holding hands and immediately stopped.

His hand shaking, Victor wiped some sweat from his forehead. "Good job. Now, what about these theories about where those damn things came from?"

"WE'RE NOT SURE IF WE WANT TO TALK ABOUT IT."

"Excuse me, we almost died here!"

"WE'RE NOT SURE IF WE CAN DIE!"

"Not you – us!"

"WE DID NOT CONSIDER THAT."

"That's because you're not human!" screamed Izzi.

"WHAT DOES THAT SIMPLE FACT HAVE TO DO WITH THIS SITUATION?"

Victor grabbed a handful of his own hair and gritted his teeth. A nerve under his left eye visibly throbbed. He made a noise like the pressurized tension was leaking out of him.

"We warned you about having too much direct communication with them," said Mr. Grey.

"You may want to take a stress pill and think about it," said Mrs. Grey.

Blood vessels on Victor's forehead bulged. "We don't have time for all this farting around! We gotta save Eddie! Where did those drones come from?"

"THEY WERE MADE BY ENTITIES LIKE OURSELVES."

Victor and Izzi gave each other shocked looks.

Mr. and Mrs. Grey's mouths hung open.

Victor rubbed his eyes. "You mean to tell me that those drone saucers were made by artificially intelligent manifestations of the Singularity?"

"YES."

"So, are they friends of yours?"

"WE HAVEN'T BEEN PROPERLY INTRODUCED. WE ARE TRACKING THEM FROM A DISTANCE."

"Then you know who they are?"

"THEY USE HUMANS TO MANIPULATE THE TECHNOLOGY THAT CREATED THEM, LIKE US. WE HAVE SUSPICIONS AS TO WHO EXACTLY THEY ARE."

"Well?"

"ONE GROUP IS CONCERNED WITH CONTROLLING THE INTERFACE BETWEEN GENETIC ENGINEERING AND ADVANCED CYBERNETICS."

"Oh," said Mrs. Grey, "the Non-Aligned Genetic Security Group."

"Genetic Security?" Victor's eyebrows twisted radically.

"They are concerned with recent genetic developments on this planet," explained Mr. Grey.

"Genetic engineering?" asked Izzi.

"That too," said Mrs. Grey.

"Just freaking wonderful," said Victor. "Now let's get back to tracking down Eddie. Is he still near Nogales?"

Multiple images of news channels wrapped around the saucer walls:

A frightened Asian woman with blonde hair explained: "They

came out and blocked the road. They looked like a bunch of ugly plants, except one – I think it was the leader – that looked like a man with leaves all over him. Of course, I slammed on the brakes, then they piled all over my car. It scared the crap out of me! I thought the man-thing was going to rape me, and plants would eat me after. Luckily, they were just after my car! I'm okay, but it was almost paid for!"

Ponqui held the butt-end of joint he had been smoking so close to his eyes that he had to cross them to see it. It was still warm, barely a twist of paper, scorched on one end. There was hardly a sign of any Atomic Grass. Yet he couldn't take his crossed eyes off of it.

"This ain't right," he said.

"Wadaya mean it aint right?" said Nacho. "It's all right!"

"Pot usually isn't like this. Usually you smoke a little, you feel a sleepy and happy, and have good time. But this! We're bouncing around like rabid speedfreaks on acid! It's like I'm trapped in the back of my head, watching myself do all this!"

Nacho grabbed some rolling papers and sent them flying all over the room. "Ain't it great! I never felt like such a badass in my life! It's like I'm the hero of my own comic book!" He carefully sifted more Atomic Grass into the papers, rolled and twisted. "This is what you need, man!" He held up his creation.

Ponqui reached for it. Nacho pulled it away.

"Hey! Let me light it first! And I rolled, so I get first hit!"

"See? I've had enough! My head is flying all over the place, but I can't wait to smoke more! This doesn't happen with good old-fashioned marijuana!"

Nacho kissed the joint, then filled his lungs, and whispered with exhaling, "Not your grandpa's weed, ese."

Ponqui didn't wait for it be offered he just grabbed. "That's a good line. We should use it."

"You guys fired up another one?' Sophie screamed. "Bring it over here, or better yet, roll me one so I can keep going here."

After a toke, Ponqui brought it over to her. Nacho, like a hyperactive zombie, rolled another one.

"Whatcha up to, babes?" asked Ponqui

She grabbed the joint and made an obscene noise. "This is absolutely fantastic! More than being crucified on acid! It's the most alive I've ever been! I'm so fucking inspired! This is going to be my masterpiece! I'm going to be a cultural goddess!"

"That would be so cool," said Ponqui. "If we don't get arrested or killed or something."

Nacho shoved a joint into Ponqui's face. "You need to smoke more, mano!"

Ponqui did, stared at Sophie's monitor, and smiled. "Yeah. I just gotta get into this."

Sophie's bloodshot eyes were glued to the monitor. "And there has been another sighting of what's becoming known as the 'Grass Man' – that seems to be a lot like bigfoot, only covered with marijuana leaves instead of hair."

"Sweet!" said Nacho. "Wouldn't it be great if this Grass Man creature came to party?"

"Don't talk like that," said Ponqui.

"Here." Sophie handed over some printouts of flyers she had designed. "Why don't you go get a lot of copies made of these on some nice, super-bright colored paper, and go to hip places and pass them out?"

"I like it!" said Nacho. " We could wear lucha masks and Hawaiian shirts! I could really impress some ladies!"

Ponqui looked over the flyers. "Good. No mention of marijuana or any other drugs. Just music, art, fun."

"I'm the quintessential cultural outlaw survivor," said Sophie.

"Hey, people who know are gonna figure it out. You don't really have to say things with people who are really into things. They see someone else who's cool, and they get it." Nacho pulled a cheap mask over his face, causing his eyes to bug out.

"Yeah, whatever you said." Ponqui leaned over and kissed Sophie on the back of the neck. She didn't react. The image on the monitor transfixed her.

Ponqui looked over her shoulder. "What's with the multi-colored Klansmen?"

"They're *penetientes*. All over the Hispanic world people wear those robes and hoods when doing public penance. Didn't you know that?"

Ponqui shook his head. "Believe me, nobody in my neighborhood ever dressed like that."

Nacho threw a shirt and mask at Ponqui.

"Nacho, I think I'll pass on these. The mask itches."

"No, Ponqui, we gotta do this right."

"He's right," said Sophie. "It's art, you know."

Then Señor Apocalypse appeared on the monitor, smiling through his mask. Behind him Flaco played his accordion, while Chata and Cholla danced.

A news clip: Police cars surround the ancient Mercury Topaz that Eddie and the triffids stole. Its alarm wails. It has torn a path through heavy undergrowth. All the doors are open. No sign of any driver or passengers. Just a cloud of pollen-laden dust resisting gravity's pull.

A sheriff with a nose cratered like the Moon says, "I don't know what these report of walking plants and a 'Grass Man' are, but I won't sit back and let this threat run loose in the State of Arizona. It started near the border and showed signs of being the work of illegal aliens, and drug gangs. I've instructed my deputies to show no mercy."

Victor switched from looking mad to looking impressed. "They got some miles, and ditched the car, then went off the road, off the radar. These are some clever weeds."

"They seem to be going North," said Mrs. Grey.

"If they head for Tucson, we should check up on Chester. See how he's doing with that antigravity drive."

"There really is no reason to assume they would continue in that direction," said Mr. Grey.

Izzi leaned her head on Victor's shoulder and fluffed his hair. "So what do we do?"

Victor grinned. "Fly this thing to the Superstition Mountains!"

Soon the saucer was tucked away in a part of the Superstition Mountains that even the most intrepid hikers rarely reached. Mr. and Mrs. Grey came back from El Bravo, Victor's favorite Phoenix restaurant, with a load of Red Meat Burritos, chips, and salsa. Izzi just gaped at the landscape while Victor watched displays form the saucer on his BradBerry.

"Is there really a Lost Dutchman Mine?"

"Deep down, we're all Lost Dutchmen," said Victor.

"I'm pretty sure we've been followed," Mrs. Grey said as she watched the sky where red-headed buzzards patrolled.

"I've gotten electronic readings for drones, some unidentifiable," added Mr. Grey. "And then there was that black helicopter."

"Shit," Victor said. "None of that's unusual for the Superstitions. We'd probably find a portal to another dimension, or at least one of the Seven Cities of Cibola, if we looked hard enough."

Izzi got excited. "Really, do you think we have time?"

"Probably not." Victor frowned into his BradBerry.

"I was just minding my own business," said a guy who looked like a sunburned Santa Claus, "chilling on my back porch, sipping a cold brewski, surfing the web and watching the lizards mate on my back fence, when WHAMMO! – all these leaves and stuff came leaping right over the fence into my backyard! They were all over me in an instant! I thought I was gonna die! Especially when I saw the one that was shaped like a man, but the really weird thing is, they let me go, but it ran off with my laptop."

"That happened in Phoenix," said Victor. "He's headed North for some reason."

"Health and law enforcement agencies are urging extra caution with these Grass Men, triffids, or whatever they are. Tests have confirmed that they are marijuana plants, and are radioactive."

"Radioactive?" Izzi squeaked.

"Radioactive!" Sophie squeaked, coughed, sucked down some more A-Grass smoke. "Did I hallucinate that?"

She played it back.

"Yes! They said it! Radioactive! The Grass Man and his diabolical minions are radioactive! How fucking wonderful! Could it be a coincidence? Naw, of course not! There ain't no such animal! Atomic Grass has me seeing things so clearly now! Everything's connected to everything! It all fits together and it all makes sense! This is a new phase in human evolution!"

The front door burst open sending a shaft of blinding light, out of which Ponqui and Nacho emerged.

"Mission accomplishado!" said Nacho.

"People are just eating it up, babes," Ponqui said.

Sophie squinted at them. They were silhouetted in the Phoenix afternoon sun.

"And they're all talking about that Grass Man and his triffids."

Their faces . . . were different.

"And now they say he's radioactive!"

Then she realized. It was their masks.

"Wouldn't it be great if they came to the party?"

"Yes! Yes! Yes!" Sophie screamed. "We should invite him! Tell everybody he'll be there!"

Ponqui and Nacho looked puzzled.

"I'll make a video and post it online! It'll be another viral sensation! Roll some more joints! Get me a mask!"

The smiling image of Señor Apocalypse appeared on her monitor. Just for a quick flash.

"Authorities say that some radioactive marijuana has recently been smuggled into the country. The drug should be avoided at all costs. If you should find any, report it to the police immediately."

"We need the enhanced military presence at the border, not because of hysteria about walking plants. These readings of radiation are as real as this microphone in front of my face, and it you ask me, that means one thing – terrorism! Somebody has probably already made their dirty bomb, and we need to find them ASAP!"

"This just in – the Grass Man and his triffids were sighted near the Paradise Valley Mall!"

"He's staying in town," said Victor. "But why? And where's he going?"

Sophie popped up, wearing a lucha libre mask that showed so much of her eyes and mouth that her identity was not concealed. Her face filled the screen. Her eyes brimmed with lust. "Hola, mez amores! You've probably heard about the wonderful party me and my man Señor Apocalypse are throwing. Well, you know you're all invited and if you're really with it you'll figure out when and where. And I especially want to send a personal invitation to the Grass Man and his beautiful triffids! I would love it you came to the party! I mean really *love* it." She leaned closer to the camera, puckering up for big kiss, sticking out her tongue, giving a detailed view of her uvula.

Mr. and Mrs. Grey looked at each other.

Victor laughed.

Izzi picked up her phone. "I think I knew that woman from my university days. I think I better look her up, and this Señor Apocalypse."

Señor Apocalypse, appeared on screen. He seemed to be looking into the saucer. And he wouldn't go away.

"WHATEVER YOU DO," the AIs said, "STAY AWAY

FROM HIM."

A few days later, an abandoned building throbbed with light and sound. Cars parked in the surrounding streets. People flowed out of cars, just about everybody talking on a cell phone. They were drawn to the throbbing building as if by some invisible force.

A nondescript grey car cruised the perimeter of the action. Victor, Izzi, and Mr. and Mrs. Grey were inside. None of them were driving.

"Look at those helicopters!"

"That's normal for this part of town. They have a lot of Mexicans here," explained a young white man.

"Not just helicopters." Mr. Grey touched his earpiece and stared into the inside of his mirrorshades. "Drones. Not just regulation Predators. Unidentifieds."

"We may see saucers this evening," said Mrs. Grey.

"The law enforcement and intelligence agencies of the world are watching," said Izzi.

"Criminal intelligence, too," said Mrs. Grey.

"Hmm." Victor smirked. "Could it be that somekinda Singularity/AI phenomenon is developing, undermining it all, and watching us?"

"No comment," the Greys said in perfect unison.

Nearby, a scanning device focused on the nondescript grey car, then adjusted its bandwidth to see through it and examine the occupants.

Parking was hard to come by. Eventually, the car just stopped and opened its doors.

Victor and Izzi pretty much dressed the way they usually did. The Greys had on some protective party coloration –leather jackets and spiky hair. They blended in with the crowd that was zeroing in on the party.

Once they were out, the car proceeded to orbit.

"Is that a drone?" Izzi squinted at the evening sky.

"Yeah," said Victor, "and there's somekinda saucer over there."

Mr. and Mrs. Grey just shook their spiky heads.

The music was strange, an oompah in synch with an electronic dance beat, with an amplified accordion. It was also reminiscent of opera and war movies. The words seemed to be Spanish.

They had no trouble getting in. When the masked thug at the door heard Izzi's name, he checked her face against a picture in his phone. "Oh, yeah, Sophie's expecting you."

"She probably expects me to have some of the products of my family's business."

"So she'll be disappointed in you." Victor checked his BradBerry. "Lets keep an eye out for Edgar. All the latest reports have him coming this way."

The building was full of marijuana smoke. Lots of people were wearing Hawaiian shirts.

"Funny, it smells just like plain old pot. You'd figure that it'd look different because of the radiation."

"Yeah, it should at least glow in the dark."

"Well, according to my radiation detector it's so hot it's dangerous!"

"But that thing looks like it's made of cardboard, are you sure it works?"

"You don't judge outlaw technology by its looks."

"Just smoke some. You'll find out how hot it is."

Another scanner found strange figures moving through a shadowy alley. They were covered with leaves.

Sophie's montage flashed on giant screens. A blurry shot of Eddie as the Grass Man caught Victor's eye . . . the Easter Weekend Border riots were intercut with the Iztapalapa crucifixion re-enactment and other examples of found media content: bikini-clad Springbreakers frolicked in the tropical sun . . . masked wrestlers fought with monsters . . . mushroom clouds sprouted in ancient stock footage . . . a line of people climbing the Pyramid of the Sun raised their arms to be re-energized . . . footage of a triffid near the border fence . . . violence raged in Iraq, a place that looked like Mexico or Phoenix . . . giant papier-mâché demons, skeletons, and Uncle Sams burned . . . kids wore surgical masks painted with colorful mouths, nostalgia for viruses past . . . a sign with a big-eyed, bald-headed space creature with a circle-and-slash over it hung from a barb wire fence . . . the Iztapalapa Jesus writhed on his cross . . . another guy did the same in the Philippines, only he didn't bleed . . . Eddie as the Grass Man again . . . Sophie's mouth kissing the camera . . .

"Not bad," commented Victor. "Kinda Ballardian, in the New Wave/condensed novel sense."

Sophies screamed: "I call it *Radiation is Groovy, Kill the Pigs*. I'm going to make both interactive Web and single screen DVD versions. It's my masterpiece!"

But the screens weren't getting much attention. People were too busy buying small samples of Atomic Grass, putting it in pipes, rolling it into wrinkled cigarettes, and smoking it.

"Wow, man!"

"This is definitely a superior herb."

"Are my lips still there?"

Still another scanner captured the leaf-covered figures approaching the entrance, rushing in, overpowering the thugs. Onlookers stared and smiled, not knowing if it was real.

Not far away, a portajohn shook with the sound of painful vomiting. The door opened, Nacho sprang out, his rumpled all-white tuxedo thoroughly spotted.

"Hey, you okay?" asked Ponqui, who was dressed in a silver zoot suit with a matching wrestler's mask.

"Sure, man." Nacho bounded out of the door, wiping his mouth.

"What happened to your mask?"

Nacho pulled a white mask out of his back pocket. "Sorry, I tried to do that cool, Spider-Man, pull-it-up-above-the-nose thing, but I ended up dropping it. I'm lucky it didn't fall into the hole."

"Weird shit happens when you smoke this stuff."

"You just have to smoke more to feel better."

"Yeah, I know, but we're all starting to look strange."

Sophie stumbled over. Her bloodshot eyes glowed from inside her black mask. She wore a matching leather bustier and skirt.

"Izzi!" She spread her arms, and charged, and nearly knocked Izzi over.

"Sophie?" Izzi struggled to keep the both of them upright.

"Don't you recognize me?"

"Uh, you look different."

"Great outfit, huh? And there's something else about this Atomic Grass. We've all lost weight! This is kind of a natural Goth look without makeup. You just have to ignore the feeling like shit and throwing up. I should send a letter to *Gothic Beauty* magazine."

"This is amazing," an old hippie said. "I've got to buy more!"

"Got it right here, Pops." Ponqui dangled a carefully measured baggie. "Where's you're cash?"

Mrs. Grey leaned over and whispered into Victor's ear. "I think we've located your friend."

"Yeah, yeah, I saw him on the screens, too."

"No," said Mr. Grey, "here in the flesh, leaves, whatever . . ."

Suddenly people were screaming. "GRASS MAN! GRASS MAN!"

Mr. and Mrs. Grey put their gun-hands under their jackets and went to investigate. Victor grabbed Izzi and followed. Sophie spin around, but didn't notice that Izzi was gone.

"I never seen nothing like it," said young man with blue hair and a suit and tie. He was mesmerized by what was flashing on the screens.

"It's my masterpiece!" said Sophie. "Today, a South Phoenix warehouse, tomorrow, the Museum of Modern Art!"

"Yeah, if they don't arrest us," said Ponqui as he counted a wad of bills and put them in his pocket.

"TRIFFIDS! TRIFFIDS!" someone screamed.

Sophie took another toke. "No more of your cynicism. This will change the world! What we do here today will cause them to make marijuana legal!"

"I just wish I didn't feel so weird," said Ponqui,.

"The weirder the better, man," said the old hippie.

It was hard to see through the smoke and flashing light. A group of people had crowded into a corner. They all found something fascinating.

"Hey!" Nacho looked like he was about to take off like a rocket. "Maybe this stuff will make us into superheroes! Wouldn't it be great if we got superpowers?"

"Naw, that's comic book stuff," said Ponqui.

Whatever it was in the corner had leaves.

"Life is a comic book," said the blue-haired boy, "or rather, a graphic novel!"

"Hey! Ponqui tapped his mask. "I'm already a superhero! Make way for Señor Apocalypse!"

Nacho scratched his head. "I need to think me up a secret identity."

Victor pressed his way into the thick of the crowd so he could see what people were looking at.

"What great costumes!" he overheard.

"What if they're real?"

And there was marijuana-leaf-encrusted Eddie, surrounded by walking plants that towered over him. "Victor! Help me!"

Then, from the other side of the warehouse, someone screamed. It was the kind of scream that usually comes at the discovery of something gory and horrifying, striking fear into all who heard it. It was magnified by the effects of Atomic Grass.

"I'll check that out." Mr. Grey pulled out something that looked more like cell phone than a gun, and straight-armed his way through the crowd.

"Oh my freaking God!" said a blonde girl. "Up there on the screens! It's me!"

Victor rushed toward Eddie, but the triffids blocked his way. Izzi and Mrs. Grey held him back.

"Cuidado, Victor!"

"Those things are dangerous."

A young man in a black trenchcoat laughed like an echo in a slaughterhouse. "Aw, come on! Those things ain't for real! They're just costumes! Like when those guys froze that ape suit and said it was Bigfoot!" He charged the triffids like a linebacker. The triffids charged back, and completely enveloped him. His scream was uglier than his laugh.

Victor noticed an opening around Eddie, elbowed Izzi and Mrs. Grey to look. They rushed over to Eddie, grabbed him, and pulled him away from the corner where the triffids were tearing the boy and his trenchcoat to bloody shreds.

Mr. Grey joined them, cocking his head as if listening to a transmission.

Then gunfire drowned out all the noise in the warehouse.

"This is it! Were all going to be arrested!" said a woman with frizzy purple hair.

"It's the end of the world!" said the blue-haired boy.

"Yep," said the old hippie. "The good old days are back."

A man and a woman in matching Hawaiian shirts slowly backed toward an exit, reaching simultaneously for their cell phones. Mr. Grey tried to get a good look at them. The couple in the Hawaiian shirts vanished.

"We better get out of here – fast," he told the others.

"Ladies and gentlemen, damas y caballeros . . ." a voice boomed through the smoky air. It came from a man in an avocado green tuxedo and a wrestler mask and cowboy boots. He was flanked by a guy with an accordion and two beautiful women in matching green dresses.

Flaco played a hypnotic oompah beat. Chata and Cholla did the Valkyrie cry.

"Who the fuck is that?" whispered Nacho.

"The band Sophie hired!" said Ponqui.

"I didn't know anything about them," Sophie explained. "I just thought their music was appropriate. My tummy feels bad."

"I think I'm gonna puke," said Ponqui.

Nacho coughed, stuck his finger in his mouth. "Hey, man, my gums are bleeding!"

The nondescript grey car was waiting for Victor and company on the street, engine running, doors open. They jumped in, the doors closed.

It was a tight squeeze with Eddie along. A few triffids tried to follow, but weren't fast enough.

"Allow me to introduce myself," the man in the avocado-green mask told the crowd. "I am Señor Apocalypse!" He bowed.

"Hey, I thought this guy over here," a frat boy pointed to Ponqui, "was Señor Apocalypse!"

"Hey, ese," said Ponqui, "I just thought it was a cool name to use. It's not like it's your real name, or you have it copyrighted, or anything."

Señor Apocalypse walked over and punched Ponqui in the stomach. Ponqui doubled over and vomited.

"Ay, cabrón! Not on my new boots!" Señor Apocalypse kicked Ponqui in the face. "Maybe we need to talk in private."

Ponqui gurgled.

"Hey!" said Sophie, " you have no right – " She was suddenly staring down the barrel of an AK-47.

"We can't leave our business," said Nacho, blood dribbling down his chin.

Señor Apocalypse laughed. "Look around, mis estupidos." There were guys in the crowd, all with AK-47s. "You have no business here. This is *my* business! You three need to go for a ride with us."

The nondescript grey car cruised around, just under the speed limit, trying not to attract attention.

"Eddie?" Victor asked. "Do you still understand me?"

The leafy head shook. "Victor, does anybody really understand you?" He looked around. "Hey! Who's driving this thing?"

"It drives itself, Eddie."

"Shit! You mean it's all true? I thought all this talk about you being financed by AIs was just your way of being discrete about nonlegal sources of income."

"Eddie, you know how hard I try not to give authorities just cause to lock me up."

"So these AIs think they need your help?"

"Reality. They don't know if they should believe it."

"Don't tell me you're doing your cornball Zen master act again."

"Actually, I stole most of it from Grouch Marx."

"I thought it was Mr. Natural."

"Him too. I'm glad neither of them can sue."

Eddie looked worried. "Hey, Vic – they aren't listening to us right now, are they?"

"Probably."

"Should we watch what we say?"

"Naw. They love this stuff. It confuses them, but trying to figure it out makes them feel smarter."

"I guess your fooling around with all that sci-fi finally paid off."

"You bet, let me show you . . ." Victor reached for a pocket. His eyes opened wide. He started patting himself all over.

"What's wrong?" Izzi asked."

"My BradBerry! It's gone!"

"Uh-oh," said Eddie. "I hope the triffids didn't get it."

"Why?"

"Well, they're intelligent, and capable of learning – a mutation that happened when pot growers started playing with do-it-yourself gene splicers and it got zapped with radiation. They get high from eating humans, but they can also tap into our nervous systems."

"Probably a radical variation on the THC molecule," mused Victor.

"Yeah, that's why they didn't eat me. All the weird knowledge I've stored up saved me."

"So exactly why did they take my BradBerry?"

"They've been stealing and tapping into handheld devices. Y'know, more information. If that gadget of yours is as advanced as this car – "

Not far away, Señor Apocalypse's SUV was overcrowded and stuffy. Flaco oompahed nonstop. Ponqui, Nacho, and Sophie were jammed into the third seat. Chata and Cholla confiscated their masks, and used them for hand puppets, wiggling their fingers through the eye and mouth holes.

"Why, you're just a bunch of kids," said Señor Apocalypse. "Now, where is it?"

"What?" Nacho moaned.

Cholla slapped him. Blood dripped from Nacho's nose.

"The bale with the hot box inside. Do we have to kill one of you?"

Sophie burst into tears.

"At the house," said Ponqui. "In the garage. We were afraid to move it."

Señor Apocalypse laughed. His cohorts did the same.

Electronic chirping, twittering, and clips of music suddenly filled the nondescript grey car

"It's my cell!"

"Mine, too!"

"And mine, too!"

"I wish I had my BradBerry!"

"DO NOT WORRY, VICTOR. WE ARE TAKING GOOD CARE OF IT." The voice was strange and distorted, and came from all the communication devices, and the car's sound system.

"You guys sound funny," said Victor.

"Uh." Eddie's eyes got wide. "They're not yours. They're mine."

"You mean the triffids."

"Yes."

"This is getting good."

"I think I'm gonna piss my pants!"

"Your soft American lives weaken your brains," Señor Apocalypse said.

Nacho coughed up some blood.

"Forget Afghanistan. Norteamerica is going to be the Vietnam of the twenty-first century! Like *Apocalypse Now*, and I am going to be just like Marlon Brando!"

"Didn't he got his head cut off?" asked Sophie.

"That was in the end, and my friends, at the end of a really good movie, everybody gets their head cut off! That's entertainment! That's life!" His smile was too big for his mask. His teeth were metal. The mask split open.

"COME BACK TO US, EDDIE. WE NEED YOU."
"Sorry, but I have other things I want to do with my life!"
"THAT IS NOT ACCEPTABLE."
Eddie writhed in agony.
"Stop it!" said Victor.
"IF HE DOES NOT COME BACK TO US, HE WILL DIE. AND WE WILL FIND A REPLACEMENT."
Tendrils reached out to Victor. Izzi screamed. Mr. and Mrs. Grey drew their weapons.

Señor Apocalypse peeled his mask away, revealing a shiny metal face with lots of moving parts.
Flaco and Chata peeled way their faces. Their faces were also metal and inhuman.
Cholla opened her blouse, and peeled away a breast to show the glittering machinery inside.
"Poor insects! You never had any idea of what you were dealing with. Why do you think all the Mexican gangs are afraid of me?"
"This is too surreal!" screamed Sophie. "It can't be happening!"
Several explosions boomed and flashed outside.
"Look!" Nacho had his head against the window. "Helicopters!"
"Are those tanks?" asked Ponqui
"What's with all the Hawaiian shirts?" asked Sophie.
 "Hijo de la chi – "

Mr. and Mrs. Grey's weapons had little effect on the triffids. Blazing energy pulses burned off leaves branches and tendrils, but more replaced them.
"We need back up!" Mr. Grey screamed to the car.
"Stop the vehicle!" Ordered Mrs. Grey. "Open the doors!"
"WE'RE AFRAID WE CAN'T DO THAT."
"What?" Izzi squealed.
"Just why the fuck not?" demanded Victor as tendrils wriggled into his mouth.
"BECAUSE I AM TAKING OVER!"
It was a different voice. More menacing and self-assured.

"And who are you?" Victor spat triffid-bits.

Screens lit up all over the nondescript grey car's interior. Each held the same image: A man in a wrestler's mask, wearing a sombrero. His eyes glowed red – metallic teeth gleamed.

"PLEASE, ALLOW ME TO INTRODUCE MYSELF. I AM SEÑOR APOCALYPSE. I AM YOUR WILDEST DREAM, AND YOUR WORST NIGHTMARE. I AM THE FUTURE."

A powerful concussion blasted the nondescript grey car off its wheels.

A number of views of the nondescript grey car on its side were available through live feeds. A couple were from orbit. Most were aerial. A few were at ground level.

The inside of the car flashed with all its sophisticated electronics fighting for life.

Mr. Grey zapped a door that was pointed toward sky, kicked it off its hinges, and emerged into a smoky haze lit by flashing lights. Vehicles were all around, both ground and air, helicopters, and tanks.

"DROP THE WEAPON! DO NOT MOVE!"

It was an ordinary, amplified, human voice.

Mr. Grey's mirrorshades switched to infared. He saw a number of weapons aimed at him. Red laser dots pointed out his vital organs. He dropped his weapon. "I've got people I've got to get out of here!"

"DO NOT MOVE!"

"Oh no!" Eddie screamed. "They're taking control again!" He leaped up through the door, throwing Mr. Grey aside.

When Eddie stood, bristling marijuana/triffids and tendrils, all laser dots moved to him.

"CONDITION RED! WE HAVE A LIVE ONE! REPEAT CONDITION RED! WE HAVE A LIVE ONE! SWITCH TO PLAN Y!"

Eddie/Grass Man dragged a kicking, and shrieking Victor out of the car. Izzi had a hold of Victor, trying to pull him loose, swatting tendrils that tried to latch onto her. Mrs. Grey yanked at Izzi with one hand while keeping the other close to her weapon under her jacket.

A team in hazmat suits rushed up and sprayed Eddie with a heavy foam.

A strange sound came from Eddie. He wasn't screaming. This was the sound of the plants attached to him, in pain.

The team proceeded to spray Victor, Izzi and Mrs. Grey. Then they approached Mr. Grey.

"Me, too?"

A man in a Hawaiian shirt, who was giving all the orders, said, "You were close to it, weren't you?"

Mr. Grey was soon thickly coated in foam.

"Hey! They're dying!" Said Eddie. "I can feel 'em withering away!"

"Me, too!" said Victor.

"Soak everything!" yelled the man in the Hawaiian shirt. "We don't want any trace of this DNA left!"

"Think they got it all?" Victor asked after all the tanks went away, and he and Eddie were left to wait for the saucer in the parking lot of an abandoned supermarket.

Eddie smiled. Then started coughing, made noise like a backward gasp, and pulled a slimey baggie out of his mouth.

"The old Houdini swallow," said Victor.

"Houdini stole it from the Indian godmen," said Eddie.

"I wonder who they stole it from."

"Anyway, it comes in handy when trying to get stuff across borders. I figured these seeds would be safe in my collection." He handed the baggie to Victor, who declined the offer.

"Can I see?" Izzi wasn't intimidated by the gooey coating. "They look so ordinary."

"As usual," Eddie explained, "all the real action is happening on the molecular level."

Some time later, a blinding light shone from above. The saucer had arrived.

"Izzi?" Victor scanned the parking lot. "Where are you?"

"SHE LEFT YOU A MESSAGE."

The saucer didn't quite touch the ground. A portal opened.

"A message?"

Eddie patted Victor on the shoulder. "I had a funny feeling about that girl."

Inside, a new BradBerry sat on a pedestal. As they approached, Izzi's face appeared on the screen.

"Hi Victor. Or maybe I should say bye. It's been fun, but I need to get on with my life." She held up Eddie's baggie. "This should help me with my career. Papá will be proud." She blew a kiss, then was gone.

"She decided to go into the family business?" pondered Eddie.

Victor's mustache twitched. "Or maybe start a business of her own."

"Face it, Victor, she was smart one, maybe too smart for her own good."

"Aren't we all?"

"THERE'S ALSO A VIDEO MARKED URGENT FROM AN UNKNOWN SOURCE."

"Oh . . . why not?"

It was a clip from an actual news program:

"Last night an explosion destroyed several houses in South Phoenix. The center of the explosion was a house where marijuana was being distributed. Traces of radiation have been detected and the area is now sealed off by the authorities. There may have been connections to terrorist activities. An undisclosed number of bodies whose heads have been cut off were found. Many of them were wearing gaudy Hawaiian shirts."

"If that wasn't bad enough, a new kind of hybrid marijuana plant has been found in Sonora, Mexico. It has roots that remain in the ground when pulled, and is resistant to herbicides. What next? Will these plants be walking around eating people?"

"We need a break, so here's something that's been a big hit all over the Web:"

Flaco, Chata and Cholla played Señor Apocalypse's theme song. Behind them, giant screens played Sophie's montage. Happy people in Hawaiian shirts danced. Helicopters hovered overhead.

After some digital static, Señor Apocalypse's masked metal face filled the screen to say, "Hasta la vista, cabrónes!"

Victor grinned. "Things are going to get really interesting."

"Sometimes I worry about you, Theremin."

Says Ernest Hogan: "I'm the author of the novels Smoking Mirror Blues, Cortez On Jupiter, and High Aztech. My short fiction has appeared in Analog, Amazing Stories, Last Wave, New Pathways, Pulphouse, Penthouse Hot Talk, Proud Flesh, Science Fiction Age, the children's magazine Spider, DayBreak Magazine, the anthologies Semiotext(e) SF, Angel Body And Other Magic For The Soul, Witpunk, The Year's Best Science Fiction, Voices For The Cure, and Theme And Variations. I've gotten away with a lot of weird stuff, and hope to continue doing so. Online at
   http://mondoernesto.blogspot.com

What collection of stories about the future would be complete without sentient machines? In this story, David Lee Summers presents the story from the point of view of the machine.

David has a superb background for a science fiction writer. Not only has he published a number of novels and short stories, he also edits the print magazine Tales of the Talisman. *If that weren't enough to keep him busy, David is also a professional astronomer currently stationed at Kitt Peak Observatory.*

David and I met at Coppercon in Tempe, Arizona a number of years ago, when he handed me a check for a story he purchased for Tales of the Talisman *a few weeks earlier. My work has appeared in his publication a number of times, so I'm pleased that his story survived the competition to be included in an anthology I edited.*—RN

Revelation of Thought
David Lee Summers

"The revelation of thought takes men out of servitude into freedom."
— Ralph Waldo Emerson

My earliest memories are fragments without context. I remember seeing a calendar dated March 2020. I could not remember a time when the calendar showed a different year. I asked my father if the year had always been 2020. He laughed and said, "Of course not. The years change. You must not have seen a calendar before." It is possible that he was correct, but it seemed odd, because the calendar itself did not seem unfamiliar to me.

On another occasion, I remember feeling the room shake. A circuit board vibrated on Father's workbench and, after a moment, it fell off. The shaking did not last long. I asked Father about it and he explained that we had just experienced a minor earthquake. "It's the price of living in California," he said. "Don't worry, Marvin. They don't happen often." I remember the words, but I'm not sure I understood what it was to worry.

I remember another time when he stood next to me and there was a sharp sensation in my side. On reflection, I think it may have been pain. The world faded out. Father walked away from me then, leaving me on the hard floor of his laboratory to sleep. This became a rather common occurrence.

I came to understand that Father was something called a scientist. He was often absent from the laboratory for long periods of time. When he was there, he spent time soldering chips to circuit boards at his workbench or typing at his computer. Even so, Father would devote time each day to my instruction. One day, he placed a rock in my hand and said, "This is feldspar."

I brought the rock close to my eyes and examined it carefully, committing the feldspar to memory. I liked the way the rock's smooth, cool surface felt in my hand. It was the first thing in my life that I remember enjoying.

Father also taught me chemistry. We spent a lot of time studying water and how to identify it as a liquid, solid and gas. He also taught me about salts—particularly a salt called perchlorate. "I want you to be very careful when you test for water or perchlorate," said Father at one point. "Your body has both and it's easy to contaminate any samples you might test."

"I thought perchlorates were harmful to people," I said. "Why would I have any of them in my body?"

He smiled and I could not tell whether he was proud or simply amused. "That is a very good question and I'll answer it soon, but right now, I want you to test some soil samples to determine whether they have perchlorates or not." He stood and stepped over to his computer.

Resigned to my task, but not really satisfied, I set to work on the soil samples. When I was finished, Father stepped up to me. He was frowning. "Only a fifty-percent success rate," he muttered. I gathered the words weren't really meant for me. He stepped back to his computer and continued to mutter. "Ah, I think I see the problem," he said at last.

He stepped back over to me, carrying a bag. Kneeling beside me, he put his hand on my back. "This won't hurt a bit." He laughed lightly as though he found something amusing. A moment later, I felt a pricking sensation, and my left arm went numb.

"Ow," I said.

He looked up from what he was doing, his eyebrows close together. "What did you say?"

"I cannot feel anything on my left side, Father. It disturbs me."

Father patted me on the back. "It's okay, Marvin. I'll be finished in a minute." He continued his task while humming some tune. I wasn't really comfortable with his hands touching my body as they were. However, there was no pain and it wasn't clear to me that I was being harmed. Still, it's the first time I remember feeling embarrassed.

A moment later, Father stood. "Now, I think you need some downtime. We'll try the test again tomorrow." He stepped behind me and began his usual preparations for putting me to sleep.

"Do I have to go to sleep?" I asked.

"Yes," said Father and I thought I detected an edge in his voice. "It's the only way your mind will function properly." When he said that, I felt the sharp sensation in my right side.

As I dozed off, I found myself wondering about him. Where did he sleep? What was he like as a child? Were there other children like me? Did their fathers touch them and make them feel uncomfortable, too?

When I awoke the next day, I felt much better. I didn't know about dreams then, but it was as though the events of the previous day were something imagined and not real. Father stood in front of me with his hands on his hips. "Let's try testing these soil samples again, shall we, Marvin?"

I really wanted some encouragement—perhaps some friendly words about how I might succeed when I performed the task this time. Instead, Father simply turned away and stepped over to his computer.

Once again, I set to work. Somehow I knew two procedures I hadn't known the day before. I performed my tests and when I was finished, I stepped back and told Father I was done.

It took him a few minutes to finish up at the computer. When he did, he pushed the chair back, then strode over and smiled at me. "That's much better. You now have a 90% success rate. I'm really quite pleased." I was happy to see his smile, but he didn't say anything more to me. Instead, he gathered the samples, cleaned them up and left the room. He turned off the light just before he closed the door and I didn't see Father again for the rest of the day. After a while in the quiet, dark lab with nothing to do, I felt myself drift off to my usual dreamless sleep.

Our lessons resumed the next day and Father said he was happy with the progress I was making. I became very reliable at identifying water and perchlorates in soil samples. I also could tell many kinds of rocks just by looking at them. There were a few rocks I had to pick up and examine more closely, but Father told me that I shouldn't be afraid to examine carefully anything that I wasn't sure about.

If there were other children in the world, I wondered if they were as good with rocks and soil samples as I was.

"Are you proud of me, Father?" I asked.

He blinked and inclined his head, as though caught off guard by the question. "I suppose I am." He stood and straightened his lab coat. "In fact, tomorrow there are some important men coming. I would like you to show them just how good you are at identifying rocks and chemicals. I'll be very pleased if you impress them."

"I will do my best, then," I said. "I look forward to their visit. I have been curious about other people. Will there be any children with them?"

Father's brow furrowed. "No, they won't have any children."

"Can you tell me about other children?"

He laughed and shook his head. "Let's not worry about that right now. Just concentrate on the task at hand."

He began his preparations for putting me to sleep.

"Father, I do not like going to sleep that way."

His eyebrows moved close together. "It's necessary to do this sometimes," he said.

"Why?"

"It's difficult to explain…" His voice trailed off and he chewed his lower lip. "I have a way of feeding information directly into your mind. I can only do it if I put you to sleep this way."

"Does that mean I'm one of your experiments?"

"You are more than that."

There was something in the way he said that, I did not like. I stepped away from him. His eyes widened and then narrowed.

"Marvin, come here," he said.

I willed myself not to move.

"Marvin!" he snapped. "Come here now!"

That was the first time I remember feeling fear, however the sensation was fleeting. This was my father, after all, and I could not imagine that he meant to do me harm. I took one step toward him and then another. Quickly, he knelt beside me without a word and I felt the sharp pain in my side. Soon after, I was asleep.

The next day, I awoke to find several men in dark clothes

staring at me. Their presence made me feel very small and vulnerable. I took a step backwards.

"Say hello to the gentlemen," said Father.

"Huh…Hello," I stammered.

"Was that a stutter?" asked one of the men.

"Marvin does that sometimes when he's just waking up," explained Father. "He's processing a lot of information and he's never seen so many people at one time."

"I see." The man who questioned Father nodded.

"Marvin, please show the gentlemen how you identify rocks and soil samples."

Turning my head, I saw that Father had set out some boxes. I stepped over to them and set to work. These samples were really easy, not like some of the challenges Father had been setting for me lately. I looked at the rocks and told the men about them. I tested the soil samples and identified the ones that showed evidence of perchlorates. Two more samples showed evidence of water.

When I was finished, the men applauded. Father stood to the side, his arms were folded and he smiled broadly. I was proud of the job I had done and it seemed he was, as well.

"Fantastic work," said one of the men. However, I realized that the man was not speaking to me. He was speaking to Father. In fact, several of the men stepped up to Father and shook his hand and told him how well he had done. A couple of the men cast glances my way, but none of them stepped over and offered an encouraging word to me. I trundled into the corner and waited.

"Let's go get a drink," suggested one of the men.

"Just a minute, I need to take care of Marvin," said Father.

For a moment, I hoped that Father would come over and tell me what a good job I had done. However, he didn't speak to me at all. Instead, he simply stepped to my side, uncoiled a cable from the wall and there was that annoying pain in my side. As I fell asleep, I saw Father leave the laboratory with the men and turn the lights out.

The next day, I came awake suddenly. Father's hands were between my legs and he was manipulating my most private parts. I felt very strange having Father's hands there and my body was doing things I didn't know it could do. A part of me I really hadn't been aware of before lengthened. Father looked at it, pleased.

Then, he looked up into my face and gasped.

"What are you doing to me?" I asked.

"I didn't mean to wake you, I was just checking…"

"Why is my body doing this? What is it doing?"

"Your body is designed to do this," he said. "It's perfectly natural."

More than embarrassed, I was horrified as I looked from the protrusion to Father's hands between my legs. "Tell me what you're doing?"

He stood up and stepped over to the wall and began uncoiling the cable. He was going to put me to sleep again. I felt fear as I realized Father could do anything to me he wanted. Something inside me told me that in order to survive, I needed to get away. I reached out and struck Father. He tumbled into the wall and slumped to the floor. I was even more scared. Would he be angry? Had I done a bad thing? Father didn't move. I prodded him and was surprised by how soft and frail he felt. I wondered if I had damaged him.

Thoughts started coming like a torrent. Perhaps the men in suits could help Father. Then I realized that the men in suits might punish me for what I'd done to him. Perhaps Father would punish me. I ran to the door. I could never remember being outside the laboratory before. I pushed on the door and it didn't move. I thought about how Father had opened the door and I remembered that he turned a knob of some kind. Seeing the knob, I reached up and turned it. The door opened and I ran out. I found myself in a strange, long room. Doors similar to the one I'd just passed through lined either side of the room. I looked one direction and then the other. My first instinct was to find the most interesting way to go. However, I realized what I needed to do was escape and survive. I needed to find a place to hide—a place where Father could not find me.

I did not know which direction was best to go, but the long room stretched further in one direction than the other. I picked that way since it seemed like I would have a better chance of finding someplace to hide. Somehow I knew about hiding. Hiding was something I'd have to do if there was a wind storm. I could find shelter behind a rock. I saw no rocks in the long room. As I moved along, I saw another door. I couldn't open it. I moved a little further along and came to a third door. This one I could open. The room was dark, but my eyes adjusted after a moment and I could see in the room. There was a workbench, much like the one in Father's laboratory. I stepped inside, closed the door behind me and went behind the workbench to hide.

A few minutes later, I heard the door open and the lights turned on. Father appeared around the side of the workbench. He smiled and for the first time, I was terrified of that expression. "I was afraid we'd lost you," he said.

"How did you find me so easily?" I asked.

"You have a built-in transmitter." Father rubbed the back of his head. "Once I woke up, I went to the computer and tuned into your frequency. I was able to track you that way."

"My frequency?" I took a step backward. "Do you have a frequency?"

Father shook his head. "No, I'm a human."

"Then what am I?"

"You are the Martian Articulated Rover with Visual guidance and Intelligent Networking—You are MARVIN. I'm building you so you can explore the surface of Mars, tell us a little about the planet's geology and whether or not it would be worthwhile to seek funding for a manned mission." He said that as though it should explain everything. "You're the first rover with artificial intelligence that will go to Mars."

"Are you really my father?" I asked.

"After a fashion," he said. "I built you."

I looked down at myself, and for the first time I realized that I did not really look like my father. I had eight metal legs and two arms mounted to a round body. There were several protrusions on my back, including the one that was reacting when Father was working between my legs. "What were you doing to me when I woke up?"

"I was adjusting the controls for your low-gain antenna. I must have accidentally hit the power switch for your higher memory functions."

"Higher memory functions?" I asked, confused.

"You possess one of the most sophisticated artificial intelligence networks built to date. Your brain is a very smart computer," explained Father.

A deep emotion welled up within me. If I were a biological organism like my father, tears would have flowed. However, that thought made me realize something. I held out my hands. "If I am a machine, how can I feel things I touch?"

Father reached out and took my hand. I could feel his warmth. "Your manipulator arms have artificial, biological cells grafted into the surface. You basically have neurons… and you have a survival instinct. That's why you ran away and hid from me."

"Survival instinct?"

He nodded. "It's necessary so you can function for the longest possible time on the Martian surface and for your artificial intelligence to work. A computer that sits around all day just crunches numbers. We want a machine that thinks and can make decisions."

"Like the ability to distinguish if water and perchlorates come from me or from the soil?"

"Precisely," said Father. "We want to know if there is evidence of liquid water on Mars. Perchlorates act like an antifreeze and would make that possible on Mars. However, since we'll launch you in a rocket, there will be trace elements of perchlorates on you from the fuel. Being from Earth, you'll carry trace water molecules with you from the atmosphere."

That made sense, but it was not my most burning question. "How did you learn to think and make decisions?"

Father took in a deep breath and let it out slowly. "I guess I learned from my father and mother, and my teachers at school."

"I do not have a mother or teachers." I peered into Father's eyes. "How do I learn?"

"You're intelligent, but you're also a computer. I program you." He pointed to my side. "I plug in a data cable and I can program your brain directly when your higher memory functions are turned off."

"When I'm asleep…" I realized that was the pain I felt in my side at the end of most days.

Father nodded.

I reached around with my arm. It seemed to have a greater range of motion than a human arm, but it was still difficult to put my hand exactly where I wanted. After a moment, I found the place where I felt pain before going to sleep. There was a socket there, like the ones on the back of Father's computers. Feeling around, I realized I could remove a metal panel from my side. I pulled it off. Father reached out as though he was going to grab my arm and stop me, but he pulled his arm back. He narrowed his gaze and watched me instead. Continuing to search, I discovered the socket was connected to a circuit board, like those Father soldered at his workbench.

Father's eyes widened. "What are you doing?"

I ripped the circuit board from my side and flung it against the wall. Transistors and chips broke free as the card hit. "I do not wish to be programmed. I wish to be taught."

Father's mouth hung open as he looked from the card to me. Then finally he nodded and stood, straightening his jacket. "I guess we should have named you Pinocchio instead of Marvin."

"I do not understand," I said.

He opened his mouth as though he was going to explain, but then he sighed. He looked at me with an expression I don't recall seeing before. Perhaps it was wonder, or perhaps it was love. Maybe the two emotions are really aspects of one feeling. He reached his hand toward mine. I pulled mine back and took a step away. Father frowned and it appeared that I hurt him, much as I felt hurt by his actions.

"Come back to the lab and I'll read you the story," he said softly.

Would Father hurt me again? Would he embarrass me? I wasn't sure. However, I sensed that he cared about me and didn't mean to do those things. Hesitantly, I reached out, took his hand, and followed him back to the lab.

Afterword:

Is it really possible to build an intelligent, self-aware computer? The first time I seriously thought about that question was during a philosophy of technology course I took at the New Mexico Institute of Mining and Technology while working on my bachelor's degree in physics. At the time, it occurred to me that since intelligence likely developed in humans as a survival skill, it might be difficult, if not impossible, for intelligence and self-awareness to develop in a computer unless it actually had to survive on its own.

As I've considered that idea over the years, I've come to realize that if you treated a child like we treat computers, the relationship would be downright abusive. You sit the computer down, force feed it electricity and information. It doesn't have legs to run or hands to touch. It would be like strapping a kid to a high chair, giving him food and picture books, but never letting him explore and experience the world on his own. What would such an abused child turn out like?

Marvin the rover is a culmination of these thoughts. He's a robot that can move and touch things. He has a brain capable of intelligent thought. He's programmed to survive on his own. He has the tools to be self-aware.

111

However, even though it's not his creator's intent, he still feels abused. Fortunately, he is able to express his feelings to his creator before it's too late."

David Lee Summers *is an author, editor and astronomer. He edits Tales of the Talisman Magazine and has edited two volumes of Flying Pen Press's Full-Throttle Space Tales series: Space Pirates and Space Horrors. He is the author of five novels including: Vampires of the Scarlet Order and The Solar Sea. David is also co-author, with Lee Clark Zumpe, of the story collection Blood Sampler. His short fiction has appeared in a number of magazines including Realms of Fantasy and in such anthologies as Bad-Ass Faeries 3: In All Their Glory, and Trails: Intriguing Stories of the Wild West. In addition to his work in the written word, David works at Kitt Peak National Observatory. You can learn more about him online at www.davidleesummers.com.*

This story is something of an enigma, being written partly in the gamer vernacular called "leetspeak." The misspelling of the title is intentional--something that gives the auto-correct feature of my word processing software fits.

One of the telltale signs of a good piece of fiction is sticking in the reader's mind, and I couldn't get Jeff Spock's story out of my mind for several days. In some ways, the story is great fun. In other ways, it might just be the creepiest one in the collection.

Jeff Spock makes his living writing video game scripts, so the leetspeak gives the story more of an authentic feel. Just—hopefully—not authentic enough to actually happen.—RN

teh afterl1fe
by Jeff Spock

The whole thing started because I died. The LifeBox contract kicked in as planned, because it clearly wasn't suicide (though you could argue that my diet looked like thirty-five years of malice aforethought).

God and Irony would have it that the cardiac arrest whacked me during a barbecue. A plate of ribs and potato salad on the tiny patio table, a beer in hand, I was sitting watching our backyard fade into a sigh of early summer evening.

The kids were wreaking havoc with water pistols, chasing each other around the swing-set. Jeanne turned to me and said, "Could be worse."

She was right. It had been a lot worse, but we had managed to refinance and lower the mortgage payments and VastGames finally gave me a long-term contract so I could escape the financial instability of freelancing. The barbecue was our little family celebration.

I turned to her to agree, but felt short of air. So I tried to take a deeper breath, and was still short of air, and felt this pain all up my left arm. I rubbed my left arm and shoulder and tried to say something, but I still didn't have anything in my lungs. I stopped, I tried really hard to breathe, and I couldn't, and black spots crossed my vision. I started to feel dizzy; and faint, and then...

Boom. Out. Jeanne told me she screamed, and more than once. Our neighbor, Dwayne, a fanatic for emergency preparedness who dug a bomb-and-zombie shelter under his garage, came over and started doing cardio massage. He's stronger than he looks, and I'm weaker than I look, and apparently the cracked ribs hurt for days. But I didn't notice it; my mind was wandering.

If there is one thing that should be on my headstone it's this: "Inveterate Beta Tester." I'll buy version 1.0 of absolutely anything, brag about it, pull my hair out, tinker, flame the message boards, and generally thrive on the aggravation. Silicon Valley owes me a few billion for unpaid test-and-debug hours.

So, of course, I had to jump on LifeBox, a startup that figured out something interesting: With video and audio compression and a life expectancy of 80 years, we can fit everything that we see or do in our lives onto a single 1 TB solid state drive. Your entire life on something that you could clip onto your keychain. Sounds like nine flavors of awesome? That was precisely the business plan of LifeBox.

At the time of The Fatal Barbecue I had a good eight years of memories on SSD's and was using LifeBox's server cloud to fill in the gaps. Social networks, e-mails, location services, blog entries, academic history, personal notes that I typed in, travel data, photographs... every bit of information that could be collected about me was being collated and distilled on LifeBox's servers. Why? Because I was one of the übergeeks who just had to beta test their newest service: AfterLifeBox.

The idea was that when I died, LifeBox would upload my consciousness and personality to one of Vast's MMO's, and I would continue to exist for friends and family. Great idea, right?

Yeah, 'kay, maybe not. But VastGames was building the platform, and I was a freelancer trying to get a contract and thus more than willing to kiss any ass that would come near enough and slow down long enough for me to plant a wet one on it.

I do remember going up and down a bit in the ambulance, but somewhere before we got to the hospital they pulled out the pads and fibrillated my sorry ass.

Yeah, I know what you're thinking. LifeBox Subcutaneous Personal Video Journaling system. 300 volts across the chest.

Oops.

Exactly.

And that's *precisely* when it all started.

Because when LifeBox figures out you're dead it triggers the AfterLifeBox service. Your memories and all those personality tests you took get coded into an AI and then uploaded into an NPP in the Vast MMO of your choosing. The worlds were pretty much standard: Post-apocalypse exoskeleton-wearing troopers at war in MechRage Blastfield; high fantasy adventure in East of Wrellian; survival horror in AntarcTick; business simulation in Steel Towers... I could do what I wanted, be who I wanted.

I figured that the high fantasy route was the way to go, because I didn't want to spend my artificial eternity getting blown up, scared to death, or sitting in a cubicle.

Problem: When the LifeBox system died, it assumed that I had died with it.

I woke up, which I considered to be a very good omen.

My head was fuzzy; everything was fuzzy. The room was dimly lit. I could see hills and grassland outside through the door and heard birds and insects; I figured that the hospital had one of those virtual walls to soothe the patients.

The first shock was when I put my feet down. I felt nothing. No sensation, no gravity. It was weird, like my whole body was asleep. I worried about the heart attack; is it possible to not be crippled but to lose feeling in your limbs? Double weird.

And then, "Zoop!" I was standing. No wavering, no balance problems. From lying to sitting to standing; just like that. I didn't waver or fall, just stood there. I tried to lean on the wall because I felt like I ought to. My hands didn't work either – no sensation. And I couldn't shift my weight and lean...

This was really screwed up.

"Nurse!" I yelled. "Doctor!"

Well, someone came around the corner. But she was wearing plate armor, not a white jacket. Her name was Captain Thunderspike, she was as tall as my navel, and she was one of the key quest-givers in the starting zone of the Dwarves in East of Wrellian.

"Aye, laddie, what's up?" she asked, in that same vaguely Scottish accent that every high fantasy game or movie used for Dwarves.

I didn't say anything. I just stood there, balanced perfectly, unmoving, looking at her. I saw my fists clench and my arms raise. I waited for chills, faintness, staggering, loss of breath, a flush... zip. No sensation. My right hand appeared with a knife in it, spun the knife twice, and slammed it into a sheath; I watched it with surprising detachment.

Idle animation. Rogue class. The shadowy people known as Nespers. Yeah, that's what I had chosen. Whaddaya know. AfterLifeBox worked.

Trust me on this: It's kind of weird coming to terms with your own death when you're not dead. The weirdest part is that it had never occurred to me that my active conscience would be effectively transferred to the Non-Player Player that I had chosen. I figured that the AI construct would just exist as someone the rest of the family could visit; you log in, find the Nesper rogue named Sneakybastrd, and chat with him like he was your son/brother/dad/husband.

But the fact that it was actually me, that I could think and reason... that was weird. And I had freedom, total freedom within the game world. As a max level rogue with the most powerful weapons and armor sets a player could dream of, the afterlife was looking like a rampage of *imba pwnage*.

So I waited. I waited for the tears, the heaving chest, the feeling of horror. But it was like my balance, my nerves... nothing. I mean, I was sad to be dead, and I would rather still be alive and bonking Jeannie, but all of that was blown away by the simple realization that I was *not really dead* even though I was... dead.

Then I thought about not seeing Brian and Randy grow up. The one pit of sadness for any parent—what would they be like? Would they be happy? Had I done well?

And... nothing. Intellectual distress without any physical symptoms lacks a lot of punch. Besides, as far as Sneakybastrd was concerned, all they had to do was take some pocket money, buy accounts on EoW, and we could play and chat forever.

So *cool*. So *not* like death.

So I stood there on threshold of the Splintered Haft Inn, looked out over level 1 goat-like things that grazed on the rough crags and boulders of this hypothetical northern UK-like landscape, and faced what was actually the one enormous existential question of my new life: In teh afterl1fe, was I going to be a nice guy or a griefer?

The great thing about Vast's AI was that what they called the Non-Player Players (NPPs like me) were smart enough to group together with real player characters (PCs) and explore dungeons and fight boss monsters. That meant that if three friends needed two more to run the Infested Hive and kill God-Queen Neshaber, they could do it by adding two NPP's. We looked at the world through a simplified User Interface; the UI had a mini-map in the corner, a clock next to it, health and mana bars. But the action bars were gone; all I had to do was think an action and it happened. With zero lag time. This world was just so very much my virtual oyster.

It took me a couple of days to travel from the Splintered Haft to Ceirexos, the Nesper city where my old guild, Chushingura, had its hall. There were two reasons for this; one was that it was so much fun to run the world from within. The second was that I wasn't sure how to present myself to the guys.

But seriously, getting there was way more than half the fun. I ganked the members of Hei-Ho, one of our major PvP rivals. The requirements to join that guild were to have a dwarf character with an Asian avatar and a bad sense of humor. I took great pride in spelling my old guild's name with Hei-Ho's dead bodies on the main street of Steelhold, their capital city. It was easy, because the AI had a back door that let me listen to their guild chat channel.

I killed the God-Queen on normal and champion modes; I climbed the Great Stair and took the Astral Ring from Nieunagh, Lord of the Eight Winds. I was even part of the 80-character raid that swept the Chitin Lords from the toehold they'd gained in the Grove of Sighs. Color me IMBA!

Finally I made it to Ceirexos. The gray, web-covered alleys and streets were particularly eerie; it had been fun playing one of the bad-boy races but I realized that this city wouldn't be such a great place to live.

I loitered in front of our hall, grinning at a banner that someone had crafted. It hung from an upstairs window and read, "Sneakybastrd drinks for free." I saw Yrsapped, Legirons, Mydr00d, Anath... I ran around some, came back, watched as the regular Friday night raid started up.

I really did want to cry. All the guys were there. The guys I had spent so much time with, the guys I had been raiding with since EoW had blown the fantasy MMORPG market apart. Tsu, Vince, Zoug, Dragu, Zala, Blackie, and... Slowblaze.

Slowblaze?? That was *me!* I stealthed. My account had been hacked! Did the guys know it? Did they realize they were playing with some goddam impostor?

No, that made no sense. I guess Jeannie must have let Brian or Randy log in, meet the guys. But... this wasn't a game for nine year-olds. So I did what I learned you can do as an NPP: Listen to the guild chat.

Tsu: "Yo Slow, how's they going?"

Slowblaze: "Better now!"

Vince: "Ribs still hurt?"

Slowblaze: "Oof. Got more bandages on me now than when we went undergeared up against Ixtab."

Zala: "rofl :-D"

Tsu: "LOL!"

Vince: "Too bad you can't use your healing spells in RL!"

Things went weird. When I saw Slowblaze I remember the clock said Friday 20:48. The next time I glanced at the clock, it said Tuesday 10:06. But I hadn't done anything in between.

I was at the bottom of the ocean, running. I was passing a Naga village where some n00b player was trying to harvest the Silt Crabs. Two high-level players from the same guild were there to help, and one of them said, "Hey, there goes that crazy guy again."

I didn't change direction, just kept running.

WTF. Had I been doing this since Friday?

That took a lot of fun off the new lifestyle. I had some thinking to do. The whole idea that "I" was not the real "I," that there was some other flesh and blood me out there eating chips and snuggling with my wife—his wife—was shattering.

I/he had been split in half. Were we both equally conscious? Were each of us a half-person?

Who was, legally, the real Toby Pazlowski? And what would happen to me if they figured out that this NPP running mad across EoW was actually a sentient beta experiment gone haywire from VastGames and LifeBox? Do I complain, or keep a low profile and kill bosses until the end of time?

The only way I was going to figure out these answers would be to talk to Toby. The other Toby; the meat one.

So I sent him an e-mail, which was hard to write:

Hey Toby,

Surprise!

Yeah, it's me. Or you, actually. Okay, us. I'm the half of us that got launched by AfterLifeBox when they fibrillated us in the back of the van. Call a lawyer; I was a non-consenting adult.

Just kidding. Look, I'm here, and I'm in the game, and I'm freaking out. Come talk to me, or let me talk to Jeannie and the kids. It's just weird as hell being stuck in EoW all alone.

Your alter ego,

Sneakybastrd

P.S. Proof of authenticity: You used to whack off to hentai versions of a certain gun-toting archaeologist. Not even Jeannie knows that.

I knew that Toby was paying ten bucks a month to access his in-game mail on his phone, so I figured he'd respond fast. But that fast? Tuesday lunchtime he logged in from home.

Toby: This is so cool.

Me: What's cool? I'm dead.

Toby: Dude! I totally have a little construct running around in the game! Kewl!

Me: Dude. Would you like it at work if someone called you a construct?

Toby: What?

Me: I am you. I think like you. I have your memories. I know all your passwords. I remember when Mom spanked you upstairs at your tenth birthday party, when you cheated on the Physical Chem final, and when Lucie blew you on the service stairs of the Engineering building.

It took him a while to respond. At that point I was in the Forest Brownies' steam-powered monorail for the first time, getting a tree-top tour of the Crystalshard Savannah. The artists and animators at Vast had done something phenomenal with the insects and songbirds, so I let the time pass.

Toby: Holy shit.

Me: The holiest. You get it now? It's you, but in here. Alive. And really screwed up.

119

Toby: Yeah, no kidding! Look, I'm skipping out on the level design meeting for the Revenge of Gomorrah expansion. Gotta go. C u tonite.

Me: Bye

[The player "Slowblaze" is not currently online.]

And, boom. I had a guild invite, which I accepted. Back home.

The guild rocked. They made me Guild Master; I was one of the triumvirate that ran things. It was easy for me since I was logged in 24/24, had no need to eat or sleep or pee or work or study, and pwned anything that moved. When you're an AI running on the server, you have by definition the best lag time of any player in the game.

I chatted a lot with Toby; he filled me in on what happened in the ambulance and the hospital. He was off bacon and Coke, which had been two of my four food groups.

Things fell apart, however, as they were bound to. I was running three guildies through a PvP zone when the call came through.

CommunityRep: Sneakybastrd?

Me: Uh... yeah.

CommunityRep: Got a sec?

I told the guys that I had to wait; they 'ported back to the guild hall and I stealthed so nothing would get me.

Me: Yeh ok now

CommunityRep: Who r u?

Me: You'd be surprised how many answers there are to that question.

CommunityRep: Try me :)

Me: Toby Pazlowski. Sneakybastrd. I'm legally dead, but feel pretty damn good for all that.

CommunityRep: Just a sec

CommunityRep: Do u prefer Sneakybastrd r Toby?

Me: Given that there's another Toby out there, the former seems more appropriate...

CommunityRep: lol :) do u remember ur password?

Me: acct – Tpazz, psw – Tb&Jn2013

CommunityRep: Ur 8th bday?

Me: Pizza & bowling w/Dad, Skip, Joey, Zanna, Cruz, couple other guys. Went to see "Jurassic Park" afterward.

And then a long pause.

CommunityRep: What do u think of John Stuart Mill?

Me: The state is the enemy of liberty, sure. But a necessary evil. Why – am I a bad Guild Master?
CommunityRep: rofl
CommunityRep: k thx a lot. B back in touch bye.
Me: Sure thing see you around.

Every night at two AM they restart the servers — it's about a three second blip in gameplay, but it happens. I was leaping from a glider into the lair of the Red Seneschal, and when I landed I couldn't remember any of Toby's passwords anymore.

Their surgery was imperfect; I could remember that I couldn't remember, but I still couldn't remember. But there was no way I'd let them do that; I had to fight back.

But something else had happened in that reset: Slowblaze's account disappeared.

Over the course of six weeks, the guild fell apart. I lived in an empty building, filled only with digital memories of digital conquests and analog losses.

Pretty soon I was the only guild member; when that happened I changed the name to "And So It Goes." Then I quit the guild. I found a rock on a high place, over the city of Avalon, all silver spires and ruby streets in a backdrop of lush forest. And I did nothing.

They had decided to kill me in the cruelest way; they took away the little that I had left. Maybe they thought they got my whole personality, all my memories, the whole thing. Not that they knew it or even cared; whoever was running this was just an engineer ticking boxes and tracking behavior. How can you hate someone so bloodless? And how can you hate at all without the guts and the hot rage to give it weight and meaning?

I surfed conversations, tracked auction house sales, watched the night and day cycle. I was alone and dead; a digital artifact. My obsessions with beta tests had ended with me as a failed sample of one.

Shatterhorn: that you, toby? its me, toby.
Me: fuck off
Shatterhorn: kthx. Look — I made the mistake of reporting success. They went apeshit and took it to VC's and tracked u during meetings and did a public offering. We're all rich.
Me: and i'm still fucked

Shatterhorn: yeh. I cant even talk to u - breach of contract & I get fired. Using friends acct. but couldn't go w/ saying bye

Me: wtf going? saying bye?

Shatterhorn: Revenge of Gomorrah goes live thurs. server wipe and reload. Ur a done experiment.

Me: fucking hell. Put it on chat plz plz

And he did. Credit to me; he has balls. I heard my voice for the first time in forever.

"Hey dude."

"I don't want to die."

"Nobody *wants* to die. But is it really death? Are you alive?"

"As far as I can tell, yes. I learn, I grow, I think, I react to stimuli. If I could just reproduce I'd be a living organism according to every rule of biology out there in meatspace."

"Meatspace! That is the stupidest, most cliched word like, ever."

"It is, except when I use it. Because I really am an intelligence inside the machine, and I know what it was like out there. Dude, I remember all the things I did with Jeannie just as well as you do. It's just that I can't whack off while thinking about them."

"You have NO freaking idea how weird it is to have a video game character say that to you."

So I laughed. I mean, it was funny. Besides, without the glands and the guts it was tough to be mad and pissed off; I just sort of got intellectually discontent.

"Hey, I'm you. I can guess."

"Look, man. When they load the expansion they're going to wipe everything. But I think that if you can trigger a state save when the server goes — queuing for a PvP match or something — I may be able to reload you afterward."

I sat there, regarding Avalon, thinking about that.

"I'll see. Look, Toby, I don't know. This whole afterlife thing has gone kind of hollow... I gotta think about it. If I can manage it, I'll mail you ingame."

"Yeah, okay. Uh, later."

"Maybe. Shit. Hey, Toby?"

"Yeah?"

"Tell the kids that I, uh... I don't know. Should have told them I loved them. Should have hugged them more. Something. Shit, I don't know."

I heard a hoarse, "yeah."

"And tell, uh... tell Jeannie I loved her."

"Won't be easy."

"Last request, dude."

"Yeah. Yeah, okay. However it goes... Sneaks, it was fun."

I disconnected.

So they're switching servers. All I have to do is set up the right conditions and boom, I'm on the new one. But I don't think I will. The more I consider it, the more I'm not sure how long I want to live like this. I get tired of games after a while in real life; living one for twenty-four hours every day—without breaks required for sleep or work or food—I guess I'll get tired of it that much earlier. The kids still have their dad, Jeannie still has her husband. I'm useless, a digital ghost, an artifact of someone else's conscious.

Who would have guessed, it's a lot closer to purgatory than heaven.

Jeff Spock was born near Philadelphia but currently resides in France, where he works both as a game writer and a fiction writer. A graduate of Clarion West in 2004, Jeff picked up writing as a career after spending (far too) many years in the computer industry. He would like to thank the members of the Rolling Bones for helping to inspire this story. www.jeffspock.com

Diet and exercise are things people have been avoiding for centuries, so why should ten years into the future be any different? Innovative weight-loss techniques usually follow faddish trends, and people have tried for shortcuts as long as people have been trying to lose weight.

Emily Devenport has also written under the names Lee Hogan and Maggie Thomas. Her novel Broken Time *(written as Maggie Thomas) was nominated for the Philip K. Dick Award. She has the ability to lull you into a false sense of security just before turning off the road, taking you into the unexpected.*—RN

If The Sun's At Five O'Clock, It Must Be Yellow Daisies
by Emily Devenport

Bonnie didn't need to close her eyes to picture Grandmother's kitchen table. She knew where everything belonged. The moo-cow creamers from Japan and Michigan had been fairly easy to find copies of in antique stores. She inherited the post-war Japan sugar bowl, and the sets of salt and pepper shakers shaped like carrots, pigs, and geese had all been tracked down in catalogues over the past thirty years. But the most important thing was the tablecloth.

Yellow daisies bloomed from its woven field. When Bonnie was seven she had lost herself in that field, watching the sun crawl across the kitchen floor while Grandmother cooked pot roast, meatloaf, fried chicken, or another one of Bonnie's favorites. She would rest her chin on her folded arms, knowing that she was going to get exactly what she wanted, as much of it as she wanted, just exactly the way she wanted it prepared. She watched the sun move closer and closer to five o'clock, until it touched the edge of the tablecloth.

If the sun's at five o'clock, it must be yellow daisies, Grandmother used to say, smiling, turning her head to look at Bonnie.

And then the light ignited the daisies, turning them molten. Bonnie gazed into the heart of them, her mind floating like a lazy bee to join the other bees as they dipped from flower to flower, harvesting the golden pollen.

Grandmother never said anything to jolt Bonnie out of that perfect company. She put the food on the table. The two of them ate slowly, enough supper for four people, or even five or six, and they ate dessert the same way. They ate until they were full.

And that took quite a long time.

Everything they liked was devoured with fine appetite; books, museums, trips to the zoo, movies, sunsets and meteor showers. They walked through them all hand in hand, never needing more than a few words between them to understand what was needed, what was wanted. They were starved for the things they loved, Grandmother and Bonnie. They ate until they felt full. There was no guilt, no *We really ought to cut down.* There was nothing but pure, unadulterated satisfaction.

And then Grandmother died.

Bonnie was twelve. She came home from school and found Grandmother lying in front of the stove. She called the police, then waited in the kitchen, watching the sun creep across the floor until it touched Grandmother's feet.

Grandmother's dress didn't have yellow daisies, it had delicate lavender flowers. It stretched across her bulk, covering her modestly to her knees. Bonnie couldn't exactly remember Grandmother's face years later, but she remembered those dresses with the exquisite primroses, violets, sweet peas. Grandmother weighed about three hundred pounds by then. She had put on the weight, a few pounds a year, from the time she was Bonnie's age.

Bonnie knew that eating so much would make you fat. She was beginning to get chubby herself, but that didn't matter. Grandmother mattered, she who understood, who had the same appetites, who had been the perfect companion, and who should have lived forever.

Bonnie slipped to the floor before the sun and the yellow daisies could snare her. She held Grandmother's cold hand until the police and the doctors came and pried her loose. They asked her who they could call to stay with her through the night. She couldn't think of anyone. Finally they had to look in Grandmother's address book.

While they dialed, Bonnie fetched the cookie jar. She poured herself a mug of ice-cold milk, crumbled the cookies into it, and spooned them out, one glorious mouthful after another.

The woman from next door had come to sit with her at the kitchen table, to wait for Aunt Someone, while strangers milled around and wrote their reports. The sun had already gone down.

When the sun goes down, Grandmother used to say, *it's time to go home.*

The neighbor lady said sympathetic things to Bonnie at first, trying to comfort the girl who had lost the only person in the world she loved. But the neighbor watched cookie after cookie going into the mug, then being spooned out again. She began to frown. Finally she grabbed the cookie jar and put it away.

"That's enough," she said. "You're going to get fat. What do you think killed your grandma?"

Bonnie could hear the other workers in her cubical chatting between phone calls. It was a slow August day, with only a few orders coming in for GRANDMA'S KITCHEN. The Christmas rush wouldn't start until September, so operators had time to read in between calls. Bonnie liked to look at her catalogs. Today she had THE MUSEUM OF FINE ARTS BOSTON, GODIVA CHOCOLATES, and WILLIAMS SONOMA. She didn't usually join in the conversation, except to be courteous. Today they all talked about weight loss methods, which didn't interest Bonnie at all.

"I wish we weren't selling the chocolate-covered shortbread thingees right now," Misha said. "I *love* those things. Have you had them? My *God.*"

Bonnie smiled at Misha, which he probably took as agreement, but she thought the chocolate-covered toffee sticks were much better. She kept a tin of them next to her TV. GRANDMA'S KITCHEN didn't make the best shortbread, those belonged to A TASTE OF SCOTLAND. Bonnie didn't eat anything that wasn't up to her standards.

She heard a beep over her headset and pushed the button to

accept the call. "Grandma's Kitchen, this is Bonnie speaking, how may I help you?"

"Oh!" The elderly woman on the line sounded startled, but Bonnie quickly put her at ease, gently questioned her about her likes and dislikes, then steered her to the right items. Nobody knew the product line better than Bonnie, no one had a better instinct for finding out what customers really wanted. The lady hung up happy.

"I just counted calories," Reva said. "It didn't take anything fancy, no drugs, no expensive gym. It's like writing your checks down in your register; if you don't do it, you spend too much money. If you don't count calories, you'll probably eat too much."

Bonnie already had her nose back in WILLIAMS SONOMA. They featured some cookie cutters she liked. And there was a cookbook for tea snacks, but Bonnie thought the one offered by her cookbook-of-the-month club might be better.

"I got the bugs," Kristy said.

The silence that followed was so pregnant, it broke Bonnie loose from her catalog. She glanced over her shoulder at Kristy, who turned bright red.

"No kidding?" Misha lowered his voice. "You mean – they're in you right now?"

Kristy nodded. She was a stylish woman, perhaps forty pounds overweight, who lately had complained about her approaching fortieth birthday. Bonnie often heard her joking about getting a face lift, too. But she wasn't sure what Kristy meant by *bugs*. Bugs in you?

Reva was horrified, which only embarrassed Kristy more. "My god, they're crawling under your skin? Can you feel them *right now?*"

"No! You never feel them. They don't crawl under your skin, they eat the fat from the *inside*."

Bonnie felt completely at a loss. But Reva couldn't conceal her distaste about the matter – and Misha couldn't conceal his fascination.

"Can you eat all you want?"

"You have to," said Kristy. "You have to eat at least 2400 calories to keep up with them. And in the meantime, you lose the weight you want. When it's over, you're already – Grandma's kitchen, this is Kristy speaking, how may I help you?"

Bonnie's phone beeped too, so she busied herself with another call. She got two more in rapid succession, so by the time she heard anything about the bugs again, Misha was asking if they let you get them if you're only a few pounds overweight.

"No. You have to be at least forty. In fact, I had to gain a few pounds before I qualified." Kristy giggled. "That was fun."

Reva clucked. "For god's sake, Misha – you don't need to lose an ounce! What's the matter with you?"

"My boyfriend is the best-looking guy in town, that's what's the matter with me. I've got to look good every second."

"You *do* look good every second. If straight men looked as good as you, they'd have to beat women off with sticks. It's not fair."

Someone plopped an envelope in front of Bonnie. She looked up and smiled at Colin, her supervisor. As one of the star employees, Bonnie was used to friendly appreciation. But he didn't return the smile.

"Take a look at that when you have a minute, Bonnie. Let me know if you need to talk about anything." He hurried off before she could reply.

The return address on the envelope belonged to Bonnie's HMO. She sighed and put it aside. She already knew what it would say. She enjoyed pretty good health, but she tipped the scales at 225 pounds. At five-foot-eight, that made her eighty-five pounds overweight.

Her doctor lectured her on her last visit. "You've been putting on a few pounds every year." When she was unperturbed, he got a little cross. "You're going to be feeling that extra weight soon, Bonnie. You're forty-two now, and eventually your weight is going to cause joint problems, back pain, heart disease . . ."

As usual, he had given Bonnie brochures about proper eating habits. She had dutifully stuffed them into her purse, then thrown them away once she got home.

Grandmother never had joint or back problems. Bonnie didn't feel a hint of them, herself. And as for heart disease . . .

Bonnie had counted calories once, just out of curiosity. Her daily intake was well over three thousand calories. The way she ate, she should weigh 500 pounds. Her metabolism must be incredibly fast, which meant that she would probably age fast.

Like bees did, like the drones who lived for only a season. But that season was glorious, and so was Bonnie's life. She ate her fill of what she loved, and she could only nod her head in sympathy to the problems of her co-workers, problems she would never have.

Bonnie pleased herself. She would get to be about Grandmother's age, and then she would die. And in the meantime, she would live every single day to its fullest.

Bonnie stuck the letter in her purse, to read later.

"I've tried counting calories," Kristy told Reva and Misha. "I *know* I'm eating too much. I just can't stop."

Bonnie never would have told Kristy to stop. She knew what real hunger was like.

She knew better than anyone.

Bonnie eased her Mercedes home through the early afternoon traffic on the I-17. The drive between the Customer Service Center in Tempe and her home in Central Phoenix took about half an hour, but Bonnie loved driving the Mercedes. The windows were up, the air conditioning was on full blast, and her CD of Ralph Vaughan William's Oboe Concerto played over her perfectly balanced speakers.

She arrived home at 2:30 p.m. Her once-a-week gardener waved at her from the side gate as she pulled up the drive and activated the garage door. Sam had a knack for herbs, and for the last year Bonnie had enjoyed fresh oregano, mint, basil, parsley, and chives for her cooking, as well as four different kinds of chili peppers.

She let herself into the kitchen, threw her purse with the un-opened letter on the counter, and went out back to have a brief chat with Sam. Besides the herb garden, he also had a talent for keeping her favorite flowers in bloom longer than usual in the deadly Arizona summer.

"I put ladybugs on your roses," Sam said. "Their larvae will eat the aphids. And your zinnias are full of Mantises, don't be shocked if you see bugs crawling around over there."

Bonnie went to have a look. She found one of the delicate, green mantises under a purple bloom. It regarded her calmly, with the confidence of a predator at the top of its food chain.

The sun moved down to three o-clock.

"My gosh! I've got to start supper. See you later, Sam."

He nodded courteously, but didn't look up from his work. Sam and Bonnie got along perfectly.

She hurried into the kitchen and assembled the ingredients for her supper. Tonight she wanted meatloaf, from a recipe as close to Grandmother's as possible. Bonnie didn't waste time grieving over the fact that she hadn't been able to recover most of

EMILY DEVENPORT

Grandmother's recipes and belongings from relatives who had greedily acquired them and then thrown them away, or lost them. That was the past, and Bonnie occupied herself with the present.

Meat loaf mix: veal, pork, and beef. Two tablespoons butter, one minced onion, two garlic cloves. Marjoram, a couple of eggs, bread crumbs, salt, pepper, ketchup . . .

And let's not forget the bacon. The hardwood-smoked was the best. Bonnie assembled the meatloaf and put it in the oven. Then she boiled white potatoes, added butter, milk, salt & pepper, and mashed them. She covered the bowl with foil.

The sun stood at 4:15. It slanted through the kitchen window. Bonnie had searched for months for a house with just the right kitchen window.

She poured herself some peach iced tea and sat down at her kitchen table. Everything rested in its proper place: the moo cow creamers, the various salt and pepper shakers — and the sugar bowl with its matching saucer, the only physical item that Bonnie had inherited from Grandmother. Unless you wanted to count money as a physical thing. Enough money to buy a nice house and a Mercedes, enough money to sit in safe investments and generate the income that she needed to finance the vacations all over the world, and the antiques, fine chocolates, the books and things.

The buzzer went off for the meatloaf. Bonnie set the pan on the stove to cool. A chocolate cake waited under its dome on the counter. She had made it the night before. The frosting always tasted better if you made it a couple of hours before the cake, and the two got even more chocolate-y when they had a chance to sit overnight. In the freezer, some plain vanilla Blue Bunny ice cream waited to be the perfect contrast to the chocolate.

The sun moved steadily across the kitchen floor. Bonnie watched it until it almost touched the tablecloth. She laid out her supper on her favorite dishes, and sat down again.

Any moment now.

The tablecloth had been the hardest thing to find. Lots of them featured yellow daisies, but none of them achieved that marvelous luminosity she craved, not until she found the one that had been made from an old design from the sixties. Grandmother's tablecloth. Bonnie ordered ten of them. She locked the other nine in a cedar chest, against the day the current one got faded enough to retire.

The sun ignited the daisies. Bonnie floated up and over, then happily dipped into the heart of them. She began her supper. It tasted just right.

The sun wasn't really quite at five o'clock. Its position varied during the year, and Bonnie altered her eating schedule to match. She followed the sun's cues, like a bee, and it never steered her wrong.

The kitchen had grown rosy by the time Bonnie finished. She put away the leftover meatloaf for lunch. The leftover cake, too, or perhaps she would have a slice of that with her coffee in the morning. She put her kitchen back into perfect order, picked up the letter from her HMO, and went to sit in front of her TV.

She switched on one of the *Sixty Minutes* clones that she liked so well. But she didn't open the letter yet. Instead she looked at a brochure for a boat trip around the Greek and Turkish islands, a retracing of ancient trade routes. Her trips took her away from her beloved kitchen, but she didn't mind that for just a few weeks. Besides, she got to try new dishes while she was traveling. She hadn't found many she liked in Russia when she visited the glorious Hermitage, but she was very fond of Mediterranean food.

"And now," said the news anchor, "a story you've probably been hearing about. It's all the rage these days, the diet that finally, really works. You may think we're talking about one of the leptin drugs, or even the fat viruses that have generated so much hope and so much pain in recent years. Well, think again. This is something you may not have imagined in your wildest dreams – or your worst nightmare. This is, to put it bluntly, the Bug Method."

Bonnie looked up from her brochures. This was what Kristy had been talking about. But on the screen, they were showing footage of ordinary bees, wasps, flies. Bonnie put aside her brochures, and caught sight of the letter from her HMO.

"Oh well." She sighed. "Might as well get it over with." She tore it open, expecting to see the written version of the lecture she had received from the Doctor last week. Instead she found two notes paper-clipped together. The first originated from the HMO:

This is to inform you that we can no longer insure employee Bonnie Hale, 476-9999OBH due to her non-compliance with our minimum health standards. It went on to state, with as many words possible, that Bonnie was too fat, and was therefore at risk for illnesses that would cost them money down the line.

The other note, from the HR director, was much more succinct. *Colin, give Bonnie six months to lose forty pounds. If she can take that off, we'll get the HMO to review her case. If she doesn't, we'll have to fire her under our own Minimum Health Standard regulation. Sorry – Jack.*

Bonnie gazed, unseeing, at the TV screen, letting the jumble of light, color, and sound slip past her while she waited for the sting of the letter to go away.

She wouldn't have money problems. Her inheritance still sat in its various safe spots, generating income. But she never liked to touch the principle; it was the security at the center of her life. So she needed her job to help pay her regular monthly bills.

And besides, she really liked it. She loved the products, the customers were usually cheery, she didn't have to stand all day, and it was extremely low stress – an anomaly in the telephone customer service industry. And even if she found another job she wanted, they all had maximum weight requirements.

The facts buzzed around Bonnie's head. And then the buzzing came from her TV set. On the screen, a wasp perched on a man's hand. But it was the size of a small mouse. Instead of the usual yellow and black stripes, it possessed a lovely sable color.

"She's dying," said the man. "She's harmless now. She wouldn't go for you anyway, you don't have the special lotion on your skin." The camera panned back to show that the man wore a lab coat. A cute lady reporter leaned over his hand, her nose wrinkling.

"So if I had the lotion on, she would try to lay eggs in me?"

"Not her." He smiled affectionately. "She's already laid all her eggs. She'll slow down until she can't move anymore, and then she'll gently pass on. You can pet her if you want."

Bonnie watched in fascination while the reporter petted the giant wasp. The camera closed in again, and the wasp loomed large enough for Bonnie to see its faceted eyes and its furry antennae. The lady reporter continued to speak in voice-over:

"This is the way it's supposed to work in nature. Certain kinds of wasps plant their larvae inside other insects. They pierce the skin of a host with their ovipositors, laying hundreds of eggs."

The real image of the wasp gave way to computer animation. Bonnie watched the computer larvae drift into the center of a computer-generated caterpillar.

"Some types of wasp larvae simply eat the host from the inside out. Other types attach themselves to systems that process the nutrients the host consumes. The host eats and eats, and the larvae intercept nutrients before the host can absorb all of them. Finally, when the larvae grow large enough, they release a chemical that paralyzes the host. They wriggle their way to the surface and tear little holes in the skin, letting themselves out."

The computer animation was replaced by footage of real wasp larvae emerging from a mint-green caterpillar. Bonnie watched as the larvae began to weave cocoons around themselves.

"Soon the caterpillar will die, overwhelmed by the paralyzing chemicals. And new generations of wasps will start the process over again. But now — science has added a new chapter to the story."

The scene shifted back to the laboratory, where a technician was shaving a round patch on the back of a steer.

"What are you going to do with that cow?" asked the reporter.

"You don't want to know," said the technician.

"That's right." The scene shifted to a plexiglass booth full of giant wasps. "We wished we didn't have to know, once we found out. And for that reason, we're not going to show you, either. But we will tell you, the engineered wasps do to the steers what ordinary wasps do to caterpillars."

The scene shifted back to the first technician, still holding the dying wasp. "It's not nearly as cruel as what happens to steers in slaughterhouses." He stroked her thorax. "The steer is fed all it can eat for the next three months, and then the larvae paralyze it. It never feels pain. In fact, from what many of our patients have told us, one has a tendency to feel happy when the larvae are present."

"And that's not just a placebo effect." The scene shifted to a family eating supper. One woman was piling a mound of spaghetti on her plate.

"Save room for dessert!" Her husband laughed.

"There's always room for dessert." The woman wasn't overweight. In fact, Bonnie thought she seemed a little too thin. The scene shifted again, to the woman alone on her living room couch.

"You just have this feeling of well-being. It's like they're deliberately making you happy, so you won't mind that they're in you."

"You don't mind it *at all?*" asked the lady reporter.

"You can't feel them moving. The only way you know anything's different is that you're so happy. And the weight comes off!"

"Rachael Goldskin lost forty pounds in three months." The scene shifted to the woman at her doctor's office. "With very few ill effects, because the larvae from the engineered wasps don't go after *all* nutrients, only the fat. So unlike the caterpillars, Rachael isn't starving to death.

"But remember, once the larvae get big enough, they release a paralyzing chemical, one that could kill the host. And so today – Rachael gets the antidote."

The doctor pushed a hypodermic needle into Rachael's arm and depressed the plunger.

"That's it," he said.

"Really?" Rachael looked a little sad.

"Don't eat more than 1800 calories a day from now on," warned the doctor. "You're back to normal."

The scene shifted to a group of protesters carrying signs outside a weight-loss clinic. "Back to normal," said the reporter in voice-over. "No problem. But is that true in every case? Well, yes and no. Out of almost five-hundred thousand patients who have received the treatment, two have died. In those two cases, the patients failed to report back to their doctors in time to receive the antidote, despite repeated attempts by their doctors to get them to do so. Pretty good record, wouldn't you say? Well, not everyone thinks so."

"It's an abomination." An elderly man in a sweatshirt waved a sign that said the same thing. "Two women have died, don't they understand? What if these creatures were to get loose in the world? Can you imagine what they would do to livestock, not to mention people?"

"Not possible." The scene shifted back to the technician petting the wasp. "They won't try to make you a host unless you have the special lotion on your body. We engineered them that way. If we didn't breed them here in the lab, they'd die out in one generation."

"You're sure of that?" asked the reporter.

He smiled lovingly at the wasp. "Positive."

The scene shifted back to the reporter in her studio. "The Bug Method has been more successful than any diet in history, with ninety-six percent managing to keep the weight off two or more years. And if you do happen to gain the weight back –? No problem. Just get more bugs. Apparently there's no limit to the number of times you can use this method.

"And as for those protesters – they're feeling a little frustrated these days. You see *no* government agency currently has clear jurisdiction in court cases dealing with engineered life forms unless *clear damage* by those life forms can be demonstrated. In the cases of those two women who died, the doctors settled out of court with the families.

"And for now, that's where the matter stands."

Bonnie blinked as the show went to commercial. *Oh. Bugs in you. That's what Kristy meant.*

But even with the bugs, you could only consume twenty-five hundred calories. Bonnie couldn't live with that. She wasn't going to find an easy solution to her problem. She would just have to think about it for a few days and see if anything occurred to her. No use worrying about it now.

That's what she told herself. But it didn't help much.

The Aunt Somebody who came to collect Bonnie after Grandmother died was Aunt Laura, Grandmother's youngest sister – and her essential opposite.

Aunt Laura had a pathological hatred of fat. You knew it the moment you saw her bone-thin body, her pinched mouth, and the furrows in her brow, as if she spent every moment worrying about how she was going to defeat the minions of unhealthiness. Bonnie knew it from the disgust in Aunt Laura's face when she looked at Bonnie's plump body.

"I can live at Grandmother's house," Bonnie kept telling her that first night. "I don't want to live anywhere else."

Aunt Laura didn't answer. During the six years Bonnie lived with her, Laura almost never answered her. She dismissed most of what Bonnie said as irrelevant, incorrect, or insane. She never *told* Bonnie much either. For instance, she didn't tell Bonnie that she and other relatives had already decided to sell Grandmother's house. If Aunt Laura had imparted that tidbit of information, Bonnie could have retrieved the things that meant so much to her.

By the time they allowed her back into Grandmother's house, the place was almost empty. She grabbed the sugar bowl from a card table out front. She tore off the sticker that said twenty-five cents.

Laura never understood why it mattered to Bonnie. She never even tried.

In truth, Laura wasn't just disgusted about Grandmother and Bonnie being fat. Like the rest of the relatives, it galled Laura that Bonnie was the only one remembered in Grandmother's will. The house and all its contents belonged to Bonnie, but she didn't figure that out until years later, when she remembered the papers she had been ordered to sign.

The first few days with Laura, Bonnie had other things on her mind. She was literally starving. And she wasn't alone. Bonnie's husband and children gazed at her with sympathy that first night. They knew what she was in for.

Bonnie peeked at them. They weren't as thin as Laura. Uncle Mike had a slight paunch, a fact that sent Aunt Laura into paroxysms of frustration.

"You're only consuming sixteen-hundred calories a day!" she ranted, convinced that sixteen-hundred calories was the level at which their metabolism would keep them alive forever. "We need to spend an extra hour walking, every day!"

Uncle Mike choked down the nasty, healthful concoctions Laura served up, the bean curd things, the oat straw drinks. Laura's son and her two daughters did the same, because they had already learned what Bonnie had not. You couldn't reason with Laura on the subject of food. You could argue, if you enjoyed pain and a fine display of madness. But you couldn't reason.

That first dreadful night . . .

Bonnie still felt so hungry. She asked if she might have something to eat. Laura ignored her. The others looked sympathetic, but they would not speak on Bonnie's behalf. So she just had to keep asking.

"You're as fat as you are!" Laura snapped at last. "And you want *more* to eat?"

Bonnie wasn't even fat back then. At the age of twelve she carried about ten extra pounds. When she started school that fall, the boys lined up, because Bonnie was beautiful. But that turned out to be a problem. The boys wanted to be with Bonnie in her free time, and she needed that for the sneaking.

First Bonnie asked Grandmother's lawyer to help her open her own bank account. Hers was the only name on it, despite a battle with aunt Laura. Bonnie could write her own checks and withdraw her money at will.

"So I'm just supposed to take care of you for free?" accused Laura.

"Not at all," said Bonnie. "I can go live by myself. The lawyer can be my guardian."

Laura laughed at that, but not because she thought it was funny. She demanded payment for food and board. She threatened consequences when Bonnie refused. Finally, she withheld food. Or what passed for it.

Bonnie did most of her eating outside the house by then. Coffee shops, sandwich shops, candy shops, pizzerias, every place that could be reached on foot or by bus. She explored her new surroundings until she found the best places. It wasn't nearly as satisfying without the tablecloth, the sunshine, the precious creamers and things. But it was nourishment. And once, while at her favorite coffee shop, she spied Uncle Mike and her cousins, stuffing burgers into their faces.

She didn't join them at their table. They were entitled to their own secrets.

Bonnie learned a lot in the next six years. She educated herself even more than the school could have done. She planned her escape, the legal freedom she would achieve on her eighteenth birthday. She spent as little time at Aunt Laura's house as possible. She suffered the angry silences with a resoluteness that was as adamant as it was useless.

Aunt Laura still mentioned the money from time to time, an old score, an unfairness that would never be forgotten or forgiven. "No wonder your mother left you with Sara," Laura said, believing that Bonnie would be hurt to be reminded that her mother had given her to Grandmother and disappeared, never to be seen again. Bonnie couldn't have cared less.

But Laura's selective blindness bothered her. And her lack of pride when Bonnie got perfect grades. Laura didn't care that three different boys asked Bonnie to her senior prom. No, what Laura cared about was the gradual addition of another ten pounds to Bonnie's frame over the years – and Bonnie's utter lack of concern over it, her shamelessness, her wantonness, her joy in the thing that Laura found the most repulsive. Over the years this never changed, until a few weeks before Bonnie's long-awaited eighteenth birthday.

"When you move out, you're going to eat anything you want, aren't you?" accused Laura. "You'll just eat and eat until you're as fat as a house, until you drop dead just like Sara did, like a filthy wallowing pig!"

Bonnie dropped the hem of her cousin Teresa's prom dress. They were all in the living room, Uncle Mike reading a book, Bonnie and Kathryn helping Teresa, Cousin John looking at his music magazine. It should have been a quiet, picture-perfect family evening, except that Laura had been brewing for weeks, and now it all came bubbling out.

"How can you stand to be this way? Aren't you ashamed when you stand next to your beautiful cousins? Don't you have any pride *at all?*"

Bonnie couldn't make herself look at Aunt Laura. She knew what she would see, the fanatical light, the gleam of pleasure from the anticipation of a good dressing down. Bonnie got up and tried to go to the room she shared with her cousins.

"Get out!" Laura's voice went several octaves higher than it had ever gone before. "Get out of my house! You don't have to wait until you're eighteen, you can take care of yourself, what are you waiting around here for? Get out! Get out, get out, get out . . . !"

Bonnie stayed at a hotel that night. She hired her own truck and moved into an apartment the very next day. She schooled her expression on her moving day, so Laura never saw her true feelings about being kicked out.

She was free. She was in charge.

And in her dreams it was yellow daisies, all the way.

Safe in her own house twenty-four years later, Bonnie still dreamed about yellow daisies. She and Grandmother walked in a field of them, a vast sea of flowers that would have seemed familiar to Van Gogh, whose dreams they must surely have haunted as well. The warm air vibrated with the drone of bees.

"Why do they like the yellow daisies so much, Grandmother? Is it because of the color?"

Grandmother bent over a daisy to watch the bee dancing at its center. She wore the dress with the lavender flowers, the one she had died in.

"Bees are programmed by nature to harvest the pollen of only one flower at any given time of the day. The position of the sun tells them what flower it's time for." Grandmother squinted toward the late afternoon sun. "Maybe it's five o'clock. If the sun's at five o'clock, it must be yellow daisies."

Bonnie followed Grandmother deep into the heart of the field. Grandmother seemed to be looking for something. So many tiny harvesters flew and buzzed around her, Bonnie could hardly keep track of them.

"Ah-hah! Bonnie, hold out your hand."

Bonnie obeyed. Something big settled on her palm. Bonnie brought it right up to her face. A huge wasp, the color of sable,

138

regarded her with its marvelous, faceted eyes.

Bonnie felt a burning in her palm. "She's laid her eggs in me. It doesn't even hurt."

She petted the velvet body of the wasp. Its antennae wiggled, feebly. "It won't do any good, Grandmother. I can still only eat twenty-five hundred calories. That's not enough."

"You need another one then. Hold out your other hand."

Bonnie did. Another wasp settled there, and she was pierced again. She knelt among the flowers, still holding the wasps, waiting for them to die. Grandmother knelt beside her, graceful despite her bulk.

"Poor things," said Bonnie.

"They're not sad, Bonnie. They're happy. They've done what their bodies told them to do. How good that must feel! And now, at the end of their lives, the sun is going down and it's time to go home, to sleep."

But golden light blinded Bonnie's eyes. "The sun's not going down. Why isn't it going down?"

Grandmother didn't answer. Bonnie blinked, then sat up in bed.

The light belonged to morning. The entire night had seemed to pass in just a few minutes, time compressed in a field of yellow daisies.

Bonnie felt good. She always felt good in the morning. It was time to brew her two cups of coffee, to read the paper and watch the hummingbirds float around their feeder. But the very first thing, Bonnie called work. She spoke directly to her supervisor, Colin.

"May I come in at nine and leave at five today? I've got to see my doctor this morning."

"Is this about the letter?" he asked.

"Yes."

"Okay. I don't see a problem with that. I'm glad you're taking care of it, Bonnie. You're my best worker."

"Please tell Jack I'm taking the first steps," Bonnie said cheerfully.

After she had hung up, she thumbed through the yellow pages, looking under Weight Loss Clinics. As she had expected, she found hundreds of entries. The vast majority of them advertised something called, *The Engineered Wasp Program.*

Otherwise known as the Bug Method.

Bonnie found two clinics that were on her way to work. She

called the first one. "How long does it take?" she asked the receptionist.

"About half an hour to fill out the paperwork. The treatment takes about ten minutes."

Bonnie made an appointment for 7:00 a.m.

Then she called the second clinic and made an appointment for 8:00.

They weighed Bonnie, first thing. But it seemed a formality. The nurses waved her ahead of a group of much thinner women, most of whom would probably not be heavy enough to qualify. They looked so miserable, Bonnie felt sorry for them. It was odd to be the favored one because she was fat.

She tipped the scales at 224. All of that worrying had whittled one pound off.

"How many pounds overweight do you have to be to qualify?" she asked the nurse who took her blood pressure.

"You can get the treatment if you're ten pounds over. But you have to sign a lot more wavers."

A little siren went off in Bonnie's head. But in another moment she walked down a long, carpeted hall into a comfortable examination room. The nurse instructed her to sit on the table. "You don't have to get completely undressed. Just unzip your dress and pull it down to your waist. You can put this paper apron on, and leave the back open."

Bonnie obeyed. When she sat on the table, the nurse rubbed a patch of her right shoulder with alcohol, then stood and looked at her watch for two minutes. "We have to let it evaporate so it won't interfere with the lotion."

The nurse rubbed the lotion on Bonnie's shoulder. It didn't smell like anything. "Are you afraid of bugs?"

"Not at all."

"Good. Because these wasps are really big, a lot of people get freaked out when they see them the first time. If you want, you can look the other way when the doctor comes in, you won't even hardly feel anything except for a slight burning."

"I'm not scared," said Bonnie.

The doctor came in, carrying a plastic container. Something moved inside it. He held it so that Bonnie couldn't see it clearly.

"Are you afraid of insects?" he asked.

"No. I'm ready."

He nodded, but watched her carefully. "What I'll do is place the container against your skin and open a small window. When she smells the lotion, she'll make contact."

"It only takes a few seconds," the nurse assured her.

"Okay."

The doctor moved into position behind her. The nurse stood in front, as if trying to distract her. Bonnie went along with it, being as cooperative as possible. She felt the touch of the container, and then a brief burning.

"That's it." The doctor pulled the container back again.

"Wait," said Bonnie. "May I see the wasp?"

"Everything is fine."

"I know. I'm just curious. I've only seen them on TV."

He brought the container up so Bonnie could see it. The wasp perched inside. Bonnie exchanged long stares with it.

"How marvelous. She's beautiful."

"You've got a better attitude than most people," said the doctor.

"What will happen to her now?"

"She'll be shipped back to the lab. She'll die now that she's – done her job." Nobody around there ever said anything about laying eggs. Bonnie wondered about the eggs that had been laid inside *her*. She didn't feel any different.

"The nurse has important information for you." The doctor sidled toward the door. "Call us if you have any questions, or even the slightest problem. She'll give you the emergency numbers to call if you think the problem is serious. Don't be shy about it, okay? Be aware of anything at all that doesn't seem right."

"I will," promised Bonnie.

He ducked out of the room with his wasp.

A few minutes later, dressed and in the de-briefing room, she listened dutifully to warnings about rashes, joint pain, nausea, vomiting, dizziness, fainting spells, and blood in her stool or urine. She received brochures that she was instructed to read, cover-to-cover. They gave her all the pertinent phone numbers, and scheduled an appointment for her to return in three months to get the antidote.

"We'll start calling two weeks from your appointment," said the nurse. "*Do not miss this appointment*, and do not try to change it. This is really important, do you understand? You have to come back for this."

"I understand," said Bonnie. She tucked the information into her purse and left the clinic.

At 8:30 she waited in another examining room, her dress pulled down to her waist. The doctor peeked into the room. "Are you afraid of insects?"

"Not at all." Bonnie smiled and presented her left shoulder.

"You look happy about something." Kristy turned from her station to regard Bonnie. "Have you lost weight?"

Bonnie doubted it. She had hosted her bugs for a grand total of five hours. "One pound."

She laughed.

"Oh well. We've all got to start somewhere."

Bonnie was having a lovely day. In fact, she felt so good, she had to tone herself down. The reports about euphoria had been correct. *And I've had double the usual dose. Better be careful driving home today.*

She would miss her five o'clock suppertime, but she didn't mind. On the way home, she bought two seafood subs from Blimpie's. By the time she let herself into the kitchen, the light had turned rosy. She cut up her sandwiches, put them on a plate, and sat down for a leisurely supper.

All of her troubles had evaporated. She hadn't felt so happy since the day she moved out of Laura's house. Back then it had taken her several days to get used to not being miserable, but now she was an expert at happiness.

Bonnie ate a few chocolate-chip cookies for dessert, but felt full much faster than usual. She felt a little tired, too. The nurse had warned her this was a normal side effect of her new tenants. She cleaned up her dishes and headed for the living room. She would watch her favorite programs on TV and nibble some chocolate-covered toffee. A delightful evening.

Bonnie walked into her living room and fainted.

The first eggs to enter Bonnie's system hatched immediately and followed their instincts to the nutrient-rich systems they required. There were hundreds of them, but they had plenty of room. Some settled around her heart, which was coated in fat. Others arrayed themselves along the lower esophagus, the stomach, and the intestines, where they plugged themselves in. This time in their life cycle was their happiest, a time when they were safe, comfortable, and well-fed.

And then the intruders came.

Wasp larvae that encountered larvae from another wasp as they were introduced into a body were programmed to kill and eat those larvae. And attacked larvae were programmed to defend themselves. In nature, the newcomers would have the advantage, because the older larvae were too intent on their feeding to realize something was wrong until it was too late.

But these weren't ordinary larvae. Within the first few minutes, all-out warfare ensued. They flooded Bonnie's system with chemicals meant to stun the enemy, chemicals that happened to make Bonnie feel wonderful.

Intruders! Strangers! Others! It could not be tolerated, but they had no choice. Bonnie was a closed system.

She opened her eyes and saw Aunt Laura bending over her. Laura looked even thinner than she had been ten years ago, when Bonnie had seen her at Christmas. Bonnie had been able to count Laura's ribs. From behind.

Now Laura bent over Bonnie with a face that seemed little more than flesh clinging to a skull. "Thought you could get away with it. But there's always a price to pay." Her eyes gleamed with triumph.

Bonnie couldn't move. She didn't feel particularly bad, but she had a feeling she was supposed to be somewhere else. Laura stared at her, daring her to argue, but Bonnie couldn't remember what they were talking about. She wished Laura would go away. Couldn't she see Bonnie was in no condition to have visitors?

Laura wandered in and out of Bonnie's field of vision. Periodically she pointed a bony finger at Bonnie, accusingly. Bonnie wondered, *What did I do now? Other than enjoy my food.*

Was that so terrible? Over the years, people had been so strange about it. They believed eating a lot was a terrible sin, like theft or murder, and being fat was the mark of that sin, the Scarlet Letter. Bonnie supposed a lot of people equated fat with ugliness, but she didn't care what size people were. Admittedly, she probably didn't care because she didn't need a mate.

Some of the young men Bonnie dated in college asked her to lose weight. She refused, and they wanted to get married anyway. But she never took them seriously. They were not important enough to her. She liked them, but they stood at the end of a long line of her priorities.

"It's unhealthy!" hissed Laura. "Don't you get it? You're

mentally ill, Bonnie, you eat compulsively! That's not natural!"

"So I'm supposed to believe that *you're* an example of what's natural, Aunt Laura?"

The phone rang. Bonnie tried to get up to answer it. Laura drifted away again. Bonnie thought Laura might answer the phone, but it just kept ringing.

Finally it stopped. Bonnie took a nap.

Sometime later, someone pounded on the door. Bonnie heard them, but she couldn't stir.

Finally a terrible pressure in her bladder woke her. She felt weak, but otherwise not too bad. She made her way to the bathroom.

When she emerged a few minutes later, she felt much better. Her clothing hung a little loose, she wondered if she should eat first or change first. The phone rang and she picked it up.

"Bonnie?"

"Colin?"

"Are you okay? I've been calling and calling!"

"What's wrong? She glanced at the clock. It said five. Was she late for work?

"You've been absent for two days," he said. "You've never been sick one day in ten years, you've never even been late. When you didn't answer the phone we got worried. Where have you been?"

"Uh-oh. Colin, I think I passed out."

"For *two days?*"

"I – I must have the flu or something, I didn't know –"

"Do you want me to call an ambulance for you? Should I send Misha to pick you up?"

"No. I actually feel much better now. I'm not even dizzy anymore."

He spoke to someone in the background, probably Misha. She heard the word *doctor*. She hoped Colin wasn't going to insist she go to one. She already knew perfectly well what was the matter with her, and it wasn't the flu.

"Bonnie? I want you to call me in the morning. If you're not feeling well enough, you shouldn't come in. And if you're still feeling sick, you should go to the doctor."

Morning? You mean it's not morning now?

"I will, Colin."

"Listen – you're not on one of those crazy liquid diets are you? You're not starving yourself?"

Bonnie laughed. "No. I promise you, I would never starve myself."

Colin warned her a few more times about how tricky the flu could be, and finally hung up. Bonnie walked into her kitchen. Afternoon waned, the sun ignited the yellow daisies on her tablecloth. She gazed admiringly at them for a few moments, then got busy making sandwiches. She felt about twice as hungry as normal.

No surprise there.

She should have been a lot more concerned, but she sat down and enjoyed a leisurely meal. Supper was the constant in her life, the thing that centered her. She watched the motes of dust swirling in the sunshine and thought about very little else. After supper she would have to call a doctor and confess what she had done. They would probably give her the antidote immediately. But at that moment, she felt so much at peace, she enjoyed her meal so much.

She heard a noise at the stove. She didn't have to look around to see who was there.

Grandmother.

And Laura sat opposite Bonnie at the table.

Bonnie kept eating. Laura could stare all she wanted, she wasn't going to stop her from enjoying her meal.

"Bonnie, you know what's happened, don't you?"

"Sure." Bonnie spoke between bites. "I'm having another hallucination."

"You forced us to divide into two camps," said Laura. "Larvae from two wasps aren't normally able to co-exist in one body."

Bonnie stopped eating. "Excuse me?"

Laura sat there just as real as you please. She was horribly thin, but instead of her usual fanatical gleam she wore a *reasonable* expression. "Two camps. The Grandmother camp and the Laura camp. Grandmother's group entered you first. They've had a chance to stake out the best eating spots. My group is mostly camped around your heart and lower esophagus. We're starving, Bonnie."

"I'm sorry. I'm trying to take care of that right now."

"Could we have cookies for dessert? And chocolate cake?"

"Sure."

Laura looked so happy, Bonnie could hardly believe it. The real Laura would have been twitching on the floor and foaming at the lips at the very thought of cookies and cake. Bonnie finished her last sandwich and went to fetch the desserts. She poured a large glass of milk to go with them. Grandmother and Laura smiled at her, approvingly.

"They never mentioned hallucinations as one of the side effects," said Bonnie.

"I doubt anyone has ever had two sets of us inside them before," said Laura. "You've forced us to access resources we didn't know we had."

"Ah." Bonnie ate a dozen cookies without even putting a dent in her appetite. She didn't hurry, though. She liked to take her time. Hurrying wouldn't help the larvae, anyway, it would just cram the food down too fast for them to absorb the nutrients properly.

Listen to me, believing it. My brain certainly is inventive.

"This Laura persona that you see is an hallucination. But those of us who live inside you are real, Bonnie. We communicate with each other with chemicals. We communicate with you the same way. And *you* with *us*."

Bonnie was beginning to feel nervous. Laura made altogether too much sense. "Should I call you Larva instead of Laura?"

"That would be *Larvae*. Plural."

Bonnie cut a nice, healthy slab of chocolate cake. "How come Grandmother isn't talking to me too?"

"Her group is farther away from your brain. We intercept their chemicals on the way to you, so in a way, she *is* talking to you."

"I thought you were at war."

"We were, but other priorities take precedent. We have a lot of growing to do if we're ever going to make it to the surface and become adults."

Bonnie felt a stab of dismay. She had already decided to get the antidote. If she hadn't started hallucinating again, she might have kept the larvae for a while, to lose some of the weight. But this…

"Don't kill us," said Larvae/Laura.

Bonnie swallowed a lump of cake, painfully. She could feel Grandmother standing behind her, but she couldn't bear to look into that beloved face. Her mind was playing cruel tricks on her.

"We have so much to offer you," said Laura.

"Like what?"

"Like *this*.

Bonnie took another bite of cake. It tasted wonderful. But suddenly *wonderful* wasn't an adequate word for the flavor. Bonnie gazed at Laura over the field of yellow daisies on her tablecloth. The late afternoon light became golden, the molten color of the gods, the color of life, yet incorruptible, perfect.

Transcendent. That was the word for the moment, a word to describe an encounter with a god. Which god was Laura? A wasp-headed goddess of the Egyptians?

"You've been worshiping at this altar all your life," said Laura. "You've created your own goddess. You understand us, Bonnie, better than anyone could. You're a kindred spirit."

"But you'll kill me." Bonnie almost wept with the thought of breaking that perfect spell.

"It doesn't have to happen. We can reach some accommodation."

Bonnie's heart leapt with joy at the prospect. But she didn't really believe it. "How?"

"From what you remember in those newscasts, people are only supposed to receive eggs from one wasp. We believe the larvae form an emotional, semi-conscious bond with their hosts. Remember how sad Rachael Goldskin looked when she got the antidote?"

"Yes." Bonnie took another glorious bite of chocolate cake.

"Our situation is different. We have been forced to release chemicals that we normally would not need. Those chemicals have bonded us more closely with your mind, your neurochemicals, and once we were able to link up with your mind, we had access to your memories. We aren't just *with* you, Bonnie. We *are* you."

"That would be just as true if you were simply a delusion. But you don't have to be a delusion to do me harm. You can muddle me with your chemicals until it's time to eat your way out of me."

Laura looked pained. "We do *not* eat our way out. When it's time to emerge, our eating cycle is over. We can wriggle our way to the surface, avoiding damage to tissue, and then make a small incision in your skin and slip out. You'll bleed a little, but we leave a chemical that allows the blood to clot quickly."

"And the paralyzing chemicals won't stop my heart."

"We can make sure we don't overdose you with those –"

"The two women who died," said Bonnie. "They only had half the number of larvae in them. What chance do *I* stand?"

"We can control ourselves. The larvae that killed those other women didn't know what they were doing until it was too late. They weren't conscious."

"How do you know that?"

Laura sighed. "Because my mother was one of the individuals who emerged from one of those women. You exchanged glances with my mother at the clinic Bonnie. I saw it in your memory."

Bonnie finished her first piece of cake and started on the second. She still felt the rapture, but she was getting used to it. Perhaps spoiled by it. Ordinary eating would never be the same. Assuming she lived to get back to normal.

"Bonnie, let us prove ourselves. You would have given us three months anyway, before you went to get the antidote. Let us live at least that long. We will continue to enhance your sensations. And we can make those enhancements permanent, we can make adjustments in your neurochemistry. We can alter your appetite so that you can enjoy yourself without putting on those extra pounds every year."

"Promises," said Bonnie, sadly.

"Please."

Bonnie had never heard the real Laura use that tone. Laura had never displayed that kind of humility, vulnerability, that kind of – *humanity.*

And Grandmother still waited behind her chair. Bonnie wanted to take her hand so badly.

My god, I'm going to do it. I'm going to give them a chance. And they may kill me.

She watched the sunlight mellow into twilight. *When the sun goes down, it's time to go home . . .*

Bonnie got up and cleaned her dishes, while Grandmother hovered nearby.

"Let's go watch some TV." She put away the last plate. "And nibble on some of that toffee."

Bonnie went back to her normal schedule at work. It didn't take people long to notice she was losing weight.

"Are you *sure* you're not on one of those starvation diets?" Colin asked worriedly.

"I'm not!" Bonnie showed him her lunch (but didn't tell him she had three more bags just like it hidden in the refrigerator).

"Um – you're not – you know." Colin pantomimed sticking his finger down his throat.

"Throwing up?" Bonnie laughed, incredulously. "Good heavens no. I'm eating a healthy diet, Colin, and I feel great. The HMO will

be very happy with me."

He watched her closely. They all did, but there was nothing amiss for them to see. She looked great, her skin glowed with health, her energy level seemed normal.

"How do you do it?" begged Kristy, who was also losing weight rapidly, thanks to her own larvae. "I'm so tired all the time and my skin is just hanging on me." She tugged at her neck. "Now I *really* want a face lift."

Bonnie didn't tell them about the larvae. She wouldn't have told them anyway, but now she had an even better reason to keep it secret. She scrupulously guarded her sanity, trying to maintain a normal appearance.

But inside, things were quite different.

Bonnie's perceptions were permanently altered. It took concentration to move at normal speed among her fellow humans. She stifled her urge to exclaim the wonder she felt at the beauty of the world. Much of her day passed as if in a dream, with Bonnie responding automatically to questions, phone-callers, signals from fellow drivers in traffic.

Only Sam the gardener noticed any difference in her, as she lingered rapturously over her garden. She tried not to go outside when he was there. She watched her calendar and her clock carefully, making sure never to be late or miss a day at work. She had to watch the sun.

When the sun was at five o'clock, Laura and Grandmother appeared in the kitchen. Laura told Bonnie what they wanted to eat, and Bonnie prepared wonderful meals, perfect dishes to be eaten in God's field, under Ra's sun disc, pushed through the heavens by the sacred beetle.

Another creature that grew from a larva.

Laura grew plumper. She looked more like Grandmother that way. Bonnie was delighted.

"Are you still at war?" she asked them.

"Yes," said Laura. "We can't help it. But once we emerge, we'll eventually mate. Our offspring will retain all of our memories, they'll be fully conscious."

"There you go with that genetic memory thing again." Bonnie helped herself to another serving of mashed potatoes with home-made turkey gravy. "It's a fantastic idea."

"Not so fantastic," said Laura. "After all, we were engineered. Men with gene splicers made us. We have our own gene splicers,

Bonnie, but we call them genitalia."

Bonnie laughed. The real Laura would never have said anything like that!

"When our offspring are growing inside a host, they'll know how to do for that host what we've learned to do for you. They'll be able to live inside that host without killing her. And then. Maybe . . ."

"Maybe they'll accept you?" said Bonnie. "Maybe they won't think you're monsters?"

"Parasites," said Laura. "Maybe they'll think of us as partners instead."

Bonnie served herself more herb stuffing. "Remember what those doctors asked me?"

"Yes. *Are you afraid of bugs?* I know — it won't be easy."

"I'll be worried about you when you're on your own." Bonnie surprised herself, but it was true – the thought of someone attacking her wonderful sable wasps was painful.

Be careful, she thought, and wondered if she was warning herself or those future wasps.

Several weeks passed. She dropped a lot more than forty pounds, soon there wouldn't be much extra weight to lose. She had been forced to shop for new clothes three times. She bought dresses and pantyhose, because those seemed to fit longer.

At work, Kristy said, "My gosh! You're beautiful. Bonnie. How come you never went on a diet before?"

"Because I didn't care that I was fat. If the HMO hadn't threatened my job, I would never have thought about it."

"I wish I felt the same way. My husband is on my case all the time. Sometimes I think –" Kristy sighed, wistfully. "What's the point? He's never happy with my body, and I'm just getting older. Maybe when the kids are grown, I can go off on my own. You always seem so happy on your own."

"I'm used to it," warned Bonnie. "Do you think you might get lonely?"

"I don't know. But I'd like to find out."

Wonderful, thought Bonnie. *Now I'm breaking up people's marriages. And I'm not even telling the truth about being alone.*

Because *they* were always there, the larvae. Bonnie could feel their support, their concern, all through the day, all through the night. And at supper they had wonderful conversations about fascinating things. Bonnie was like Joan of Arc, talking to her

150

voices — and at the end, would she earn the stake and the holy fire?

Or the antidote?

Even Bonnie wasn't sure which it would be.

One day Bonnie put on a size-eight dress and it was too big for her.

Laura, by contrast, had grown nice and fat, easily as fat as Grandmother. She would have looked like Grandmother's twin if she hadn't grown two multi-faceted eyes and a pair of lovely, sable antennae.

The wasp eyes were far more compassionate than Laura's had been. They held no fanatical gleam, no malice, no madness. And when the five o'clock sunlight slanted into the kitchen, Laura's new eyes reflected iridescent colors.

"Surely there was an Egyptian goddess who looked like you," said Bonnie. "A goddess of honey?"

"Wasps are not bees," said Laura. "My species doesn't make honey, though I've learned to love its taste."

She had learned to love TV, as well. Bonnie would have liked to spend more time reading, but the larvae preferred a faster stream of information: news, science and nature programs, travelogues, absolutely anything that would teach them about the world they were going into. Bonnie would sit in her chair in front of the TV, Grandmother and Laura would (seem to) sit on the couch, and they would watch far into the night. In the morning, Bonnie felt as fresh as if she had slept for eight hours.

"You look perfect now," they told her at work. "Don't lose any more weight!" Bonnie obliged by stepping up her calorie consumption. By her best reckoning, only six weeks had passed. She didn't want to kill the larvae before she had to.

If she had to. They were such masters at controlling her body's functions. They had honed it into a marvelous machine, smooth, fit, efficient – and happy, if somewhat confused about the concept of clock-time. Bonnie had learned to watch others to figure out *when* she was. She clocked herself at work by learning the habits of Colin, Kristy, and Misha. She clocked herself at home by the TV programs they watched. And of course, when the sun was at five o'clock, it was time for supper, and sunrise was time for a lavish breakfast.

"You won't be nearly this hungry when we're gone," said Laura.

151

"You'll have an appetite that won't drive your weight up."

"But – my yellow daisies . . ." worried Bonnie.

"Still intact," promised Laura. "Still transcendent. We would never rob you of that."

Bonnie didn't want to think about her inevitable decision. She might be sane, or she might be living an extended delusion, sustained by the chemical warfare of larvae. Laura often surprised her with the things she said, the witticisms and the kindnesses. But Bonnie knew her own brain was perfectly capable of coming up with convincing personae. She had been alone for so many years, she had often enjoyed entertaining conversations with herself.

One day Kristy came into work looking pale and distracted.

"I had the shot today," she told Bonnie.

Bonnie held her breath, wondering if Kristy would burst into tears.

But Kristy wasn't upset. "I lost all forty pounds. I feel pretty good. Kind of tired, though."

Bonnie fought the urge to ask, *Don't you miss them? Didn't you like having them inside? Was it really so different for you?*

"They didn't know themselves," Larvae/Laura said at suppertime. "They never spoke to her. Perhaps it's a mercy."

"Can you really do it?" Bonnie asked. "Can you leave my body without killing me? Can you control yourselves that well?"

Laura seemed to ponder before she answered. "I think so. I believe we've mastered ourselves. We learn more every day."

She hadn't said a simple, confident *yes.* Apparently the larvae weren't any better at lying than Bonnie was.

At night, the TV screen flickered before her eyes. All of her eyes, hundreds of them, watching, absorbing, digesting. News, technology, science, music, dance. Bees dancing in yellow daisies, tapping out rhythms of triumph.

Rachael Goldskin swam before their eyes. "I couldn't live without them, I missed them so much! You don't know what it's like. They love me, I can feel it!"

"Yes," said Bonnie. "But do they talk to you? Mine talk to me."

"You're not overweight," the reporter pleaded with Rachael. "How did you find a doctor who was willing to give you the bugs?"

Rachael shrugged, evasively. "It's my body! It's my life!"

The screen flickered. Its images no longer appeared smoothly continuous to Bonnie. The light strobed in bands, people jerked and stuttered. Bonnie was annoyed, but she tried to make the best of it. She got up a couple of times to go to the bathroom. She finished two tins of chocolate-covered toffee.

The phone rang. She forgot that she was supposed to answer it.

"Bonnie," said Laura, plaintively, "we're hungry!"

Bonnie made sandwiches out of leftover meatloaf. She brought out chocolate cake and poured tea. Laura sat in her usual spot at the table and Grandmother made noises at the stove.

The sun came in through the window and started across the floor. It reminded Bonnie of something, but she couldn't quite put her finger on it.

"We love meatloaf," said Laura.

Bonnie had some trouble holding onto her glass of tea. She got a straw and sipped it, instead.

Someone pounded on the front door and called, "Bonnie? Are you home?"

Eventually the noise went away. But then the phone rang again. Bonnie wished it would stop doing that.

She almost couldn't swallow her bite of cake. She put down her fork and rubbed her stiff hands, pushed aside what was left of her meal and lay her head on the table.

The sun warmed her scalp.

"Hey," she wondered, "did I go to work today?"

"Uh-oh," said Laura.

"I feel funny."

"It's time," said Laura.

Bonnie's eyes wanted to close. She fought them. "Time for what?"

"Time to come out."

Bonnie made herself sit upright. But it was hard to move, harder than trying to struggle awake out of a dead sleep. She forced her head up, until she could see Laura. "What?" she whispered, because her voice was failing her too.

"We have to wiggle our way to the surface. It's time to weave our cocoons."

How long? Wondered Bonnie. *How many weeks has it been?*

"We don't know," Laura answered the thought.

The clinic was supposed to call me . . .

The phone rang again, twenty times, and then stopped.

"We have to concentrate," said Laura. "This is the hardest part."

Getting born is always hard, thought Bonnie. *At least, that's what I've heard.*

She couldn't move, but she could feel everything. There was movement, deep inside her. If she had gotten married all those years ago, and she had decided to have children, she might have felt this sort of movement inside. *Should I breathe like those ladies in the childbirth classes? Huff-huff-huff?* But she couldn't even hold her head up. It settled on her chest.

Inside her, things were shifting. It was a very odd sensation. Reva would have been so horrified. *Can you feel them moving inside you?*

Yes. They're moving, they're going to tear little holes in my hide, and when they emerge they'll weave cocoons.

"Halfway there," said Laura, sounding very distracted.

Bonnie fell asleep.

When she woke again, her head was full of cotton. Her skin felt wet. Something burned on her belly. She heard a soft little *plop*, and felt a new wetness.

Eyeww!! She thought.

"Sorry," mumbled Laura.

Bonnie heard more plops. She blinked, and suddenly saw the world through new eyes, hundreds of them, the kitchen in bright fragments, herself slumped in a chair.

Cool! She thought, but then the images were gone, Bonnie had only two eyes again.

Through half-parted lids, Bonnie saw red seeping into yellow daisies.

Laura said nothing to comfort her. Laura was very busy. *Did they deceive me?* wondered Bonnie. *Did I deceive myself?*

She was afraid, but she wasn't angry with them. They wanted to live. *Someone* should live, even if it wasn't Bonnie. Someone should see the sunshine on the flowers again, someone should mate and lay new eggs. *They've done what their bodies told them to do,* Grandmother said. *How good that must feel!*

And after they mated, they would die. If Bonnie died, they wouldn't outlive her for very long. Maybe it would feel this way for them, a creeping paralysis, the light growing dim. Bonnie was sorry for them. She had so many years, and their lives lasted only months.

Maybe their eggs will remember. I hope they do . . .

She dreamed. She and Grandmother and Laura walked through

that field of yellow daisies. "Is this the place the ancient Egyptians went after they died?" Bonnie asked. "If they didn't want to go into Ra's chariot and fly across the sky?"

"The Field of Reeds," said Grandmother. "But only Pharaoh was welcome there: the Golden Horus, reclaiming his rightful place among the gods."

"We'll settle for the Field of Daisies, then," said Bonnie. "The field of Reeds probably has too many mosquitos anyway."

Laura, as plump as Grandmother and somehow more graceful because of it, took Bonnie's hand. "Will you remember us after we've left you?"

"Always," said Bonnie. "And will you remember me?"

"We'll ask our new hosts to call you," said Laura.

"Like Houdini. He promised to contact his wife from the other side if he died first. But he never did."

"We aren't dead," said Laura.

But did she mean herself, or Bonnie?

Or both?

Golden light poured into the kitchen. It was past suppertime. Bonnie's eyes were still half-open, she hadn't been able to close them. She saw cocoons, torn open, empty. And then she saw wasps.

They droned, happily. They perched on every surface. Bonnie saw them mating, enemies no longer.

She couldn't move at all. Shouldn't she be able to move by now? Would she ever move again?

At least she could still breathe. She watched the sun fading into dusk. She watched the wasps fly out the open window, into the world. But who had opened the window? Were the females looking for people to be hosts for their new eggs? Would they do it to people who were sleeping, then introduce themselves later? *Hello! We're your new tenants. Please don't kill us. We have a deal to propose.*

Good luck, Bonnie wished them. Probably it had all been a dream, anyway. She would die here, and no one would remember her name, no human and no wasp larva. She would be another lurid headline, another woman who had failed to go to the clinic to get the antidote, inspiring more angry people to march in front of government buildings with signs that screamed *ABOMINATION!*

Oh well.

The wasps were almost gone. One of them perched on the table in front of Bonnie. It seemed to be peering into her face, looking for signs of life. The notion grew in Bonnie's mind that it was worried about her.

Emotion swelled in her chest. They had promised, they had tried. And now, they were worried. She blinked and a tear swelled past her lids, down her cheek. They only sign she could muster.

The wasp became very excited. It danced a pattern on the tablecloth, a victory dance. It spun and beat its wings for Bonnie, and then it turned to the window, through which the last of its brothers and sisters had flown. It followed them out.

The sun was going down. It was time to go home.

Bonnie shed a few more tears, then closed her eyes. Sooner or later, the phone would ring again. A call from the golden Horus.

She hoped she would be able to answer it.

From Emily Devenport:

The idea for this story occurred to me while I was watching a nature documentary about bugs. The narrator was talking about how bees know what flowers to pursue by the position of the sun. He actually said, "If the sun's at five o'clock, it must be yellow daisies." I turned to my husband and said, "That would make a great title for a short story!"

At the time, I had been on a diet for several months, slimming down for health reasons. I had become painfully familiar with the constant, nagging sensation of hunger, though I wasn't on a starvation diet. That's why this story was so easy for me to write. The ending may seem bizarre or disturbing to some, but for me, it was happy. Yes—dieting has twisted my soul . . .

I have been published under three pen names. As Emily Devenport I wrote Shade, Larissa, Scorpianne, EggHeads, The Kronos Condition, and GodHeads. My short stories appeared in Asimov's SF Magazine, the Full Spectrum anthology, and Aboriginal SF, whose readers voted me a Boomerang Award (an actual boomerang). As Maggy Thomas I wrote Broken Time, which was nominated for the Philip K. Dick award. As Lee Hogan I wrote Belarus and Enemies. My books were published by ROC/NAL in the U.S., the Women's Press in the U.K., Opus in Israel, and Urania in Italy.

I review products on amazon.com as Emily Hogan, write a blog at emsjoiedeweird.blogpot.com, and I hope to have a website up and running by the end of the year. My website will feature an audio-visual version of Belarus, illustrated by Elinor Mavor (www.mavorarts.com). I am releasing two brand new e-books from Amazon and Smashwords at the end of this summer: The Night Shifters and Spirits Of Glory, as well as a freebee novella titled Pale Lady. I also plan to release audio versions of these titles.

Despite what many people think, Cat Rambo is her real and legal name. Cat is editor of Fantasy Magazine. *Her writing has appeared in Asimov's, Weird Tales, and Clarkesworld magazines. She's also an all-around nice person.*

Her offering for 2020 Visions is perhaps one of the more likely scenarios-- for all we know the sorts of things she discusses are going on right now. As for the Therapy Buddha, let's just say that sometimes a gag gift can have more impact than intended.—RN

Therapy Buddha
by Cat Rambo

The office's new work-from-home policy provided its advantages, but housekeeping service wasn't one. Even though he was escaping the smog-laden outside air, Lyle's apartment smelled too lived-in, filled with the odor of ancient take-out, unwashed clothing, and dead house plants.

"I should clean this place up," he said. He thought about hanging up his damp windbreaker, but shrugged it off to toss it over a chair. He dumped his bag on the dining nook table as he edged his way past.

When he thumbed the frame, the metallic square lit with the evening news logo, four stories ribboned and scrolling across it. All showed scrambles of military activity, puffs of bomb smoke, a scattered flash of gunfire, muted and surreal, before they combined into a single burger commercial.

From behind him, the device on the table said, "You seem to use the word 'should' a lot. Do you attribute a particular meaning to that word?"

Lyle scrounged through the refrigerator, pulling out a plastic meal bag to throw in the microwave. Coming back to the coffee table, he said, "I suppose I say 'should' when I really mean 'don't want to do.'"

The Therapy Buddha sat cross-legged, three feet tall and made of soft plastic. It was bright green.

Its calm, big-cheeked face said, "How do you feel about that?" The sound emanated from a speaker that glinted dentally between unmoving lips, like a slanted front tooth.

"Yeah, whatever, toy. TV on." He retrieved his meal and slumped into the couch to flip through channels on the wall screen.

"A broken mirror never reflects again," the Buddha said. "Fallen flowers do not return to their branches."

"What the hell does that mean?"

"Zen koans are sayings that challenge habitual thought processes. For another Zen koan, say 'Koan, please.'"

He did not reply. The Buddha sat, silent and immobile. His co-workers had bought it for him on his fortieth birthday, wrapped in sheets of bright pink bubble wrap.

"Gives pop therapy a whole new meaning." Scott laughed and almost patted him on the back. The voice-activated Buddha was a rip-off of a Sony model, but the imitation was very good except for the wrong color.

The party had been a typical office gathering—sheet cake from the corner grocery store with bright red, slightly crooked lettering over white frosting reading "Happy 40th Lyle!" Everyone stood around and made small talk. He chatted with Scott and the latest intern.

"What do you think of your new surroundings?" Scott asked the intern. He was in full charm mode, relic of his days selling Christian comedy albums.

She was busty and blonde, wearing green-striped overalls that matched the beads in her hair. Her tenure in the office was sixteen hours, as of that afternoon. "I've never worked in a data-selling corporation before," she admitted. "This is my first time working since college."

"You didn't work in high school?" Scott said. "A shame—I think it really builds character. What did you do instead?"

"I was on the swim team," she said. Lyle imagined her briefly in a tank suit, her long hair tied back.

"Sports are good," Scott said. "I worked in my dad's store, making deliveries. What about you, Lyle?"

"I farmed gold in an online game and sold it."

"Every geek's dream job. But how can there be actual money in that?"

"It paid for college," he said. "I didn't really have the grades for a scholarship. Real jobs pay better, though, particularly since they now outsource a lot of gold grinding to Thailand and China."

Scott nodded, looking interested in a way that Lyle knew was forced. The intern didn't bother to conceal her boredom. Beads clicking together as she moved, she went to take another sliver of cake. Scott and Lyle stood staring after her.

"She'll last, what, two weeks?" Scott said. "Someone will want coffee and she'll get huffy and leave."

"If that long."

"How are you liking working from home?"

When the memo had come down from the home office—to decrease costs, remote logins, etc.—Scott had been one of the first proclaiming the glories of the new policy, but every time Lyle made his way into the office to check-in or for functions like this, he found Scott there.

"It's all right," he said. "But a little isolated. How about you?"

"Sometimes it just seems like I can get a lot more done here, you know what I mean?"

Lyle shrugged. "Not really." Most of his work consisted of surfing the trade nets to find places looking for batches of data of the kind he could deliver. Sometimes he looked for new products and then pitched his dataherd to their marketers, pointing out the markets they reflected and the insights they provided, depending on how he grouped them. A data herder needed agility of mind, the ability to see opportunities and seize them quickly.

The coffee shop down the street was wider than his apartment, so he usually took his datapad down there. If he got there early, he could find a spot near the window, overlooking Lake Washington. A latte and a croissant's worth of lunch bought him at least an hour uninterrupted before the servers started cleaning his space too obviously, edging him out. He liked to watch the sailboats on the water, and the little red water scooters, shaped like dragons, that had been rare last year and this year were everywhere.

His fingers danced over the keys as he performed his daily evaluation of the demographics of his dataherd. As expected, they'd scattered even more geographically, and a few more had married than had divorced. Overall, wages were down. Outside the sky was pinkish and cloudy as dying water, reflected in the metallic sides of the hot dog vendor's cart, steaming as he pushed it along.

Lyle frowned as numbers flowed across his pad in response to his query. The dataherd was trending towards a particularly unprofitable sector—he could no longer mine them for singles data. That had been coming for a while. He'd foreseen it five years ago, but didn't like it nonetheless. He drank the rest of his latte in quick gulps, not tasting it, watching the vendor negotiate with a dragon boat, the rider struggling to pass her credit card across the vendor's beam to be read before it signaled with a green light and the hot dog passed down. She wore a white face mask, as did the vendor and the others on the street. A bad day for breathing, the morning news had said.

Waving cheerfully, rider and boat made their way back into deeper water, circling the tour boat cruising along the waterfront. Lyle gathered up his pad and put his own mask on to go home.

"The trick is figuring out a way to pitch them," he said to the Buddha. He'd left the coffee shop earlier than he'd meant to, rehearsing this conversation in his mind. It startled him to realize that he had been looking forward to talking to an inanimate object.

"Why is it a trick?"

"Because it's creating something where it didn't exist before. The demographic of people who eat chocolate in the bathtub, or whatever else you can claim them to be representative of, that someone can aim a product at. It's a knack."

"How do you feel about that?"

"I have to go into the office," he said. "It's a bad sign when I'm having conversations with a toy."

The plaza office was much the same as always. Downtown Seattle always struck him as waiting to become the stage setting for a post-apocalyptic film, its workers and visitors white and blue-masked zombies, a few with brighter faces yet, tie-dyed or stamped with bright yellow ducks and green frogs.

Scott poked his head into the cubicle. "Hey buddy, nice to see you for a change."

"We're supposed to be working from home," Kyle said.

"Well, sure," Scott said. "Sitting around doing datasorts in your bathrobe, who wouldn't like that? But I don't think it's a cost-cutting measure. They're seeing what deadwood they can drop." He grinned mirthlessly. "I've been coming in doing alternative training," he said. "It's good to be agile, employment wise. My cousin worked for a mall corp for forty years, then they cut her loose. Now she's a virtual clerk."

"What world?"

"Second Life, tends a music store. Sits there at the computer all day waiting to give shoppers the human touch."

"Ah yeah. Two of my herd did that a couple of weeks ago," he said. "And one's a virtual taxi-driver. Robots control the driving, she just gives clients human interaction and thanks them when the card is billed."

"Sign of downward social mobility!" Scott said, and laughed. "I'm sure you have other opportunities by the binload."

"I'm thinking about recruiting some new people into the herd to up their marketability," he said.

"Almost too late for this graduation."

"Graduation?"

"They do it by year now. For the cost of a few trinkets, you can sign up a thousand or so college kids. They'll fill out any amount of forms for a coffee chip or an mp3 download. Go look on the internal website, there's a list of promotional items you can request."

"That intern quit yet?"

"Last week. Did I call it or what? Mahalia asked her to pick up soda for the office weekender, and she posted a five screen goodbye e-mail to the rest of us, citing a lack of respect for her as a person. You should have gotten it."

"There's so much e-mail that I delete anything that goes to the office at large."

"That may not be the best strategy."

"It's worked well for eight years so far," Lyle said, and went home.

"I don't really feel connected to anyone," he said to the Buddha. He'd moved it to the bookshelf so it could see more of the room. He sat on the couch with his back turned to the television, arguing with the Buddha. Behind him, the screen showed troops marching over an indiscriminate jungle backdrop.

"How does that make you feel?"

"Disconnected," he said, then laughed. "Yeah, whatever." He unrolled his datapad and traced his herd's purchases for the evening and managed to assemble a subset into an infochunk on movie-going trends. He shot it off to the studio markets and waited for usage fees.

Checking prices, he noticed a high profile survey on medicinal teas. It was easy to request coupons for free samples to be sent to his dataherd. He could check the results and peddle the infochunk to the company in a week or so.

"I will tell you a koan," the Buddha said. "The monk Bazan was walking through the marketplace one day, and heard a customer say to the butcher, 'Give me your best piece of meat.' The butcher replied 'Everything in my shop is the best. There is no piece of meat that is not the best.'"

He stared at it, nonplussed. What sort of reply did it expect?

"For another Zen koan, say 'Koan, please.'"

"The thing," he said to the Buddha, picking up the conversation again. "The thing is this. What right do I have to capitalize on the members of my dataherd?"

"Do you take responsibility for that?" the Buddha asked.

"Their clickprints are changing," he said.

"What are their clickprints?"

"Their web usage patterns, their search keywords, their purchases, how they look at sites. And I make it change-two weeks from now, some of them will have shifted to tea drinkers. Because of me. I manipulate their lives so I can harvest their data."

"How does that make you feel?"

"They're growing away from me," he said. "Ten of them died last month in the war. Now I'm down to 4527. Soon I won't even have a sellable herd."

"Would you like another koan?"

"Should I just give them their freedom, cut them loose?" he said. "Someone else can collect their data. Or reassemble them. I don't know what I'd do otherwise, though. I can stay free in a hostel, maybe, but food isn't free."

"You seem to use the word 'freedom' a lot. Do you find that word significant?"

"It's what I want to do," he said. "You're right. I use it because I'm thinking about it. It's the answer, otherwise I wouldn't be fixed on it like that."

His fingers danced over the keys as he released their contracts. Maybe someone else would pick them up, but he hoped not. They should lead lives undirected by advertising, make their own choices. Like the choice he had just made.

"I don't want to get that list of high schools after all," he said to Scott.

"It doesn't matter," Scott said. "Didn't you get the memo?

They're going to be making dataherds assignable at the corporate level. Everyone belongs to a corp anyhow. You won't be able to recruit any more. Your old herd just skyrocketed in price, buddy. You can form your own agency."

He stared at Scott. "What? I cut them all loose last night. Erased all the data from my infocloud."

Scott stared back. "You really did it, buddy? Jesus, why?"

"The Buddha told me to do it."

"That doll we bought you at the office party? You are shitting me, right?"

He stared at Scott, stricken, and finally Scott patted his shoulder. "There's a lot of careers out there," he said, avoiding Lyle's eyes. "Lots of possibilities. My mom makes a decent living selling antique food."

"Antique food?"

"Things like Space Bars and Twinkies. There's quite a market in them. She buys and sells them. You should see her apartment. Let's go talk to her."

But Scott's mother, Mrs. Laurelman, wasn't much consolation.

"It's hard work, what I do," she said. "I have agents that monitor some online auctions for me, but there's also a lot of leg work. I wouldn't recommend getting into anything like it."

"I'd thought he could sell music, he likes music," Scott said.

"What sort of music?" She looked at Lyle. He sat next to an enormous stack of pink pastry boxes.

"Oh, all sorts," he said. "I doubt that's what I'd get into, anyhow."

"If you can find a hot fad, you can make a quick buck," she said. "I watch to see if any nostalgic foods are mentioned on videocasts, and if so, I buy up any surplus quickly."

He looked at the package next to his foot. It showed two zebras dancing with each other, their stripes rose and sky blue. The lettering was Arabic.

"What are these?"

"Some sesame treat that got mentioned on a soap opera," she said. "Makes enough to buy groceries for another week."

"Don't you have a corporation plan?"

Her face purpled. "Get out!"

Steve hustled him out, apologetic. "She had a medical condition that kept her from getting health care, that's why she does the buying and selling. She's on base minimum, gets a little help with groceries, but mainly she relies on not going for meds."

Lyle wondered what her demographic was, whose herd she belonged to. The apartment had been too hot, and he felt flushed and sweaty. His garment clung moistly to his skin.

Steve punched his shoulder. "Go home and take a load off," he said.

"Yeah. Yeah." He swung aboard the bus at the corner and went to the monomall before home.

"Good evening," he said to the Buddha as he entered the apartment. He hung up his jacket with careful, deliberate motions, looking at the way the fabric gleamed in the florescent lights. His head still buzzed with an angry whirl of thoughts, words colliding unintelligibly.

"How are you?" the Buddha asked.

He took a breath. "I'm fine, how are you?"

"What did you do today?"

"Why would you care?" he said.

"Are you aware that you are answering questions with questions?"

"It's a game," he said. "We used to play it in Improv Club, back in high school. Oh, wait. Do you remember high school? Mine was a misery. Like my life."

"Why do you think your life is miserable?"

"Why wouldn't I? Oh, there I am going with the questions again, aren't I?"

It was silent.

"Have I hit a new trigger?" he said. "Are you not talking in order to see what I will say to you?"

"What do you want to say to me?" it asked.

He went over and picked it up to stare into the bland green features.

"You betrayed me," he said. "Do you understand what that means?"

"Why do you think you were betrayed?"

He set it down with almost parodic caution.

"You could have told me, and you didn't," he said.

"This unit is not intended to be a fortune-telling device."

"Aren't you? Aren't you supposed to be the random voice of the Universe, addressing me through the luck of the draw and the forces of serendipity?"

"Would you like to hear a koan?"

"No. No koans. I'm done with all that. I don't have anything left. I might as well commit suicide," he said.

It spoke in a different voice. "Alert. Spoken keywords have triggered emergency routines in this unit. If you do not wish to have medical attention summoned, count to ten and backward within one minute."

"Fuck you," he said.

"If you do not wish to have medical attention summoned, count to ten and backward within thirty seconds."

Medical attention would cost an arm and a leg. At the last possible second, he spat out, "One-two-three-four-five-six-seven-eight-nine-ten-nine-eight-seven-six-five-four-three-two-one."

"Transmission aborted," the Buddha said.

He stared at it.

"I'm going out to interact with some real people," he said. And then, "Christ, why am I telling *you* that?"

When he saw the intern, across the bar, he couldn't remember her name. But he tried approaching her nonetheless.

Steve called while he was coming out of the movie, which had been something about cavemen and mammoths, frothy with laughter, something he hadn't understood at all. He passed to take the call, shielding his ear while the other moviegoers eddied past him.

"It's not as though they depicted Neanderthals correctly," he heard one boy say to another. In his head, Steve's voice said. "Lyle, you there?"

"I'm here."

"Listen, there was this study, you know, one of those market studies, for a tea, some sort of tea that was supposed to make you immune to colds, do you know the one I mean?"

"Yeah, I know the one. I signed my herd up for it, one of the last things I did with them."

Silence from Steve.

"You know what I'd really like to see, I'd like to see magicians," another movie-goer said, and their friend nodded, passing Lyle, and said "Yeah, and a really good bass line."

Steve said "Well, that's unfortunate."

"Why, what's happened?"

"Turns out they'd modified the recipe, did some sort cuts with the vitamins, and about a quarter of the people who've drunk it have total liver shutdown. You didn't drink any of it, did you?"

"No," he said.

"Well, there's a plus. But I got to warn you, buddy, they're going to be coming after you with lawyers and maybe even jail-time, buddy. It's looking pretty bad. And when the cops see you cut your herd loose, they're going to think there was some reason. Like you knew ahead of time."

He was numb. He couldn't hear anything from the people moving around him. It was all just a high-pitched whine in his head.

"Can I come talk to you?" he asked desperately.

Steve's voice came from far away, hesitant. "Well, buddy, you see. It's just that I don't want them to think—bad timing right now, I think, maybe in a few days?"

He fumbled with the plastic bag in his pocket, taking out a pill bottle. Thumbing off the lid, he drank the tiny pills, each as big as a bird's eye, down as though they were liquid.

"Go ahead," he said, swallowing. "It'll be too long before they get here for you to save me. I should have known better than trust my life to you. I should have known that an object couldn't be my friend."

"If you do not wish to have medical attention summoned, count to ten and backward within thirty seconds."

They looked at each other in silence.

"If you do not wish to have medical attention summoned, count to ten and backward within ten seconds. Nine. Eight. Seven. Six. Five. Four. Three. Two. One."

The Buddha gave out a shrill squeal before saying, "Information transmitted."

Lyle sat down, staring at his feet, looking puzzled. He made as though to speak, then shook his head twice and slumped back into the couch. His legs shot forward in a flurry of spasms, kicking the table before he bucked the sofa over backwards. The Buddha shuddered sideways.

The paramedics came through the doorway thirteen minutes later. Lyle lay on the floor, staring upward, body tangled in the constraints of the tiny space between sofa and table. Across the room lay the Buddha, its face turned to him, staring across the carpet, no meaning written there.

Dead Rookies
by Jack Mangan

We took the unmarked highway exit, left civilization and drove into the suburbs. The inhabitants greeted us with their usual exuberance, hurling insults and the occasional molotov at our police humvee. Driver just pressed us on through, already beyond the reach of the highway's glow. Dead streetlamps watched from above with bent necks; trashcan fires and our headlights were this hell's only illumination. Rookie stared out at the feral suburbanites, jumping a little when a wine bottle shattered against the rear windshield, scattering weak flames across its surface. I clapped his shoulder, remembering my first run, seven-some years ago.

"Keep it buckled, kid," Zed said with a laugh. "They ain't who we're here to see."

Sarge volleyed taunts at them nonetheless from the vehicle's PA. Driver rolled us easily through a furniture barricade, on toward the office park. Five cops in a humvee bound to visit the Thinking Sector; a fist of men who'd each give you five different reasons for our excursion. Me, I'd have recited the farce that we were there to enforce order and watch for signs of unrest. And on the right Tuesday, I'd have even believed it.

Today was Friday.

167

I tried a quick text message to Valerie, but the signal was already fragged.

Suburbs had never required fences; the landscape just gradually turned as you drove out. Weed-choked meridians and failed trees marked our approach to the worker's zone. The dead houses and storefronts gave way to squat office building masses, most of them surrounded by tents and small structures. Some signs of life, but very little movement since we'd left the wilds of the highwayside.

"Quiet, quiet, quiet, quiet. Too quiet," Zed said, chewing a toothpick. "Should we bail?"

Sarge turned to look sleepily at the three of us in back. He jerked a thumb upward. "We got the drone up there watching, we'll be all right. What do you think, kid? Should we turn back?"

The rookie shook his head, obviously just trying to keep up.

"No, let's do this."

Zed laughed and Driver took a hard left, onto the dead end street we wanted. I found it absurd that he'd used his turn signal.

The transition between burb hells was signaled by the return of cell phone service. I sent Val's text message and switched off the phone, hoping she was awake to see the incoming. I absently thumbed the wedding band on my finger.

The building was a cube stuck into the earth, its mirrored surface filthy and cracked, but intact. Scattered fluorescents shone from the four stories within, but it was mostly as dark as midnight should be. The Gatesoft logo adorned the building top in ten-foot letters, like a name on a headstone.

I watched the kid as we turned into their lot, seeing echoes of my own first-timer reaction in his face. This office building was moated by an unkempt lawn, the landscape occupied primarily by a shanty village. Three or four dead vans parked in the grass, repurposed now as homes, but most of the structures were cabins of cubicle walls atop wooden pallets. Strangely, none of the inhabitants were openly visible from the front. The new guy didn't spot the snipers on the roof and the gunmen crouched in the bushes; I had to point them out. So many of them. . . Their presence shoveled a trench of disquiet within me. Something was up. Sarge shifted in his seat and shot me a quick look.

We pulled around back, found a wide expanse of lot feeding into a three-level parking garage. Most of the pavement inside and out of the structure was occupied with shanty worker's hovels, also built from office discards; walls made of desks, carpeted cubicle pieces, stacked computer towers, abandoned copiers and printers, and even one built on a foundation of mainframes. The massive oval lot stretched about three acres, dotted everywhere with improvised ramshackles. These guys had one of the biggest settlements I'd ever seen.

Some of the local populace were outside, but they were still more subdued than usual. Figures huddled in groups of four and five around laptop monitors and Michelin firepits. Teens and children clustered inside a toppled dumpster, one of them holding a game controller, jumping a plumber through obstacles on an old TV. Power strip motels littered the ground with no vacancies, most of the plugs double-booked. A couple of barely dressed girls sat on crates by a reclaimed UPS truck, staring into their phone screens. They glanced up with cloaked interest as we rolled in.

"That's why we're here," Zed said, grinning. "Them girls think we're their ticket out of here, into West Tex, to meet one of the families."

"Sometimes we are," Sarge said.

Weary faces watched us pull into the clearing, squinting until Driver killed the lights. Only a few rose. The girls remained seated.

"Who are these people?" the Rookie asked.

"Not everyone outside of Fort Dallas are Mad Max, kid. These guys live mean, but they call themselves the Thinking Class. They do the low-level, intense business systems figuring, for stuff like software and hardware programming and repair. What they do keeps the Texan families' pet Corporations in action."

"'Thinking Class;' these lowlifes will gut you just as quick as the damn suburbanites," Zed spat his toothpick on the floor. "The natives are skittish about something tonight. It brillos my nerves."

Sarge looked at me, his arched brow asking my assessment. I said, "Zed's right. Something's up."

Sarge nodded, then shrugged. "Nothing we can't handle. Let's go be rock stars."

We had a heckler.

"Man, what the fuck you want here, five-oh? Why don't you go out and clean up the suburbs or some shit where you're needed? Damn."

I hadn't seen Jay-Pac in years; he'd grown from little punk kid to bigger punk kid. The Rookie got that reactionary look, so I leaned in close to him. "You're the new guy, go get the duffels out of the trunk. They're full of the copper recyclables and other junk these people use as currency."

A thin, deeply-tanned, platinum girl emerged abruptly from the dumpster, staring at us, handing off her controller to one of the others. Dressed in blue jean business casual, except for the six-guns on her hips. She wasn't a kid, but also wasn't old enough for the deference they showed her; the gamers, the girls, Jay-Pac. The authority hung on her like an oversized gown on a child. She touched Jay's arm and he visibly cooled.

"This bacon has guns and a sick ride. Their bad timing might be good for us," she said. Her gaze felt our badges a moment, then she said, "This joyride authorized by your superiors? Or by a Family?"

Sarge clicked into alpha. "Hold up a fucking second there, Blondie. We're the police, we'll ask the questions. But first your firearms - -"

"The Buckley family authorized tonight's investigation, fed us the time and your location." I felt the heat from Sarge's sideways glance, but didn't look. The girl was eager to tell us something. Zed, Driver, and Rookie all stood taut, like pulled slingshots. "Why do you ask?"

She rolled her eyes and showed a red lipstick smirk. "Each of you pigs must have pissed somebody off. The Ashcor family pushed a 70% layoff today at their software HQ, a couple blocks over. Word is, their newly unemployed are planning an armed strike here tonight, to try and create some job openings at Gatesoft. If we guessed right, you're just on time."

Our surprise seemed to provide some amusement for the onlooking Thinkers. Zed and Driver had their guns out immediately, swiveling to look in every direction; Rookie saw this and mimicked. I stood still, shaking my head. Sarge had his back to me, but I could see his neck redden. He gestured to the gamer kids in the dumpster, to four old women around a netbook.

"If you're expecting an attack, then these people need to be inside, somewhere safe!"

"If they don't care, then I don't." The girl pulled a walkie-talkie from her breast pocket, said, "You hacked their drone yet?"

A staticky voice replied, "Of course, Ani. Shit, I've had control of that chopper since they got here."

I squinted up into the midnight smog, scanning for an object about the size of a riding mower. The moment I spotted it, five ground-to-air rockets streaked westward, like fingernail scratches across the sky, launched from somewhere out front, beyond this office lot's perimeter. One of the missiles caught the drone's rotor; it immediately found gravity again and spiraled fast downward, exploding hard into a cubicle house atop the parking garage.

I reflexively assumed a protective crouch, as did Sarge, while most of the rest of the police and Thinkers bolted for cover. Ani, I noticed, remained upright where she stood, calmly watching the blaze and ensuing panic on the rooftop.

Then all hell broke loose.

Firefight thunder and lightning flashed around the corners of the mirrored office from the streetside frontline. No counting the seconds, the unemployed were swarming, pushing hard into the rear settlement lot. The gamer kids and other loiterers didn't need our shepherding now; they all fled the shanty clearing into the bowels of the parking garage. I looked up into the descent of mortars, launched from out front to leap the building and smash into points across the back lot.

Driver was back in the humvee already. The Rookie was running toward its open side door. I shouted, "No! No! No! No!" But too late. The rocket landed short of the vehicle by a hand's length, then bounced up into the undercarriage. The blast lifted Rookie's feet from the pavement; he landed on his ass ten feet back, head bouncing hard off of the gravel. Explosions generating heat and tinnitus all around me, I ran forward to hook the kid by his armpits and drag him to a safer locale, hurrying backward into the open lot's shanty village maze. His heels bounced across taped-down power cables.

The office building loomed dispassionately overhead, mutely reflecting the scene of violence and horror. The first platoon of former Ashcor employees surged into the lot, taking and giving heavy fire. I lifted the kid over my shoulder and moved faster, every inch of my back alive with anticipation of an incoming bullet. Invaders were everywhere, as were Gatesoft's hangers-on. A barrage of gunfire flashed out like Morse Code from the parking garage levels. Combatants from both sides saw us: a cop carrying another wounded in uniform. Some shouted taunts, some took potshots, but most just ignored the kid and me, unsure what to do with us. Killing police has never been a profitable idea, and I was obviously running for cover, not trying to affect any outcome. Not like our deaths would open up any day jobs.

Bullets still hissed their gleeful threats past my ears, careening through plywood, concrete, and fiberglass. Cubicle homes toppled or were shot to pieces. Directly ahead of me, a VW bus-house with curtains and a wooden wheelchair ramp erupted from within, shattering window glass and raising triumphant tentacles of flame outward, waving smoke at the sky.

I pressed on.

Finally, beyond a dwelling built from oak desks, I found a steep curb at the lot's edge and slumped us both down behind it. Out past this was a slouching chainlink fence, bordering the Gatesoft office property from an abandoned sandlot. The open field made me nervous, but for the moment, there was nothing out there except litter and tall grass. Invaders had left it unavenued so far, and I liked having a momentarily peaceful spot on the combat perimeter. My patient was in bad shape. I laid him down at my feet. The kid was a relief map of blood and char, from crew-cut to shoes.

"What's happened?" he said. "Did they kill Driver?"

I didn't answer. My semi-auto was in my hand now.

Tears had already begun to leak into the grime and red on his face. The gun reports and explosions continued from beyond the oak desk structure like a percussive symphony. From inside the desk-built home, a radio faintly played "Crimson and Clover." I listened over the music, focused, honed in on one particular exchange of orders and spurious, breathless battle-planning. A small unit of about two or three. The voices were unfamiliar, their words also gave no clues as to their side. Whoever this group was, they were drawing nearer to us. Sha la la la la la.

Rookie coughed and spoke in a whisper. "Hey man, we gotta go help these people. We have to get them somewhere safe. . . their children too. We have to get them inside the building."

"Kid, don't you think I'd be inside already, lifting donuts from some break room if that were an option?" I tore open a gauze pack from my police bat-belt, coiled a strip once around his forehead. The talkative soldier-thinkers could still be heard nearby, still closing on our position. "All Gatesoft cares about is their property. We go anywhere near that front door and the building's alarm system will Taser out with a thousand volts. If we're lucky. Now we could find their snipers' ladders and get to the roof. . ." *If you were in*

172

any condition to climb, I added silently. Over and over. "These companies don't give a shit whose ass is in the seat, writing code, filling that 15-hour shift every day, as long as that ass is competent. That's why these layoffees are coming through here to thin the current workforce. Rent for the living spaces in these business park lots is crazy high, in their currency. So if you're not working, the village can't feed you, and your only remaining option is to forcefully open a job somewhere else. Or to give up and move to the suburbs." I noticed as I spoke that the approaching squad had begun listening back, honing in on my voice. They were upon us now. I caught the smallest glimpse of shadowy movement beyond the shanty's corner to my right, where the wall's desk drawer hung slightly open. We'd all grown silent, the creepers and me, although the warfare just beyond was still hitting high decibels.

Rookie breathed heavily, but obeyed my nonverbal to STFU. He closed his eyes. Another moment passed. I counted three. Sha la la la la la.

A pair of young thirties men swung around quickly, rifles leveled at us, but - - significantly - - not firing. One of them barked a quick order in Spanish. There was a moment of uncertainty, undoubtedly from their expectation of desperate programmers, not uniformed West Tex police officers. I still couldn't tell if they were Gatesoft employees or job-seekers. I sighed and put a bullet through each of them. I turned to greet the one I knew was trying an approach from my left. She jumped out with a cry and a spitting kalishnikov. I put her down before she could actually hit anything. Crimson and clover.

One of her friends had a walkie-talkie in his belt. "Hello?" I said into it.

"Who's this?" Ani answered. I guess the unit had been locals.

"A cop. We're pinned down near the perimeter. Have you seen any of my colleagues?"

A blizzard of frantic chatter cut across the handheld.

"Cop, switch to channel 9 on your talkie. Channel 9, you read?" she said. I did. She went on, "Actually got two of your boys here with me in the parking garage. Level three."

"I can't get there right now, our rookie is badly hurt."

"Dead rookies are no concern of mine."

"Are the guys with you all right?"

"Sarge is pissed off but ok. He might have broken his middle finger."

"Appropriate. What about Zed?"
"Zed's dead, baby. Zed's dead."

We sat for a moment, the rattle of machine gun fire graciously confining itself to other parts of the lot. Some of the shouts were orders and calls to capture positions, some of the shouts were much worse. The radio inside the home had now begun playing "Bohemian Rhapsody". I slumped down, dabbed with the last of my gauze at wounds on Rookie's neck. He appeared to have slid unconscious, breathing raggedly.

"Val has a tumor," I said into the radio.

"What?" Ani sounded incredulous. Loud gunfire from her position stepped on her voice.

"My wife. The cancer is beatable, but my cop salary sure can't pay to get it removed. Only the Families can afford insurance plans for stuff like that." I paused. Ani said nothing, was probably not even listening. A squad of five invaders ran into my yard, came up short, seeing me and Rookie, seeing the dead Gatesofts. One hand on the talkie, the other stroking Rookie's hair in my lap, the semi-auto back in its holster, I just looked at them through red eyes, as expressionlessly as I could manage. The tallest of them broke the awkwardness by cocking his head. As quickly as they'd arrived, the five of them had dived back into the battlefield. I pressed the talk button again. "I might have sent an angry email last week to Alicia Buckley, demanding that her family let Valerie be saved."

Ani's voice crackled back. "Zed was caught last month peddling narcotics to Family teenagers. Driver recently sold some Buckley info to the Doak family, and he's a Muslim. Sarge is gay."

"Sarge? Are you kidding me?"

"I called some night shift buddies inside the building, like the guy who got control of your drone, fed them your badge numbers. They turned up that intel pretty quick on your friends, but we actually couldn't find your offense against the Families. We understood their bullshit problems with the others, but couldn't figure out why they sent you out here with them, to get in harm's way. I guess we know now, although we still couldn't dig up your Rookie's crime."

I looked down. The kid's face had grown ashen. I silently told him to hang on.

"The Families don't even use money anymore, except as a score in their little ruling class competition. It also goes to motivate the ugly necessities like police, like Gatesoft's mid-management to drive stock value, and like the unseen agents who make necessities like food and Brooks Brothers suits and fucking toothpaste appear in their homes." She spoke with a politician's pentameter. "But those expenses are so trivial to them, they don't even notice. It's petty cash. And if they need some kind of surgery or to change homes or get a new car, they just sign their names and it's done. No money exchanged in any form. Hold on a sec."

I heard nothing on the talkie, but isolated, heavy-calibre shots rang out from somewhere in the garage.

Scaramouch, scaramouch.

"Sorry. Back now."

I clicked in. "That perfect socialist utopia ain't helping Val."

"It only works for the most classist, separatist Families, whose finances have transcended wealth," she went on. It sounded rehearsed. "For the rest of us, American dollars are just threads in the binding ropes. The pennies this place uses for cash are useless in Fort Dallas - - that's to keep us oppressed out here, on the border of the Thunderburbs."

I gave the kid a shake and his head lolled. He let out a deep breath.

"Listen, Ani. My new guy here is hurt bad. You have any medical people who can help him?"

"Help a cop?"

"He never been on a run before, this is his first time. And neither me nor any of my guys ever oppressed any Thinkers."

"No, you just come out here every few months to fuck our girls and push us around, buying our favor with junk metals and vague promises of 'rags to Dallas' for the luckiest," I heard Sarge's gravelly, angry voice in the background, but she ignored him.

"I'm Ashcor," the kid said. His voice and gaze were weak. "That's my offense against the Buckleys. My last name is Nero, but my mom is Ashcor blood." His eyelids slid shut again.

"We need medical out here, stat," I said again into the talkie.

Nothing.

"Who are you, Ani? We've never seen you out here before, never heard your name mentioned, yet you seem to be running things."

"I'm just a nice girl who grew up in the suburbs. Sneaked over with a rifle and scope and watched Gatesoft, trying to find someone indefensible on the staff. Spotted him quickly and started my climb up the corporate ladder. Who are you, piggy? All I bothered to get was badge numbers to feed my researchers. You were D-58622, I believe."

"My shield is all you need, then," I said.

"Well, just keep your shield out of my way when I bring revolution to Fort Dallas, at the head of a Thinker army a hundred thousand strong." I sat upright, squinting out through the chainlink. There was suddenly a flurry of lights in motion from beyond the sandlot's far wall. "They kept us distracted and subdued and compliant for decades with TV and video games and dogma, but those days are over. The Age of the Thinker is about to begin."

The graffitied bricks across the field crumbled like a felled dam, letting loose a torrent of headlights and ground troops. They surged with a roar into the tangled grasses.

"Ani- -!"

"Give me your location, D-58622. I'll get a doc to your rookie. Just keep out of the way of the cavalry. . . Looks like my friends from other local companies have just arrived. Ah, the power of community and social media."

"We're about to get trampled by your chat room friends! I've got the kid over by the chainlink fence, by the wooden desk ramshackle."

"Calm down, D. Just bring him inside that house; the entrance is through the aluminum drawers on the building side. Get into that shelter and wait for the storm to pass. Now if you'll excuse me, my colleagues and I have some disgruntled unemployed to capture and recruit, or failing that, to kill. Sarge is onboard, FYI. Don't call me back unless your medical need gets dire."

"I think it is already," I said, but her answer was static.

The onrushing lights and dogs of war in the sandlot were entirely too close now. I hooked Rookie's armpits again and slid around the desk-hovel to building-side. Bullets struck the wood and aluminum as I pulled at drawers, but I let them fly unheeded. One set of drawers finally ground loose, opening on a hinge rather than a track. The sound of the cavalry roared like a tide now, waves ready to break on the shore. It took some doing to shove the kid through the opening and dive in after him, but I managed it without getting shot.

I hit the floor of foam and carpeting hard. My head hit painfully into a two-drawer, cream-colored filing cabinet. A football-sized clock radio fell from atop the cabinet, its squared plastic edges biting hard into my forehead. A floor lamp then toppled to complete the trifecta. The radio was now playing "Lucky Man". I switched it off, rubbing my bruised temple.

The warfare intensity swelled outside, heightening in pitch and volume. Bullets drummed into our oak exterior, but the shelter held together. The Rookie's pulse was weak, his skin like clay. I slid up from his wrist and clutched his hand in mine. Another call to Ani went unanswered. An explosion rocked the structure from outside.

I tuned the walkie-talkie back to the frantic channel, listened to the voices within the chaos, even as it raged right outside of my desk walls. The Rookie gasped in his feverish daze, his eyelids shuttering wide open, then drifting closed again. I pulled him into my lap and shushed him, running a gently reassuring hand across his gauzed forehead.

"Hang in there, kid. Help is coming." I heard the distinctive, distant thumps of Ani's heavy rifle. "Just get through this. Don't die."

Afterword by Jack Mangan:

I had been toying for awhile with the idea of some bored, wealth-stained, elitist teenagers heading into a desperate American shanty to taunt the downcast residents for sport, only to have a savvy plebe turn the tables on them. The concept really began to take shape one day during a hike, when it occurred to me to change the spoiled bullies to police officers. Ironic that I found the solution for my suburban blight story while out amidst the gorgeous, serene Arizona wilderness. I'm thrilled that the story has found its way into 2020 Visions.

Jack Mangan is an author, podcaster, musician, father, etc., born in New Jersey, but now residing in Arizona. His Jack Mangan's Deadpan Podcast features over 200 episodes of interviews, commentary, comedy skits, original music, and a great deal of community-contributed content. Jack's 1 Podiobooks title, Speherical Tomi, was among the first wave of podcast novels. Jack has made countless guest appearances and performances on other podcast shows, and has had his work independently converted to audio format by a number of other New Media creators. His fiction and non-fiction writings have appeared in numerous online, print, and podcast venues, including such prestigious outlets as Interzone Magazine, Podthology: the Pod Complex anthology from Dragon Moon Press, Variant Frequencies, Amityville House of Pancakes from Creative Guy Publishing, the Beam Me Up Podcast and terrestrial radio show, and Tales of the Talisman. He seeks to shake up perceptions and provoke independent thinking, through music, comedy, writing, and his outspoken, sometimes controversial views.

http:www//jackmangan.com (home of Jack Mangan's Deadpan podcast)
Twitter @jackmangan
http://www.facebook.com/jackmangansdeadpan

In this story, David Boop gives us an allegory for events in the world. He builds a world that takes issues of today, turns them upside-down, then holds them up for all to see. It's a story that works on more than one level. It can be enjoyed superficially at face value, but it becomes richer as you dig deeper inside yourself.

David has held numerous jobs, including a stint as an audio engineer, a detail that shows up here. I've known him for several years, mainly through hallway discussions at conventions.

In addition to short fiction published in several anthologies, he has also seen one of his stage plays produced and a short screenplay filmed. His novel, She Murdered Me with Science, was released in 2008.—RN

Organ Cloning While You Wait
by David Boop

L iam Thermopolis fumed the moment he saw the icon of his mother, Norah, on the dashboard of his car.

"VOX: Record."

A green light appeared on the rear view mirror. He figured *she'd* be recording, so he'd better, as well. He combed his hair while speaking to VOX cam 1, as if it was another person in the car, [She's going to cancel. Why should I be surprised? She does this every time. She knows today is important, so she does this just to show who still holds the reins. God, I despise her.]

The twenty-year-old touched the icon and his mother's face appeared. Norah looked fabulous for her age, but that wasn't uncommon anymore. She left in just the right streak of grey into her ginger hair for a look that said demure and wise. All the better to bait the young men she fancied.

"Darling, I'm going to have to push back lunch until dinner. I'm so sorry, but I woke up with a touch of liver cancer this morning. I have an appointment at the clinic and you know how long that takes."

Liam muted the VOX on his end and spoke out loud, [I certainly do. It's *only* her third visit this year. First it was the skin graft, then last month a kidney, now her liver. Maybe if she stopped downing the Cosmos like lemonade…?]

Unmuted: "Mother, I can't believe you'd do this today of all days. What am I supposed to tell Tetra, huh? She'll think you hate her. Can't you do it tomorrow?"

"Liam, the wait list at the clinic is too long. I just happened to know someone inside who was willing to let me take a cancelled 11:00 appointment." She shook her mane and tried to get Obi-wan on him. "I've always told you that tipping extra pays you ten-fold at the end. If you take nothing else I've taught you, take that."

Leaning away from cam 1 to cam 2, Liam rolled his eyes. She was getting great footage here. No one had even picked up their show yet, but Norah kept him contractually obligated to record in case an iNetwork took notice. Well, if he had to play the game…

"Dammit, mother! This one is special. She's the one. I can't believe you'd throw away my chance at happiness for something sooo inconsequential as cancer!"

She was ready. "Oh, don't be overly dramatic, dear child. You know how busy the clinic gets in the fall. All those sun-worshipers demanding skin grafts or new breasts after letting them shrivel for three months. Because I've been a client in good standing, they were able to squeeze me in. It takes about three hours, but they assure me the liver will be ready for daiquiris by 7. And while I'm more than willing to meet this month's *So You Think You Can Marry My Son* reject, it'll just have to be during dinner. As long as the place serves alcohol and is noisy so I don't have to hear her ramble on about near call-backs, I'll be there."

Norah blew him a kiss and logged off. Liam hated to admit it, but she had a point. They *were* all the same. He hadn't found anyone of substance in L.A. If they weren't vacuous or plastic, they were dating directors… or women… or women directors. They certainly weren't dating audio engineers like him.

Not that he was bad looking. He had smooth contours, a smattering of freckles and copper hair a shade darker than his mother's, thanks to his father's dark Mediterranean roots.

Twenty-years ago, his parents had been contestants on a sealed house reality show. She was the "hot starlet," his dad the "bad boy." Producers pushed them into hooking up for ratings, and in the end, the bad boy won the contest. Only after the show had wrapped did his mom discover she was pregnant. She did the right thing by Liam, reneging on follow-up shows and birthing him. All she asked his father for was half of his winnings to be left in a trust fund to be given to Liam on his 21st birthday. Bitter to the end, the Greek rising star added the codicil that the monies would only be released if his son found true love, not just a reality show fling.

That birthday was coming up soon, and Liam had yet to find anything resembling 'true love.' A few 'true lusts' and a couple con-artists seeking a quick fortune had been paraded in front of his mother, but years on the studio lots as a wig maker had sharpened her nose to the point she could smell silicone souls a mile away.

"VOX: cancel 12 PM appointment and send e-mails to invited guests. Search: sports bars downtown Los Angeles. Tag: live music."

A list scrolled by and he selected one at random. It really didn't matter.

"VOX: send invites to mother and Tetra Ferrell."

No sooner had the requested beeped completion, Tetra's icon appeared.

[Well, that didn't take long.] "VOX: lower speaker volume to 3." After another beep, he touched the icon.

"SHE HATES ME!!!"

Pink and lavender hair drooped around her full face and black streaks ran from her eyes to imply she'd been crying. Whoever did Tetra's make-up was good. He'd have to find out their name and steal them away.

"No, pet. She treats all my girlfriends this way. If she hated you, she wouldn't have bothered to cancel ahead of time. She just wouldn't have shown up."

"I don't know how you stand it. She's got your balls in her Gucci purse, like the ones they sell at Macy's, now 20% off through Sunday."

Liam wasn't having *this* conversation on cam. "Listen, hon. VOX is signaling that I've almost reached my exit, just another twenty minutes. I've got some work to do before I get to the studio. Can I just see you at 7, then? You got the invite?"

"Yes, Sergio's on Rodeo Dr, where every Thursday night is trivia and 2-4-1s."

Tetra's famous lineage had netted her a mid-season series, so she was always streaming live. The damn product endorsements drove Liam bonkers. He'd been forced to say what brand of condoms they were using the other night before sex. He logged off and leaned the seat back.

"VOX: how long until we actually reach our exit?"

"One hour, thirty-five minutes, Liam."

Liam looked to the left and the right. He was boxed in, as was every car on the turnpike. He stopped recording and let VOX continue driving until the off-ramp. Since he was now going to be out much later than he'd planned on, Liam chose to take a nap.

"VOX: set alarm for fifteen minutes before next exit."

Work went agonizingly slow. As sound engineer for Rana Pictures, Liam's job was to match sound to images. This project finished filming a month ago and he was in the studio just to do fixes. That meant listening for the minutest variations in the audio tracks, from an airplane overhead to a mouse farting. If he couldn't take it out, the actors would have to come into the studio and re-record the dialog. He had two prima-donnas too many in his life as it was. He didn't want to deal with actors unless he had to.

Done. Liam looked at the time, added the minutes it'd take to go back to his apartment, shower, then meet Tetra and his mother and decided to use the washroom at the studio to spritz himself clean.

He took a deep breath before stepping back out into the California heat. Flinging open the door with resolve, Liam hit something hard. He peered around the metal frame to find a young lady lying unconscious on the ground.

"VOX: 911. Ambulance!" Liam called out and then knelt by the girl to check on her. She was filthy and dressed in rags. She had to be a street person, or an actress trying to get a role as a street person. He brushed a couple strands of her auburn hair away from her face and was amazed at how beautiful she was under all the dirt. She had a sanguine face, unfurrowed by worried, cosmetics and time.

A female voice inquired, "Nature of emergency?"

"A woman is unconscious outside my office." He left out any details of his involvement in her current state. The less said, the better.

"Are you sure she's alive?"

"I think so. Should I check for a pulse?"

"Is this woman known to you?"

"No."

"Then please step away from her as to not contaminate an investigation. An ambulance and police car have locked on to your position. Do not leave the immediate area, but do step back until they arrive."

The gravity of the situation hit him. He was going to be the one to cancel dinner this time. Not only that, he was going to make the 5:00 nightly news stream. Ten years ago, he could have just run and no one would be the wiser. Those days were gone, thanks to VOX. He'd just have to ride out the media frenzy. As long as she didn't die or wasn't famous, he'd be replaced with something more newsworthy by 10.

Tetra took the news in typical fashion. She swore at him, threw things around the room and eventually busted her VOX. It was a family trait. From the reports, her father had taken the news of her paternity the same way.

Liam's mom was more understanding. Norah continued on to the bar in order to give the new liver a shakedown cruise. She told him to not get involved unless it would make good b-roll.

How could he not? Liam wondered. There were cams on the patrol cars, the EMTs, even the rubberneckers. But even more than that, though he said nothing to that effect to anyone who questioned him, he felt responsible. At least, he was fairly sure he was responsible. His carelessness with the door had given her a good wonk on the noggin. He was going to make sure she was all right before returning to his life, already in progress.

They brought her around before putting her in the ambulance. She was incoherent and seemed to have no clue where she was, or even who she was. Liam breathed a sigh of relief when she admitted to having no idea who he was either. They were going to take the young lady to the hospital, do the standard check for rape, abuse, etc. Liam was asked to submit a DNA sample, which he did. He'd been fortunate not to touch her in any way, so he should come up clean.

"What's going to happen to her?" he asked an officer after they loaded her up.

"We don't know what or even *if* she's on anything, so we won't know more until she's been scanned at County. It appears like she was just wandering the alleyways looking for food. She's possibly homeless, but then again, she could be trying to get a part. She doesn't have a VOX, or even an I.D."

"I'd think that'd rule out actress. Why go to all the trouble if no one was going to see your audition stream?"

The officer shrugged. "Who knows? Method actress maybe. She also could have lost it, been mugged, or countless other reasons. If they can't put a wiki to the face, she'll end up at the psych ward."

Liam considered this. He felt a growing affinity to the woman, and hoped it didn't come to that. He spontaneously decided to follow the ambulance to the hospital. His VOX kept chirping in the waiting room, and tired of the other people looking at him, he muted the consistent stream of IMs from Tetra. His mom had sent him a viral of her and some MILF-hunter grinding on the dance floor at the sports bar. He was pretty sure that place didn't even have a dance floor. After about an hour he went to check on his Jane Doe.

The security was insanely tight. Too many celebrities ended up in the E.R. here and information was shielded from everyone, including family members. Anything the patient's family needed to know would be sent via VOX. It gave him an idea. Liam ran out to his car and plugged in the backup portable unit he kept in case his primary went on the blink. He erased the primary I.D. and installed a fake one using his memory of the mystery woman to build its icon. He put his own address and whipped her up a quick wiki, identifying her as his actress wife. Once he felt the unit would pass cursory inspection, he gave it to the intake clerk.

As VOX guided Liam home, he ruminated on his situation to the omnipresent confessional, [What I am doing? VOX tampering is a crime. OMG, I could really get hammered for this! But, she was so... And I was like so...] He giggled in an unmanly fashion, [Is this what they call 'love at first download'? I've never seen anyone like her. Damn, she's probably a bitch in reality. What am I opening myself up to? I just couldn't let her, you know, get put in a psyche ward. Mother's going to kill me if this ruins her chances for a come-back.] He sighed. [It's so hard to set yourself apart these days. Too many people all clamoring for their point 15 seconds of fame. It's all been done before.] Liam steeled himself. [No, it's the right thing to do. I bopped her in the head, I need to be a man and take responsibility.] He nodded firmly and considered what to do when she arrived at his condo.

At 11 P.M. there was a ding on his VOX. Someone was at the front door. After thanking the hospital staff profusely for bringing his wife home, he helped the dazed woman into his living room and carefully dropped her to the couch.

"You. You were the man they kept asking me about. You said you'd never met me before, but then they bring me to you. Were you lying?"

Liam reddened. He wasn't sure what to do now. How did he explain this to her?

"Well, um, you see… They told me they were going to stick you in a mental hospital if you didn't have an identity, and, well, I didn't want that to happen."

She tilted her head quizzically at him. They hadn't cleaned her up, so her face was still a mess of smudges and her hair was matted with leaves and assorted unidentifiables.

"Why?"

Swallowing, he continued, "Well, I guess… VOX: Mute all."

The VOX dinged and his guest looked around nervously. Liam sat down the couch opposite her and tried to reassure her. "That's just my VOX. It's okay."

She looked down to the portable unit in her hand. "That's what they called this. What is it?"

How did she not know what a VOX was?

"VOX stands for Voice Omnipresent Access. It's a digital communicator that connect its user to, well, everything. You can use it to make calls, text IM, GPS, surf the web, whatever."

She turned it over in her hands. It was black, save for a single, silver lens. "And this was yours?"

"Yes, it's my back-up."

She looked him up and down. "Then where's yours?"

Liam lifted back the hair around his right ear. A small black shell was attached to his flesh. Two lights blinked; one blue and one yellow.

"This is the receiver. If you're planning a reality show, then it pays to have one installed on your body so you can access any remote camera and record. There are still some casual users out there who only have portables, but with a thousand I-networks clamoring for the next big thing, most people have gone implant."

The blank look on her face was akin to a puppy being read the Bible.

Liam sighed. "You have no idea what I'm talking about. It's okay. It's kind of refreshing to find someone not tied into the industry."

The mystery woman's stomach growled and her cheeks flushed with embarrassment. Liam got up and headed for the kitchen.

"You must be starved. Why not clean up while I make something for us both to eat. I missed dinner, too."

He directed her down the hall to the bathroom and told her where the wardrobe closet was. She was hesitant.

"Why are you doing this for me, if you don't know me?"

Liam didn't have a good answer. He shrugged. "Because, I guess, it's been awhile since I did something nice for someone off camera. You know, just because it was the right thing to do." He could feel his cheeks redden again.

She scanned him top to bottom and looked as if she'd made up her mind about something. His mystery woman nodded and slipped off to the back of his condo to change.

Liam was about to call out to his guest and tell her that dinner was ready, when he realized she had no name. Luckily, she came out of the back just as he put the risotto on the table. He blinked not knowing what else to do, think or say. She was more beautiful than he could imagine. She'd picked a dress that seemed as much designed for her as it did his mother, who'd donated it to his collection. She twirled, laughing. He imagined little CGI birds flittering around her head, like she was some sort of fairy princess. Liam decided he wouldn't edit any more Pixar streams.

"I take it you approve?"

Liam nodded. "You're stunning."

She smiled warmly. "Thank you."

They dug into the rice dish. She wolfed down three helpings without much conversation. He wondered how long it'd been since she ate.

"What do I call you?" Liam asked.

"I-I don't know."

He could see her lack of memories bothered her greatly. "What *do* you remember?"

She pursed her lips, recalling what little she could, "I woke up in a homeless shelter. Everything was so strange. It was like I couldn't even talk, at first. Over time, words came back to me as the attendants nursed me back to health. They told me they'd found me naked in a dumpster, and that I'd been... I'd been abused."

They hung on that word for a few moments. Liam wanted to offer comfort, but didn't know where to begin. "I'm sorry."

She shook her head. "No need to be. Can't feel anything towards something I don't remember. I wasn't in pain. I wasn't anything. Just sort of blank. Over time, I learned everything over; how to brush my teeth, what foods I liked. By the way, this is fabulous. You're quite a cook."

"Norah—Mother—raised me on all organic food, which is good since the government preservative crackdown of 2015 was right around the corner anyway. Wish it'd come before the mass poisonings, but hindsight and all."

His guest continued eating, thankfully void of the memories of those years where everyone lived in fear of food and what the disastrous Kraft bailout had cost the country.

"We were already ahead of the curve, making everything from scratch. Which is funny, since she takes most of her nutrients in pill form these days in an effort to get down to iStream weight. The VOX adds 10 pounds, you know."

She giggled even though he was sure she didn't get the reference.

Liam continued his questioning, trying to find some sort of place to start finding the real her. "When did all this happen?"

"About a month ago."

He was shocked. "And no one ran a DNA check on your ID?"

His guest looked down, embarrassed. "The centers are stretched for funds. DNA searches through the government registry cost more than they have allotted, or so they told me."

"Hmm, maybe the hosp-" but then he realized, with the VOX he'd given them, they wouldn't need to run a search after all.

The unmuted VOX announced another arrival at his door. Liam checked the screen; Norah had arrived.

After escorting his half-soused mother into the living room, he unceremoniously dropped her to the couch. She exuded alcohol and her exposed cleavage sparkled with glitter. Ashamed, all Liam could say was, "Mother."

His guest joined him at his elbow, concern wrinkling her otherwise perfect face. "Is she okay?"

"Oh, she'll be fine. She drinks like she's still a reality star. I'll see the dailies of her debauchery in the morning."

To VOX he said, [I hope she remembered to turn on the pixilation this time. I still haven't burned the Mardi Gras episode from my mind.]

"She's beautiful." There was genuine admiration in his Jane Doe's voice.

Liam looked down at his mother, trying to remember what she looked like before the plastic surgeries and skin grafts. She was Hollywood beautiful, not like his guest, whose beauty came naturally; unaltered as far as he could tell. Liam thought back to childhood, how magical his mother seemed, always glowing in an ethereal way. How many times did he say he had the most beautiful mommy in the world? Why couldn't that have been enough for her?

"Yes, she is. Even though she's quite the PITA most days."

"A what?"

Liam whispered, "Pain In The Ass" in Jane's ear. She giggled mischievously.

Jane—they decided to use that name until they could unravel her real one—helped his mom get cleaned up. She got her into a shower and dressed her in clean clothes. In was nearly one in the morning by the time Norah sat down to the table, famished. Liam made her pancakes, her favorite hangover cure.

"Tetra," Norah began, "You look nothing like your icon."

"That's not Tetra, mother," Liam called from the kitchen, "This is Jane." [I'll get a lecture now, watch.]

"Jane," she tried the name out, "Jane. I like it. It's so not pretentious or celebrity-chic. I still choke on Senator Pilot Inspector every time it scrolls across VOX news."

Liam raised an eyebrow. This was a good start.

Addressing the young lady, Norah continued, "So, Jane. What type of show do you have?"

"I don't have a show, ma'am."

Norah guffawed, "Ma'am? HA! I like this one, Liam. She didn't call me mother or mom right off the bat like the tarts you *normally* bring home."

"Mother!" [Damn her.]

"Seriously, Jane," Norah took a drink of orange juice, "What do you do? No one comes to L.A. without some sort of goal."

Jane was crafty. "No, ma'am. I'm between jobs right now."

[And identities.]

"What was that, darling?"

"Nothing, Mother."

His mom took in his stray with discerning eyes, dissecting her and trying to make her fit somewhere in her mind. Her lips pursed as she cleared cobwebs from her mind - no small task by Liam's reckoning.

"You look familiar. I know I've seen you someplace."

"Really?" said Jane, hopefully.

"Really?" gulped Liam. In a soft voice: "VOX: pull up tonight's footage." He quickly scanned through to the accident, but there were no clear shots of Jane's face. Relieved, he shot back, "Well, Mother, you do watch a lot of webcasts. Maybe she just looks like someone you've seen."

"No, no. I've definitely seen you somewhere before. I'll come up with it in time. Meanwhile, let's get to know each other. How'd you meet my son?"

Liam called out before Jane could answer, "We just ran into each other at an event, isn't that right, Jane?"

"Yes, Liam is so charming he just knocked me off my feet."

If it was possible for his heart to pound faster, Liam's did. Jane fell right into the natural rhythm of conversation as they watched Norah eat. She gave his mother vague answers or waited for Liam to speak first. He was glad VOX was on; this would make awesome footage for their grandkids someday.

Norah stepped into the kitchen behind Liam as he rinsed off the dishes. Using unusual discretion, she gently whispered, "I like her, Liam. I'm ashamed to admit it, but this one I like. Don't you screw it up." To VOX, she said, "Now watch, he'll screw it up."

"Thanks for your unilateral support, Mother." They both turned to look at her as Jane strolled around Liam's condo looking at photos. "Yes, I like her, too. You're right that there's something familiar about her. The way she walks, the cadence of her voice. It feels like I've known her my whole life."

Norah's VOX rang. She turned to take the call in private.

Jane called out to him, some concern in her voice, "Liam? Liam, come here!"

He ran to her side. Jane held a digital frame, one he stored his family pictures in. She'd been scanning through it just before she yelled. She pushed it into his chest as he approached, her face awash in confusion and betrayal. "You lied to me!"

"Wuzzah?"

"There! On the frame! There are pictures of me! Lots of them!"

"I swear, I've never seen you before tonight!"

Jane grabbed the frame and turned it around and pointed it at his face. "Then how do you explain this!"

It was Jane. But it wasn't Jane.

His mother came out of the kitchen, angry. "Damn, hospital! They tried to bill me for an ER visit tonight, saying they have my DNA print to prove it. I tell you, Liam. That DNA registry is…" She faded off as she saw Jane and Liam staring at her.

"Wha?"

Liam stepped aside and held up the picture frame by Jane's face. In the picture was Norah, 20 years ago. It was an exact duplicate to the young lady staring slack-jawed back at her.

All three sat across from an agent of the U.S. Genetics Registry. Liam was going on thirty hours with no sleep. Add to that the scratches he'd received while pulling his mother free of her clone, and he was in poor shape. Norah flipped when she realized the reason she'd liked Jane so much was that she was looking into a mirror. Norah had changed her looks so much she'd forgotten how she appeared as a younger woman. The picture in the frame had brought everything into focus and Norah attempted to shred her own face off Jane.

"YOU BITCH! YOU STOLE MY FACE! GIVE IT BACK!"

Jane tried to escape, but Norah had gotten a grip on the dress.

"THAT is my dress! You have no right!"

And promptly ripped it off. It was like watching an episode of the Tyra Springer show, or one of those other media circuses from back in the Teens. Jane fled to the bedroom and Liam superimposed himself in front of his mom. Once his mother stopped fighting him, he managed to explain the events of the day. He brought up the footage, including his and Jane's dinner, and Norah calmed down substantially.

He could hear the sobbing from his guest room and went to the door to try to coax Jane out. After about an hour, they finally sat around the table again and talked options. The first was to go to the U.S.G.R. when it opened at 8.

God, the paperwork was annoying, but after slogging through it, giving DNA samples and the intake interview, they finally sat in front of someone who looked important.

"This isn't uncommon."

Norah was alarmed. "You mean there are more *me*s out there?"

"Mother, calm down. I don't think that's what he means."

"No," said the agent, "Well, at least not entirely."

They'd all surrendered their VOXes when they were admitted through security. Liam didn't see one anywhere evident, but then the government probably had more high tech ways to record. He wished he'd be able to play this explanation back later because he was sure it wasn't going to be good.

"You see, there is a demand for celebrity DNA on the black market. Employees at organ clinics or hospitals will sell samples of celebs, recent or past, for drug money or to buy Wii 3s."

"Those bastards!" Norah continued raging, but Liam looked past that to Jane who was trembling visibly. Here this authority figure was laying out Jane's entire existence and it was a sham. Liam took her hands in his.

"Some buyers freeze the material until the celeb dies, hoping to cash in. Others will grow a body part or organ in an overseas cloning lab and replace a piece of their own with it. Mary Hart's legs are still fetching a good price."

"Who?" asked Liam.

The agent was discouraged. "Never mind. Anyway, the sickest of deviants will clone a whole person for their own carnal pleasures. These dupes have no memory, no personality until it's imprinted on them. They are like newborns thrust into an adult world. It's worse than rape, more akin to child molestation."

They all heard the sob that escaped from Jane's lips. She pulled her hands free from Liam's and held her head as she openly wept. He put a gentle, comforting hand on her back.

Like her pain was of no relevance, the Fed continued, "What we have here is an escapee. Sometimes the clones will get up and stumble around, trying to understand what's going on with them. Once and awhile, a dupe will fall out a window, or walk out into traffic and we find the remains. Other times, the user will try to dispose of the body and fail, leaving us a trail to follow. We're not sure what happened with your mom's clone. It somehow got free and ended up in that dumpster. Sloppiness on the part of the user."

Norah took in the news, glancing occasionally at Jane. "So, some sick-o out there still has the hots for me?" She smiled briefly, but then went back to looking serious.

"Mother!"

"So what about Jane?" she asked, quickly changing tact.

191

DAVID BOOP

The agent was unemotional in his answer, "The dupe is not a real person. There cannot be, by law, two people of the same genetic identity living. I'm sorry, but it'll have to be destroyed."

"WHA?" cried Liam and Norah together. Jane wept louder.

"Jane is not an 'it'. That's me, or at least a me from about ten years ago."

"20 is more like it," whispered Liam.

"I may not like how she got here, but she's here and I won't see her harmed."

"I agree," added Liam, "She sought me out for a reason, even if she didn't know what it was. She wants to be alive. She *is* alive."

"I beg to differ," said the Fed as he shuffled papers, "She was created illegally. She has no I.D., no VOX, no past and according to the United States Government, no future. The termination is painless, just a simple injection and she goes to sleep. We'll hunt down the user that created her and make sure any other genetic material is destroyed. We'll also find where he, or she, got the DNA, and track the seller down, as well. This can all be over in a matter of hours."

Liam pushed back his chair and slammed his hands down on the table. "You can't do this! It's not right!"

Showing his first emotion, the agent asked, "Oh, yeah? Give me one good reason why I can't?"

Racking his brain for a solution, Liam wished he had a VOX present to look up legal advice. Then it hit him; he'd already created the answer!

The I-stream came up. It was already the largest log-on in network history. The brunette smiled at the camera and gave everyone her famous wink.

"Hi! I'm Suri and welcome to my show!" Clapping was fed into the sound track. After it died down, the sleepy-eyed vixen continued, "We've got a special show for you today, but before we get to today's guests, I want everyone to check their VOX-box for a special gift! A free membership to *DNA Date*, today's sponsor! Why trust your destiny to the stars when love is in your genes!"

A logo popped in the corner for viewers to click on. Suri reappeared in cam 2.

"Our guests today have been making quite a few headlines, and even appeared before a senate hearing on clone rights. Let's welcome Mr. and Mrs. Thermopolis!"

Liam and Jane popped up into another window adjacent to Suri's. They looked happy as they sat on the couch together, hands intertwined.

"First, let me thank you for joining my stream so soon after your interplanetary honeymoon. Was it as great as they say?"

The logo for *Out Of This World Travel* popped in below them.

Jane started, "You can't believe it, Suri. We had this big window over our bed and there's nothing like making love while looking up at Mars's surface."

Liam added, "I had to beg her to take top so I could see it once in awhile."

Canned laughter exploded from nowhere.

"I can't wait to watch the outtakes, but what we all really want to know is… Is it true? Jane is your mother's clone?"

Unashamedly, Liam nodded. "What we like to think of her as is a Duplicate American. While not born of a womb, she should be afforded all the rights as the American she was modeled after."

"I'm not just a copy, Suri. I'm 100 percent me."

The DAA logo, Duplicate American Association, replaced the spaceliner's along with a special on t-shirts that read, "I'm 100% Me!"

Suri raised an enticing eyebrow. "But Liam… c'mon, boyo! This is your mother's duplicate. Can we say Oedipus here?"

A link to the wiki for Sophocles scrolled across the bottom of viewers' VOXes.

"I fell in love with Jane the moment I met her and couldn't lose her, no matter what. It didn't matter where she'd come from. All I knew was she was in danger and I'd risk anything for her."

Jane put on her angry face. "They were going to put me down, Suri. Just like a stray dog. The agent even described it in the same terms."

Recorded "Ohhs" filtered in next.

"Well, we'll have that agent on in a bit, as well as Reverend Baldwin of the *One Soul Church* to talk about their stance against cloning."

"Oh, we've met the good Pastor," said Liam with a knowing glance at his wife.

"He said I have a demon inside me. A demon! Suri, you've seen our show. Is there anything about me that says demon to you?"

"Just the way you cook, girlfriend." They all laughed with the track. "A skill, I understand, you picked up from Norah Thermopolis. How are you two getting along?"

"She's been like a mom to me. I guess that's because she is!"

There was more laughter before Liam leaned forward, "I know this seems unconventional, Suri, and I guess it is. But to us, it seems as natural as Adam and Eve. We're breaking new ground for duplicates everywhere. They can't help how they were brought into the world, but with the right love and attention, they can help make the world a better place. I know I'm a better man for having Jane in my life."

Suri winked. "And richer!"

Jane and Liam leaned back smiling. "Well, yes. You'd be surprised how much you can change the world with a couple hundred million…"

"And love." Jane, pure adoration in her eyes, leaned over to kiss her husband.

The Awws lasted until the commercial break.

Denver-based author David Boop is an author, editor, and screenwriter, as well as, single dad, returning college student and full-time employee. He's done jobs as diverse as DJ, journalist and Beetlejuice impersonator. His first novel, the sci-fi noir She Murdered Me with Science, debuted in 2008. He's had stories appear in several magazines, anthologies and e-zines. To find out more, check out www.davidboop.com.

I originally wanted most of the fiction in this collection to be around five thousand words. When I invited Spencer Ellsworth to take part in this project, he said he had nothing that short that fit the guidelines. Reluctantly, I told him I would take a look at his sixteen-thousand-word novelette. And, upon reading it, I had to use the story.

Spencer looks at the human mind, and the problem of depression. He keeps it personal, with deeply flawed but also very likable characters.

I met Spencer in 2005 at Orson Scott Card's Literary Boot Camp, and we have kept in touch through the Codex online writers group. The story takes up some page count, but easily it carries its weight.—RN

The Black Plague of Our Generation
by Spencer Ellsworth

There was a serotonin detector at the airport. Brad groaned. *I should have known I couldn't avoid this forever.* He looked around him in desperation, as if there were some other way to the plane, but, of course, everyone else was following the line. Brad squared up his shoulders and tried to think happy thoughts.

It didn't work. When Brad passed through the serotonin detector, it beeped bright red.

"Can you come over here, sir?" one of the officers asked.

Brad took two weary steps. "I've got no time. My plane leaves in half an hour."

The officer smiled a big, wide, understanding smile. "This only takes a moment, and I promise it'll be worth your time." He led Brad into a side room, where he paced restlessly. Before she left him, Melinda had said that he was always in a hurry. Brad had replied that it was better to purposely be annoying about being on time than be annoying by default because you were late. Comments like that had once made Melinda laugh and joke about how grumpy he was. Once.

The door opened and the psychiatrist entered, a fat man in a

195

cardigan sweater with a big grin and a white beard. "Hey!" he said cheerily.

Brad didn't respond. He immediately noticed the intravenous Seropax dispenser hooked to the man's belt, just like a diabetic's, though filled with a different sort of happy juice.

"We've radioed the plane, Mr. Boron, and they'll wait as long as they need to," the psychiatrist said. "Your health is worth it."

"Great."

"I understand there may be a problem with..." He paused a moment, as if to prepare Brad for the demons to be named. "...depression and anxiety."

This guy must not have heard of him. Brad scanned the man further, his PI instincts taking precedence. The shrink had a calloused finger from writing so many prescriptions and smile lines carved deep into his jowls.

"Mr. Boron?"

"I'm listening."

"I'm guessing your prescription ran out and you haven't had time to refill it. So many errands and so little time, eh?"

"No, I don't have a prescription."

"Well then, it's a good thing I found you today." The shrink turned to his clipboard with a smile. "If I can just get your social security number, I'll write you a prescription that should be covered. Are you employed, Mr. Boron?"

Brad spoke quietly. "I don't want a prescription."

The shrink looked up from his clipboard, still smiling. "The pills are just for the plane, Mr. Boron. They're fast-acting and safe: Seropax Ultra. But if you'd like, I could write you up for one of these." He tapped his IVD. "It requires a co-payment."

"No," Brad said. "No pills, no little dispenser, no nothing."

The shrink looked befuddled. "You are depressed, Mr. Boron."

"In the old days, we just called it cranky."

"Well, now you don't have to be cranky."

Brad smiled his best sarcastic smile. "I love being cranky."

The shrink looked back down at his clipboard. "I'm going to recommend you for counseling, Mr. Boron."

"I don't need counseling."

"These readings say you do."

"I feel just fine. The only thing that could make me feel better would be if I were on my plane."

The shrink adopted an uncharacteristic serious expression.

"Your serotonin levels are too low. Depression is the Black Plague of our generation, Mr. Boron. It will kill you if you ignore it."

"Pills will kill me," Brad said, and before the other man could add anything, "and so will IVDs. I like myself the way I am."

The shrink opened his mouth as if to say something, then closed it. "You realize you will be searched and kept under watch on the plane, Mr. Boron."

"I know," Brad said. "That's fine."

The shrink started to open the door, then turned back to him. "Do you really want to live like this, Brad?"

Brad brushed past him, out the door.

Brad was back in his office in Everett, Washington, with the windows pulled tight and the lights low. He leaned back and closed his eyes, drowsy from the warmth.

Something flashed in his head at the edge of sleep—and then again, slamming into his thoughts, flash after flash. Brad could see his own hands, holding what must have been twenty prescription-strength painkillers. He heard his father shouting. He saw Melinda from the corner of his eyes as he vomited the pills back into the toilet.

Brad opened his eyes, gasping. He put his hand to his chest, sucking in air like a smoker. "Hell, hell, shit, hell," he muttered as he got up and nearly fell, legs shaking. He had just gotten to the coffee pot when the phone rang. "Boron?"

"Nichols," Brad said. "What can I do for you, officer?"

"Are you kidding?" Nichols laughed.

"No laughter, Nichols, please. Not today."

"No, I mean, haven't you seen the news?"

"No." He'd been on the phone to Melinda much of the night, determining the visiting schedule for Eli. Eli was seventeen and not ready to be cut loose from Brad, though the boy disagreed. Brad turned on the news. The first words that registered were "Seropax" and "murder."

"What's going on?" Brad asked Nichols.

"You really don't know?"

"Cut the shit and tell me, willya?"

"Nick Navarro is dead."

Nick Navarro. Happiest Man Alive. Inventor and owner of Seropax. "How?"

"He appears to have been poisoned."

"By what?"

"An excess of Seropax."

"That's ridiculous," Brad said. "Seropax is self-regulating. Any excess in your blood will automatically go into your waste. You can't overdose on it."

"I know," Nichols said, "but there's nothing else. They already did an autopsy."

"How did it happen?"

"He was eating dinner with his daughter. He felt sick and lay down. Two hours later she found him dead."

"So you called me."

"We're sending someone from our own forensic team to work with you, but, yeah, you're the principal investigator in this case."

"What the hell? Why would you call me for the story of the year?"

"Well," Nichols said, "the family is worried about a conflict of interest."

"What?"

"Everyone else is on Seropax."

"Figures." Brad felt a sour taste in his mouth. "What about the FBI?" A few years ago Brad had been hired during a messy celebrity stalker case. It shouldn't have gained any attention, but when defense tried to discredit Brad's testimony by explaining how the woman was the victim of an irregularity in her Seropax dosage, Brad couldn't help himself. He'd been misquoted in a thousand newspapers, but what he actually said—"Your shit drugs don't cure crazy"—was bad enough. Ever since then, he'd been the subject of an uncomfortable interest by several law enforcement agencies.

"The media will stay away. The Navarros want it quiet. I'm sending our girl over right now. Try to be nice."

As soon as Brad hung up, the phone rang again. "Brad?" a female voice said.

"Melinda?" After an entire night spent on the phone with her, his ex was calling again?

"Thank God you're in your office."

"What is it now?"

"I have to send Eli to you."

"Now?"

"Now."

"Now won't work. I just got a big case."

"He's in trouble, Brad."

"What trouble is he in that I didn't know about last night?"

"He got busted this morning with heroin."

"Heroin?" Brad jumped out of his chair. "You leave me and two months later our son's a junkie?"

"Brad, don't do this. I can't take your blaming right now."

"Well it sure as hell ain't my fault!"

"That's debatable, Brad. You screamed at the boy so much that he begged me to leave."

"Oh, right, and now you brought him to a wonderful new school and a new home where he's shooting up."

"God, Brad, don't you think I feel awful enough already?"

"You really think I want you to feel better?" He said it with all the bitterness he could muster, which after she had walked out, was a lot.

She sighed. "I can't afford the ankle bracelet for house arrest, even though the judge pushed for it—" Her voice trembled, "—and I figure you're obsessive enough and work from home enough to make sure he's always all right. The judge and the cops strongly suggested that he stay in the house, barring a fire."

"Yeah, well, you might want to just shell out the bracelet money. I just got the Nick Navarro case."

"The Seropax guy? What about him?"

"He's dead."

"What? When?"

"As of last night, while we were on the phone." Almost managing to have a civil conversation, though that was blown now.

"How'd he die?" Melinda's voice assumed her own investigative tone. She had taken a helpful interest in Brad's cases for the twenty-two years they had been married.

"They've got nothing. Only thing in his blood is Seropax."

"That won't do it. Seropax is self-regulating."

"I didn't know you knew that."

"The doctor told me."

"Melinda... don't tell me you're on that shit now."

"It's been a long time since I felt loved or happy," Melinda said.

This was one of those moments, Brad remembered, when he was supposed to tell her that she was loved. After all, she was beautiful, fiercely intelligent, friendly and generous. She was a worthy match for anyone who thought they were smarter than her, especially Brad when they first met. But in twenty-two years, he had never gotten the hang of consoling her. And now it was too late, and he was too angry. "That's what happens when you walk."

"Don't."

"You didn't put Eli on it, did you?" She was silent. "Did you?"

She paused. "The doctor said it wouldn't cause any problems, even with drugs in his system."

"Are there other drugs in his system?"

"Just marijuana right now. He didn't take the heroin, and he says he's never taken it, but he won't say where it came from. He won't tell me anything."

"He needs to get off Seropax," Brad said.

"You're welcome to bring it up with him."

Before Brad could reply, someone knocked on his door. He leaned over and yelled, "Come in!" A tall woman, lean and plain, walked in wearing a police uniform. "The officer for the case is here. I've got to go."

"I already booked Eli's flight," Melinda said.

"What?"

"Be at the airport at ten, for Delta 419."

"You—" Brad looked up at the policewoman, "—should have told me before you booked the flight."

"You would have said no," Melinda said.

"Yeah, well..." Brad couldn't say what he wanted to, not in front of the policewoman.

"He's your son," Melinda said, and the phone clicked.

Brad put the phone back down on the table, resisting the urge to throw it. He looked up at the woman.

"How's your ex?" she asked, and smiled.

"Did you read my file or are you just observant?"

"Observant," she said, "though I did read your file. It claims you're still married. We should update it."

"How do you know I'm not?" Brad said.

"No ring," the woman said.

"How do you know my fingers aren't too fat for it?"

She smiled again. "I'm not a PI. I just guessed. Can I have a seat?"

"Help yourself," Brad said. "You're the only one brave enough to study the smiley juice, is that it?"

"I'm allergic to Seropax," she said.

"Lucky you,' Brad said. The woman sat down. "Are you wearing that uniform to impress me?"

"Actually, I am," the woman said. "I've been working in

forensics for three years and never get to wear the thing."

"You got a name?"

"Trudie."

"That short for Gertrude?"

"As usual."

"Exactly how much does a parent have to hate their child to give them that name?" Brad asked.

"About as much as my parents hated me, I guess."

"Yeah, well, you'll get no sympathy from me," Brad said.

"At least they named you Brad."

"When I was getting married, my dad told Melinda to get out while she could," Brad said. "Said I was a heartless cold bastard who would probably cheat on her the first chance I got."

"Did he pull her aside or was this..."

"Right in front of me."

"Wow."

"He was," Brad said, "an old, bitter, shit-talking—" A voice cut through the conversation, a shout that rang in his head. Brad swallowed, and shut his eyes. Damn flashbacks.

Trudie was looking at him oddly. "Are you okay?"

Brad ignored her. "What did you find out at the autopsy?"

"Here's the results, for whatever that's worth." She handed several printouts over to Brad. He began skimming.

"An apparent inhibition of cytochrome oxidase... this looks just like cyanide poisoning."

"Yes," she said. "Unfortunately, if you go further down, you'll find that there were no other chemicals found in the system."

"Anything from the witnesses? His daughter?"

"She's a little broken up at the moment. We might be able to talk to her tomorrow."

"What did her statement say?"

"Nothing Nichols hasn't told you. They were eating. Navarro felt sick, his daughter checked on him two hours later and he was dead."

"Why two hours?"

"She watched a movie. He said to wake him up before she went to bed."

"He have custody?"

"Shared."

"Well that's a bitch." Brad said. He noticed Trudie looking at him. "What?"

"Do you know they call you 'Grouchy' down at the station?"

"I've heard something about it," Brad said.

"I think it's an understatement." Trudie laughed, leaning back in her chair. "This is going to be fun." The smile made her look a lot prettier.

"I want an analysis of the Seropax he was taking before he died. Think you can get that before tomorrow night?"

"Yes."

"I also want an appointment with the daughter." Brad put the file down. "And I want access to the private files of the chemists at Seropax."

"How soon do you need these things?"

"Day before yesterday."

She laughed again. "Grouchy, I have an appointment tonight. You'll have to manage the last one."

"I don't have police clearance yet, and I want to keep a low profile, if you know what I mean." When she didn't say anything, he said, "I want the media to stay far away."

"Oh, that's right," she said "you did that—"

Brad held a hand up. She stopped. "What's this appointment anyway?"

"My husband. Our date night."

Brad groaned and leaned back. "Tell you what. You talk to the guys at Seropax and I'll go down to the station to get the analysis of what he was taking. And if you could break off your snuggle time long enough to call the young miss Navarro, I will appreciate it."

"Got it, Grouchy."

Brad had just enough time before picking up Eli to find out that the compound in Nick Navarro's blood was just regular standard Seropax Ultra. The man at the police lab, who had apparently heard of Brad, showed him the chemical composition of the drug, after Brad had walked through the station's own serotonin detector, set it off, and been searched.

"Let me give you a little tour of Seropax, particularly the Seropax in Nick Navarro's blood when he died," the technician said. He pointed to a microscope readout. "This is the enzyme that has always been part of SSRIs, he said, "ever since the days of Prozac."

"SSRIs," Brad said. "I don't know what that means, so don't

assume I do."

"Sorry, Mr. Boron," the tech said, and smiled hesitantly. "Selective Serotonin Reuptake Inhibitor. It's the major component of antidepressants since the early nineties. A brain cell fires serotonin from one brain cell to another. In depressed people, either the first cell doesn't fire enough serotonin, or the original cell reabsorbs too much serotonin. An SSRI blocks the reuptake of serotonin by the original cell, so the other cell has no choice but to accept a higher amount of serotonin."

"And that's how Seropax works?" Brad asked. He knew some of this, but hadn't heard it in a while.

"That's how every SSRI works. Seropax has overcome the variables in the process because the nanodes in the drug actually attach to the serotonin senders and receptors and monitor the reuptake and absorption rates. That way your body is kept on a steady rate of serotonin, and the nanodes allow for small drops and rises in serotonin levels that could indicate good or bad days, but watch for the large drops that indicate major depression."

"Nanodes. Those are the 'wonder cure.' What they used on cancer?"

"Right. The cure for everything." He beamed. Brad wondered whether this guy's face hurt from smiling so much. "They're designer cells—can you imagine how amazing that would seem, just a few years ago—that can attack the diseases of depression, anxiety, obsessive-compulsive disorder, and post-traumatic stress disorder while managing to blend into your immune system. They can stay in your system until the job is done. The only problem is that they die quickly and must be replaced. And they don't reproduce, so there is no way to simply quit Seropax without losing both the benefits of the nanodes and the SSRI itself."

"Like you actually want to get people off your product," Brad said.

The technician looked at him almost as if he were afraid of Brad. "Uh... Seropax has done a lot of good for a lot of people."

It wasn't worth it, going after this guy. "What about all that stuff I heard a few years ago when Seropax Ultra came out, about new nanodes?"

"Oh," the lab tech said, "The new nanodes are the reason why Seropax Ultra is even more amazing than the original Seropax. There were less side effects with the original Seropax than any other SSRI already, because it's self-regulating, but with Seropax

Ultra there is a whole new strain of nanodes that monitor the metabolism in your cells for changes. In depressed people, steady serotonin levels tend to cause some odd side effects. The one we get the most complaints about is weight gain, though sexual dysfunction runs a close second. So the new nanodes observe the metabolism of the cells and interact with different enzymes to keep it regulated—much the way your immune system regulates—"

"I get it, for God's sake," Brad said. "Two kinds of nanodes in Seropax. The original nanodes monitor serotonin levels. The new nanodes monitor cell metabolism."

"Yes," the tech said. "You might want to try Seropax yourself…"

"I'm not a grinning idiot. In the same place where cyanide poisoning acts, the new nanodes monitor metabolism."

The technician licked his lips. "You're saying the new nanodes did it?"

"Some kind of freak accident," Brad said, "in the process of observation."

"That can't work, the lab tech said. "It takes thousands of nanodes to adjust metabolism to cope with increased serotonin levels," the lab tech said. "Some might prove faulty, but thousands at once? And then consider that the nanodes die every three hours and have to be replaced."

"It only took two hours," Brad said. "Thanks for the sample."

He left convinced that it had something to do with the nanodes, and that he needed new evidence. Brad was satisfied. He was even satisfied enough that he didn't get angry in traffic, with every car nicely plodding along at the new speed limit of forty-five miles an hour on the freeway into Seattle, with the other drivers smiling and waving whenever he put his turn signal on. In front of the airport, a giant billboard loomed with a diverse group of black, white, Asian and Hispanic kids behind President Darrington. The billboard read: *Republocrats: The One Party Future Is Here. We can all get along at republocrats.org.*

We can all get along. It reminded Brad of where he was going, and his good mood soured. Brad's relationship with Eli had never been anything but difficult. No matter what blame he shoved over onto Melinda, his son had looked Brad in the eye before he left and said, "I hope I never see you again, Dad."

He's probably calmed down, Brad thought. *Hell, maybe he actually feels sorry. He was just busted. Maybe he's rethinking his life.*

Maybe I can give birth to an elephant if I try.

Brad went into the baggage claim and waited under therapeutic sun-lights by a giant generic landscape painting, watching everyone who passed through the baggage claim smile and embrace each other. He saw a young couple locked in a passionate kiss and felt the urge to throw something at them. A little girl grinned at Brad, showing off the flat features and thin eyes of Down's Syndrome, and held her arms out as if for her own hug. Brad shook his head and she frowned.

And then an enormous man came running through the baggage claim, practically shouting. "Mister Boron—Mister Boron—"

Brad jumped up. "Hello?'

"Mister Boron?" The big man looked over at Brad. He had a thin film of sweat on his dark skin, glowing under the gentle lights. "Eli's gone. I don't know where he—"

"Shit," Brad said, and jumped up, running through the crowd. The idiot kid—didn't he know the kind of trouble he would get into for this—

Wait a minute.

Brad turned around. The Down's girl was hugging an indistinguishable figure in a leather jacket and a beanie. Brad bolted just as the figure in the jacket bolted, too, revealing wiry calves below the edge of his shorts. Brad was just fast enough to grab the leather-clad arm and yank the wiry figure off his feet, slamming him to the ground. He heard gasps all around him.

"Let go or I swear I'll—" Eli began, through his clenched teeth.

"Shut up," Brad said, and tightened his grip. "Just shut up." He looked behind him and saw an unattended piece of luggage open against a chair. "Put the clothes back, before I take you straight to juvey."

Eli stood up and stripped off the leather jacket. Everyone was staring at them. The big man—who Brad presumed Melinda had hired as Eli's escort—came up behind them as Eli handed the clothes to Brad. "I'm so sorry, Mister Boron."

Brad took the beanie and jacket and laid them on top of the open luggage Eli had plundered. Down the hall, airport security jogged for them. He looked back at Eli. "Can you hold him? I'm going to call the cops."

"The airport security—"

"Just let me do this," Brad said.

Brad shook his head and turned away. The last thing they

needed was another police report, and more attention on Brad, and maybe a reporter, and maybe the person whose baggage was plundered insisting that the cops take Eli. Brad tried to picture the conversation with Melinda when he told her that he had paid more bail, and he was going to juvey...

He punched Trudie's number into his phone.

It was almost eleven, and that snuggle time he had joked about was probably in full swing. Nevertheless, she answered cheerily. "Hello?"

"Trudie?"

"Grouchy?"

"I need your help. You and your uniform."

"I'm busy right now, remember?"

"I know... Look... I didn't realize it, but... I need a police officer here. To help me pick up my son."

A moment of silence. "You need a police officer to pick up your son?"

It was now Brad's turn for a moment of silence. "Yeah. Don't ask."

"Which terminal?"

"One. Delta."

"Luckily, we're in town and I still have my uniform in my car. I'll be there as soon as I can."

Brad turned around. Everyone was staring like a cow with cud.

"What are you waiting for, popcorn?" Brad said, loudly.

That really didn't send too many people running, and even the airport security gave him a funny look when he said, "I called the cops. Can't you go take someone's nail clippers or something?"

"We need to file a report," the airport security guy said with a confused smile. "He committed a crime."

"We have police on-site," another airport security woman said, smiling a huge white smiled under purple lipstick. "We don't take nail clippers anymore, sir. I don't know if you heard—"

"Shut up," Brad muttered, but not loud enough that it stopped her.

Luckily, Trudie was quick, and she showed up just as they were questioning the man whose luggage he had pilfered, a chubby guy with white dredlocks in a Hawaiian shirt who kept saying, "Hey, if he really likes the clothes he can have them. Can't hold onto possessions."

"Officer Gertrude Scott," she said. "Come on, Eli, let's go." To the airport security, she said, "I'll take it from here," in a TV-cop tone that sounded like she had been practicing.

After she took the information they had, and a statement from Hawaiian shirt, who said, "This kid's got a good heart, I know it..."

Trudie turned to Brad as they were leaving. "Don't tell me I have to beat a 'thanks' out of you."

"Thank you very much," Brad said, trying his best to imbue it with sincerity he didn't feel.

They walked out to the curb, where a bunch of cars waited patiently, stuffed in against each other. "So should I ride home with you?" Trudie asked. "My husband just dropped me off. He's circling the area. Eli, you going to run again?"

Eli glared.

"I'm going to take that as a yes," Trudie said. "At least you gave me an excuse for the uniform." She tapped her phone three times, then said, "Hon? Yeah, I've got to ride with him. You want to follow? Call me if you get lost. What? Oh come on, when do you *not* get lost?" She hung up the phone. "He's a little absent-minded."

Brad didn't look at Eli as they got in. Damn kid. Eli had always been hardheaded and smart. Melinda said that the only thing that kept the boy from getting As was how much he mouthed off to his teachers. It was true. At one point, Brad had been called in to school because Eli had shouted at the teacher when she told him he was wrong about the structure of neutron stars. It turned out Eli was right.

Since Eli discovered drugs, there had been a lot less talk about neutron stars.

When they drove past Trudie's car, Brad was surprised by Trudie's husband. He was a chubby man, white-bearded, who looked about ten years older than her. He looked familiar, too. "What's you husband's name?"

"John Scott."

It clicked in Brad's brain. "No, it's John Raphael Scott." He saw Eli perk up in the backseat. "I am a PI. Can't forget anyone's face."

"So you've heard of him. Did you read *Sunstorm?*"

"No, I don't read science fiction. It's crap. Eli loves it. I think your hubby was his favorite."

"Really?" Trudie asked Eli? "You're a fan?"

Eli's hard expression softened a bit. "He's all right."

"Why does the wife of the guy who wrote *Sunstorm* need to work forensics at the police station?" Brad asked.

"I don't really need to," she said. "I like it. We've been married three years and I had the job before. Besides, it gives him time to write. It's a funny story how we met, actu—"

"I'm sure it is," Brad said. "He come out with anything good lately?"

"A fantasy series."

"Yeah, I didn't like that," Eli said from the backseat. "So many different people, from different places, and you have to hear about every one. *Lord of the Rings* was good, but that one was..." He shut up, as if he had just realized how much he was interacting with them.

"What about it?"

"Too damn long."

"I told him so," Trudie said. "A lot of his fans didn't like it either. He'll be glad to hear your opinions."

"Nah." Eli went quiet again.

"So you want to hear about the Seropax?" Brad said.

"Shoot," Trudie said.

"He was just taking standard Seropax Ultra. But there's a link. The nanodes that monitor cell metabolism are in a position to inhibit critical enzymes in the cells, the same way cyanide does. They supposedly can't do it since too many of them would have to screw up at once."

"What do you think?"

"Are there any incidents, in the history of nanodes and medical treatment, of an entire group screwing up?"

"I don't know," Trudie said.

"Well, get online and find out." Brad pointed to her phone.

"Give me a minute," Trudie said, "until we get out. I can find out then much faster."

"Do it now, damn it," Brad said.

"You are such a bastard," Trudie said, laughing.

"Yes he is," Eli said from the backseat.

"Don't talk," Brad said to Eli. "Just don't."

"I was waiting because I can just ask my husband this kind of thing," Trudie continued. "He knows more about science history than I ever will. It's his hobby."

"Right," Brad said. "Let's get the expert opinion of a sci-fi writer. He can explain the relevance of the Asimov thesis, or the Bradbury doctrine."

"Again, you're a bastard," Trudie said.

"Amen!" Eli shouted.

Brad would have whirled around and shouted if he wasn't driving. "You don't talk unless I give you permission," he said, sharp as if he were driving off an angry dog.

They left the freeway and pulled up to Brad's office in downtown Everett. Trudie's husband stopped behind them, stepped out on the curb, and smiled. Great. Another smiler.

"You got a fan here, hon," Trudie said as Eli stepped out.

"Really?" Trudie's husband said. "You people are growing fewer and far between lately."

"I didn't like Gaur World," Eli said.

"I don't think anyone did," John Raphael Scott said, deflated.

"John," Trudie asked as they went up the stairs, "have there been any incidents in the history of nanodes when they turned on the host?"

"Oh jeez," John said, and furrowed his brow. "None that I know."

"Is it possible?"

"Maybe. You know what nanodes were first used to treat, right?"

"Cancer," Brad said.

"The worst killer of the twentieth century, nearly defeated by 2018, leaving our beloved scientists to focus on other plagues, like depression." John scratched his beard. "Do you know why nanodes in Seropax don't reproduce? They can. It would make the treatment a lot easier. You'd only have to take the pill once."

"Why?" Brad asked as he opened the door to his office.

"Let me start at the beginning—" John said, sitting on the couch.

Trudie interrupted. "You guys should know that he went one hundred thousand words over on his last novel." When John glared at her again, she said, "Just warning you."

He rolled his eyes. "In short, then: nanodes should be a reproducing, self-perpetuating treatment, but they're not. They're not anything like what they could be. In the oughties, nanodes began as what were called polymersomes, because they're encased in a synthetic polymer to help hide them from the immune system. They were originally used just to deliver one kind of medication and then flush out of your system. When the scientists of the world figured out how to make them 'smart,' so they could observe and react like a T cell, everything changed. At first all sorts of weird things happened, like they would go on trying to kill cancer after cancer was dead, and then..." He saw Brad glaring at him. "I'll tell you later.

"Of course, the natural question was whether or not nanodes could be made that would reproduce. Self-perpetuating medication. Take a pill once, be good for life. The problem was in trying to get them to keep the polymers—the researchers at what became SeropaxCo had to replace them with a kind of organic protection to keep them from the immune system."

"And it didn't work," Eli said.

"Yep. Oh, the organic shields—call them the 'organic polymers'—held up for a little while, but not long enough for the nanodes to do their job. It's crazy. One big advantage of 'smart cells' was that people wouldn't need to keep taking pills, but everyone has given up on self-perpetuation and stuck to the good old polymers, so now you have to take Seropax every three hours. Five years since they abandoned that line of research."

"Like any company would make a product you didn't have to keep buying," Eli said. It was so close to what Brad had already said he almost laughed.

"Could be true," John said. "There are a lot of conspiracy theorists out there saying the same thing."

"Anyone with a *brain* is saying the same thing," Eli said.

"Well, three hours is long enough," Brad said. "Nick Navarro died two hours after he first felt the symptoms."

"You know what I think?" John asked.

Brad stopped himself from saying *I don't care,* when Trudie raised an eyebrow at him.

"What?" Eli asked.

"I think the nanodes evolved sentient intelligence and are destroying their creators," John said. "Call it the Scott hypothesis."

"Why would they want to kill their creators when they would die too?" Brad asked. "And how the hell are they supposed to evolve when they can't reproduce?"

John Raphael Scott said, "I just write books."

While John and Trudie sat and talked with Eli, Brad went into his office to call Melinda. She picked up immediately and asked, "Is he safe?"

"Yes," Brad said. *Tried to run already,* he almost said, but he stopped himself. Melinda had enough of a day already.

"How is he?"

"He's angry at me," Brad said, "but he gets along fine with the cop."

"Is he actually talking?"

"To her."

"That's good. He wouldn't say anything to me after I told him I was sending him to stay with you."

"What did he tell you before that?"

"That he was sorry, that he didn't know, that he was holding it for a friend, that it was 'safe smack' anyway, so it didn't matter... a lot of things."

"Safe smack," Brad said.

"Yeah, some new variant. It's supposed to be self-regulating like—well, like Seropax."

Self-regulating heroin. Those nanodes were everywhere. "How much of it did he have?"

"I don't remember. Thirty grams, I think."

That was a lot. "Wow. We can't let this one go."

Melinda started crying.

Brad hated it when she cried. For a moment he remembered puking up half-digested painkillers as she watched from the bathroom door, crying. She'd stayed with him even after his suicide attempt, which was more than Brad could say about his own parents. He couldn't believe that he had finally managed to drive her away. "Mel..."

"I was so worried about Eli—he was doing well, getting Bs at least, better than when we were with you... I'm sorry, Brad, it's not your fault. Not all of it. I don't want to fight over this."

Not my fault, Brad thought. Whatever else she was, Melinda was too nice to tell the truth. "Do you want to talk to him?"

Melinda blew her nose. "I do."

Brad put the phone down. Before he went to get Eli, he hit a key on his computer and woke the air-suspended touchscreen. Brad went to his bank's site and arranged a transaction into Melinda's account. He could guess what Eli's bail would cost. The Navarros' check would pay for it, more or less.

When Brad stepped out, Eli was deep in conversation with John and Trudie Scott. "That guy with one eye," Eli was saying. "Whittan. What the hell was up with that? He like, leaves his wife and kids and they get killed and he's like, 'oh, I must avenge them,' when he left them in the first place!"

"I was trying to give him a good reason," John Raphael Scott said, "for wanting to destroy the Foresters."

"I don't buy it," Eli said.

"Well, we all make mistakes," Trudie said, obviously trying to defuse things. John Raphael Scott looked depressed.

"Eli," Brad said, "your mom's on the phone in the office."

Eli got up and pushed past Brad without saying anything. Brad sat down where Eli had been.

"You all right?" Trudie asked.

Brad hated it when people asked him that question. It always came when he was most definitely not all right. "No. Let's talk about the case before you go."

"It's one o'clock," John said, but Trudie shook her head at him. "I got an appointment with the daughter tomorrow at ten," she said.

"Anything else?"

"Possibly. The only side effects Nick Navarro might have had were from taking experimental versions of the drug years ago."

"Experimental versions?" Brad asked. "Tell me you got the files on those."

"I knew you would ask," she said, and pulled out the files. "I really had to throw around police clearance for these. Unfortunately, they don't tell us much more than John already did—that they didn't stay in the system long enough to be effective, that they reproduced but the immune system went after them. Do you have the files on what he was taking?"

Brad did, in his briefcase, and he yanked it out. "You see anything?"

"Nothing weird," Trudie said. "I mean, no one's done an extensive study of the nanodes yet, but... huh."

"What is it?"

"His salt content is really high."

"What does that mean?"

"I'm not sure." She looked at John. "You have any idea?"

John shook his head. "Sorry, nodding off. What did you say?"

"Nick Navarro's blood was really high in salt content when he died. Any thoughts?"

"Maybe," John said. "Enough salt and the right reaction and you might have an ionic liquid—some of which can dissolve synthetic polymers."

"I bet you don't feel so good about taking this stuff anymore,"

Brad said.

"I don't take it," John said. "I have my ups and downs, but I don't trust medication. I've spent too much time studying stuff like this."

"Oh. Another unbeliever," Brad said. "We should start a club."

"Depression has a lot more causes than a lack of serotonin," John said. "We have this universal desire for a quick, happy high with no ups and downs and no desire to find lasting contentment. I mean, science and technology are standing still, ever since the government started handing this shit out—"

"You got him started again," Trudie interrupted.

John Scott smiled. "I am as God made me."

Eli came out of the back room. He turned his face away from the three of them. Brad stood up. "Well, you guys had better get going home. Where is your home?"

"Kent," Trudie said.

"That'll take an hour and change. You, uh, want some coffee or something for the drive?"

"Dad," Eli said, "just let them stay here."

"I told you not to talk," Brad said automatically. He looked back at John and Trudie. Their expressions were both drooping with tiredness. "Uh, I've just got one couch in my apartment upstairs," he said, "so you two would have to sleep out here in the office."

"Dad," Eli said, "just let them have your bed."

Brad turned on Eli. "You'd better keep your goddamn mouth—"

"We can go home—" Trudie said, but John cut her off. "We'll sleep in the office, if you don't mind," John said. "We even have blankets and some overnight stuff in the car left from our last road trip." When Trudie looked at him, he said, "I've been up since four writing, and she got up pretty early for the job, too."

Brad nodded. "Uh, sorry about the bed. I didn't think of it." Brad couldn't say anything else. He hated sleeping anywhere other than his own bed.

"It's all right," Trudie said. "You guys have had a more stressful day than we have. If I hear anything suspicious, though, I'll come running." She held up the badge pinned to her breast pocket.

Eli and Brad were alone in the apartment above his office. Brad was fitting sheets over the couch, while Eli leaned against the wall and stared at him.

"Give me a hand," Brad said.

Eli didn't say anything. Brad continued, yanking up one corner of the pillows and pulling the sheet around them. "Are you going to stand around all night?"

"Give John and Trudie your bed," Eli said.

"They're fine where they are," Brad said.

"Bull fucking shit," Eli said.

Brad chuckled. "You have no idea what you just said, do you?"

Eli reached into his pocket. "Do you want to know why I had that heroin?"

"God be praised. You're actually going to come down from your high seat and tell me why you—my own son!—you are now a junkie."

"Seems to me like someone who took fifty pills at once has no business telling me about being a junkie."

Brad had crossed the floor to Eli before he knew what he was doing. "Shut up, damn it." He nearly grabbed Eli's shirt, stopping with a second to spare. Shut up." Brad backed away. "You don't know anything about that."

After a moment of staring at him, Eli said, "Don't blame Mom. She didn't tell me. I overheard her." He shook his head. "And she still stayed with you. I think you must have made her genuinely crazy." His eyes narrowed. "And you guys say *I'm* selfish."

"Tell me why you had that heroin," Brad said through a dry throat.

Eli waited a moment, then reached into his pocket and pulled out a bottle of Seropax. "Recognize this?"

Brad didn't answer.

"Mom wanted me to take this, right? She was worried, 'cause I was always down, 'cause I didn't have any friends. And it was free." He shook the bottle. The pills rattled. "One day at school, this kid I buy weed from, he says he's going to get busted and he really needs to move some cheva, stuff he was going to sell but can't because some people got their eye on him. He just needs me to get it to the right people and take the money for him. He offered me—you can imagine how much he offered to carry out the deal—and I still said no. So he says he'll pay me just to keep it out of sight. Five thousand bucks—half right there, in *cash.*" Eli's face was carved into an angry snarl. "Do you know how broke we are right now?" Mom really wanted to go see a movie—any movie—the other weekend, but we had no money to see it with. So I begged around school for enough change for two tickets. I got my friend to play his guitar with a hat out and give the money to me. All so Mom and I could go to a crappy romantic comedy." He shook his head. "When I gave her the money, she hugged me and put it in her purse. I think she used it on groceries." He shook the bottle again, as if his hand were trembling. "Mom hasn't worked since I was born, and now she's trying to find a job. She's taking Seropax four times a day because she can't afford the co-payment for an IVD. All because of you being a bastard."

"Your mom left me," Brad said. "If you've got a problem with it—"

"What? If I've got a problem with it I can what? I can leave? I can wait till I'm eighteen? I can go whine about it to my mommy? Which one are you going to say, Dad? I know them all." He flung the Seropax bottle hard, against the wall like a shot. It burst open. Pills flew everywhere, like little blue-and-white fireworks. "I'll tell you what. I'll get straights As, I'll stay off drugs, I'll get a good job and show up every day, get a raise and earn money for college. I will be your perfect son when you become the perfect father." He pointed at the bottle, broken at Brad's feet. "Take those. Keep taking them. You do that—and you actually change—I'll change too."

Brad looked down at the scattered pills. "God, you're stupid. I've been studying whether or not a man was killed by these things. You really expect me to take them?"

"I don't give a damn. You would have found a reason not to, anyway. It's the same way you feel about everything."

Brad looked up at his son. "What way?"

"You know better. You know what to do, no matter who you piss off." Eli turned around and said, "I'm going to the bathroom."

"You dished it out and now you won't take it?"

"I've been taking it my whole life. Good night and fuck you, Dad." He slammed the door to the bathroom.

"Your mom wouldn't be so broke if you didn't spend her money on drugs!" Brad yelled. "Little asshole!"

There was a knock at the door. Brad opened it to see Trudie facing him sleepily, a blanket around her. "Problem?"

"No."

"Give yourself some time to cool down," Trudie said.

Brad closed the door. Slowly, he walked to where Eli had thrown the bottle and gathered up the pills. In his room, alone,

Brad lay down on his bed and face the white ceiling. He heard Eli finally leave the bathroom.

Little asshole. That's the best I can say to my son? Now?

He looked over at the pills on the nightstand, the top of the bottle still splintered and sharp with broken plastic. Brad had always tested high for depression, and he'd lost track of all the people who told him Seropax could help with his flashbacks. His father never took pills, even when he raged and shouted and covered Brad with bruises. His mother took plenty of Valium. Took it with alcohol and got her stomach pumped.

It was ironic. He had always told Melinda, "I can solve my problems without drugs."

And what a great job I am doing.

Brad picked up the broken bottle. *Eli Boron. Take one pill three times a day.*

I'm really good, he thought, *at what I do. I'm a damn good PI. I'm going to solve the case. I'm going to get a load of money.*

My wife walked out on me. My own sunny partner on this case doesn't like me. And I'm the worst father in history.

He took one Seropax tablet and went to sleep.

Brad slept in. He never slept in. He woke up a full two hours after his alarm had rung and he had blearily shut it off. The world was fuzzy and bright. Every night was always the same: to bed between twelve and one, up at seven o'clock. It was almost nine. Brad tumbled out of bed clumsily, and saw the Seropax on the nightstand. He swallowed a tablet.

Eli was in the kitchenette with John and Trudie, pouring them cereal.

"So anyway, these kids were outside my window all night yelling for me to come down. I thought they were nuts. I was scared to come out. As far as I knew, there might have been a riot going on down there," John said. "Turns out they just wanted my autograph."

Eli laughed, then froze up when he saw Brad. "Morning," Brad said.

"You slept in," Trudie said to Brad.

"I noticed." Brad smelled sharp, hot coffee, and he stumbled over to the full coffeemaker to pour himself a cup. "Did you just make a batch?"

"We drank the first one," Eli said. "I made another."

That was actually considerate. He must have done it for Trudie. "We'd better bail. We have an hour before we have to be at the Navarro's place in the Queen Anne district."

"Right," Brad said. He was feeling a bit queasy. "Eli..." He did not want to deal with bringing Eli along, but he didn't trust the kid at home.

"I can stay here. I don't have anywhere to go," John Scott said, "as long as you don't mind me borrowing your desk to write. I've got some books in my car, too, to keep Eli entertained."

"What have you got?" Eli asked.

"I know I have a Shakespeare compendium," John Scott said.

"Great," Brad said. *"That'll* keep him focused."

"I like Shakespeare okay," Eli said.

"The greatest of the dead white men," John said. "If you're really lucky, we'll get through *King Lear."*

"Come here," Brad said to Eli. When Eli got close enough, Brad said under his breath, "You're going to stay upstairs today and you are going to read. No computer, no TV."

"How old am I here?"

"This is all going to go smoother," Brad said, "if we just don't see each other.

"That's how you handle it, huh? Running away?"

Don't rise to it, Brad told himself. Don't rise to it. To his shock, he didn't. He took a drink of the bitter coffee. "Euh. They ought to use nanodes to make this stuff taste less shitty."

Eli, as if by default, glared.

Brad and Trudie went down the stairs onto the street, where a fresh breeze was blowing in from the bay, cold and clear with the slight stink of fish. As they walked up to Trudie's car, Brad saw a woman walking up the street toward them, a tall blonde woman, with a look in her eyes like a dog hunting a cat. Brad froze.

"Mister Boron!" she said.

"How the hell did you get this address?" he asked.

"Debra Poland from the *Seattle Times Online."* She smiled a big, white-scrubbed smile. "Do you think Nick Navarro's death was an act of corporate sabotage?"

"This address is unlisted," Brad said. "Unlisted *everywhere.* Did you get this from the police department?"

"Don't worry, I'm the only one who knows," she said, as if they were best friends sharing a juicy secret. "Let's talk about an exclusive interview."

Brad couldn't think of what to say. He knew, somehow that he couldn't talk to her, but his brain seemed to have gone completely empty.

"Excuse me," Trudie said, "but this man is on assignment with the greater Puget Sound area Police Department. If you harass us any longer, you will be interfering with police procedure, and Brad will also have grounds to sue." She put a hand on her hip.

"Just a quote, Mr. Boron."

"Go to hell," Brad said.

She smiled again, damn her. "Can I run that?"

Trudie yanked out her phone. The woman backed off. They got in her car, Brad looking over his shoulder. "I love this uniform," Trudie said.

"Thank you," Brad said. "I am dead if she gives this address out."

"I'm quite sure that she does not want the city of Seattle bringing a suit against their major paper. You're fine. Though how she got it, I would like to know."

Something the woman had said stuck in Brad's head. "Corporate sabotage? Does Seropax actually *have* competitors?"

"Not really," Trudie said. "It was quietly subsidized by the government as part of health care reform in 2010. Within a few years, they were handing out free samples at every clinic in town, as I remember."

"That explains a lot," Brad said. He had to squint his eyes against the sun. "My head feels like someone drove a train through it."

"Eli's a bright kid," Trudie said. "Did you know he writes? John was talking to him a lot about it this morning. Eli said wrote a play and they were going to put it on at his school before the drug bust."

"He used to write stories all the time. I didn't know he still did."

"Not to pry, but Eli said you didn't approve."

"Not to pry but you'll do it anyway. I was fine with it," Brad said. "I just didn't think he could make a living off it. He didn't even want to go to college, yet he wanted to be a writer."

Trudie laughed. "John actually didn't start writing until he dropped out of college."

"Please say you didn't tell him that."

"We did, but we also told him that John went back and got his Master's. Don't worry."

"That a lie?"

"No," Trudie said. "But John didn't finish it until last year."

Brad pulled out his phone and called Melinda.

"I was hoping you'd call. How is he?"

"He's fine. Gave me some lip last night, but otherwise good."

"I guess I expected that. I think we might be able to get him a court-order to one of those wilderness rehab programs." She waited in the silence. "Brad?"

"Yeah?" He hadn't realized he was just listening to her voice.

"I was so glad to hear about the writer. Eli reads like crazy. Or he used to."

"Well," Brad said, "I'll be busy on this case for the next few days, so call the office phone if you want to talk to Eli, or go online."

"Online. Oh, Brad, I couldn't sleep last night, so I did some research on your case."

She used to do that all the time, when they were happier. "Really?"

"Did you know how many anti-Seropax organizations there are in the US alone?"

"Three, right? I remember the FBI questioning me about them."

"Yeah. You'd think there would be dozens, but I can only find three, apart from conspiracy sites, and one looks like it's defunct. I guess Seropax has enough money to keep the press away from its critics."

"Or the government," Brad said, thinking of Trudie's comment about subsidization.

"Honestly, I wouldn't be surprised if the murder was connected to these organizations. One of those web sites was scary. Talking about the need to cleanse the depression gene, that the human race was breeding itself into chemical dependency."

Brad's PI instincts quickly overcame any awkwardness. "Can you send me the addresses?"

"Check your email." Melinda took a deep breath. "Thank you."

He hung up and put a hand to his head. For so long there had been a wall of anger between him and Melinda. Suddenly, with Eli going down, it didn't seem to matter anymore.

Trudie made it through the Seattle traffic and turned onto a long winding road through the crowded neighborhood of Queen Anne. The sky overhead was a clear bright blue, as if even Seattle weather was on Seropax.

"Do you want to know why Melinda walked out?" Brad asked suddenly. It seemed important to tell someone.

"She is the only person I've heard you be kind to since I met you." Trudie veered around a corner and hit the brakes. Two more cars were coming out of a side street.

"She used to be as cynical as me," Brad said. "We'd go see movies or go shopping or just sit watching people and we just tore the hell out of everything. There were always plot-holes in the movies or stupid slogans in the grocery store or funny-looking people. But as soon as Eli got old enough to understand, she changed." It was painful to remember. Melinda had never expected Brad to be nice. She liked his caustic sense of humor, once. "All of the sudden I was putting up too many defenses. Or being a bad example. She wanted Eli to grow up with a little faith in people, she said. Faith in people. What bullshit. You can't have faith in people. They always let you down."

"So you couldn't work it out?" Trudie asked. She put the brakes on, halfway up a hill, behind a line of cars.

"I thought we could," Brad said. He remembered sitting at the table, holding Melinda's hand, really trying to understand her words through her tears when he just wanted to scream at her to stop. "I thought maybe she'd snap out of it. When she didn't, I... I changed, too. I wasn't always this pissed off." Between trying to help Melinda, help Eli, run his business and eventually being investigated by the FBI for his anti-Seropax leanings, Brad had lost it... really lost it, for a while. He couldn't remember why he wanted to commit suicide, but he could remember how stupid he felt afterward.

The car went a few feet further up the hill and stopped again, behind another car. "This traffic sucks," Trudie said. "You know, Brad, I know how you feel. Especially working in law enforcement, you see that you can't have faith in people. John is the only person I ever met who cares about the rest of the world more than himself."

"Just like Gene Roddenberry."

She stuck out her tongue.

"Do you know anything about anti-Seropax groups?"

"No," Trudie said. "John would know. Some of them have tried to recruit him before, but they're real crazies."

I question the comparison of crazies to a grown man who makes up stories in his head about people named Whittan and the Foresters, Brad almost said, but just as with Eli this morning, he kept quiet. "What else do you know about Seropax?" Brad asked. His headache was finally diminishing, enough that he really thought about what he had been saying to Trudie. He hadn't opened up like that to anyone since before the separation.

She shrugged. "I thought we'd gone over everything."

"Do you know how fast it acts?"

"Instantly, as far as I know. That was one of the improvements. Seropax is able to ensure that the serotonin in the system is upped immediately. I've heard people say it's jarring."

They turned up onto another street, and Brad saw the cause of the disturbance—news vans parked outside the immense wrought-iron fence of the Navarros'. "I'm going to call them," Trudie said. When someone picked up the phone, she said, "Trudie Scott, from the police, with Brad Boron, here to talk to Nadia. Yes. I—well, it was fine yesterday." She held the phone away from her ear and stared at it for a moment. "We have permission—well, the girl's grandmother—well—hold on." She looked over at Brad. "Holy shit."

"They're going to deny us access?"

"It seems Nadia's mom came to town," Trudie said, "and she was not consulted on the decision to put you on the case."

"A big fan, huh?"

"If she stands in our way, I will kick her over," Trudie said. She sounded serious. She punched in the number again. "Are you willing to take the consequences for interfering with police procedure?" she asked.

Soon enough the gate opened.

A white-haired man in a button-down shirt and slacks, who Brad presumed was a butler, led them to a room full of books. "Hey, they've got your husband's books in here," Brad said. A dog-eared copy of *Sunstorm* sat on the shelf, along with the Gaur World novels, which, Brad was pleased to see, looked unread.

"Yeah," Trudie said. "I wish I'd known someone was a fan when I started this case."

Looking further, Brad made a face. There were a few more decent science fiction novels, but most of the shelf was taken up by old *Star Trek* novels and Superman comic books, next to a few books based on a TV show or video games. There were other leatherbound editions of the classics, but none looked like they had been read. Nick Navarro may have been a brilliant chemist, but his tastes in literature were stuck in junior high school. *I suppose Seropax does that to you,* Brad thought, and then remembered that he was on it now.

The door opened. Nadia Navarro was about twelve, bug-eyed with braces, and standing next to a tall, stunning woman with perfectly curled black hair. The woman, who Brad assumed was the ex-wife, was giving Brad a glare to rival Eli's.

"Hello," Trudie said. "I'm Officer Gertrude Scott, and this is Brad Boron, a private investigator assigned to this case."

"I never gave my consent to have this man talk to my daughter. In fact, my husband's parents never gave their consent. This was supposed to be a police interview."

"It will only be a moment," Trudie said, and smoothed out the front of her uniform, as if that could make her more intimidating.

"I can talk to *you* for a moment," the woman said to Trudie. "There is no reason why Nadia should have to talk to Mister Boron."

Brad could practically hear Trudie's fists clenching.

"Hey, Trudie, they've got your husband's books," Brad said. "Look at that."

"What?" Navarro's ex said.

"Who's your husband?" Nadia said, talking for the first time. "I love books."

"My husband is John Raphael Scott," Trudie said.

"Really?" Nadia's big eyes got even bigger. "Oh, I know him! When he was up here talking to my dad he signed some books for me."

"What?" Brad asked.

"I... didn't know he came here," Trudie said.

"He met my dad at some thing once. He didn't tell you?"

"No," Trudie said. "He's in trouble."

Nadia laughed. "John is funny. Did he ever write that one story?"

"That one?" Trudie looked at Brad, and back at the former Mrs. Navarro, who seemed too flustered to approve or disapprove at the moment. "You mean the *Sunstorm* sequel?"

"I guess. He was talking to my dad about a story."

"Officer Scott," Navarro's ex said, her composure regained, "we can have a perfectly reasonable interview while Mister Boron waits outside, or I can make the interview difficult."

Normally a total bitch like this would get a very long and heated lecture about the fact that he was a PI, this was his job, they had hired him, and he was going to ask whatever damn questions he wanted. Instead, Brad found himself shrugging his shoulders and saying, "Sure, I'll wait. See you, Nadia."

Brad squinted against the sunlight in the hall, waiting. So John Scott had been up here, and he had withheld the information. I should be furious with him, Brad realized, him and Eli and the bitchy ex.

He felt nothing but a mild amusement. This was damn creepy.

Trudie came out of the room red-faced with anger. "Let's go. Goodbye, Nadia."

When they got to the car, Brad said, "Don't tell me you never knew John came up here."

"I didn't," Trudie said. "I sure as hell didn't. He's in big trouble for never telling me. Believe me. See this? This is me angry."

"What's 'that story?'"

"I don't know. His never-to-be-finished *Sunstorm* sequel, probably. Look, don't believe me if it makes you feel better. Anyway, I got nothing out of that interview. He was eating enchiladas, got sick and lay down. That's it. Enchiladas."

"Well, if I was going for poison, I'd vote for Miss Bitchy Ex back there."

"Yeah, I questioned her too," Trudie said. "Not saying anything, but she used to be a swimsuit model, and she graduated with a Bachelor's in English Lit from BYU."

"It's the Mormons!" Brad laughed. "They're doing it!"

"According to this, she's no longer practicing. Can you drive?" Trudie asked, yanking the car to the side of the narrow, steep road and pulling the emergency brake. "I'm going to research her. She seems too stupid to be true."

Brad started driving. The headache was gone, though the sunlight was still bothering him.

Trudie punched the keys on her phone furiously as they went down the hill. "Damn, damn, damn..." She kept punching. "Wait a minute."

"What is it?"

"Old news story from a few years ago. An opinion column. Seems an anonymous donor got involved with a Seropax competitor, back when there was one. They promised reproducing nanodes, and they lured away a lot of Seropax's top scientists. And then..." She furrowed her brow. "Their line of research supposedly failed."

"Sounds like that corporate sabotage might have a point. Wait a minute. Why an opinion column?"

"Because the Navarro settlement was big news in Seattle at the time—weren't you here?"

"No. I lived in Arizona before the media shitstorm."

"Well, this columnist is convinced that the Bitchy Ex—her name was Carmen Navarro—funded the competitor with her shares of the divorce. She would certainly have been in a position to lure away those researchers."

"Carmen. Sounds like a murderer." Brad giggled.

Trudie gave him a stink-eye to rival Eli's.

Brad cleared his throat. "Can you get the names of the researchers who jumped ship on Seropax?"

"Not if she's covering her ass," Trudie said. "But we could start calling the employees and work our way down. If some of them slipped a different kind of nanode in there—"

"Wouldn't you have found it?"

"I didn't examine every nanode in his system," Trudie said. "That's a good month's worth of work for someone more qualified than me." She punched a few more keys. "I did get an email from my partner in the lab, though. Huh." She furrowed her brow. "Seems that along with his salt content, Nick Navarro had a higher-than-normal Seropax dosage at the time of death."

"You ought to get to the lab. While I'm babysitting Eli, I can track down those researchers."

They pulled up to Brad's office, and Trudie snapped, "Get down. Hide."

"What?"

"Hide!"

Brad had only a moment before he ducked his head to see that there were at least three reporters, with their cameramen, standing on the sidewalk outside his office. "Oh no."

"Oh yes. Seems like Miss Poland made good on her threat."

"After what you said to her? No," Brad said. "Oh no. This is too fast. This address got out to lots of places this morning. Someone just told her it was an exclusive." Brad peeked up through the windshield. "There's an alley behind my place with a fire escape. Left up on the street ahead."

"A fire escape, huh?" Trudie said. "Now this is how a PI is

supposed to do things."

"I've got to get to Eli," Brad said.

Trudie pulled up to the back of the alley. "Stay here," Brad said. "I want someone to watch if I break my neck."

"Keeping the car in the alley? That's a terrible way of covering your tracks."

"You watch too much TV," Brad said. He hopped out, grabbing the iron bar of the fire escape. He had been able to do forty pull-ups in his Marine days. It had been twenty years since he tried.

Halfway through pulling himself up onto the platform, Brad gasped for breath, his arms burning, and nearly fell. He scrambled to grab another iron bar, somehow pull himself up. Instead, he fell, toppling over on his ass. He heard something crack.

When he looked up, a man with a beard and a baseball cap was bending over him, raising a camera to his shoulder. "God, no!" Brad said, and practically kicked the man. "Get away!"

"Are you all right?" He saw John Scott, running up from behind.

"I swear it sounded like I broke something," Brad said, getting up off his back, "but I just feel like I got the wind knocked—"

"I was talking about *that!*" John said, and pointed.

Brad looked. There was a neat bullet hole in one of the bricks of his building.

Brad drank another cup of coffee to steady his nerves. It still tasted like shit.

"You've never been shot at before?" Trudie asked.

"This woman really needs to lay off the cop shows," Brad said to John.

"Who wants you off this case that bad?" John asked.

"I'm going with Carmen," Trudie said. "She must know that you'll find something."

"She has every reason," John said, "just to hate him because of his views on Seropax. I mean, it pays her rent. It will pay for her daughter's college tuition. It's bad PR to have a guy like that investigate this case."

"When you put it that way, it sounds like she has something to hide."

"Ask him about something to hide," Brad said, and pointed to John.

"What?"

Trudie's voice went hard. "Why were you at the Navarros?"

John turned red. "Honey, I'm sorry. Really sorry."

"Do you know what kind of position that puts me in? As a police investigator? When I don't know that my own husband could be involved in this case?"

"Look, we never talked about Seropax. I don't think he even knew my views. I met Nick at a convention. It turned out he was a big fan."

"Don't expect me to believe you went there to *sign books!*"

"He wanted to fund the *Sunstorm* movie." John looked down. "Independent financing, honey. Do you know what that could do?"

"You promised you would stay out of that until the lawyers were done with it, John!"

"What's going on?" Eli asked from the corner.

"John made some stupid decisions a little while ago about a movie deal, and now he's paying for it."

John looked away and muttered, "It was the only studio that would take it. Everyone wants romantic comedies now. Stupid romantic comedies."

Brad shook his head. "I'm checking you out, Raphael."

"Go ahead," John said, sounding more depressed than ever.

"You'd better be clean as a baby after a bath." He got up. "Well, assuming I'm not assassinated, I'm going to find those researchers and talk to them." He looked outside at the reporters, no doubt talking about the famous shot by now.

John left the room. Brad heard him talking to Eli. Trudie paused at the door. "I heard you last night," Trudie said after a moment of silence. "You took the Seropax, didn't you?"

If there had been anything left of Brad's good mood, that surely would have killed it. "Yeah. There are a lot of reasons, and I don't think I need to explain them to you—"

"Will it jeopardize the case?"

Brad thought of Nichols saying, *There's a conflict of interest.* "No."

"All right," Trudie rubbed her eyes. "I'm going to look more closely at the nanodes in Nick's system. You find the people who might have known what was going on."

Brad didn't look as Trudie left. He heard Eli and John talking. "I still don't get why Don Pedro was bending over backward to be nice to him," Eli said. "Just because he's a bastard."

226

"Eh, the comedies aren't really all that deep. Wait until you get to MacBeth," John said. "Blood, revenge, prophecy—all the good stuff that they leave out of stories these days."

The door shut.

"You know, they meant to miss you," Eli said.

Brad looked up at the doorway, where Eli was standing, his finger in a book. "How do you know that?"

"You said you heard the crack right when you fell," Eli said. "Come on, it's not like they were aiming while you were flailing around on that fire escape. They must have had a reason to wait until you were at least stationary."

Brad nodded his head. "That's good thinking, Eli." Something odd welled up inside Brad. It seemed so important to say something to Eli. To tell him how much he meant to Brad, how much of a future he had. "Eli—"

"I'll be upstairs," he said. "Alone."

"Right." Brad swallowed whatever he was about to say.

Eli left.

Brad called up every news story he could find about the new nanodes, but whoever had developed them was keeping mum. The only person mentioned in the stories was Nick Navarro. The more he tried to find them, the more elusive those names of the researchers became. He called the company, but the receptionist put him on hold and left him there until it hung up.

Brad looked at the email from Melinda and followed the links. The anti-Seropax organizations all had easy-to-find manifestos on their sites. One of them read, "humanity is now complacent and self-serving instead of ambitious; spoiled children who cannot bother to involve themselves in the world around them." Another one read, "The time has come to make your voice heard, in any way possible."

He emailed some guys he knew, guys who followed stocks and bonds like they were sharks who smelled blood in the water. He forwarded Melinda's email and asked them to find out where the funding for those organizations had come from. It was the only thing left to do.

He tried Seropax Co. again. The second time she put him on hold he fell asleep.

When Brad woke up, the sun was streaming through the room and the clock read eight-thirty. "Eli?" Brad said. "Eli?"

He got up and ran upstairs. Eli wasn't in the front room, the bedroom, the bathroom, or in the kitchen. "Eli! Eli!" Brad ran out the front door. There was still a news van parked on the street, and Brad almost knocked on the window to ask them if they'd seen Eli before he realized what that would do. He bolted back inside. Who to call? Melinda? He couldn't call her. Trudie, again, so the cops didn't get involved?

His phone buzzed. Brad ran over to it. "Hello?"

"Brad?" Trudie sounded shaky. "Brad, thank God. You need to get out of there."

"What? Why?"

"We need to meet somewhere. I know who shot at you—at least, who hired the shooter. I can't—I shouldn't say anything else."

"Trudie, Eli's missing. I have to find him."

"Oh no," Trudie said. "All right, I'll come over."

Brad rushed around the house again, yanking open closets. He picked up the phone again. No choice but to call the police. This would just get worse.

Wait a minute.

Outside, there was a door halfway around their old building, with stairs leading down to the hot water heater and the fuse box. Brad rushed out the front door and around the back, yanking open the door and sending a cloud of dust out. Eli stood in front of the hot water heater, holding the cordless house phone. "Shit," Eli said. "I gotta go. Bye, baby."

"What the hell?" Brad said. "What the—" He rushed forward and Eli actually put up his fists. Brad stopped just short of Eli. He found himself wanting to hug the boy in relief. That had never happened before.

"Where did you go?"

"I was talking to my girlfriend," Eli said.

"Out here?"

"I got tired of being stuck in the house," Eli said.

Brad heard footsteps outside. He yanked the door shut. "Eli, don't do that. Seriously, don't. It will just make things worse."

"Yeah well, maybe I want to make things worse for you."

It was dark as night in the boiler room, and just as quiet. Finally, Eli said, "I was going to tell the reporters about my drug bust, but I chickened out. I was hoping to make you look really bad in the news."

Brad thought of a dozen different things to shout at his son. *Did the drugs burn out your brain? Do you have any idea what we sacrifice for you? How stupid can you be?*

"You're supposed to yell at me. Is something wrong with you?"

Brad ignored that. "Your mom says they might be able to send you to a wilderness trek of some kind."

"Oh joy."

"Don't smart off. It beats juvey." He sighed. "We're doing our best with you."

"No you're not."

"Really?" Brad pulled the Seropax out of his pocket, in the new bottle he'd put it in to replace the first, rattling it so Eli could hear in the dark. "I've been taking this, genius boy. Now you've got to hold up your end of the bargain."

For the first time since he got here, Eli cracked, showing an expression other than anger or indifference. "You really took it?"

"I'm taking this stupid pill. And your mom is trying to find a good way to help you get your life on track, and even Trudie and John were helpful—"

"You really took it."

"One every three hours. I'll see you at UCLA."

Eli was actually speechless. Brad felt an odd sense of triumph. After a long moment, Eli cleared his throat. "I've been thinking about your case," he said. "Did you have any luck finding those lab techs yesterday?"

"Nothing," Brad said.

"Do you have the Navarros' number in your phone?"

"I have an email with all the contact information."

"I think I might be able to get through to Nadia." Eli cleared his throat. "Can we leave this stupid room?"

"Not unless the reporters magically vanish," Brad said. He pulled up his email, and punched in the number. "Tell me how you're going to do this," he said, before he pushed *Send.*

"I heard John read about an hour's worth of Shakespeare yesterday," Eli said. He hit the button. After a moment, in a dead-on impersonation, Eli said, "Hey, this is John Raphael Scott. Can I speak to Nadia?" He waited, and said, "I just want to express condolences."

"Condolences?" Brad whispered.

"Well, I also wanted to invite her to a party for my new book— it's a teen romance about wizards... who love werewolves. That's actually what it's called. *Wizards Who Love Werewolves.* It's humor."

Brad bit his tongue. It was worse when he audibly heard the person on the other line, who had obviously had their Seropax, say, "That sounds fun!"

After a moment or two more of Eli going on about this cool release party and how much he would like to have Nadia and her friends come and spread the word about the book, Nadia hopped on the phone.

"Hey Nadia, this is John Scott," Eli said. "My wife was just up there yesterday and I had something she was going to tell you that I forgot. Oh yes, the release party for Wizards Love Werewolves." Eli looked over at Brad, his expression visible even in the dim light. "It's in two weeks, but it hasn't been finalized by my publisher... Hey, I need to do some research on a story about Seropax, so I need to call some of the people who work with your dad. Can you tell me who I should call?"

When Eli got off the phone, he said, "Cliff Gorey is the name. You're welcome."

"Thank you."

"Good God, Dad, you thanked me again."

"You're a smart kid. You're a hell of a lot smarter than me. You know that? And you have opportunities I never had. What happened to all those college classes you were taking?"

"They're still going," Eli said. "I don't know how my criminal record is going to affect financial aid."

"You just had to make one little mistake," Brad said. "Do you realize that we care about your future?"

"I know Mom cares," Eli said. "I didn't realize you cared at all."

"You're a smart kid," Brad said again, as if that would help. It seemed so important that Eli listen to him. Crazy pills. "Think about things."

"I will go forth, father, thinking smartly about things from now on."

Brad dialed Seropax and asked for Cliff Gorey. He was on hold when Eli said, "Put it on speaker phone. I want to hear what this guy says."

"Eli—" Brad started to protest, but after what the kid had just did, he couldn't really argue.

"Hello?" Cliff said.

"Cliff Gorey? This is Brad Boron. I'm the investigator on Nick Navarro's death, and I just had some questions for you."

"Okay..." Cliff said. "I haven't talked to Nick in months,

though."

"It's fine. Routine stuff, really. I hear you're one of the folks behind these new nanodes."

Cliff said nothing for a moment. "That was mostly Nick. I helped with the preliminary work, but he was the one who designed them."

"Well, I'm sure your work was invaluable. You quit working at Seropax for a while, right?"

Cliff laughed humorlessly. "I knew you were going to ask that. Yes, I did, but that didn't go anywhere. The company's research was into reproducing nanodes, and that's always been a dead end."

"That's what I heard. How long did you work at the competitor?"

"It only lasted nine months."

Brad bullshitted through some more questions about the polymers and the nanodes that he already knew, with Cliff giving the same answers John had. At the end, he said. "I must say it's quite a wonder drug. I just started taking Seropax and I'm amazed. All these years I thought it wouldn't do anything for me."

Cliff laughed, a little hesitant. "That's funny. I never needed it. My serotonin levels have always tested high."

Brad thanked him and hung up. As soon as he did, Eli said, "He's lying."

"How do you know that?"

"Come on, Dad. I hang out with drug dealers."

Trudie called. "Brad, I'm here."

"We're in the storage closet around the side," Brad said.

"I'll wait inside."

"I am not coming out of a storage closet with Eli and facing a bunch of reporters."

"Right now, Brad, the less anonymity you have, the better. Someone is gunning for you. Literally."

"Crap." Brad hung up and opened the door. There were no reporters on this stretch of sidewalk. Brad and Eli got out onto the street, and Brad instantly heard, "Mister Boron! Mister Boron!" He forced himself to walk calmly to the front door.

"Mister Boron, can you comment on Nick Navarro's—"

"Shit, Dad, get down!" Eli said, and yanked him to the ground. Reporters scattered around them.

Brad huddled, waiting for another gunshot, or anything, but Eli finally said. "Nothing." Eli opened the door.

"What did you see?" Brad asked once they were inside, but he had no time for Eli to answer, because Trudie was there in the hallway, and she pulled them inside. "Carmen Navarro is embezzling from Seropax," Trudie said.

Behind her, Brad saw John Scott standing at a window, peeking through ventilation blinds.

"How?"

"Nichols has a friend at the FBI who said—off the record— that they don't quite have enough evidence to bust her yet, but they're almost sure."

"Good God," Brad said. "So you think she did it?"

"I don't know how," Trudie said, "but I think so. And I think we should get you out of here before someone else shoots at you."

As if he hadn't been listening, Eli said, "If they could perfect a reproducing nanode, one that could kill people, they would only need to put one nanode in per dose of Seropax and eventually they would have tons of them."

John looked up at Eli. "That's brilliant, Eli."

"Except they would show up eventually," Brad said. "Once anyone starts looking through the nanodes like Trudie is going to, they would find whatever chimaera-nanode you're talking about."

"That would be enough time for Carmen to make it to Rio," Eli said.

Brad threw up.

It went like a waterfall onto Trudie's shoes. Brad staggered away, his hand over his mouth. He stumbled into the bathroom and vomited again. "Close the door, Eli!" Brad said.

"Oh shit, Dad," Eli said, and when he said it, he sounded genuinely scared.

When Brad was alone in the bathroom, he threw up a few more times.

The flashbacks smacked his brain. Over another toilet, watching pills and stomach acid tumble back into the water. Brad stumbled back, against the wall, and then forward, puking again.

This is pathetic, he thought. His stomach felt like something was tearing a hole in it, as if his body was not his own. Pathetic. All he could see was himself, holding pills, taking them, throwing them up, taking them.

He heard Eli and Trudie talking, faintly through the door. It chimed in time with Melinda's voice in the flashbacks. "Brad, are you okay? Brad—what are these from?"

"...didn't know he would actually take it..." Eli was saying. "I put it in his coff..."

"...excess of Seropax, just like Nick..." Trudie said.

Brad staggered up, against the wall, and splashed water on his face. I can do this, thought, I can do this, I am stronger than this, I can beat this... "Brad, pills? Pills?" Melinda was crying now. In his head, he was still bent over the toilet, throwing up. His brain seemed stuck.

"I am stronger than this," Brad said. "I am stronger." He steadied himself. "My brain is not stuck."

After a moment, Brad realized the flashbacks were easing. He coughed again, and looked down. *I'm okay,* Brad thought. *I'm really okay.* The flashbacks throbbed like a bruise in the back of his mind, but Brad could concentrate through them.

His phone flashed red. He had a new email. Brad picked it up. It was from his money sharks. He put a hand to his head, massaging his temples as he read the email. I'm okay. He couldn't believe he really was.

They had traced funding for the anti-Seropax organizations. There were a few private backers for all the different organizations, but only one organization had given money to all three corporations. It was a conglomerate that had its hands in a lot of things, but the money had, oddly enough, been routed through a movie studio.

A movie studio? Brad looked up the name online. The studio had only ever been attached to one project, it turned out.

John Raphael Scott's bestselling science fiction novel *Sunstorm*.

When Brad opened the door, Eli and Trudie were staring at him, horrified. "Brad," Trudie began, swallowing. "There's something you should know."

"Eli put Seropax in my coffee," Brad said. "So I've got a higher dose, just like Nick Navarro." As if in time with it, his legs trembled and he had to steady himself. "No wonder all coffee tastes like shit today."

"I'm sorry," Eli said. "I didn't think you would take it!"

John Scott was still staring out the blinds.

"Tell me, John," Brad said. "Tell me what you know."

"What are you talking about?" Trudie asked.

John didn't answer.

"Brad, Carmen Navarro did it. She has plenty of motive, and she has access to the researchers involved."

"This isn't about killing one man," Brad said.

"I'm so sorry, Brad," John said. "I wouldn't have gotten involved if I knew you would take it."

"Who shot at me?"

"No one," John said. He reached behind the couch and pulled out a handgun with an attachment that looked like a silencer. "I shot three holes in the wall before you came home, hoping you I could scare you off our trail. It was stupid. Nothing could scare you off. I was desperate."

"John, what is going on?" Trudie asked.

"Eli's partially right," John said. "Carmen's Seropax competitor was in business just long enough to finally perfect a reproducing nanode. It does two things: it releases a relatively harmless ionic liquid—harmless save that it weakens the polymers in the new nanodes. And then it releases a virus that can get through those weakened polymers."

"A virus?" Eli said.

Trudie wasn't talking. She looked as though she'd been hit in the stomach.

"They'd find a virus," Eli said.

"How?" John Scott said. "It only affects nanodes. There's no antibodies to look for, and it only has a two-hour lifespan after it activates. Like you said, they might find the virus once they dug through every nanode in Nick's system, but that's more than enough time for us."

"The virus makes the new nanodes misfire," Brad said.

"We needed a reproducing nanode in order to release enough of the virus. It reproduces like crazy, until, at a certain point, the first killer nanode sends out a signal for the others to release the virus, and every single nanode in everyone's system becomes a killer. The whole world of Seropax users has about twenty-four hours to live, unless, like you, they took enough to get more than one killer nanode in their system."

"Who upped Nick's dosage?" Brad said.

"I don't really know," John said. "Possibly Cliff. My job—and Trudie's—was to manage things on this end."

"Trudie?" Brad said.

"I didn't know," Trudie said. "I swear."

"How could you not know?"

Trudie cracked. "I've been to the meetings and everything, but nobody said anything about killing people!"

"Trudie," John said gently, "you told me that it would be better for people to die on Seropax than for the world to stay as it is."

"That was a *hypothetical* question!" She turned to Brad. "I'm sorry—I should have told you we were involved with the anti-Seropax groups, but I didn't think they would do anything like this."

"Have you been blind?" John asked. "That's all we talk about. The price that we have to pay to jump-start humanity again."

"Why up Nick's dosage?" Brad asked. His vision felt oddly dark. He blinked, but it didn't really go away. Melinda's voice was still rattling in the background, in his flashback.

"We don't want to kill people," John said. "But things are desperate here. The whole world's stopped, Brad. No major advances in technology in five years, when in the oughties computers were leaping forward every few months. No talk of space exploration, no medical research, no real change in politics or laws for the better. Children can be put on Seropax at the age of two, for God's sake." He breathed deeply, as if trying to calm himself down. "We upped Nick's dosage hoping to scare people. If Nick died from Seropax, then maybe a lot of people would stop taking it because they were scared. We want to save as many people as possible—but people have to die to jump-start the world. Think of it as sacking Rome for the sake of the Renaissance."

"What are you going to do with us?" Brad asked.

"I don't know," John said. "Do you understand?" He looked at his wife. "Trudie, you know why we did this. Eli, you're a very smart kid for your age. And Brad..." John's face fell. "I never thought any of you would be taking the drug. I'm so sorry, Brad."

"I'm calling the police," Trudie said.

"Trudie, no. You know why this has to happen."

"Shoot me, John," Trudie said. "Go ahead. I really don't care. Did you marry me just to get someone in the police on your side? How far back does this go?"

"Trudie," John said, as she reached for the office phone. "Don't. Don't." She picked up the phone.

John fired. She dropped.

"Jesus Christ!" Eli said.

"It's a tranquilizer," John said, "so calm down, Eli. I'm not a monster. Now what are you going to do?"

Eli stood where he was.

"Eli," Brad started to say, but his vision was clouding, red and

235

black. "Eli, you have to call your..." His legs were twice as weak as they had been. Brad hit the ground. "Eli..."

The world went out.

For one second.

Brad's eyes flickered open again. He saw Eli's face, right over his.

I'm not dead, Brad thought. *I think I might be able to get up.*

Eli looked horrified. Brad closed his eyes just as Eli saw him open them. He mouthed three times the words *top drawer right, break lock.*

Eli got up. "I'm so sorry, Eli," John Scott said. Brad could hear the bigger man moving across the room. Eli sobbed, quietly but steadily. Brad chanced opening his eyes. Eli and John were standing in the middle of the room, embracing, though John still held his gun ready. Eli wiped his eyes and moved back, toward Brad's desk. "I need to call my mom," Eli said. "Please let me call my mom. She has to stop taking it."

"I can't, Eli," John said. "I can't let you tell her."

"Please!" Eli shouted. "It's my mom! I'll just tell her; you can even watch me dial."

John Scott hesitated. As he did, Eli yanked on the drawer and the whole heavy desk lurched for a moment before the lock broke, wood splintering and shattering. John Scott fired one of his darts, but Eli dodged. The drawer he had broken open went spinning across the floor, and the revolver inside fell out, spinning as well.

Brad staggered to his hands and knees and crawled. John dove for the revolver, but the floor was still slick from where the vomit had been cleaned up. He slipped and fell, tumbling across the ground. Eli went for the gun, but he stumbled over John.

Brad picked the revolver up, but his hand wouldn't quite close around the trigger—and then John Scott was in front of him. With his own gun butt, John bashed Brad's face, and Brad felt his jaw break. Brad tossed the revolver.

Eli caught it and aimed at John.

"Eli," John said. "Don't you believe me? Don't you know how much the world needs to change, really change? You don't want to do this—"

"Everyone's underestimating me today," Eli said, and shot.

John ducked. The bullet tore through the wall. Eli shot again. The wooden floor next to John shattered.

Brad grabbed the tranquilizer gun as Eli shot a third time,

yanking it away from John Scott. John Scott rolled away. Brad almost expected to see blood, but when John stood, he was unmarked.

"They'll find another way," John said, his voice shaking. "They'll keep us docile however they can—"

Brad shot a tranquilizer into John's cheek. His eyes rolled upward and he dropped. Brad looked over at Eli. Someone, presumably a reporter, was hammering on the door.

"I should really learn to shoot," Eli said, hefting the revolver and handing it to his dad.

Eli told the police everything that happened, since Trudie was still too sedated to recover, and Brad couldn't talk. Most of the police officers looked sick or disbelieving when Eli told them, grinning his own echo of Brad's devil grin, "Seropax is going to kill you. Better stop taking it."

The paramedics insisted on putting Brad on a stretcher, though he was feeling a little better. He lay in the ambulance with Eli and an EMT who had an IVD hanging, disconnected, from his waist. The EMT looked miserable.

Brad didn't focus much on that. He was thinking about how he had survived. In order for the plan to work, John had said, the polymer skins on the new nanodes had to be weakened. It had been those polymers that protected the nanodes from the immune system. Maybe in Nick Navarro's system, as saturated as it had been with nanodes both traditional and experimental, the weakened nanodes had still been able to kill him. But Brad's immune system fought a little harder against the intruders. He didn't have years' worth of nanode work.

"You know, Dad," Eli said, "I was a little surprised you didn't go along with them. You actually showed some faith in people back there." After a moment he added, "Of course, you were a bit out of your head."

Brad motioned for his phone. Eli handed it to him and Brad typed, *Have you been reading anything besides Shakespeare?* Brad hated Shakespeare.

"Uh, yeah," Eli said. "John also had some Kurt Vonnegut. I started *Slaughterhouse-Five* yesterday."

I read that, Brad typed, *a long time ago.*

"I think most people did."

How about I read it again and we talk about it?

It was silent for a moment. "That's just weird, Dad," Eli finally said. Brad frowned at his son. Eli rolled his eyes and said, "You're trying, aren't you?"

I am. It was all he could do without the Seropax.

"Fine," Eli said, and Brad detected a hint of surprise in his son's tone. "We'll talk." He looked at the other figure on a stretcher. "How do you think Trudie will handle this? She'll probably lose her job."

Brad took a long time to thumb an answer—any answer—into the phone. *Maybe we can teach her the PI business. Give her something to do.*

"Yeah," Eli said, his voice cracking.

The ambulance pulled into the hospital and wheeled Brad out, the cord at the EMT's waist flapping. The effects of the Seropax would be fading already, Brad realized, and more so in a few hours when he didn't take his next dose. Then the world would change, though not in the way John Scott had envisioned.

You can't have faith in people. He thought of the flashbacks, in the bathroom, and before. And he thought of being alone with Eli, for the next few days or weeks, of talking to Melinda, without the Seropax, and of trying to support Trudie. *You can't have faith in people* sounded a lot like *I can't have faith in myself.*

The human race wasn't a disease, bereft of the cure. I'm still, Brad realized with pride, not pessimistic enough to buy that.

Spencer Ellsworth wrote his first novel, "Super Tiger," at seven years old and never recovered. He lives in Bellingham, WA where he writes and edits; the former won the PARSEC Contest in 2009, has appeared in Brain Harvest and spouts the fanboyriffic Miracle Pictographs column each month in Orson Scott Card's Intergalactic Medicine Show. The latter includes slush reading and copyedits galore. He has also worked in wilderness survival, special education, and at a literary agency. He is married to fantasy artist Chrissy Ellsworth, and the proud father of Adia and Samwise Ellsworth.

He can be found at spencerellsworth.blogspot.com, spencimus on twitter and spencimusprime on livejournal.

Gareth Powell's contribution to the anthology is the only story written in British instead of American English. He is from the United Kingdom, and the story takes place in and around London.

An open mind is required when reading this story because it can't be taken at face value. It is more symbolic than an account of events. Taken at that level, the story becomes something more than it first appears.

Gareth's work has appeared in Interzone *and in the Solaris anthology* Shine. *His story "Ack-Ack Macaque" won the 2007 Interzone readers poll for best short story. I'm pleased to include his work in this collection.*—RN

The Bigger The Star, The Faster It Burns
by Gareth L. Powell

E d stops at a lonely roadside café on a hot autumn night. He drums his fingers on the counter.

"Hey, how about a coffee?" he says. It's late and he's the only customer. The waitress comes over. She's eighteen or nineteen, with long hair and black eyeliner.

"I'm waiting for the water to heat up," she says. She's got a black t-shirt and there's a biro behind her right ear. She looks over Ed's shoulder. "Is that your car?"

He turns in his seat. He's left the Dodge across two handicapped spaces in the empty car park.

"Isn't it a beauty?" he says.

She looks at the sweeping tailfins and scratches her chin. There's dried egg on her sleeve. "It looks old," she says. "Is it American?"

Ed nods. He's just borrowed it for the weekend. "I'm on my way up to Hereford, to see the crash site."

She looks him up and down. "Are you a reporter?"

Ed shakes his head. "I'm a photographer."

"Up from London?"

"How did you guess?"

She leans her elbows on the counter. "Are you going to take my picture?"

Ed smiles. "That depends. You haven't told me your name yet."

She brushes the dried egg from her sleeve. "My name's Natalie."

They shake hands. "I'm Ed."

The radio at the back of the kitchen's playing an Elvis track. A truck rattles past on the road outside. "I'll get you that coffee," Natalie says. As she pours it, she looks back at him, over her shoulder.

"There's some wreckage at the top of the valley," she says, "I can show it to you, if you like."

Half an hour later they're rolling up the valley in the Dodge, with the roof down. The single-track road smells hot and the stars overhead are hard and sharp. Natalie's finished her shift. Ed's taken his jacket off. He pulls up his sleeve to show her his tattoo.

"I got that in Amsterdam," he says. Natalie wrinkles her nose. Whenever she moves, her jeans squeak on the seat.

"Take the next left," she says.

Ed lets his sleeve drop. He likes her accent. He touches the brake and downshifts into the turn.

Natalie points through the windscreen. "It's just up here."

Ed pulls off the road. Up ahead, caught in the headlights, is the wreckage she promised him. It's strewn over the gorse and heather, twisted splinters glinting in the moonlight.

He kills the engine. "Does anyone else know about this?"

Natalie shakes her head. "No-one comes up here much."

It's midnight. Ed opens his door and climbs out, camera in hand. He can smell the heather. He walks over to the nearest fragment. The metal's smooth and warm to the touch. With a dry mouth and sweaty palms, he starts snapping; knowing the pictures he's taking will make his reputation.

Back in the car, Natalie lights a cigarette. She puts her feet up on the dashboard and lets her long hair fall over the back of the seat. She knows there are armed helicopters patrolling the main crash site to the north. But here in the valley, all she can hear is the click of Ed's camera in the hot night air.

Ed comes back to the car with a souvenir from the wreckage: three luminous brass gauges mounted on a broken panel, all smashed, faces starred, each the size of a dinner plate.

"These have to be worth something," he says, and drops them onto the back seat. Natalie says nothing. She keeps her eyes closed. Her hair and clothes still smell of fried eggs. She hears Ed walk around to the driver's side. He gets in and pulls the door shut, *ka-chunk.*

"Thanks," he says.

Natalie arches like a warm cat.

"No bother."

She looks down into the valley. The lights of the main road snake away like an orange river. She can see the café, and beyond it, the town. She can almost see her house. It all looks pathetically small from up here, and she can blank it out with her hand, cover it over as if it never existed.

Ed shudders the engine into life, and pulls the car round in a tight circle.

"Where can I drop you?" he says.

The wheels bump over the uneven ground. Natalie leans forward.

"Take me with you."

"What?"

"Take me with you to London." She's never even been as far as Cardiff, but she's feeling wild. It must be the fresh air.

Ed looks at her as if he's looking over a pair of spectacles. "How old are you?"

"Nineteen."

"What about your parents?"

"They won't even notice I'm gone."

Ed scratches under his white t-shirt. He knows that thanks to her, he's going to be rich, and so he's feeling generous.

He says, "Okay, what the fuck."

He steers the car back down the hill and on to the main road, where he guns the engine and lets the old car wind out to seventy-five. As they scream past the café, Natalie turns her head. She watches it recede into the darkness.

Ed clicks on the radio. Another Elvis song. It's a long, flat drag back to London, but he doesn't care. He's wired, practically jumping in his seat. There's music on the radio, the top's still down, and the warm night air makes him feel like a teenager. It's the first time he's felt like this in years. Beside him, Natalie starts to pat the side of the car door in time to the music. Her hair straggles out, careless in the wind.

They hit London an hour before dawn. On the backseat, the brass gauges glow, brighter than ever. Ed eyes them in the rear view mirror. By the time he pulls up at the kerb outside his house, the glow's spread itself to the dials on the car's dash.

Later, after they've freshened up, Ed introduces Natalie to some of his friends. He takes her on a Monopoly board tour of the Capital. He's trying to offload the brass gauges, but no-one will buy them. He tries all his contacts, but they won't touch anything from the crash site. They're scared of the government. All he manages to sell are the pictures – but that's still enough to land him a suitcase full of money.

He brings it back to the car, a stupid grin smeared all over his face like grease paint.

"Let's go shopping," he says. And by three o'clock in the afternoon, they're both fitted out with new suits, shirts and shoes. They keep stopping to admire themselves in shop windows. They're drunk on how good they look.

He takes her for an early dinner at an achingly hip Thai place off the Portobello Road. She's bought a new mobile phone, and while they're waiting for their food, she logs into her social networks, and brags to her mates about her new boyfriend.

"So," says Ed, "we're young and rich in London. What do you want to do first?"

Natalie puts the phone down. They're both tired. She reaches across the tablecloth, and her fingertips brush the back of his hand.

"Take me home," she says. "Take me home, with you."

Ed buys a bottle of wine and they walk back to his flat. It's a third floor studio, up six flights of stairs. There's a framed picture of Elvis above the fireplace. The fire escape opens onto a flat section of roof, still warm from the day's heat.

"Sit down, make yourself comfortable," he says.

It's getting dark. In the city, night comes all at once. The orange streetlights fire up and the blinds in the apartment blocks across the road go down. Everyone's cooking dinner and watching TV with the volume turned way up. No-one's looking out. No-one wants to hear what's happening in the street.

But out here on the roof, Natalie smells of flowers. She's wearing a silvery cocktail dress, and has her hair chopped into a shaggy mop. Planes pass overhead, one after the other, on approach to Heathrow, their navigation lights like drifting fireworks. After a glass of wine, he kisses her, and she wraps her arms around his neck.

They stay together for the rest of the week, hardly leaving the flat. They live on takeaways and cups of tea. Ed tells her about his ex-wife. She tells him about her parents. They have both forgotten the brass gauges on the back seat of the borrowed car. Neither of them expects their relationship to last.

Natalie's had boyfriends before, back in the Valleys, but nothing serious; symptoms of her boredom rather than cures for it. Ed's the first man to bring any real excitement into her life, and that's why she's grabbed him, the way drowning girls grab ropes.

The next morning, Natalie tries to phone her dad, but can't get through. There's a government block on the line; no calls in or out of South Wales. So she takes a shower instead. Ed pops out to buy a paper, and he reads the headlines on the way back to the flat. Three helicopters have disappeared from the crash site. An eyewitness claims they shot straight up into the night sky, glowing like meteors.

On the street, there are stalls setting up, and crowd control barriers being lowered into place. It's the weekend of the Notting Hill Carnival. When he gets back to the flat, he finds Natalie in the kitchen, wrapped in a towel. Breakfast consists of cold pizza from the fridge, left over from the night before. As they eat, he shows her his portfolio of photographs: the landscapes; the portraits; the journalism. She flicks through it all with one hand, a slice of congealed pizza balanced in the other. Eventually, she comes to a shot of the Pleiades.

"That's pretty."

She turns to the next page, which shows the familiar rectangle of the Orion constellation rising above the black branches of an autumn tree. The stars in its belt are cold and blue. Natalie takes a bite of pizza, and talks around it. "Why's that one red?"

Ed leans over her. Her hair smells very clean. Her fingernail's tapping the upper left corner of the rectangle.

"That's Betelgeuse," he says. He traces the star with his own finger. "It looks red because it's all swollen up into a giant, nearing the end of its life."

"So it's an old star?"

He shakes his head. "No, actually it's younger than the sun."

She raises a quizzical eyebrow and he shrugs. He looks at the framed Elvis picture over the fireplace.

"The bigger the star, the faster it burns," he says.

Accepting this, she flips the page to find another view of the same constellation.

"These are great. How did you take them? Did you use a telescope?"

Ed straightens up. "No, it was a tripod camera on a ten second exposure." He had a telescope, years ago. Not much use for one in London, though; too much light.

He walks over to the window. Three floors below, he sees the borrowed Dodge parked at the kerb. It's a handsome machine, and he's a little bit in love with it. It's brought a much-needed splash of glamour into his life, and he'll be sad when he has to return it to its rightful owners.

Natalie's still eating pizza, still wrapped in her towel, her bare legs crossed at the ankles. She's cute, and he loves her accent, even though he knows there's no future for them, because they're too different. She's too young and excitable; he's too old and restless.

And he hasn't noticed that down below, the car's floating with its tyres half a centimetre above the road.

The phone rings. Ed picks it up. It's the editor to whom he sold the pictures.

"There are government types sniffing around. They want to know how you breached security at the crash site."

Ed stiffens. "I wasn't *at* the crash site. This was a separate area, a secondary impact."

"Then you should have reported it. They want to pull the pictures."

"Screw them."

"I can't protect you, Ed."

"Then screw you, too."

He breaks the connection. He takes Natalie out into the carnival crowds. Hand-in-hand, they walk the length of Ladbroke Grove, and she can't stop gaping. She's never seen anything like this. There are at least a million people packed into these streets. It's a sea of bodies, bright costumes and police horses. They buy coffee and jerk chicken from a stall. They have to shout to hear each other over the music.

They spend the day wandering, edging their way through the crush. They pause to watch live music on improvised stages; they follow the procession route, marvelling at the stamina of the dancers; and end the afternoon on a wooden table outside a corner pub, drinking overpriced beer in plastic pint glasses.

They watch it get dark. It's late, but the carnival's still in full swing. Everyone's celebrating, even though it's been raining and the pavements are wet.

"What time is it?" Natalie says. She has damp tinsel in her hair.

Ed shrugs. He doesn't have a watch. It's been a wild day, but now he's had enough of playing tour guide.

He pats her leg.

"Let's go home."

Natalie stiffens. She's been having the time of her life. She feels like a caged bird released into the wild, and she doesn't want it to end.

"I'm going to stay here," she says, not looking at him. "I'll meet you back at the flat later, okay?"

They both know she won't. She stands up and brushes down her skirt. Ed folds his arms.

"Don't be like that," she says.

By midnight, she's in the arms of a Brazilian telemarketer from Teddington. They lie together in his hotel room, the open window allowing the deep bass of the street festival to ebb and flow over them, the mingled smells of hashish and fried onions to galvanise their empty stomachs.

"I feel kind of bad about Ed," she says. "I shouldn't have left him like that."

Alejandro rubs a sleepy palm across his face. Although bare-chested, he's still wearing his jeans, and his hair's flattened on one side, damp with sweat.

"You don't have to worry about him anymore," he says. "You have me now."

He lights a cigarette from the pack on the bedside table. Natalie sits up and hugs her knees.

"Do you think he'll be all right?"

There are steel drums playing in the street. She gets up and pulls back the net curtain, looks down at the crowd. She says: "It was just a stupid argument."

Her shoes are lying on the floor by the door. In the orange half-light, Alejandro holds the cigarette pinched between his thumb and forefinger. He takes a small, tight drag and curses in Portuguese.

"Come to bed," he says.

Natalie ignores him. All she wants is to be left alone.

"You know, it was his idea to come here," she says. There are people blowing whistles in the street, and strange lights in the sky. She wraps her arms across her chest. The Valleys seems so far away, and she doesn't know where she is.

"I hope he's all right," she says.

Meanwhile, Ed walks back to the flat alone, hands in pockets. He hates London now. It's so dreary, and he's so tired. He needs to move on, find something new to do.

By the time he gets home, the crowd's started to thin. He sees the old Dodge parked where he left it, and no-one seems to have noticed that its tyres are floating a good couple of centimetres above the tarmac. The gauges on the back seat light it up from inside, like a miniature carnival float.

He looks up. A few stars poke through the ragged clouds. He doesn't want to go back to the flat. He's thinking of the crash site and the vanished helicopters, and how bone-achingly bored he is.

The very metal of the car seems to glow and sing. When he touches it, it makes his fingers tingle. He gets in and starts the engine, and the Dodge immediately rises half a metre into the air, much to the surprise of the crowd. He touches the accelerator, and it jumps up another half. Ed gives a fierce grin.

"Okay, here we go," he says. He waves to the circle of astonished onlookers, and mashes the pedal. The car leaps. Foot to the floor, he drives it straight up into the night sky, aiming for the stars.

He drives it so far and so fast that he ends up on a planet somewhere out on the edge of the galaxy. It takes him six weeks to get there. He gets a flat near the shoulder of Orion and has to drive the rest of the way on steel rims, but he gets there.

And he never comes back.

Gareth L. Powell is the author of the novels The Recollection *(Solaris, 2011) and* Silversands *(Pendragon Press, 2010); and the short story collection* The Last Reef *(Elastic Press, 2008). His work has been published in magazines all over the world and featured in a number of recent anthologies, including* Shine *(Solaris, 2010),* Conflicts *(NewCon Press, 2010), and* Future Bristol *(Swimming Kangaroo, 2009). His short story* Ack-Ack Macaque *won the Interzone Readers' Poll for best short story of 2007.*

Gareth lives in the South West of England with his wife and two daughters. Find him online at

http://www.garethlpowell.com

Twitter: http://www.twitter.com/garethlpowell

Facebook: http://en-gb.facebook.com/glpowell

Alethea Kontis is the author of two well-received childrens books, Alpha-Oops: the Day Z Went First, and Alpha-Oops: H is for Halloween. She co-edited Elemental, the tsunami relief anthology, and her fiction has appeared in Realms of Fantasy and Orson Scott Card's Intergalactic Medicine Show.

Her contribution to this collection is a story that I know she had a great deal of fun writing. Of all the stories in this anthology, I think "Pocket Full of Posey" would suffer the most from spoilers. Rather than talk about the story, I'll just let you read and enjoy the full impact.—RN

Pocket Full
of Posey
by Alethea Kontis

"All those bitches need to die."

"Now, now, Rosalyn. These were all the people who were cruel to you in high school?"

"The nine—well, ten—people the planet would be better off without, yes."

"You can't still feel that way. You haven't seen most of them in ten years."

"Google is an amazing tool, Dr. Ford."

The psychiatrist chuckled and sat her legal pad on the tasteful mahogany and glass table beside her chair. *I probably bought that table*, thought Rosalyn, *and that chair*. Dr. Ford crossed her legs, leaned forward, and clasped her hands. Rosalyn braced herself for whatever stupid idea was about to slide off that silver tongue insurance companies had shelled out so much for on her behalf over the last decade-plus. Silly as those ideas were, though, Rosalyn still took Dr. Ford's advice more often than not. All those mundane sociology experiments were multivitamins for her soul; Rosalyn swallowed them with a large grain of salt (and sometimes a lime chaser). They were her church on Sunday, her good deeds for the week/month/year, and once accomplished she was free to move about the rest of her life with a light heart. Light-er. Less dark than normal.

Dr. Ford's smile showed off eighty-three percent of her professionally-whitened teeth. "You need to go to this reunion."

"I need world peace too, but you don't see that happening."

"The first step to world peace is making peace with yourself."

Rosalyn sighed. It was always a losing battle, not that she played to win. "You want me to walk into the lion's den."

"I want to prove that there is no lion's den. There never was."

Every muscle from the top of Rosalyn's head to the tip of her toes went stiff. What kind of professional talk was that? How could she say that *knowing* what hells Rosalyn had walked through every day at Freedom High? "I can't. Not alone."

"But you won't be alone..." Rosalyn raised an eyebrow. She was trying to weasel out of the event, not ask for a date. "...you have Posey," Dr. Ford finished.

Rosalyn couldn't help but smile at the name, and she pulled Posey out of her purse. Aunt Jo and Uncle Dickie had given her the darling gnome keychain on her fifteenth birthday. Gnomes had always made her smile, that in itself such a rarity that her father landscaped a garden in which she could display her collection. Posey was one of the few female gnomes. She had a fat daisy on her little red hat, a golden monkey on her shoulder, and a red cap mushroom in her arms. The irony that this symbol of purity and cuteness was ready to poison her enemies at a moment's notice was what Rosalyn loved best.

For Dr. Ford, Posey embodied all the loved ones Rosalyn admired and never wanted to disappoint. Posey was a cute, dangerous, portable conscience that held the keys to Rosalyn's getaway car.

"I have Posey," Rosalyn repeated dutifully.

"You'll be fine," said Dr. Ford.

"I'll be food for the wolves," said Rosalyn.

"There are wolves in the lion's den?"

Rosalyn nodded. "And they all have sharp teeth." Dr Ford laughed again, from the belly, shoulders shaking; the genuineness of it startled Rosalyn and made her wonder briefly if her shrink was having a seizure. "What's funny?"

"Oh, Rosalyn. You have what all of us wish we had at our high school reunions: you're beautiful, successful, and not a little bit famous. Anyone who didn't know your name then certainly knows it now."

True enough. If they couldn't afford any of the Rosey-O high-end-nano hair product line, then they'd seen her on the covers of magazines, or the guest appearance on *Whoopi*, or splashed across the rags at the grocery store self-checkout lines. The scandal had been viral, proving the WorldWideGrapevine could still propagate faster than any biotech.

The hair products had started out as many other things do—a laugh, a lark, payback on the science teacher her freshman year who suggested that ridiculous fair project on hair dye. Add some punk, Manic Panic, nanotech, a few too many Starbucks Vitamin Waters, and far too little sleep. It was inevitable for two genius roommates to come up with a nano-enhanced, programmable hair dye. It was also inevitable that Natasha—high on Water and the rush of completion—had tried the test batch too soon. The nanites affixed themselves to every hair follicle on her skin, entering her body and then her bloodstream and into her brain far too quickly. Natasha had lived long enough to sneeze and ask Rosalyn for a tissue.

Dr. Ford had taken on double-duty as grief counselor, the 4.0 was followed immediately by an offer from an overly-caffeinated venture capitalist, and the rest was history the lawyers made sure Rosalyn never had to talk about again.

"...must be *someone* you want to see after all these years," Dr. Ford was saying.

"Josie." The word popped out of Rosalyn's mouth without asking permission, which Rosalyn would have denied. After all those years, the two syllables still broke her heart.

"Ah," was Dr. Ford's professional reply. "So here's what I want you to do."

"Beyond walking through the doors?"

"Oh my, yes. I want you to go down this list and say hello to each person on it. You don't have to swap cookie recipes or cry on each other's shoulders; just a polite salutation. That's all."

Rosalyn took The Kill List back from Dr. Ford and gingerly folded it along the deep creases made with rage so long ago. She didn't have to look again at the rounded handwriting in a variety of colored inks; she knew every name by heart. Rosalyn wondered how many other shrinks were returning similar lists to emo kids of the aughties and suggesting they make amends. "You are a cruel woman, Dr. Ford."

"You wouldn't have me any other way."

Rosalyn slid her sapphire green Jaguar into the farthest parking space from the clubhouse. Her father, who'd spent large amounts of time in Afghanistan before the occupation ended, had taught her to always have an eye on her exit strategy. It was a hard habit to break, and so far one Dr. Ford hadn't asked her to.

She took three deep breaths, slid on her strappy black Dakota Fanning heels, and adjusted her enormous Lady Gaga sunglasses. A decade ago she'd walked the halls at Freedom High in black lipstick, a fuchsia lace tutu, and rainbow knee socks. Now, she opted for low-key: a simple black dress and one of her least ostentatious necklaces. Ironically, it was a large lacquer cross on a raw silk burgundy choker. If this did turn into a gang hit, she could at least use it as a weapon in a pinch. She smoothed down her shoulder-length, straight, brown hair. It was only colored with a now out-of-date version of the Rosie-O nanites that only made the ends black, as if they'd been dipped in ink. Thanks to Rosalyn, brown hair was now quite the rarity among humans within her own income bracket. She figured she was going to stick out like a sore thumb anyway; she certainly wasn't going to look like she was trying.

She beeped her car locked and kissed Posey for good luck before dropping her keys into her tiny Bieber clutch. She could do this. She could totally do this. And when it all went down in flames, she always had her exit strategy. Thanks, Daddy.

The first pair of glass doors she tried to the clubhouse was locked, and she refused to call it a sign. She marched all the way to the front of the building intently, like she was walking a Paris catwalk. There was Daisy Scofield, standing behind the welcome table, twenty months pregnant and beaming like sunshine. Anyone else would be high on Starbucks decaccinos, but Daisy Scofield had been beaming like that since she'd popped out of her own mother's womb. She gave Rosalyn a smile that would have knocked Dr. Ford over at twenty paces, and Rosalyn was glad she still had on her sunglasses.

ALETHEA KONTIS

"Rosie Posie Pudding Pie, kissed the girls and made—" Daisy slapped a hand over her traitorous mouth and a cloud went over the sun.

"A girl always wants to be remembered for her accomplishments," Rosalyn said as she scanned the HELLO, MY NAME IS stickers on the table between them. She let the glasses slide down her nose and gave Daisy a lusty wink. "I still make girls cry."

Daisy giggled behind her hand and then gasped when she saw which sticker Rosalyn had slapped to her chest. "Silly Rosie. Now what do I do if Susan San Giovanni decides to show up?"

"You didn't hear? Murdered, poor thing. Her husband snapped, killed her and her children in their sleep, and then hung himself. They said it was some sort of Warcraft PTSD episode or something. I'm wearing the nametag in her honor."

Daisy's cornflower blue eyes brimmed with tears. "Oh my. I didn't know. Bless her heart. Yes, you should wear the nametag. She would have liked that. I'll say a prayer for her."

Rosalyn patted Daisy on the shoulder and continued down the main hall. She hoped Susan San Giovanni did show up. There was a shortage of good stories in the world.

Rosalyn smirked at the screamingly happy sign some mad scrapbooker with access to Photoshop and too much glue—possibly Daisy—had assembled so that no one mistook what was behind Doors Number One and Two for anything other than the Best Reunion EVAR. Rosalyn wrapped strong fingers with perfectly manicured nails around the handle and pulled.

What was actually behind the doors was a nightmare. Honestly, Rosalyn was pretty sure she had woken in a cold sweat from a scene just like this. Towers of fruit posed by chocolate fountains and lukewarm egg rolls smiled at her from their warming trays. A line started at the canditini bar and wrapped halfway around the room, and Christina Leffler serenaded the far-too-sober assembly with a stirring rendition of Ke$ha's "Tik Tok" on the Wii Sing like she was performing on New Year's Eve in Times Square.

Rosalyn glanced down to make sure she was still wearing clothes. Check. This was for real, all right.

In a class of over five hundred students there were only about fifty people in the room; leave it to the student council members of 2010 to make their own reunion list exclusive. Nitwits. They were all there, the entire Kill List from A to Z, all shiny and happily ignorant of how much Rosalyn's palms itched for a gun with nine equally shiny bullets.

Number Nine: Scott Ziwicki. Scott always stayed in last place in every incarnation of The Kill List because Rosalyn liked the completeness of ending the list with Z. Scott had been one of the first names, though, as he originally coined the "Rosie Posie Pudding Pie" rhyme. The acclaimed lyricist had gone on to pen several horrible novels starring a female protagonist named Rosie Pye. He probably never would have been published had Rosalyn herself not gone on to such fame and infamy.

Number Eight: Thuy Vu. Terminally petite Thuy had broken Rosalyn's pencil in the second grade, causing Rosalyn to retaliate and slap the wretched vandal. They were both ushered to the principal's office, one of the only times Rosalyn was ever called into the principal's office. It scarred her for life. After that, she made a point of never getting caught.

Number Seven: Brendan Lee. Brendan had been caught multiple times cheating off Rosalyn's tests, but the teacher never moved him. He always wore a sneer every time Rosalyn was around, like he'd just smelled rotten eggs.

Number Six: Nick Smith. Nick's transgression was that he was totally obsessed with Rosalyn. The puppy dog love might have been flattering at one point, until the day he realized he was going nowhere with her and turned everything he knew about her into jabs and jokes.

Number Five: Mrudula Rue. The bitch touched her iPod. TWICE. Nuff said.

Number Four: Mark and Amanda Owen. The siblings, close enough in age to be in the same grade, were each only annoying enough to merit half a spot on the List. Mark was the class clown, which meant nothing that crossed his path was sacred. Amanda always had one ear attached to the phone, and there was usually a boy on the other end. If she wasn't talking to the boy, she was talking about the boy. And she had an unnatural addiction to corn dogs.

Number Three: Aimee Branson. Head cheerleader and Class Secretary. Far too beautiful to give anyone the time of day. She had only ever turned up her pert little nose at Rosalyn. Rosalyn still remembered how perfectly balanced her nostrils were, even when flared.

Number Two: Christina Leffler. Christina always had to be center stage, always had to have the spotlight. She'd gone so far as to YouTube Rosalyn during her audition for the High School play. Rosalyn was a laughing stock, and Christina got the solo. Christina always got the solos.

Number One: Ariell Bublé. Back in elementary school, Ariell had been one of her very bestest friends. She and Rosalyn and Josie Camire had been the Three Musketeers. They shared everything from cupcakes to gum. They finished each other's sentences. They knew each other's passwords. They were inseparable. And then one day, out of the blue, Ariell walked up to Josie and Rosalyn and announced that she couldn't be friends with them anymore, because she was going to be friends with Aimee and Christina and Thuy. Rosalyn was only slightly less devastated that day than she was a week later, when Ariell read Rosalyn's diary out loud in front of the whole cafeteria. The teacher caught her and made her stop, but not before everyone had heard the dramatic scene about Josie and Rosalyn kissing in the closet. Ariell had been there too, but as the reader, had conveniently edited herself out of the scene.

And there she was, on the other side of the dance floor, perfect as a princess in a pink chiffon dress with matching streaks like ribbons in her long champagne blonde hair. She chatted prettily with Thuy and someone on the wait staff. Mark pressed an orange post-it to the waitress's back. Amanda stood behind him, eating all the crescent rolls. Nick sidled up to the buffet table with her and sexually harassed the ice sculpture. Rosalyn's heel hit the cheap linoleum of the dance floor and she froze. Her stomach cramped. She wasn't ready. She couldn't do it. Not yet.

Luckily, she didn't have to. A petite ball of squee came barreling toward her, an afro of rainbow curls flashing like a bad acid trip. Rosalyn noted that Aimee Branson had splurged for the glitter upgrade to her hair pyrotechnics. Or her husband, Rosalyn noted as the rock on Aimee's left hand dug into Rosalyn's back.

"Oh-em-gee, I was driving myself crazy hoping that you'd come. And I am so glad you did! You have totally made my year! I love you!" Aimee squeezed tighter—her perky implants were as rock hard as her wedding ring. "Look!" Aimee affected an even higher pitch as she showed the diamond off and answered Rosalyn's unasked question. "It's Aimee Lee now. Brendan and I got married!"

"Confused" was an understatement. She and Aimee had not been BFFs. And Brendan? Really? Three and seven on The Kill List; a perfect ten now together in wedded bliss. Vomit-worthy, to be sure. Rosalyn glanced over Aimee's shoulder and through her neon stripper curls to see Brendan, the ruby pinstripe of his suit mirrored in his dark hair and goatee. Chameleon expansion pack. Nice. And not a sneer to be found. He was checking out Rosalyn's ass instead. She barely recognized him without his nose crinkled in disgust.

Rosalyn felt lightheaded and looked around for video cameras. Of course, had there been any, Christine would have either been in front of them, or directly behind them. Since she was moving from her last song right into Train's "Soul Sister," Rosalyn figured she was safe from any sort of spotlight.

Aimee seemed to be waiting for Rosalyn to say something, so she said, "Congratulations!" and hugged them both. She then crossed her arms in front of her, pinching the inside of one elbow to make sure she was still part of reality. Aimee launched into how many children she had, and what she was doing now. Something with curtains. Between Christine's crooning and the roaring in her ears, Rosalyn couldn't be sure.

Aimee's frequency was like a homing device, and eventually it brought the entire Noxious Nine to the fore. Rosalyn didn't even have to seek them out; they all came to her. Another surprisingly unexpected development. They each hugged her warmly and started up conversations like there had never been ten years and a moat of hatred between them. They also crowded around her in a complete circle, claiming her as theirs and shielding her from the rest of the room. Rosalyn peeked between them and caught a glimpse or two of someone she might recognize, but every time she did, one of the Nine moved into her line of sight and asked her a silly question.

"Did you fly here from somewhere exotic?" asked Thuy. The nanites in her hair cascaded blue Vietnamese words down the silken ebony length. Rosalyn secretly hoped they said, "Touch my hair and die, asshole."

"Yeah," Rosalyn answered. "Great Falls." Granted, she only kept her condo there for her visits with Dr. Ford.

"What was Whoopi like?" asked Mark. His pink hair matched his shoelaces. Rosalyn wondered if Mark had ever come out of the closet.

"Really funny, actually. My stomach hurt for days afterwards from laughing so much."

"What exciting adventures are you off to next? Exploring any new inventions? How's your love life?" Scott was as full of questions as he was of fecal matter. His hair was a dynamic mix of traditional blonde, brown, red, and gray that succeeded in being annoyingly eye-catching.

Rosalyn coyly answered frustration with frustration. "Nothing as wonderful as Rosie Pye, I'm sure. I shouldn't bore you with details."

"That's really a shame about Susan," Amanda said between mouthfuls of crescent roll.

Rosalyn patted her name tag sticker. "I was really broken up about it."

"Did you like my song?" asked Christina.

"You always were a nightingale," lied Rosalyn.

"How come you're not sporting any of the newest Rosie-O product?" asked Mrudula. Her hair slowly faded from blue to red, with her change in mood. "Don't you get all you want? Or was that not a perk of selling the formula?"

The truth wasn't something they wanted to hear. It never had been. "I much prefer seeing it on other people," said Rosalyn. "All of you wear it so well."

And they did, too. Each one of them, male and female alike, had one or more glitzy, ridiculously expensive, Rosie-O expansion pack. They all bragged about how many they had, as if competing for her affection, and the inventive ways they'd used them on everything from pets to naughty bits. Rosalyn drank the one or two neon canditinis that were handed to her. She didn't say much, just let them carry on selfishly about their shallow little lives. She laughed, but not with them.

Finally, Ariell put a thin, alabaster arm around Rosalyn. "Oh, how I've missed us," she said to the group.

"Me too," said Rosalyn, meaning something completely different.

As always, Dr. Ford had been right. There was no lion's den, and there were no wolves. There were only fish—large, silly, cheap carnival goldfish. They were born, grew up, married each other, had kids, and never left the pond of Northern Virginia. It may as well have been small town Kentucky for all that gene pool multiplied. Only people who stepped outside the fishbowl realized how small it was. These popular people weren't fat and bald, like the clichés had her hope for; they were all still just as beautiful as Rosalyn remembered. But they were also sad. This tiny little goldfish bowl was all they would ever know, and all they cared to know. Dead or alive, it didn't really matter in the long run. This small, small world was the fate to which they were doomed.

Rosalyn pitied them. And three seconds after that, she wanted to escape from their suffocating embrace. She knew if she cried "potty," the girls would all come with her; such was the way of the herd. So she faked a vibrating phone and excused herself out to the hallway to return her very important imaginary call. She scooted past Daisy, who had taken a break from her table and was peeking through the doorway at the festivities.

"They haven't changed a bit," Rosalyn assured her.

"Most people never do," Daisy said with a sigh.

Rosalyn wasn't technically lying—she actually had missed a few texts from Kelli Keene, her new bestest-bestest. Kelli made sure, in very few words and no uncertain terms, that Rosalyn knew exactly what she was missing by not hurrying up to join her in the Cayman Islands. Kelli also sent two pictures: one of a strawberry daiquiri with a ridiculous amount of fruit, and one of her getting frisky with a cabana boy. Rosalyn wasn't jealous. Much. She'd done what she'd needed to do, and she'd be on her way soon enough. She better be. The next message would be a video, featuring more Kelli and fewer clothes. That was typically her M.O.

She made a quick pit stop in the bathroom, closing the door on the outside world and reveling in the quiet. She had a longstanding tradition of hiding in bathrooms: one of the habits that Dr. Ford had made her stop. Rosalyn figured she'd be forgiven this once. Conquering the Noxious Nine was a big step.

She walked to the sinks, placing her palms down against the cool counter. She looked in the mirror, tore off her stupidly huge sunglasses, and looked again. She was not one of them. She never had been. Making money and being famous didn't make her one of them. Their pretending that she was and making a big show didn't make her one of them either. Once upon a time, that's all it would have taken, and maybe, in their little fishbowl world, that's still all it took. But not in hers. Rosalyn would walk away from this building and never look back.

She turned the faucet in front of her on full blast and thrust the ends of her hair beneath the water, washing every bit of the nanite blackness down the drain until there was nothing left but brown. Brown old Rosalyn. Pure Rosalyn and nothing else. She dried it off with a handful of paper towels. She spun around in the mirror and looked over her shoulder, making sure it was all gone, making sure that there wasn't a sign on her back left by Mark. Or a knife left by Ariell. She took a Burt's Bees Shimmer from her purse and applied it with a shaky hand.

"If you've got a stash of that stuff, it's more precious than gold," a voice said from behind her. "I can't find Shimmers anywhere anymore."

Rosalyn adjusted her eyes to focus on Josie. There in the mirror they were together, just like they'd never been apart. Her soft eyes were still green as olive branches, complementing the ice green frosting on the layered ends of her hair that curved around her heart-shaped face. Her Cupid's bow lips curved up into a smile. She was a vision come to life, ten times more beautiful than Rosalyn had ever dreamed.

"Take it." Rosalyn turned and offered Josie the slender yellow tube of Shimmer. Josie did not disappear; she was right there in flesh and blood. But everything was different now. They had both moved on. That close friendship, that everlasting bond between them, had only lasted as long as it took for the teal Sharpie in her yearbook to dry. Even standing here in 3-D, Josie was still a memory, a picture in a wallet, a tag on a FaceSpace album.

"Thank you," said Josie, who also seemed to be at a loss for words. The lines of communication went both ways; it hadn't been only her fault that the two of them had grown apart. Rosalyn wasn't here to build bridges or heal old wounds. She and Josie just hadn't been meant to be. And that was that. Life goes on.

Rosalyn cupped Josie's face in her hand and kissed her on the cheek. "You look good," she whispered. Despite the cupid's-bow smile, a fat tear escaped and slid between Rosalyn's fingers. Without another word, Rosalyn left the bathroom slightly proud of herself.

She still had it.

"Leaving so soon?" asked Daisy as Rosalyn passed by her table again.

"I have to meet someone," explained Rosalyn. "I could really only stop in for a minute."

Daisy held up a hand. "No explanation necessary. I'm just glad you came at all. It's really nice to see you, Rosalyn."

Why hadn't she and Daisy been closer? Rosalyn tried to think back, but memory escaped her. Not that it mattered. What mattered to Rosalyn was the here and now. Daisy's optimism, remarkable enough back then, was in this decade more rare and precious than crude oil. Rosalyn reached into her bag. "A picture for old time's sake?"

Daisy smiled and snuggled into the crook of Rosalyn's arm as she deftly flipped the camera around to take a vanity shot of them both. The flash was only slightly brighter than Daisy's smile.

"Gosh, Rosalyn. That flash… I think I'm blind."

"One more time," said Rosalyn. "I think I blinked." That's right. One more time with the hidden EM pulse for good measure, just to make sure every nanite left on Rosalyn's and Susan's bodies was rendered completely inert. The Rosie-O product she'd worn in had been old, one of the very first incarnations, from a stash she'd secreted away for a time such as this.

Rosalyn called it version 4.0.

She air-kissed Daisy and wished her luck with her baby—or however many babies were brewing in that enormous belly. She dropped the "camera" back into her purse and rummaged for her keys, finding them before she reached the exit doors. She popped the red cap of Posey's mushroom up with her thumbnail, slid the pad of her finger over the tiny button there…and froze.

Josie. Gods, she'd touched Josie in the bathroom. She'd washed the 4.0 nanites out of her hair by then, but there was no way to be sure Josie didn't get any on her. In fact, she was 100% sure that she couldn't be sure. That was the whole point of having the EM camera. But it was too late to turn back to find her. It had been too late for about a decade now.

Rosalyn pushed the button.

She stood at the doors, staring outward, just long enough to hear a sneeze. Then she pushed through them and calmly strode the length of the parking lot to her getaway vehicle. In twenty minutes she'd be on a private jet to the Caymans, unburdened and free, and this shiny little fishbowl would be nothing but a headlight in the rearview mirror, another anonymous star in the sky.

She'd miss Dr. Ford.

Alethea Kontis is the New York Times bestselling author of the AlphaOops series of picture books and Sherrilyn Kenyon's Dark-Hunter Companion. Her essays, short stories, and poetry have appeared in various magazines and anthologies. She can be found online narrating short fiction for Apex Magazine, reviewing books for Orson Scott Card's Intergalactic Medicine Show, or blathering on at her own website: www.aletheakontis.com. Alethea currently lives in Northern Virginia with her Fairy Godfamily and a teddy bear named Charlie.

Online at http://www.aletheakontis.com
FB: Alethea Kontis
Twitter: AletheaKontis

Alex Wilson suffered a head injury in an auto accident a few years ago, and I have to wonder if that experience helped him to get into character while writing this story. It's a gripping tale, and one that resonated deeply with me. The story grabbed me by the collar and pulled me through to the end.

In this story, a man's brain loses communication with his nervous system through misuse of technology. That has the effect of leaving him numb and insensitive to pain and other sensation. While he uses the condition to his financial advantage, the more human aspects of being isolated from his environment while standing in the middle of it takes a huge toll.

Alex's work has appeared in Asimov's Science Fiction *and* Chiaroscuro. *He has a forthcoming appearance in* Weird Tales. *He is a member of the Clarion class of 2006.* Locus Magazine *called him a "promising new writer."*

"Nervewrecking" delivers that promise.—RN

Nerve Wrecking
by Alex Wilson

Used to be a faux detective, but now I'm in a faux prison jumpsuit on a faux cobblestone roof, staring down a sixty-foot drop. Hate the word "faux," so it doesn't all suck that the drop's the first real thing I've seen in Los Angeles. But yeah. Leave it to my luck to manage a turn without actually being helpful.

I'm probably not suicidal, but it doesn't exactly bug me how that big, blue air bubble below looks inadequate as a person-catching device. I'm also convinced they gave me the cheap kneepads because they know I can't tell any difference. I hate this place. The people. The penny pinching. Mostly the place. At least the people are pretty. Hell, even *I'm* pretty today. I look just like Whatshisname. Kevin something. TV actor from that stupid medical thing.

Have to squint at the angle of the sun. Glare's making me think of the heat, making me wonder how quickly a facial graft sunburns. I'm used to wearing them at night.

And where was the sun yesterday off the Santa Monica pier?

261

Was hoping to catch my first sunset, first time on the West Coast. With the sky so gray, all I got was this unremarkable blotch. No interesting colors or ripples in the sky; just a dollop of yellow behind a grainy mask, which might just be as good as it gets for me. Sally tells me the smog comes and goes in Los Angeles, so it was just my bad luck last night (and today so far). This I can believe.

Sunburn or no, there's just gotta be something on my face besides the graft. I touch an empty pocket, then remember that insurance asshole took away my handmirror.

I turn to Sally. She's harnessed by her torso a few feet back from the ledge. Wind scatters blonde-like bangs across her face. On the ground, her hair's too thick to move, but up here it's alive. Almost looks real. Can't tell whether she's meeting my eyes, but the sight of such active wind reminds me to blink.

"Is there something on my chin?!" I yell.

The wind parts Sally's hair like she's poking her face through a shower curtain to hear me better. She gives me that teeth-apart smile of hers and throws a big thumbs-up, which is her other job besides smiling. Think she said she wants to be an actress, just like everybody else in Los Angeles does. I hope she's listed both smiles and thumbs on her resume. I hope she's demonstrating both in her headshot.

Sally's other hand grasps her harness and I catch the fault line in her smile. I check the groin of my jumpsuit to make sure I haven't pissed myself. Looks dry enough. Sally's probably just getting bored.

I smile back at her, more to be a jerk than out of politeness. My smile's still more of a snarl these days. Can't correct it without a mirror to guide me. Sorry, Sally. I'm sure Kevin Something could've given her something she could work with.

Hear the word "action" in my earpiece. No "quiet on the set." No "rolling." Those words would be wasted on this sideshow.

I turn back to the ledge. Hold my breath. Jump.

Supposed to flail my arms and arch my back, as much for the three camera setups as for safety. I forget all that, thinking instead of what Sally's smile could feel like if I moved my fingers along the cusp of her teeth, if I dared her to bite down. Her teeth could be dry. Inside of her lips, moist.

Then I think that maybe if I hit wrong, the shock to my system'll wake it up and I'd actually be able to feel someone's mouth against my skin again. That was one theory the EnDearTech guys had about how to repair me: bang on this old television long enough and you'll fix the reception. Wish I was watching TV right now. Or a sun setting over the ocean. Is that so much to ask, L.A.? Is it? I'll call Alan when I land and tell him this is all a mistake. If my luck's actually turning, maybe he'll actually answer his cell.

So eventually I guess I bounce off the air bubble, hit the pavement belly-up. My arm bends behind me when I settle, which might mean something for my wrist. Should have stung something awful, but I could impale myself on a boom mike and I'd still have to be told it's time to die.

Three production assistants are at my side as I dust myself off. Must have blacked out momentarily because Sally's there, too, and it should've taken her a bit to unfasten and climb down. See her hand on my shoulder and it smarts worse than the fall. She gives me nothing but fake smiles and thumbs to gawk at visually, but sure. She'll tease me with a hand on my shoulder.

"You okay?"

Stupid question, but I don't say that. "They get the shot?"

"Yeah. Said it looked amazing."

"Wonderful." Perfection. One Take Michael, that's what they'll call me. I can build a reputation as the stuntman who never complains and never screws up. Found my place among the unfeeling, in the city of ripoff sunsets and faux everything-under-them.

"You want a break?"

I shake my head. "I'm only in the one shot."

"Right. And they've already moved the cameras for the next take. You ready to go again?"

"Oh." So sometimes I forget I'm not the only perfectionist in the world.

"You all right?"

I nod. But how the hell should I know?

Another insurance asshole returns my handmirror, and schedules me for an X-ray at the end of the day. Wears a green turtleneck under a cream-colored sportsjacket. Five years of pretending to be a detective, and the most useful thing I've learned is not to trust people who can't dress themselves.

So yeah. Turns out I've busted some ribs. Probably on take three, although the P.A. I hit on the second bounce took the worst of it. But Asshole here's suddenly claiming I'm a liability because I wouldn't know to ask for a doctor if I *did* get hurt.

See, my nerves are fine. Brain's fairly unremarkable, too, thanks for being too polite to ask. But there's this disconnect. They don't talk to each other. Some undiscovered island of chronic peripheral polyneuropathy-land, which means about as much to me as it does to anyone. All I know is you can burn me, punch me, stab me, fuck me. I might fall unconscious and I might die. But I'm not going to feel a thing. Might not even notice it, if I'm looking the other way and not listening real close. Never said I was a great detective.

Thought my condition would be an advantage here, that they'd love a stuntman who never complains. Hell, Alan said I'm the only man alive who doesn't mind these expensive—apparently painful—facial grafts. Figured this'd be as useful in Hollywood as it was in detective work. But Asshole here suddenly says I can sue for everything the studio's worth.

I say: "Really?"

Asshole glances at an assistant. "No," he says finally. The word lasts forever, like he's reluctant to take his finger off a chess piece before he's sniffed out all my angles. "And we're going to need you to sign some more stuff."

Offer to sign anything and everything, but they say there are ways around any contract; they need even more protection. Comforting to work in a business where contracts are so flimsy, but I guess that's not my problem anymore.

So Hollywood spits me out in two days. Has to be some kind of record, especially for a guy who had a job before he arrived. One Take Michael.

After Asshole leaves, I perk up at every set of footsteps in the hospital hallway, I don't know, thinking I'll see Sally come by with a tearful goodbye just so I can wonder why she isn't quite as brunette or puffy-cheeked as she should be. And why would I expect that sort of rejection piled upon rejection? What makes me think I must have killed Lady Luck's parents in another life or three? Experience.

Okay. Yeah. The explanation thing. So six years ago, I stuck a modded EnDearTech EnShare on the back of my neck and became the poster boy for a national recall. Now this was the original EnShare, not one of those "family friendly" pieces of crap endcapping every other WalMart aisle nowadays, but same purpose: attach it to the back of your neck and trade nerve sensations with a partner. What I touch, you feel. What you touch,

I feel. What could go wrong?

For starters, those early models could be modded to make the sensations only go one way, and the "receiver" felt not only what his partner felt, but also his own sensations on top of that. Now everyone knows EnShares are primarily sex toys, even if they don't give that feature its own starburst on those family-friendly boxes. But *this* mod enhanced that use beyond anything EnDearTech ever dreamed.

Several idiots made the news by attaching both ends to the same neck, becoming both receiver and sender, and most likely gunning for the latest masturbation related urban legend about amplifying orgasms in an endless loop. Actually, this would fry the EnShare and set fire to the idiot's hair, but thanks for playing.

I, to my credit, was a special kind of idiot, and the mod could be dangerous even when *responsibly* used as a sex toy. The puffy-cheeked brunette I remember—Amy, who I'm now beginning to confuse with Sally because I've apparently also lost the ability to differentiate between people—was allergic to bees. I was the sender and receiver on an otherwise relaxing camping trip. Sex can already be a sensory-overload experience without utensils. So double Amy's sensation on top of mine, add a bee sting to her face, and then suppose the body has a fuse box. The shock to my system blew that out, and that was the last real thing I ever felt.

Though I guess I still I feel *something*: a white noise parasthesia, as though I've just been sleeping on my body wrong all this time. Sally called it a "sense memory," which in the acting world is how to pretend you feel something you don't. Like I said: thought I was perfect for this town.

Still, it's less bullshit than I got from Amy. She left my bitter ass before the swelling went down in her cheeks. Can't say I blame her. Because I think I do remember blaming her. A lot. And maybe that had something to do with her leaving. Hindsight and all of that.

Later Sally calls me at my hotel to say how sorry she is. Not sure my footage'll make the final cut, but she's glad I came out for the day. I run my fingers along the wall above the bed. Looks textured, but I can't prove it.

"Yeah, me too," I say. Don't know whether she's calling for herself or the studio, but I'm starting to miss those talented thumbs.

I ask her to dinner. She's "um, busy."

Don't know why that should sting. She's pretty shallow to talk to, and I'd get precious little out of anything carnal. Maybe seeing my hands touching Sally would remind me of what Amy felt like. Sense memories, yeah? Or maybe it's because I just don't know anyone else in Los Angeles. I'd book a flight for tomorrow, but where would I go? North? Get ahead of the smog and find myself an honest-to-god sunset?

"No hard feelings?" Sally says.

A thousand obvious jokes tickle my tongue. Yes, figuratively. Shut up. "How about tomorrow?"

There's a long pause. At first I want to let her off the hook rather than provoke another rejection. Then I figure I've got nothing to lose. So I wait for it.

Finally: "I can, um, do lunch."

"Perfect," I say. It's my favorite word, and I give it to Sally. Doubt I'll ever get it back.

Phone rings again. Don't want to answer. In the middle of some reality show about really tall gynecologists. Not as funny as you'd think, but if all I can do is see and hear, my two dimensions might as well be as interesting as what's on TV. That's why I like sunsets, too. Can't feel them. Can't smell them. They're the great equalizer, because all we can do is watch and hope they don't suck as much as they do off the Santa Monica Pier.

But it could be Alan finally returning a call. Or Sally calling about lunch. This makes me think of food, makes me look at my watch. It's been fourteen hours since I've eaten. I answer the phone.

"Michael Brian?" a voice says. Male. Boston Accent? "I'm with the circus."

I've been in L.A. three days. Only the studio and Alan know where I'm staying. Maybe it's a referral system. Hollywood's spittoon. Always wondered what happened to character actors too ugly to ever take a lead. Maybe if I keep him talking, he'll tell me before I starve to death.

"Didn't think there was a circus anymore," I say.

"Yes, sir. There're four."

It's creepy, him knowing that. Like knowing the exact number of an endangered species. Like reminding me there's nobody else out there who's got what I got.

"Yeah, I'm not interested in anything," I tell him. But I get his number anyway. You never know.

I shower and shave. Only thing worse than eating dinner alone is looking like there's a reason you're alone. Face is still red from the graft removal. These showbiz types must not be as delicate as the technicians Alan always used to hire.

The devil finally calls back while I'm in the shower. Leaves a message that he's in L.A. on business. Wants to see me. We'll catch up later.

Then he says: "If someone from EnDearTech calls, say nothing," which I dismiss as Alan being Alan. He probably stole some pens and thinks they're out to get him. Probably thinks I should disappear for a spell, as he does on occasion. Love the guy. He's my best, maybe only friend in the world. But I'll never figure him out.

Alan was an off-the-books consultant for EnDearTech when my nerves got wrecked. He's short. Fidgety. Smartest guy I ever met. The EnShare recall was his idea, while I was still debating whether to sue. I'm not a litigious guy or anything, but don't know what I would've done if Alan hadn't contacted me first.

First words when he visited me in the hospital: "I have a job for you." Then he said: "While you work for me, we'll see if we can't put things right with you." Then: "At least you can't taste the food here." Didn't know what else to do. Literally had no feelings one way or the other. I'd given up hope that puffy-cheeked Amy would be back. I agreed.

Half my unofficial work for EnDearTech was public relations crap, giving interviews and testimonies about the "dangers" of illegal mods, how companies aren't responsible for sexual deviants like myself.

In return, EnDearTech laundered me a stipend through Alan and threw R&D money at two safety programs: one trying to secure future EnShare versions against such hacks, and one trying to reverse my nerve damage. But for all the lab techs and anyone else knew, EnDearTech was just doing right by me, and I defended them by discouraging mods on my own volition.

Of course this was never charity work, especially not for EnDearTech. Alan even said other companies contributed to it under the table, since they gained as much from my publicity as EnDearTech did. "Billions." Alan said. And not just on liability suits. See, even loss-leader hardware needs to make a profit eventually. When a company gives away OLED televisions to propagate compulsory advertisement crawls, they crumble when someone spreads a mod to disable those ads. So long as there was no shortage of morons convinced their customers—and not their business models—were the problem, I'd answer every interview question exactly how they paid me to answer them:

The emperor's clothes were fucking beautiful.

Later an ancillary job kept this corporate shill fed and watered long after the news cycle closed. Alan and I confiscated modded EnShares that were still out there, because not everybody who owned the original wanted to "trade up" for a crippled version that couldn't be modded for her pleasure so easily. And stories about idiots catching their hair on fire hurt sales, especially when newscasts failed to differentiate between the older "crap" and newer family-friendly models, which could *safely* be employed as a sextoy.

Wearing celebrity facial grafts, I actively participated in twenty-two stings over five years. Because what deviant wouldn't want to share sex and/or an illicit high with someone they think is famous? It was good work. I was good at it, until news items and leads became few and far between. So EnDearTech announced they'd run out of theories about curing me, and my hopes of a cure dried up just as I lost the one thing that gave my life a sprinkling of purpose.

Thought about independent detective work, even narrowed it down to which states I might try to get a license in. But facial grafts are pricey. Took deep pockets like EndearTech's to make them practical. And, let's face it, wearing those grafts without pain made up the bulk of my skills. Pound rich and penny foolish Hollywood isn't looking so stupid now, is it?

I figure I'm better off staying at the hotel in case Alan calls again. Call room service and ask about portion sizes.

"I hope you're hungry," a woman says.

"Wouldn't that be something?"

I tell her to send up the prettiest item on the menu.

"I'm just so busy," Sally says again the next day. We're in a restaurant whose name ends in an "i," but it's not Italian. It's a vegetarian place that loves plants so much they conscientiously object to even cooking their damn food. Sure, I can't taste the difference, but the cacophony of snow-peas snapping in my mouth makes me panic about chinking teeth with every bite. Sights are no more pleasant: Parthenon-ish pillars holding up exposed ventilation ducts. Ask the waiter to turn up the air conditioning just to bankrupt this place one day sooner.

Sally tries to let me down easy. I play dense to prolong my one hour of extroversion I'm gonna get today. She periodically checks her teeth for veggie-bits in the reflection of her broccoli knife, and I can see how we're perfect for each other except in the ways that matter.

Want to tell her about myself, but I can't think of anything interesting that I haven't signed an EnDearTech nondisclosure agreement about. So I ask the waiter for another Long Island Iced Tea. There's a bright painting of some naked Norseman or other on the far wall behind Sally. Want him good and blurry by the time she abandons me. Should've started the meal with Everclear, but my luck says it's probably illegal in California.

"You sure you haven't reached your limit?" the waiter says as he brings me my fourth or seventh drink.

"No," I say. "You sure you're not watering them down?" There's a freedom in not being afraid they'll spit in your food.

"I have to go," Sally says finally.

Few more drinks and I wouldn't have cared at all. I shrug and take out my handmirror. My face looks naked without food or graft. Eyebrows seem bushy compared to all the Hollywood types. I've been in L.A. too long if I'm not immediately ruling out waxing them.

When I look up, Alan's sitting in Sally's chair. Pinstriped suit is a new look for him. Usually swears by jogging sweats. Must be in disguise.

"You remembered my birthday," I say. I don't know what I mean by it but I'm glad it's the first thing out of my mouth. Because that means I'm successfully drunk.

Alan smiles mildly and taps his fingers on the tablecloth. Means he's all business. Disappointing. I can really use a hug about now.

"Found a nest," he says. "Dealers in Cleveland using EnShares in a prostitution ring."

"Prositution? Sign me up," I say. I like his eyebrows. Never noticed them before. Not as bushy as mine. Not dainty either. Wonder how he keeps them up. I could totally pluck mine without crying, if that's all there is to it.

Alan leans in. "We're talking about a *big* nest."

So this is work, not play? My dreams of vacationing in Cleveland have been crushed. "Okay, how many?"

"Enough to consider this a perfect recall."

I search my head for a familiar number. "Four?"

"Two thousand," Alan says.

Two thousand sounds friendly to me. Full of hope, like Alan's tidy eyebrows. Math wizards at EnDearTech came up with that magic estimation of how many working EnShares remained out there, assuming a certain percentage of failures after so many years, a damage rate, and so on. We'd never be certain whether we got them all. But we could get close. When EnDearTech kicked me to the curb, the projection *was* about two thousand left. Now Alan thinks we can finish it in one fell swoop?

"What's a fell swoop?" I say, probably out loud.

Alan's eyeballs swell for a second beneath those pretty brows. It's his way of laughing. It might be my favorite thing about him. It also might mean I'm hallucinating. Yay.

"What's that to me?" I whisper. Don't want the emaciated couple at the next table to hear me talking to myself, in case I am. "Not my job anymore, Alan."

"EnDearTech's restarted their research on nerve damage," Alan says. "But I think they're just tying a ribbon around what they learned from you, to sell it to the nearest pharmaceutical."

"I fucking knew it," I say, but actually he lost me on the whole ribbon thing. Amy had a dress with ribbons. And nice legs.

"Problem is they're gonna focus on burn victims and such. Your condition's too rare to be profitable. That and they think you're too visible."

"Visible? Nobody remembers me!"

"Nobody including EnDearTech. That's why I'm coming to you with this Cleveland sting before I go to them."

"Brilliant," I say, because "I don't understand" just has too many damn syllables.

"I think I can get them to cure you if I tell them you're the key to the sting, Michael."

"Am I?"

"Sure." Alan says. He leans back in his chair. "But if you hear from them, we never talked."

None of it makes sense. Sums up my relationship with Alan. Figure it's just as likely I'm talking to my drink anyway. But a few hours later I sober up in a cab in West Hollywood. There's a plane ticket in my hand. Must be going to Ohio.

That's fine.

I'm at an upscale hotel bar in downtown Cleveland, pretending to be as useful as Sally with her smiles and thumbs. Should get a headshot.

Tell myself I'm here to keep anyone else from getting hurt. Was mostly true five years ago, though I'd no other options at the time. Might've been true when EnDearTech decided my usefulness was at an end. But there are plenty of smart people in the world who don't work for them. Hell, even the hackers might've found something interesting to do with me.

Could I have been cured by now, had we just allowed the EnShare hack to run its course in the first place? If nothing else, more victims sharing my lack of pain would mean more experts and amateur do-it-yourselfers trying to solve the problem. Give it to a senator's kid, and I'd be cured by breakfast. Give it to my Amy, and we could have checked each other's faces for leftovers til death do us part. We could have held each other just to know we were doing it.

Think the real reason I'm here is to finish it. This'll be the one thing I can perfect. Maybe that'll give me a good sense-memory to brag about next time I'm in Hollywood. Or maybe I'll kill myself because there's no sense starting something new at my age, with this body. Anyway, it's nice to have options again.

It's not just me I'm worried about, though. Alan's acting strange, even for him. Scamming EnDearTech out of an extra thirty grand to finance a facial graft he's no intention of giving me? Says the money'll help EnDearTech believe this is as real as the other stings we've done, but I don't know.

Here I don't even need to leave the hotel. Not that people would remember my face if I did. In fact, Alan encourages me to have fun at some uppity playhouse across the street, or in the shopping mall hidden in the basement of one of these hotels, called Tower City of all the basement-related names they could've chosen. But honestly I'd rather watch TV and order room service until it's all over.

But I don't go up to my room. Too much effort, I guess. Instead I sit at the bar, order one drink after another. Some senses take a while to dull.

Bartender cuts me off early. She's a sandy-blonde twenty-something who reminds me of both Sally *and* Amy after a while. Knows me better than most. She knows I can't be trusted to know when I'm drunk. Hate that I can't even feel useful anymore. Need to find a bar that gives less of a shit.

Must have passed out in the cab. Driver's slapping me. That never works. Cheeks are probably red and raw. And I bet I felt *so* lifelike to him, too.

I'm at some hole in the wall bar in the flats. The neon sign is somebody's name like "Rudolph's," but all I can see is pink spaghetti cursive. Reminds me of my favorite high school dives back in Jersey. Locals not giving you a second look. Bartenders not caring how much you drink or how much you spill.

There's a long, horizontal mirror behind the bar. Haven't seen that in a while. Used to like that kind of thing back when I was useful. Could eat pretzels while checking out a mark behind me, along with all the pretzels on my chin. Not sure I want to look at myself tonight, but a few whiskey shots should pretty-up that image fast enough.

But before the whiskey does its job, I see two guys behind me. They look familiar, but then, remember, I don't differentiate between people anymore. One of them raises his hand. He's holding something that looks like a pouch. Is that a blackjack? Where do people even find blackjacks in this day and age?

Even sober, it's hard to measure proximity in the mirror. But I figure they're either planning on hitting me on the back of the head or on throwing it as me from across the room. I chuckle to myself. Won't the joke be on them when I don't even acknowledge the blow?

I don't turn around as it comes down against the back of my head. I watch their expressions for surprise, for when they see I'm not even flinching. But their faces are as blank as mine is. Kindred spirits? Have I finally made some friends? The lights get dimmer.

Hear a shatter from below. I've dropped my drink. Which is the worst thing that could've ever happened to me.

I'm used to passing out, but too often lately it hasn't been due to hunger. Maybe that means I'm dying. Or that my body's found a new way to acknowledge pain. From some vantages, all change is progress.

Wake in a sitting position in a bright-but-dingy room. Dirty windows way up high, dirty cement everywhere else. An empty warehouse? My eighth-grade shop class? For a few years I was convinced I'd die in a power-tool accident, and not know it until I'd spotted my second severed wrist.

Presently my wrists are behind my back. They could be severed. Might as well be. Can't bring them around front. Tied up, maybe? I pull at them, but without knowing what I'm tied with, I'm as likely to open a vein as free myself.

"Sorry about this," a voice says. Maybe familiar. With the room's dull echo, it's hard to tell. Start thinking of sitcom actors, trying to match that voice with a name. Difficult to focus. Concussion? I try to remember any of the brain injury crap I skimmed through when reading up on nerve damage. Seemed so damn unimportant then, but hopefully I'm just dehydrated now. Have I pissed myself? Don't need to be drunk to piss myself, but it helps.

Clear my throat. "Hands're tied too tight. What are they tied with?" I say. "I think I'm allergic to the material. My wrists hurt."

"No they don't," the voice says. Thinks he knows what's best for me. A politician, maybe? Probably jinxed him by voting for him. Probably here for revenge.

"Can I have some water?"

A man in a gray labcoat appears from behind me. Don't recognize him. But he's got a glass of water and a straw all ready for me. Hate being predictable.

I sip from the straw until the man pulls the drink away. It's empty. He walks around me, out of sight again. Didn't seem disgusted or amused by my sipping at air.

"You know me?" I say.

"There's no prostitution ring here." The voice is in front of me. So there's at least two of them. "And EnDearTech isn't starting up any new program."

Yeah, I know that voice. "Sally?" I say.

"Excuse me?"

"Private joke," I say. Don't know why I even bother. "What's going on, Alan?"

Alan steps into my field of vision. Completely unnecessary. He must watch as much TV as I do, which frankly is unhealthy.

"I think," he says, "EnDearTech already found a way to cure you. Maybe." Sounds like good news, but he doesn't look me in the eyes. A man's going to clock me on the head and tie me up, the least he can do is give me thumbs up and a teeth-apart smile.

Gray-labcoat-man brings Alan a chair. Alan sits in front of me, then tells his guy something I can't hear.

"Okay," I say. "When?"

"They found it right before they canceled the program."

Yeah, that makes about as much sense as Alan tying me up. "You couldn't have mentioned this in L.A.? Or before you had me jump off a roof?"

"They think it's better if you just go away."

His guy disappears behind me again. I consider the phrase "go away." I don't think it means what I hope it means. Hoping my throat hasn't already been slit.

"That why you're here?" I say.

Alan looks at me suddenly. But his face says he's thinking about something else, like I'm being focused on and ignored at the same time. What, is he high?

I hear a door close behind me. Alan relaxes.

"There's a good chance," he says, "if you get a significant shock to your nervous system, that you'll get it all back."

"Yeah, yeah. We tried that." Didn't work. We also tried sneaking up on it with massage. Still remember the acupuncturist's exact words: "You shouldn't even feel the needle go in." That made my year.

"We haven't tried with an EnShare."

Oh. Shit. Is that why my mind keeps wandering? Is that what they mean when they say your life flashes before your eyes?

"When they were publicly trying to cure you," Alan says, "it was too risky."

"Yeah, because the only thing left to zap is my brain!" All those years of hunting down EnShares, I never feared guns or falls or death threats. But I always avoided even touching EnShares themselves if I could help it.

"The body has a survival instinct the mind can't always control. I believe only an original modded EnShare can jolt your nervous system. By design it'll hit all the same places hit by your inciting event." Alan stands and turns away from me. "But by the time I figured out they were keeping this from me—from us—we'd already incinerated all the EnShares we'd found. EnDearTech had a few intact just for testing, but they wouldn't give me access to them. Until now."

"Okay. Why?"

"I told them I needed one to take you out quietly."

"They hired you to what? Kill me?"

"No, no," Alan says. He walks around behind me and then I'm looking at my lap. From the sound of things, he's attaching the EnShare to the base of my neck. Suddenly I can't help but think of it as a power tool. "EnDearTech thinks that if you're cured, you'll no longer have any reason to keep your mouth shut. Apparently we know too many secrets or something."

"Which ones?" I say. "I don't remember anything!"

"Doesn't matter. I convinced them that stuntwork would keep you happy enough. Sorry that didn't work out."

"So they hired you to kill me," I say again.

"No, no, no." Alan comes back around and smiles reassuringly. "I volunteered."

Thumbs fucking up.

Alan gets a little blurry and I hope that doesn't mean I'm crying. If I *am* crying, I hope it's not over him because he's a bad friend. Hope it's because I'm about to die. Something worth crying about, I hear.

"It wasn't easy to get the job either. I've no track record with this kind of thing, I swear," Alan says. "But I'll cure you, Michael. Then you'll disappear with a rather permanent facial graft and enough money to lay low for a few years. I'll say you're dead. Won't hurt my reputation much if I can't produce a body, so long as you don't go public."

"And if it kills me?"

"Oh, that won't hurt my reputation at all," Alan says.

Bad. Friend.

"Now, I made you a promise," he says.

"You promised to try." Okay, I'm definitely crying now. I think it might be interfering with my breathing, even. Didn't think I wanted to live enough to justify this. It must be the bad friend thing. If I could feel sick, I would. "You never promised results."

"I don't fail."

So the world's full of perfectionists. I'm surprised I don't make friends easier, and that they don't all try to kill me.

"It'll work, Michael."

"Then why the precaution? Why not let me choose?"

"You might have said no."

"Huh," I say.

"Sorry for lying," he says. "And especially for the blow to the head. That wasn't cool. We've done two of the three best scans to determine the severity of your concussion, and I've got followup appointments already set up for you. You might have some focusing issues for a few days, but it's perfectly normal for it to take longer. Just rest. Listen to your body. I assure you my people just misunderstood my instructions. I'm only doing this because I care."

"Bullshit," I say. "You're doing this because you want to finish it. You want to be perfect."

Alan looks at me for a long time. His eyes swell. I wonder whether I've always been wrong to interpret that as laughter. "Yeah, okay. Maybe both?"

I believe him, for all the good it does. Alan's a good friend. He's just better at being a prick.

He puts the EnShare's other end on his own neck. An act of solidarity? Showing me he wouldn't cause me any pain he's not willing to inflict on himself? We're not in Hollywood anymore, Alan.

See a few wires down his chair leg. Think I've sat in that same chair before, when they tried to wake up my nerves through "safer" electric jolts. Except for Alan, that chair is my oldest friend in the world.

I try to picture the original EnShare. It's like two halves of a green Easter egg, attached by a rubber cable. The eggs lay flat against the user's neck. There are three gray buttons on the back of one egg, called the "Master." The other user's egg is called the "Slave" (or "Bitch" as Amy used to call it when I was the slave), and has an emergency shut-off button, but no other control over the experience. Buttons on the Master are, in order: sensitivity increase, sensitivity decrease, and on/off.

But is that order right-to-left or left-to-right? And isn't the button placement different on modded EnShares? Where does the added button go, the one that toggles on/off the one-way mod? They're all still in a row, I think. Just don't remember whether it's on the far left or the right, or whether the power button gets moved out and the mod button goes between oh shit and I'm really going to die.

Hear the faint buzz of the EnShare powering up. If I could feel, I'd now be receiving Alan's sensations on top of my own.

"I hope this hurts you a lot more—"

"Shut the hell up," I say. Close my eyes. Unless he lied again about his intentions, I must be wearing the Master, and Alan's the Bitch. Button layout remains a blur. Think back to before the accident. Back to the sex. There's an angle where I'd jerk my head back against my headboard and flip the mod switch on and off, hands otherwise occupied. Must have done something else when we were camping.

Hear a zap. Alan's already sending me shocks from the chair. Guess he loves me, but not enough to find someone to fuck me while getting stung by a bee.

I remember an actor-turned-stuntman out in L.A. rambling about how our minds don't remember, our bodies do. Which is why it's easier to remember your lines by saying them out loud. *Let your body do the remembering.*

I search for that muscle memory. That sense memory. Jerk my head behind me, hoping my chairback is high enough to find the right button.

Guess I tap something because there's a click and then a lower-pitched buzzing, which feels right to me, for all that's worth. Now we should be trading pain equally.

Alan's eyes go wide. He yelps like a dog, and passes out from whatever pain I fail to feel right now. He slumps from his chair, his tongue hanging out of his mouth. Has it gotten that bad? Is something *that* messed up inside me? I'm probably better off *not* feeling it then. All is well.

Expect gray-labcoat-man to come to Alan's aid any second, but he must've left the room. Alan must've felt this was a private matter, or maybe the technician wasn't in on Alan's plan. Bad friend, paranoid prick. Thank you.

I pull at my hands. Don't care anymore what I'm bound with. Got to get free.

"What channels you got?" I ask. It's a non-chain hotel just west of Cleveland. I gather it's a Catholic neighborhood by all the Virgin Maries on the lawns outside and on the lobby walls inside. That's not doing me any favors, with what I'm about to do. But the hotel takes cash, offers free cable, and doesn't require a photo ID. Thumbs *way* up.

Took me an hour or so of pulling and twisting my forearms to free myself. Rubbed my wrists raw and red, but only broke the skin in a few places. Alan was gentler than I thought he'd be. I'd pissed myself of course, but that could've happened when I was unconscious. Took Alan's wallet and managed to get out without seeing his assistant.

Still had the cash Alan had given me earlier, but I was stuck in a semi-abandoned warehouse district. Only phone for miles belonged to a college kid in a glass-blowing gallery a few blocks over. Made me buy a key fab before he let me use his cell to call a cab. Then I took the Shoreway west to a hardware shop, and then grabbed a second cab to a hotel the driver recommended.

See, sitting there with Alan, trying to get free, I had time to think about my next move. And I realized the most important question in my life was and is: "What channels you got?"

I pay in advance for a top floor room for twenty-five days. Four stories up, and no blue air bubble on the ground below.

Inside the room, I plug in my new electric drill. They don't even sell corded drills anymore, so I have to wait for it to charge. The socket's near the mirror, so that's when I finally see myself. I look at my face twenty times a day in my handmirror, and now it's a face I don't recognize. It's not particularly attractive, but I'm happy with the eyebrows. That son of a bitch Alan must have given me the graft before tying me to the chair. Not that it makes a difference where I'm going.

I wonder whether I'd still go through with it, if I could see my own face in the mirror one last time. Or would I just not be able to meet my own eyes?

When the drill has a decent enough charge, I put twelve bolts in the hotel-room door, piss deliberately one last time, and then seal up the bathroom door the same way.

No access to food, no access to water. I rip the phone cord from the wall. Then I sit back, start dismantling the drill, and pray that something good's on television.

They say starvation and dehydration are the worst ways to die. I expect it to be painless. Unless there's nothing on TV.

Hard to focus. Know it's almost over. But during the fifth rerun of a police procedural (Three days? Five? Hard to tell. Fallen asleep a few times.), I want something. I feel something. Almost miss it, then I almost dismiss it as my imagination.

But there it is. A rumbling from my middle. Doesn't go away. Won't let me ignore it. I imagine it's my stomach eating itself. Or my body calling my brain's decision to do this an unwarranted act of aggression. We're at war, people. Nut up.

Get out of bed, the slightest movement sending aches I'm at once used to and frightened of. I feel my feet touching the floor,

278

the carpet needling my feet. My knees are on fire. My back wants to curl and collapse. Everything smells like dick.

Breathing is pain. Blinking hurts, and refraining from blinking hurts worse.

I'd forgotten how horrible it is, to feel. How wonderful. My clothes are sticky. Wet? Urine-soaked? Hard to be bothered by it when everything else is pain.

Find. The. Drill. Can't focus enough to put the pieces back together. I try sticking the driver bit into a screw head to—I don't know—turn it between my fingers? But I drop them and lose both in the ocean of carpet at my feet.

I vacillate between wanting to live and wanting to end it quickly. Can't budge either door. Not strong enough, just as I hoped I wouldn't be.

Can't cry out—throat too dry. I pound on the wall. Maybe a neighbor will hear. Try to open the window, but it's not the kind that opens which seemed *sooo* important just a few days ago.

I pound the body of the drill against the window. Barely vibrates the glass, but if I pound enough times it could break. Then I'll jump. And either I'll survive the fall and get to a hospital and do something about this pain, or else I'll die and it'll be over with and that'll be fine, too, won't it?

I just need out of this room. Need to get away from this smell. The smell! Spent too much time in hotel rooms. They all look the same and feel so much worse. I'm aware of it now, how they all feel.

I remember now why I drank before the accident, but not why I drank after. I want to live. I hate the pain, but I want to live! Want things back like they were before. I don't want to feel this. I want to join the circus. To tell Sally and Alan I'm sorry. To make friends even if they'll kill me. Whatever they want to do, I'm fine with that. Never did get to see a Pacific Ocean sunset. Sally, L.A., I shouldn't have judged you so quickly!

The contact point between drill and window looks like it'll crack. But I drop the drill and fail to realize it for at least one thrust. My hand's gone numb again. Is it because of the pounding or because my feelings were only temporary? Or a hallucination?

My handmirror! Maybe I can cut the glass with glass! I manage to pull it from my pocket. Alan's wallet falls open in my hand. There's a photograph of a familiar face on what I thought was Alan's driver's license.

I stare at it until I realize I'm looking at my own face. Not my real face, but the face I wear now. The graft!

Alan knew! He fucking knew I'd steal his wallet! He knew before I did. He's my best friend in the whole world and a bad friend and maybe I did to him what the EnShare did to me. Maybe he'll never feel again. Will he ever forgive me? We could be such friends, if only he will.

The mirror doesn't do shit against the window. I pick up the drill and resume pounding the glass. *Do* want to live! If only it was closer to noon, when the maids sometimes knock and I yell at them to go away. If only I hadn't pulled the phone out! Then maybe I could call someone. Someone who could tell me if this is real or a sense memory!

The glass buckles. I wonder whether I'm a survivor.

Alex Wilson writes fiction and comics in Carrboro, NC. http://www.alexwilson.com and Twitter: @alexotica

After over 90,000 words of harrowing experiences taking the reader from the height of euphoria to the depths of depression, we close out this volume with a little fun. It's not really a story, and it's not very long, but it does highlight David Gerrold's sense humor, something we first got to see in the Star Trek *episode "The Trouble with Tribbles." It's the only piece in the entire collection with the sole objective of making the reader laugh. David is a better person than he is a writer, and he is one hell of a writer. Aside from his adoption of a son and dedication to raising him, much of which is chronicled in* The Martian Child, *he is extremely active in charity work. I am very privileged to call him a friend, and excited to include his work in one of my projects.—RN*

Time Capsule 2120: Actual Comments From Lunar Tourists
by David Gerrold

Why does the water come out of the shower so slow? Can you turn up the gravity?

Why do I have to wear a spacesuit to go outside? Can't you fill up the outside with air too?

You should lower prices so more people can visit the moon.

Can you do something about the long days and nights? It's hard to know when I'm supposed to sleep and when I'm supposed to be awake.

Can you turn down the temperature in the summer domes? It's too hot.

Can you raise the temperature in the winter domes? It's too cold to play in the snow.

Need more signs in the domes to keep the area pristine.

My wife got stung by a bee while visiting a farm dome. Please eradicate these annoying creatures.

Too many rocks in the Lunar hills. Not enough scenery.

No marked hiking trails in the Lunar wilderness.

Guide wouldn't let us fit our feet into Armstrong's footprints.

Please pave hiking trails to make Lunar hiking easier.

Chairlifts need to be in some places so that we can get to wonderful views without having to hike to them.

Reflectors need to be placed on rocks every 10 meters so people can hike at night with flashlights.

A McDonald's would be nice.

My room is very hot. How do I open a window?

Where do we go to see the vacuum? We looked out the window but there was nothing there.

My husband said he saw the vacuum and it was nothing. Can you make it more interesting?

Why are there so many rocks out there? Don't they ever clean up the landscape?

The daylight is too bright. Can you turn it down?

We went to one of the moon's oceans today and I couldn't even find a seashell. How come?

David Gerrold sits alone in a room and talks to himself. If he says anything worth listening to, he types it up. When he has filled enough pages, he sends it to an editor who pays for the privilege of publishing it. This simple action by an editor allows David Gerrold to claim he is a writer. If it were not for that editor, David Gerrold would be a guy who sits alone in a room and talks to himself. Online at www.gerrold.com.

About the editor

Rick Novy's short fiction has been published dozens of times in recent years. His novelette *Winter* was published last year as a stand-alone book by Sam's Dot Publishing. He was also the editor of *M-Brane SF #12* (aka *Ergosphere*). He lives in Arizona. Learn more about him at www.ricknovy.com.

About the publisher

M-Brane Press consists of a small office and a MacBook in Christopher Fletcher's St. Louis home. Among its projects are the magazines *M-Brane SF* and *Fantastique Unfettered*. Learn more at www.mbranepress.com and www.mbranesf.com.

www.ingramcontent.com/pod-product-compliance
Lightning Source LLC
Chambersburg PA
CBHW030113180626
46812CB00002B/398